TRUCKED OVER ROYALLY

Neil's attention was caught by something behind the truck. "McKee, come here," he said sharply. He was bent over, feverishly brushing snow away from something.

I looked at Stu across the nose of the pickup. He shrugged and went back to look.

"Do you always drive around with one of these?" Neil asked Stu quietly, pointing to whatever he'd uncovered in the truck box. If Neil had found a shovel back there and we could have rescued ourselves hours ago, I was going to be royally pissed.

I was already beginning to shiver in the frigid early morning sunlight. I leaned over to see what had caught Neil's attention.

It was a human hand.

Which was unmistakably attached to an entire human body.

Other Tory Bauer Mysteries by
Kathleen Taylor
from Avon Books

SEX AND SALMONELLA
THE HOTEL SOUTH DAKOTA
FUNERAL FOOD
MOURNING SHIFT

KATHLEEN TAYLOR

COLD FRONT

A TORY BAUER MYSTERY

AVON BOOKS
An Imprint of HarperCollinsPublishers

AVON BOOKS
An Imprint of HarperCollins*Publishers*
10 East 53rd Street
New York, New York 10022-5299

Copyright © 2000 by Kathleen Taylor
ISBN: 0-380-81204-5
www.avonbooks.com

First Avon Books paperback printing: October 2000

Avon Trademark Reg. U.S. Pat. Off. and in Other Countries, Marca Registrada, Hecho en U.S.A.
HarperCollins® is a trademark of HarperCollins Publishers Inc.

Printed in the U.S.A.

WCD 10 9 8 7 6 5 4 3 2

Without Jane Dystel and Carrie Feron, this book would not have come to be. They never stopped believing, and together they worked a small publishing miracle.

....

Prologue

There is no subject as near and dear to a South Dakotan heart as the weather.

Oh we bitch loud and long about politics and the Vikings and the wretched state of [fill in the blank] today. We happily dissect our own sex lives (or in my case, the complete lack thereof) and the supposed excesses of our neighbors'. But there is no conversational gambit as apt to command the complete and total attention of one and all as a comment about the weather.

Whatever Citibank and Gateway 2000 and our governor would have you think about the industrial and business potential of the state, South Dakota has an agricultural economy. Here in our northeastern corner, we live and die by the farmers.

And the farmers live and die by the weather. A good year, with the right amount of moisture at just the right time, will leave us all smiling, our larders and bank accounts filled to face another season.

A bad year, a year with too much rain, or too little rain, or too much snow or not enough snow, or more wind than we need, or an untimely hailstorm, or a badly placed tornado, or a weather pattern weirdly out of whack—or, to put it more simply, the kind of weather we get most years—can send many a depressed farmer and small town businessman scuttling for bankruptcy court. Or swallowing the contents of an aspirin bottle.

Or contemplating the shotgun in the corner.

When all goes well, the weather is our friend.

And as I watched freshly drifted snow feverishly shoveled from a man who was already far beyond our help, I realized that the weather can also be our worst enemy.

In order to survive a South Dakotan winter, you have to keep your wits about you.

In order to kill in a South Dakotan winter, you only need the critical mass of old grievances and new insecurities.

And a full-out blizzard.

1

....

When it Snows, it Pours

I've heard that Eskimos assign to each variation of snow its own distinct and descriptive name. In their assorted languages, the splotchy flakes that fall gently from a slate-gray sky have nothing in common with the deep powder accumulations prized by the owners of ski resorts. And except for a color and temperature similarity, neither of the former bear the slightest relation to the frozen granules that pelt anyone unfortunate enough to stand next to large northern bodies of water in the middle of winter.

English, on the other hand, is not so specific. Whatever the size and texture, most Americans lump all cold, white precipitation into a single meteorological category.

But Delphi is not most of America. In our corner of northeastern South Dakota, we have a few distinct and descriptive terms for snow too.

"Piss, shit, goddamn," Del said, glaring out the cafe window. "Fuck."

It had been cold, bitterly cold, with daytime highs well below zero and wind chill factors exponentially lower. We'd had blowing and drifting snow and a winter storm warning in place for several days already, with another cold front scheduled to hit just before midnight.

I didn't care. The best entertainment Delphi had to offer on New Year's Eve was karaoke and drinks for a buck at the bar—an enticement that left me more than satisfied to burrow in at home with a book, even without a blizzard.

Del, however, had a date coming up from Sioux Falls—a guy she'd met through a personal ad in the newspaper. She'd regaled us for two weeks about this paragon of desirable manliness: flashing his picture and speculating wildly on his other attributes.

In fact, his photo showed him to be of better than average build and looks. We'd all memorized his stats long before Del read his perfectly charming letters out loud for the twentieth time, and could quote right along with her his claim to be a divorced professional man with a fondness for children and dogs and translating French poetry, not to mention a craving for long walks on the beach at sunset.

While maintaining indifference to the whole enterprise, Alanna Luna, ex-stripper and new co-owner of the cafe, managed to broadcast frequent warnings about the stupidity of meeting losers culled from the newspaper. But Rhonda, our twenty-year-old relief waitress/temporary cook's helper was delighted at the possibility that the well-traveled, forty-something Del might finally settle down with one man. An unmarried one at that.

Neither young nor naive enough to subscribe to that notion myself, I still had to admit that I was looking forward to getting a peek at the paragon who was set to arrive soon with a white carnation pinned to his coat.

If he could only get here.

Del's highly anticipated, and minutely discussed, New

Year's Eve First Date was now endangered by the governor's mandate to restrict highway traffic to emergency vehicles only. Ian Douglas O'Hara (who even had a handsome, manly name) needed to travel one hundred miles of drifted interstate before turning onto another hundred-mile stretch of badly plowed two-lane in order to arrive before five P.M.

"I wouldn't worry," I said to Del as she continued to peer anxiously out the window. "A man with the intestinal fortitude to appreciate unadulterated Baudelaire should be more than equal to a blizzard."

"You know, Ted Bundy was smart too," Alanna drawled innocently, from behind the counter as she refilled the napkin dispensers.

"Yeah, and so was the Unabomber," Ron Adler laughed, blinking.

Small and trim, with an undershot chin and a receding hairline, wearing insulated coveralls unzipped and peeled to the waistline, Ron drank coffee, told bad jokes, stared at Alanna's overhung bosom, said sarcastic things to Del, and in general wasted time as he waited to be paged again. His garage/gas station had been inundated with service calls to start frozen vehicles all day. His pickup sat warm and idling, jumper cables at the ready, diagonally parked in front of the cafe.

I used to think that the facial tic that caused Ron to blink wildly every third word was triggered by proximity to Del and his long-term unrequited crush on her. But since that particular itch had been scratched to no one's satisfaction a few months ago, and then rescratched every so often since with the same result, while the blinking continuing unabated, I had to conclude it was just one of his more lovable traits. Along with the need to prove to one and all that twenty-five years of mooning notwithstanding (most of that as a married man), he had never really been attracted to Del in the first place.

I sometimes wondered why Ron still spent so much time in the cafe given his newfound and obvious dislike of Del.

But mine was not to wonder why. Mine was to wander with a pot of regular in one hand and a pot of decaf in the other filling up cups, hoping against hope that the nastiness would not escalate beyond a few verbal jabs.

"So whose picture did you use to lure him here?" Ron continued for the cafe's benefit. "Raquel Welch?"

It was proof of Del's superhuman restraint that she had yet to pour a pot of coffee on his head.

Not that it hadn't occurred to her.

Or me, come to think of it.

The sporadic laughter in the cafe withered under Del's glare, though Ron continued to chuckle weakly to himself, and Alanna grinned behind the counter.

Bad weather notwithstanding, it had been a busy shift, with people rubbing chapped hands, blowing red noses, and stomping new snow off old boots in the doorway all day. As the afternoon wore on, the local businesses closed early, because of both the snow and the impending holiday. The cafe filled with local lollygaggers waiting for enough time to pass so they could have that first celebratory drink without feeling guilty.

Not everyone felt the need to wait.

"Sit down honey, and rest a bit," Eldon McKee said, patting the seat beside him. "You look like you could use a pick-me-up." He pulled a small silver flask from his jacket pocket and topped off the coffee I'd just poured into his cup. He'd been sitting in a window booth, gazing out at the snow for over an hour already.

A year ago, a mild stroke had left him with a drooping eyelid, a crooked smile, and a less than efficient business sense, which had resulted in the return of his married son to run the Feed and Seed Store across the street.

Which had messed up my life pretty well completely.

It would, however, have taken a large stretch of my imagination (and a major case of denial) to blame Eldon for the heartbreak and confusion caused by my relationship with Stuart McKee. Or its subsequent end. Eldon was a slightly lecherous Old Fart. A cafe regular. A pain in the butt but a predictable one, and kind of sweet at that.

"What's in that? Whiskey?" I asked, peeking to see if Alanna or Del had spotted Eldon's flask.

"Yup," he said, grinning. "Grab a glass and we'll toast the new year."

I sighed. "I'm working. I'd better not," I said, mightily wishing that were not the case. "It wouldn't do to get caught drinking on the job."

"What are you gonna do, fire yourself?" Eldon cackled.

He had a point. As a new and reluctant co-owner of the Delphi Cafe, I had no one to answer to and no one to please, except myself. Well, myself and the other new co-owner, who seemed to rank annoying me second only on her list of entertainments to needling Del. And Del, whom Aphrodite had been able to control far better than I had realized, was currently unpleasable.

The only thing that had made Del smile since the death of Aphrodite Ferguson was her anticipation in meeting Ian O'Hara. Said meeting was now in danger of being postponed, or canceled completely. And since Del would take a no-show personally, even if the weather was the culprit, my chances of spending New Year's Eve with a thoroughly disgruntled trailer-mate were growing by the minute.

In fact, the only employee in the cafe displaying even a modicum of holiday cheer was Rhonda, who had been temporarily pressed into service as an assistant cook to help Alanna's son Brian.

But since Rhonda was on Christmas break from her university classes, and wildly infatuated with Brian to boot, she didn't resent the sudden change in duties. With barely a week before her classes started again, we were desperately hoping our own newspaper ads for a relief cook would produce results before I had to go back into the kitchen.

My last stint there had been a disaster of biblical proportions, a fact that engendered some unrepentant anger at Aphrodite for getting herself killed and dumping Delphi's only cafe in my lap.

Well, mine and Alanna's laps, either of which should have been ample enough to deal with the sudden burden.

And maybe they both were. But what we weren't able to deal with was each other or our unexpected and undesired fifty-fifty ownership of the cafe. At least not comfortably. Or happily.

"Tory," Alanna called from behind the counter, "can you come here a minute? I need to talk to you."

Del turned and made a face that I could see but Alanna couldn't. Ron watched Del, blinking impassively. Eldon sipped his whiskey-laced coffee and stared out the window. Rhonda and Brian giggled in the kitchen as they cooked. Everyone else was engaged in complaining about the weather. Even Del's son, thirteen-year-old Presley, who was usually impervious to the cold, sat on a stool in the kitchen just to warm up. Or maybe it was to get a better view of Rhonda in her lime-green T-shirt.

But whatever Presley was doing in the kitchen, he didn't need me at the moment. And neither did anyone else. I had no meals up, no cups to refill, no one to ring out, and no emergencies to deal with. I therefore had no excuse to avoid Alanna.

I sighed. And sniffed. And sent another silent grievance to Aphrodite, wherever she was, for putting me in this position. And then I set the pots on the warmer behind the counter, and turned to Alanna.

"What's up?"

"Well, here," she said, tucking a bleached blond tendril behind one ear as she bent over a ledger that was open on the counter. "I've been going over expenses and I think we have a problem."

Considering that we had barely enough money for the day-to-day operations of the cafe, and not enough help and nowhere near the kind of experience necessary to run a business—alone or in tandem—I wasn't surprised.

"Tell me something I don't already know," I said, not

even trying to keep the weariness out of my voice.

"I am only trying to make this a goin' concern," Alanna said sharply, her Okie accent rising to the surface as it did whenever she was on the offensive. Or being seductive. Or angry. "I did not *ask* to be your business partner."

Rhonda caught my eye and set a burger platter on the stainless steel counter that divided the kitchen from the cafe. I nodded, and turned to Alanna. "Listen," I said quietly, "I'm *not* criticizing you. What's the problem?"

She peered at me, eyes narrowed, and then flashed a tight smile of faux friendliness that set my alarm bells ringing. "You're not doing anything tonight, are you?" she asked sweetly.

"Yes," I said firmly. "I'm going home and fixing myself a drink. Then I'm going to listen to the wind howl and read a mystery."

"I mean, you're not going out or anything, right?" She was still being sweet, which meant that she wanted something from me. The Southern accent deepened and the chest expanded and the eyelids fluttered. "Well, you know what I mean," she continued, when I didn't say anything. "You're not doing anything important. You don't have, like a date. Or anything."

It was a statement of fact, not a question. All of Delphi, including its newest residents Alanna Luna and her son Brian Hunt, knew beyond a shadow of a doubt that I was no longer dating the very married expectant father Stuart McKee. And they all knew that I had no one lined up to take his place.

In Alanna's universe, as well as Del's, no woman was actually doing anything important or meaningful unless it was with a man. Their mutual desire for, and determination to have, any breathing male who appealed to them was the one thing, besides being flashy middle-aged single mothers of handsome sons, that they had in common.

Neither of which caused them to form any kind of bond.

"No," I said, rubbing my forehead. "I don't have a date. But I *am* doing something tonight. I am going to read a book and drink to the new year and enjoy the blizzard. By myself."

"Well, that works out really good," Alanna said, smiling, "because I do have a date. And her too," she said, frowning across the cafe at Del. "And Rhonda and Brian are celebrating together." She shot a genuine smile at her son in the kitchen.

"None of which has anything to do with what I'm doing tonight," I said, edging away. My burger platter was getting cold.

"Well, in a way it does."

I didn't want to ask.

She waited. I waited.

I caved.

"How does it matter?"

"Well, all of us," Alanna indicated everyone in the cafe, and probably the rest of the world, "have plans tonight. You know, *formal* plans with other people and all. And we're all likely to be out late. And maybe we'll all celebrate a bit too much . . ."

She let the sentence hang.

I let her sentence hang too.

Rhonda caught my eye again and pointed at the congealing burger and fries.

Presley, assuming that Rhonda needed assistance, poked his head around the divider and hollered, "Tory! Burger."

I shot a warning look at Pres, who grinned and ducked back into the kitchen.

Alanna hemmed and hawed and hesitated and tucked her blouse in and patted her very large hair and avoided looking me in the eye. "You know we're having, um, financial difficulties here. You know we've discussed several ways to bring in more cash. You *know* we need the business."

She was starting to plead. My heart sank. Whatever she was leading up to, it was bad.

Alanna pointed out the window. "And with this storm coming in, most folks are going to stay right here in town. No one is going to chance the roads with a blizzard. Even on New Year's Eve."

Her voice trailed off again.

From across the cafe, Ron shouted, "If that's my hamburger sitting up on the counter, you can just throw it away. I'm not paying for a cold one."

I rubbed my forehead, wishing it was time to close. Wishing I lived in Hawaii and had never heard of Delphi, South Dakota.

Or at least the Delphi Cafe.

"Should we make another one?" Rhonda asked from the kitchen.

I nodded and then fixed Alanna with a steely glare, daring her to complicate my day any further.

She did.

In a rush, with almost no accent at all, she said, "Mostly no one is going to leave town tonight but they're all going to go out and get drunk. And they're all going to be hungry when the bar closes."

I groaned. "We've been over this already. There isn't any way we can expand our hours to stay open in the middle of the night. Drunks are impossible to please— they throw up in the bathroom when they're not punching each other in the booths. Besides, there's no one to work a midnight shift."

"But we need the money and we need the customers," Alanna said defiantly, standing up to her full height, which with the addition of piles of blond hair, was considerable. "I already posted a sign up in the bar saying that we're going to open up at midnight tonight for a special New Year's breakfast."

I stood with my mouth open, flabbergasted. *"You what?"* I said, much more loudly than I'd intended because the cafe went suddenly silent.

I glared at the room in general, which shamefacedly went back to normal.

"We'll pull in two grand, easy. Two grand that we

need desperately if we're going to make bills this month," Alanna said quietly, smiling. "No one tips like a drunk, you know that."

Still flabbergasted, I bit back a retort about not being as adept as strippers at manipulating tips from drunks. And another about one partner making arbitrary business decisions without consulting the other. And my cutting comment about her assumption that I'd give up my New Year's Eve plans just because I didn't have a date.

Well, actually I was going to say that last one out loud just as soon as I started to breathe normally again, but Del squealed.

"He's here. He's here, he's here, he's here," she chanted excitedly, ducking into the bathroom to recheck her makeup and fluff her perfect red hair and loosen the top two buttons of her artfully tight shirt. She reemerged and danced nervously, knowing that not a single eye in the cafe was on her.

They were all watching out the window as a craggy-faced man wearing a cowboy hat, gloves, and a perfect Marlboro Man sheepskin jacket with a white carnation pinned to the lapel strode across the street toward the cafe.

It is safe to say that Del has had the experience of many men, some of them certifiably gorgeous, but I'd never seen her in this kind of state, hyperventilating like a sixties schoolgirl who'd just caught a glimpse of Paul McCartney.

Alanna craned her neck to look out the window, feigning boredom, an expression that was quickly replaced by surprise. "My God, he *is* gorgeous."

The cafe door swung open as Del turned away swiftly and pretended to arrange Eldon's placemat.

The rest of the cafe didn't even pretend to be doing anything else. The locals had been evenly divided between thinking that Del had woven Ian from whole cloth, and predicting that if he was flesh and blood, that he'd be seriously unimpressive in person.

Not a single person, myself included, thought he'd

turn out to be a blend of Clint Eastwood and Harrison Ford, only taller, with a little Robert Redford thrown in for good measure.

We were impressed.

Hell, we were stunned.

And we were quiet, quieter than any roomful of curious South Dakotans had ever been, in the entire history of the state.

The tall handsome man that we all assumed was Ian Douglas O'Hara removed his hat, fingered his boutonniere and cleared his throat.

"Um," he said. "Pardon me."

Even his voice was handsome. And if I was not mistaken, English. Or at least English by way of PBS. It was certainly not an accent one would expect from a man who looked like he'd be perfectly at home on a horse.

Alanna groaned. Or maybe it was a moan.

He tilted his head her way and said, "Ma'am. Maybe you can help me. I am looking for a Miss Delphine Bauer."

Alanna swallowed, unable to speak, unable to smile, and unable to take her eyes off the stranger. She grimaced and nodded in Del's direction.

Del herself was facing Ian, and smiling. And blushing.

Ron Adler scowled, blinked, and mumbled something that sounded suspiciously like "Limey cowboy," which jump-started activity in the cafe again. Silverware clinked, cigarettes were lit, conversation began again where it left off. But all eyes were still surreptitiously glued to the pair standing in the aisle—the middle-aged glowing redhead and the smiling, possibly English stranger.

Well, all eyes were on them for about four seconds until I heard a muffled yelp from the kitchen.

Alanna, concentration focused, had obviously not heard the sound. And neither did anyone else in the cafe as they watched Del and Ian, their heads full of sweet thoughts of romance.

Or not so sweet thoughts.

Ron sat glued in his booth, glaring at the pair, not blinking at all.

Sighing, I pushed through the swinging half-door that divided the cafe from the kitchen proper. Rhonda and Brian stood close together, examining something that Rhonda held between them.

"You all right?" I asked Rhonda, who jumped guiltily, and hid something behind her back. "I thought I heard someone scream."

"I'm sorry Tory," Rhonda said, red-faced, hands behind her back, looking down at the floor. "I didn't mean to scare you." She shot a glance at Brian. "Well, we were just . . . well, you know . . . and I sorta hollered without meaning to."

Blond and pretty in a sturdy corn-fed way, twenty-year old Rhonda blushed furiously. Twenty-six, tall, handsome, and old enough to have outgrown such things, Brian blushed too.

Ah, young love.

I shook my head, too tired even to think about the health-code ramifications of romance over the grill. "Can we get back to work now?"

Rhonda nodded and turned to the grill where a couple of hamburger patties sizzled merrily on their way to becoming charcoal.

"Jeez Tory," Presley said, sliding off the wooden stool where he'd been sitting for the last hour or so. "You're sure mean lately."

"Yeah, and I'm about to get a whole lot meaner," I said sternly to him. "Don't you have somewhere else to be?"

"Nope," he said forlornly. "This is one dead town."

"You know, even bored, normal boys don't enjoy hanging out at their mother's place of employment," I said, hoping he'd take the hint and go be bored somewhere else. It's not that he was in the way as he sat on a stool and gazed longingly at Rhonda, wishing for excitement, it's just that I had more than enough to worry about without a juvenile civilian hanging around the kitchen.

He grinned, drew himself up to his full height, which was these days a couple of inches taller than me, and threw an arm around my shoulder. "Yeah, well, I'm not normal and I'm not a boy," he said, deepening his voice manfully. "And you're not my mother."

"She's not that far away, you know," I said, giving up.

Presley grinned an irresistible grin and kissed me noisily on the forehead.

Deciding that I would never understand the vagaries of the male pubescent mind, I pushed back through the swinging door into the cafe.

Del and her admirer had done a good job holding the attention in the cafe, which was running smoothly at the moment. Ron and Alanna were sitting in a booth together in deep conversation, shooting alternate venomous glances in Del's oblivious direction.

I poured myself a half glass of Diet Coke with ice and sat wearily across from Eldon McKee.

"That drink offer still open?" I asked.

"You damn betcha," he said grinning. "It's after five o'clock somewhere."

"Cheers," I mumbled to myself as he poured whiskey into my glass. I didn't care who saw him do it either.

"Well you know what they say," Eldon said cryptically.

I stirred the drink with a straw and then swallowed a large gulp, wincing as the whiskey burned down my throat. "No, what do they say?"

"It never rains but it pours," he said.

"Well, I think it's poured enough for one day," I said, taking another, smaller sip. "Things should calm down now."

"You might be just a bit premature on that one, sweetie," Eldon said, grinning even wider.

"Nah, a handsome stranger and a sudden change in business hours are more than enough to whet my appetite for adventure," I said, finishing my drink in two more big swallows.

Eldon *tched*, a noise that clearly indicated that there were wonders on heaven and earth that I had not yet witnessed in my less than half-century of observation.

I'd been hearing that sort of admonishment from the older generation my whole life, and so I didn't pay strict attention to Eldon, who continued to talk. I was far more concerned that I hadn't brought more than one glass of pop with me from the fountain.

". . . in fact, I think things are just about to get excitin' again," he said pointedly, indicating the street outside the cafe window. "Right now."

I turned to see plump and pretty Gina Adler, Ron's long-suffering wife, march purposefully down the street toward the cafe. Her face was set in grim determination and her long pink bathrobe flapped open to reveal a worn, flowered, flannel nightgown.

Despite the cold and snow, she did not wear a hat or gloves, and her fuzzy bunny slippers were most emphatically not snow boots.

She did, however, carry a Louisville Slugger gripped tightly in her right hand.

Without even a glance toward the cafe, she planted her feet wide, and swung the bat from an overhead stance—a powerful blow that struck and shattered the windshield of her husband's idling pickup.

2

Women Are From Mars, Men Are From Sioux Falls

Females on this planet bear the reputation of being the kinder, gentler sex. We're automatically expected to be weaker, calmer, more nurturing, and better with a dust mop than carbon-based life forms who do not happen to carry the double X chromosome.

This genetic code, we have been told, compels us to fuss over children and homes far more than our pretty little heads bother about our mates' equally coded tendency toward wandering eyes and other assorted body parts.

We're sweetness and light, they're piss and vinegar. Sugar and spice versus snakes and snails. Biological clocks pitted against mid-life crises. And all the while, we're supposed to look pretty and keep the house clean and supper warm in the oven because it is our destiny to do so.

Such theorizing looks good on paper, and in the sociological and anthropological journals (not to mention the nonfiction best-seller list), but anyone thinking that females are inherently more passive has not paid attention. Just ask a black widow spider with a full stomach and a smile on her face if the female of the species isn't occasionally more deadly than the male.

And given the proper incentive, your average female can swing a pretty mean bat too.

Usually docile and cheery, patient and uncomplaining, concerned primarily with her home, adolescent son, and the care and feeding of a husband coming off a long-term attraction to another woman, Gina Adler had evidently found enough incentive to smash the shit out of Ron's work truck.

Swinging furiously in her nightgown and bathrobe, she'd turned the windshield into a zillion sparkling crystals and had begun working on the headlights before anyone else noticed the activity outside.

As I hesitated, trying to decide whether to call the police, who would take a minimum of fifteen minutes to arrive, or go outside and try to disarm Gina without becoming a casualty myself, someone from across the cafe cleared his throat loudly and announced, "Uh, say Ron, I think your old lady wants a word with you."

Though Ron had been sitting in a window booth that afforded a perfect view of the carnage going on just outside, he'd been too deep in conversation with Alanna to notice the commotion. He shot a confused and slightly guilty glance at the speaker, who grinned and pointed out the window.

By the time Ron turned to look, the whole cafe was gasping, and enjoying the spectacle of Gina playing Casey at the Bat, though unlike Mighty Casey, La Adler never ever missed.

Ron squealed in horror, grabbed the top half of his coveralls, and tried desperately to jam his arms into the sleeves as he ran for the door. Within moments, everyone in the place had followed him into the cold, though

I doubt anyone noticed the below-zero temperatures or the fierce wind.

Cafe patrons were not the only Delphi residents attracted to the scene. Early New Year's Eve revelers poured out of the bar and across the street, cheering and whooping. All three employees at my Uncle Albert Engebretson's insurance office stared goggle-eyed as Gina brought the bat down squarely on the hood of the Ford, which was still gamely idling. Out of the corner of my eye, I saw Stuart McKee, wearing a Cargill jacket and a pair of jersey gloves, trot across the street from the Feed and Seed Store he ran with his father.

Curious, and delightfully horrified by the unexpected display, the onlookers gathered in an informal, shivering circle around Ron's truck, close enough for a good view of the proceedings while maintaining a healthy respect for Gina's unexpectedly powerful swing.

"Gina! Honey! Dear, what are you doing?" Ron danced frantically around his truck, trying to get his wife's attention. "Honey, calm down. Calm down, please. Gina, sweetie."

Oblivious to his pleas, Gina aimed another blow that dented the driver's side fender. Ron flinched as though the bat had been aimed at him.

"Honey, you gotta stop this!" A side mirror flew into the air. "Jesus." Ron's voice rose and cracked in desperation. "Dear, you're ruining my truck."

Neither Ron's anguish, nor his statement of the obvious, had the slightest effect on his wife, who continued smashing her merry way around the vehicle. A rolled-up window withstood the first two whacks, but a carefully aimed third sent the whole thing flying into the driver's seat.

Finally realizing that he wasn't getting through to her, Ron appealed to the crowd. "Someone's gotta help me stop her. I don't know what's wrong with her. I think she's gone crazy."

I don't know whether Gina heard Ron's earlier conversational gambits and just ignored them, or if his last

statement was the only one to get through to her, but
she whirled around suddenly, and advanced on her husband.

"Crazy, huh?" she shouted. "Crazy? I'll give you
fucking crazy." She swung the bat menacingly in Ron's
direction.

Now there are women who salt their conversation
with the "F" word like sailors on leave. And there are
women who use it for emphasis in extreme situations.
And there are women who suddenly find themselves co-
owners of cafes in small towns who use that word (and
others of the same ilk) far more often than previously.

But there are even more women who are physically,
morally, and completely incapable of forming that syllable.

I'd have sworn that Gina Adler was one of them. And
up until she uttered that particular Anglo-Saxon vulgar-
ity, I had assumed there was a conventional explanation
for her behavior, like the presence of pods in the Adler
basement.

But once Gina shouted *that* word, a term she'd never
even hinted at in our more than twenty-five years' acquaintance, I knew that Ron was right. Gina had traveled
completely around the bend.

"Crazy? Did I say crazy?" Ron asked, wide-eyed and
backing up, stuffing his hands into his coverall pockets.
The circle of onlookers backed up a step with him. "I
didn't mean crazy. Not really crazy. You just surprised
me, that's all."

Gina lowered the bat and stared at Ron, who stood
his ground. "If I'm crazy, it's your fault," she shouted.
"You made me crazy. You, and . . ." Gina hesitated and
scanned the crowd, and then pointed. "You and *her*."

She meant Del.

The crowd actually gasped, as though Del and Ron's
affair was news.

In reality, their affair was such old news that the fact
that it had cooled off into almost total animosity wasn't
even news anymore.

However, it was news to me, and to the rest of the crowd, judging by their reaction, that Gina thought the affair was still an ongoing concern.

We stood outside in Delphi's main drag in the middle of an incipient blizzard, with the wind whipping our hair, snow whirling around us, with frostbite imminent, and still no one moved. As if watching a tennis match, the collective gaze turned back to Ron to see how he'd volley Gina's shot.

His relief was evident as he took a tentative step toward his wife. "There's nothing going on between Del and me," he said, blinking soothingly. "You know that was over a long time ago, and it was a terrible mistake."

I heard a small growl behind me, and turned to see Del, arms wrapped around herself for warmth, shooting death rays at Ron.

Ian O'Hara, whom I'd forgotten in the interim excitement, stood by Del's side looking studiously ambivalent, perhaps considering a shade too late the wisdom of finding dates through personal ads.

Ron, emboldened by Gina's silence, took another step forward, which move she countered with a sudden one-armed swing of the bat that missed his forehead by bare inches. Ron squealed and jumped back.

"*Over a long time ago*, my ass," Gina spat, voice increasing in volume. "If it was over a long time ago, where were you last night? Where were you *both* last night?" she shouted. "*All* night?"

The crowd murmured, and then split, half waiting for Ron's rebuttal, and the other half staring at Del.

Now Del has some heavy sins laid against her, not the least a few afternoons spent in the company of the married Ron Adler (and a goodly assortment of other men, some married and some not). But I happened to know that Gina was off base, at least as to the timing of that particular accusation.

Last night Del had been at home, puttering joyfully around the trailer, speculating ad nauseam about her projected meeting with Ian O'Hara. We sat up together yak-

king until I finally went to bed at midnight. Unable to
sleep, Del had covered up with an afghan on the green
vinyl couch to watch old movies, where she'd still been
at three A.M. when I got up to go to the bathroom. At
six when I left for work, she'd been snoring peacefully
in her room.

It was not beyond Del's skills or morals to sneak out
of the trailer for a quickie in the middle of the night,
even in the middle of winter—but considering her excitement over the proposed meeting with Ian, and Gina's
emphasis on the "all" part of *all night*, I was fairly certain that Del had not left the trailer between supper last
night and breakfast this morning.

A belated sense of propriety toward her son, especially since Presley and John Adler were good friends,
had kept Del from inviting Ron home for any of their
sporadic trysts—so I was equally certain that Ron had
not spent the night in the trailer.

With my mouth running far ahead of my brain, I
stepped forward without thinking and said, "You're mistaken, Gina."

She whirled around, and for the first time I saw in her
eyes the look of a woman who'd been pushed to the
limit.

And in the snowstorm, with flakes swirling around
her, I saw behind the current rage and temporary insanity
an intense and enormous hurt, a pain so raw and familiar
that it twisted my own heart.

I reached toward Gina, saying, foolishly it turned out,
"Del was home with me last night. I swear."

Gina's eyes narrowed and she sneered. "Of course
you'd say that. You home wreckers all stick together."

I pulled back, startled by the sudden attack.

"Aha," Gina pounced. "Hit you where it hurt, didn't
I?"

Confused, I stared back at her.

The crowd's attention was now focused on me, something I found distinctly unpleasant.

"Yeah, everyone thinks you're so sweet. *Ooooh poor*

Tory," Gina sing-songed, her words pouring out in a rush. "*Isn't it terrible that Stu McKee's wife left him? Isn't it nice? Isn't it wonderful that Tory and Stu are seeing each other? Tory realllly deserves some happiness after her awful marriage.*"

Gina smiled a terrible smile.

I pulled back, breathing heavily, not wanting this conversation to continue and unable to stop it.

The crowd, huddling in the cold, stood like statues waiting to hear what I knew Gina was going to say next.

"How many of you know that Tory and Stu were seeing each other before his wife left town?" she asked the crowd. "How many of you know that they spent all last summer shacking up in motel rooms?"

Evidently one use of the word *fucking* was all Gina would allow herself per public breakdown. But it didn't matter. No matter what term she used, everyone got the point.

Other than Stu and me, only three people knew that our affair had started before Renee's temporary sojourn to Minnesota. I figured that Renee herself would keep the secret. And I knew that Neil Pascoe would never tell anyone.

I thought I had known the same thing about Del.

Struck dumb by the venom, and the accuracy, of Gina's unexpected attack, I shot a glance back at Del, who had the grace to look guilty before she shot an equally venomous glance at Ron Adler, who blinked furiously and looked away.

Loose lips had certainly sunk my ship.

I could not bring myself to look at Stu, though I sensed the crowd had no compunction about doing so.

Unable to form a reply, a denial, a response of any kind, I stood mute and obviously guilty in front of a jury of my peers, whose dawning understanding of the situation was transparent on their chapped and raw and completely surprised faces.

I looked back at Gina, whose face suddenly went slack, her shoulders slumped, the rage drained from her eyes. She slowly turned around, as if seeing the crowd, the wreckage that had been her husband's truck, and the bat in her hand, for the first time. She looked down at her nightgown and slippers, and then up at the gray sky, and then desperately at me.

She dropped the bat, only dimly aware, I think, of the spectacle she'd just created, and even more dimly realizing what she'd done to me. Her face crumpled as she dissolved into miserable, racking sobs.

Surprising us all, Ian O'Hara stepped forward and enveloped Gina in his arms and began to murmur soothing sounds, rocking her slightly.

Rhonda, bless her heart, stepped through the crowd and gingerly picked up the bat, and then placed a comforting arm around my shoulders, saying loud enough for the others to hear, "She didn't mean it, Tory. You know she was out of her head when she said those awful things."

Still unable to speak, I nodded numbly and turned to go back into the warmth of the cafe but caught sight of Presley shivering in the cold. He'd witnessed the whole confrontation.

His face contorted in anger and disgust, misery, and complete disappointment. Too young to have to deal with more than his mother's indiscretions gracefully, he silently pleaded with me to contradict Gina's accusation. If I'd had another couple of minutes to compose myself, and if he'd been any less aware of the foibles of the adults around him, I could have lied well enough to fool him. At least for a couple more years.

But I didn't have time, and Presley's a smart kid.

He turned and ran off through the swirling snow.

"Let him go," Del said quietly. "He'll get over it."

I was too upset to answer Del, though I knew she was right. At least about letting Presley go. It was anybody's guess as to whether he'd ever get over it.

I watched him disappear down the street, wondering how a perfectly ordinary day had become so very interesting so very quickly, hoping that would be an end to the excitement for one winter afternoon.

Unfortunately, hope in one hand and a quarter in the other won't even get you a cup of coffee these days.

3

....

Fire and Ice

It is the pleasure and the bane of small-town existence to know the details of one another's lives. We understand the workings of one another's brains. We recognize one another's grandparents, and can rattle off their political leanings, weight, and checking account balances—sometimes without the formality of familiarity with the facts.

In knowing so many intimate details about those around us, we come automatically to assume that we know everything there is to know about one another.

And often we do know everything.

Or we know what amounts to everything. Or we know enough of everything that we really don't need the rest of the details immediately.

Sometimes the most shocking revelations, the sneaky last pieces to interesting puzzles, come when they're least expected.

Unfortunately, embarrassing secrets don't have an expiration date, so a juicy tidbit about an already defunct relationship has the power to hold the collective interest just as surely six months after the fact as new gossip hot off the press.

I had known, of course, that the truth about when my relationship with Stu McKee had really begun would come out.

I knew the truth. And it goes without saying that Stu knew the truth. Renee knew it. Neil knew it, and unfortunately so did Del. That was four more people than the highest number able to keep any one secret.

The rest would have found out eventually that I was sleeping with Stu before his wife left him.

But given my druthers, it wouldn't have been today. And it wouldn't have been in the middle of the street, in front of the whole town. And it wouldn't have happened with both Stu and me in the audience.

Our relationship had been wrong from the beginning (as everyone in Delphi would know by this evening), but it had had its moments. And I missed those moments, though this was probably not the time to wax nostalgic.

Ostensibly buzzing over Gina Adler's astonishing performance with the Louisville Slugger, I detected many a speculative glance as the crowd dissipated.

Several lady friends pried Gina away from Ian O'Hara's obviously comforting arms. Ron took a tentative step toward his weeping and disconsolate wife, but the women who surrounded her turned on him and actually growled. He stepped back in alarm, blinking rapidly, as they formed a protective huddle and hurried her down the block.

Cold, confused, and possibly in shock, Ron stood staring bleakly at his ruined truck. A few guys hovered valiantly nearby, but none said a word.

Vastly entertained, and sorry the show was over so quickly, the bar crowd whooped their way across and down the street into the comforting smoke-filled warmth of Jackson's Hole. Uncle Albert, who carried the insur-

ance on Ron's truck, reentered his agency with a worried
expression on his usually mild face. The cafe patrons
filed back inside noisily.

I studiously ignored all inquiring glances. Peripher-
ally, I could tell that just as many glances were being
shot at Stu, though I couldn't look at him directly, and
therefore could not see how he weathered the scrutiny.

Suddenly aware of the bone-chilling wind and my
own complete weariness, I sighed and went back into
the cafe.

After being outside, the indoor heat felt tropical and
oppressive. Though the chatter didn't evaporate when
the door closed, it definitely paused for a moment before
resuming even more loudly.

Del, standing by one of the tables with Ian, motioned
me over but I waved her off. There was nothing she
could say to take back what had just happened, and I
had no desire to make her feel better about it.

I would like to have gone home and mourned the loss
of my undeserved Good Girl reputation, or better still,
gotten rip-roaring drunk and thought about nothing at
all. But there were tables to clean and orders to take,
and details of the New Year's Eve Feed From Hell to
iron out.

Somewhere in between Gina Adler's one-woman de-
molition derby and the shattering of my dignity, I had
realized that opening up late in order to feed the drunken
hordes was a distasteful, but necessary move if we
wanted to stay in business. Even if it was Alanna's idea
and I had not been consulted in advance. Even if it
meant that I could not hide out in the trailer this evening.

"So, exactly what did you promise the multitudes by
way of food tonight?" I asked Alanna, who had been
whispering worriedly with her son behind the counter as
I approached. Brian nodded somberly at me, and returned to Rhonda in the kitchen.

Sensing correctly that I was not in the mood for play-
ful Southern seductiveness, Alanna answered me forth-
rightly, and with a minimum of accent. "It'll be best if

we limit the number of choices. I figured we'd cook up a mess of scrambled eggs, sausage links, and bacon, and then let 'em choose between hash browns and pancakes. And toast of course."

"Of course," I said. "And how much are we charging for this little repast?"

Junoesque, with bleached blond hair in haphazard piles on the top of her head, Alanna stood to her full height, threw her shoulders back (which always caught the attention of any males in the vicinity), and winked. "It'll be enough, believe me."

I didn't have the energy to play coy or beg for details. And suddenly I didn't care whether we broke even or not. The cafe had been Aphrodite Ferguson's baby. She had somehow single-handedly made it a going concern that not only paid our wages, but had supported her in the manner to which she had become accustomed for more than twenty-five years.

Alanna and I had been responsible for the day-to-day operations of the cafe for two months now, and under our tender ministrations, the business was precariously close to closing its doors forever. If Alanna's little fund-raising idea paid off, fine. If not, we would be that much closer to shooting the whole thing in the head and putting all of us out of our misery.

"Okay," I said, squinting up at her. "Do we have enough supplies?"

"I ordered extra last week. We got plenty of eggs and pancake mix," she said triumphantly, which meant she'd planned this shindig in advance and still waited until this afternoon to tell me about it.

Over by the till, the pay phone on the wall rang.

"Who else is working this with me? You know I can't do it by myself."

The phone continued to ring.

"Well?" I prodded.

"I'll be here, at least part of the time," she said, licking her lip.

"Wrong," I pounced. "You'll be here the whole time. From midnight until two, right?"

"Well, I don't think I can be here the whole time," she whined.

The phone was still ringing. I shot a murderous glance at Del, who scurried over to answer it.

Maybe I could play her guilt to my advantage for a while.

"If you're not here, I won't be here," I said, smiling dangerously.

Alanna swallowed, and then nodded.

"Who's cooking?"

"Well, there's a little problem about that," Alanna said.

The door opened and a tall woman wrapped in several layers of bulky coat, scarf and mittens, with a folded up newspaper under her arm, entered.

We all shivered as a gust of wind whipped around the interior of the cafe while the door closed. Del huddled closer to the wall, talking seriously into the phone.

I raised an eyebrow at Alanna. "Well?"

"Well," she said slowly. "We have a small problem about cooking tonight. Rhonda had offered to come in for a while . . ." Her voice trailed off.

"Rhonda knew about it?" I asked, sending a glance of my own at the traitor in the kitchen, but Rhonda and Brian were again examining something in Rhonda's hand, and did not notice. "When did you tell *her*?"

"That's beside the point now," Alanna said in a rush, "because Rhonda burned her hand and she can't cook."

I pushed through the swinging half-door that divided the kitchen from the cafe. "Are you all right?" I asked Rhonda. Maybe it was more of a demand. "When did this happen? Let me see."

Rhonda, embarrassed, held out her right hand. Her entire palm was an angry red, and blisters were forming in a ring around an area about two inches in diameter. The skin wasn't peeling or cracked, but it was obviously painful. No wonder she'd picked up the bat so gingerly outside.

"Oh hon," I said, instantly contrite. "You need to put some ice on this right away."

I shot a significant look at Brian, who headed out to the ice hopper behind the counter.

"When did this happen?" I asked Rhonda.

"This morning, just after Del's date got here," she said, voice trailing off. "I was trying to get a good look at him and I accidentally splashed hot grease on my hand. And that made me jump and I spilled more on the grill and it flared up and burned my hand. I sorta screamed a little. I think you must have heard me."

I'd heard her, and had thought that she and Brian were practicing new and dangerous courtship rituals over the grill.

Brian returned with a cup full of ice chips and a clean washrag which he assembled into a cold compress and gently applied to Rhonda's injured hand.

"Why in the hell didn't you tell me that you were hurt right away?" I asked.

Rhonda and Brian exchanged guilty glances.

"Well, we knew that Mom had planned to stay open tonight," Brian said slowly. "And we knew you wouldn't like the idea. We figured you'd like it even less if Rhonda was too hurt to help you."

"We didn't want to complicate your life any more than necessary," Rhonda said.

"Too late," I said. It was possibly the understatement of the day. "I appreciate the thought, but you won't be able to cook. In fact, you should have a doctor look at it."

"That'll have to wait," Brian said quietly. "There's no travel advised, and we'd be nuts to try the highways now."

We couldn't see the windows from the kitchen, but we could hear the wind howl, and feel the building shake with each gust. Brian was right, nothing but a life-threatening injury would be worth the risk of traveling fifteen miles to the nearest emergency room.

Cursing everything that had brought us to this point, including the big fire that had killed Aphrodite, and the little one that had burned Rhonda's hand, as well as the blowing and drifting snow, and the ice-packed roads that kept her from getting the injury treated, and ensured that the local drunks would stay strictly local, I nodded at Brian. "You're right."

To Rhonda I said, "Go home and keep that thing iced and hope the weather clears tomorrow so you can get it looked at."

"Tory," Del said through the opening that divided the kitchen from the cafe. "Tory, I need to talk to you about that phone call."

"Just a minute," I said to Del without looking at her. "Are *you* going to be able to cook tonight anyway?" I asked Brian.

"I'd love to," he said. "I really mean that, but I sorta promised to help the DJ at the bar with karaoke stuff." He shrugged helplessly. "By the time we're done over there, you won't need me here. Sorry."

"Well, I guess I can cook," I said, sighing. We all knew how well my cooking went over with the general public. "But you," I said to Alanna, who'd been watching everything from the doorway, "can't do all the tables by yourself."

We all turned to Del.

"Nope. Uh-uh," she said, furiously shaking her head. "No way. I have *plans*."

We all knew she had *plans*; we'd heard endlessly about her *plans* for a good long time. And we all knew exactly what these particular *plans* meant to Del.

As much as I would like to have shamed her into working, and as much as we needed the help, forcing Del to miss her wildly anticipated evening of romance would ruin the rest of the month for all of us.

"All right," I said, giving up. "We'll figure out something."

We were interrupted by a sharp rapping on the stainless steel divider.

The tall woman who'd come in earlier had removed several sets of outerwear to reveal a lanky figure wearing a sweatshirt and jeans. Short shaggy faded brown hair cut in no particular style framed a smiling face covered with a fine tracing of wrinkles but devoid of makeup.

She slid a folded newspaper across the counter to me. Circled in felt pen was our ad looking for a cook.

She pointed at the ad, and then at herself.

I looked at the woman, who smiled even more widely.

"Can you cook?" I asked.

She nodded.

"Can you start tonight?"

She nodded again.

"Good then," I said. "You're hired."

4

....

Deus Ex Machina

I have a fair amount of practice in the willing suspension of disbelief. I was a book-a-day reader from the time I figured out that it was the black marks on the printed page, and not the spaces in between, that mattered. I often believe six impossible things before breakfast. And when Nick was still alive, I worked on believing even more impossible things after supper, especially when he'd amble in six or seven hours late with a cockamamie story about a flat tire.

That said, I do prefer my plot twists and conundrums to fit realistically into the story at hand. I cast a suspicious eye on the sudden appearance of long-lost evil twins, or the transfer of ancient but heretofore unknown titles and grand estates. And though I'd personally love to have a fairy godmother, I don't really believe in them.

However, we were in dire need of a relief cook, and if the gods had seen fit to open a hole in the cafe ceiling and lower one down to us on a cable, I wouldn't have blinked twice.

As it was, at the exact moment when all seemed most bleak, one entered our lives by the mundane method of walking in off the street. I was not about to look a gift cook in the mouth.

"In fact," I said to the smiling woman, "if you want to start now, you're more than welcome."

She nodded.

"Whoa, just a minute here," Alanna pulled me aside and said sort of quietly. "I think we need to get some details worked out before we hire some stranger without references or anything."

"Yeah," I said tiredly. "Important details like who's going to cook tonight since Rhonda can't. You want the job?"

"Well." She bit her lip and patted her hair. "Not really."

"Me neither," I said. "So it's settled?"

"We don't even know the woman's name yet." Alanna pouted. "Or if she really can cook."

"We know she wants the job and she's willing to start right away. It's a sure bet that she can cook better than me, right?"

Alanna squinted over my shoulder at the woman, who stood her ground, smiling. "Oh all right," she said, sighing loudly. "I just hope that she doesn't poison anyone."

"Me too," I said, turning to the woman.

"Looks like you got yourself a job starting immediately," I said to her, holding out my hand. "I'm Tory Bauer, co-owner of this magnificent establishment with that lady there." I indicated Alanna with my other hand.

"Alanna Luna, glad to have you with us," Alanna said grudgingly.

The woman's eyes widened just a tad at Alanna's improbable name. Though we were used to her, we'd forgotten that both Alanna's name and her aspect trumpeted her former profession loudly.

She looked, walked, dressed, and sounded exactly like an ex-stripper from Oklahoma.

"And this," I said pointing into the kitchen, "is

Rhonda Saunders, our injured temporary relief cook, and
Brian Hunt, Alanna's son."

Rhonda and Brian smiled and said hello.

"Over here is Delphine Bauer, our other waitress.
She's also my late husband's cousin. We share a trailer
out on the edge of town." I figured I'd save some time
and start with a little of the genealogy right off the bat.
"This is Ian, and he's new here, and probably a little
overwhelmed by all our small-town excitement."

Del managed a tight smile, and edged a little closer
to Ian, who looked uncomfortable being included in cafe
business. The woman shook hands with everyone and
smiled, and looked around the cafe with satisfaction.

Several people were standing at the till. Del harrum-
phed a bit, and then began ringing them out. Rhonda
slid a meal for me across the counter. On the way to
picking it up, it occurred to me that we didn't know our
new cook's name yet.

It also occurred to me that we hadn't heard her speak.

"Why don't you come on over here and we can get
your numbers and things down so you can get going,"
Alanna said from behind the counter. She opened a
drawer and sorted through a pile of papers. "It'll be easier if we carry you off the books for the rest of today,
just to save some tax hassles, it being New Year's Eve
and all," she drawled, not looking up. "We'll just start
you on the payroll nice and proper tomorrow and pay
cash for your hours tonight."

I hoped our new cook wasn't an undercover IRS
agent.

As Alanna searched for a formal employment application, the new cook caught my eye and winked, and
then deliberately covered her mouth with one hand and
shook her head slightly.

I tilted my head and looked at her quizzically. She
repeated the gesture.

I raised an eyebrow and touched my ear. I don't know
sign, but she understood my question and nodded back.

I gave a very politically incorrect sigh of relief, and then immediately felt guilty for being relieved.

Keeping one eye on Alanna and the new cook, I set the plate down in front of Eldon McKee. "Have we had enough excitement now?"

"I wouldn't bet on it, toots," he cackled. "You up for one last bump?" He patted the flask in his pocket. "I think I can spring for another round before I need to head out."

"Sounds lovely, but I think things are going to get busy again in a minute," I said, indicating Alanna.

Eldon, who didn't miss much, nodded sagely. "She don't need to talk right now. She just needs to cook," he said.

"You wanna explain that to Alanna?" I asked.

"Nope, I'm having enough fun looking out the window. Always something to see."

Through the window, we watched Ron struggle valiantly to pull a dented fender away from the tire so he could back out and drive what was left of his poor pitiful truck down the street to his garage.

"Always good stories to tell about the things going on around you. Want to hear something interesting?" Eldon grinned wickedly.

"Tory, honey, could you come over here a sec?" Alanna said urgently, with more than enough accent to fill those syllables to overflow.

"Maybe later, Eldon." I sighed. Any time Alanna tossed an endearment in my direction, we were in for trouble. "You sure you don't want to take over?"

"You're younger 'n me, go to it," Eldon said, grinning lopsidedly.

"Tory." Del grabbed my arm on the way past. "I need to talk to you a minute about that phone call. Also, it's time for me to leave."

"Leave?" I was confused.

"My shift is over. I'm off. I have a date, remember?"

How could I have forgotten? "Okay. Have a good time," I said. I even meant it. "I'll see you later then."

"No, this is important." Del insisted.

Whatever was bothering her, it was serious.

"Tory, I need you," Alanna said, just a little more loudly and with a tad more Southern in her voice. *"Raht naow."*

"Tory," Rhonda sing-songed from the kitchen, pushing another plate across the counter.

What I wouldn't have given to have been this popular in high school. I blew out all my air and decided that Alanna had first priority.

"Tory," Del began, but I interrupted her.

"This first. I'll only be a second, okay?"

Del clenched her teeth and nodded.

"And take my meal for me, would you? I'll be fast. I promise."

Amazingly enough, most of the cafe was buzzing among themselves, paying no attention to Alanna's conversation behind the counter with the newcomer.

She cornered me by the kitchen. "Do you know what you went and done?" she demanded, handing me a business card.

"Actually, yes," I said, glancing down at the card. "We needed a cook really badly, so I hired one."

The card read: *Hello. My name is Dorothy Gale. I am unable to speak, but can understand you completely.*

Dorothy Gale? The new cook's name was actually Dorothy Gale? Dorothy Gale who wasn't in Kansas anymore?

I raised an eyebrow at Dorothy, who waited patiently behind the counter. She smiled broadly and pantomimed a flip-flop gesture.

I turned the card over. And then I laughed out loud.

Printed on the card back in italics was: *No I'm not from Kansas.*

"Do you realize that this here woman can't speak?" Alanna's voice rose. I think she was beginning to hyperventilate. "And what in the hell is so funny?"

"Yes, indeed. I realize that Dorothy Gale cannot speak," I said. "But you should lower your voice a little.

I'm pretty sure that she can hear." I peeked around
Alanna, and caught Dorothy's eye and said, "You *can*
hear, can't you?"

Alanna turned and caught Dorothy's big nod.

The cafe door blew open, and Ron Adler shuffled in
dejectedly with a gust of wind and a swirl of fine powdery snow. All conversation halted for a moment before
continuing.

"Fine," Alanna said distractedly, "you think this is so
funny. You deal with it."

She rushed over to commiserate with Ron. Almost a
full head taller than he, she wrapped a motherly arm
around his shoulders, and ushered him to an empty
booth.

I rubbed my hands together and turned to Dorothy.
"You need anything special before you start?"

She nodded no in reply.

"Well, let's get you situated in the kitchen, then."

"Tory," Del said urgently.

"Just one more thing first," I said to Del, holding my
finger up.

We pushed through the swinging half door into the
kitchen, and I completed Dorothy's introduction to
Rhonda and Brian.

"Good enough," I said to the trio who were grinning
broadly at one another. "We all set now?"

Everyone in the kitchen nodded.

"No more emergencies? No more excitement? No
more nasty surprises?"

They all nodded again.

And for a minute, a wonderful fleeting minute, I believed them.

"*Tory,*" Del said insistently, leaning over the stainless-
steel opening between the cafe and the kitchen. "I have
a message for you from Junior."

"Junior?"

My dreaded cousin Junior Deibert had given Del, of
all people, a phone message for me?

Pregnant prissy annoying Junior, mother of four

mostly perfectly behaved children (three of those triplets), wife of the Lutheran minister, pain-in-the-butt Junior who absolutely hated Del?

And Del, who had no love for Junior, her church, her
ideals, or her children, and who would just as soon tell
Junior to sit on it and spin, had actually taken the message?

This did not bode well.

"Your mom called Junior's mom," Del said softly.
"And Junior called here. It's your grandma. She's
slipped into a coma and they don't think she'll last the
night."

5

....

Featherstonehaugh

There is never a moment in South Dakota when the weather is not the final arbiter of all things possible. No outdoor wedding, no indoor reception, no community function of any kind is ever penciled in without casting a wary eye skyward. For the best-laid plans of mice and men can be, and frequently are, waylaid by a fickle high-pressure system.

And for the smaller milestones—that first date, a wildly anticipated concert two hundred miles away, the delivery of a long-awaited package or simply a trip to the grocery store, you can bet that Mother Nature will fool you every single time.

Especially in the winter.

On the other hand, once in a while the joke is on Old Mom.

I would have trudged on foot to my mother's farm to attend the protracted death of my grandmother if I possibly could have. Both a love for my mother, who was taking care of Grandma in her final hours the same as she had during the last twenty years, and a fondness for the woman my loony old grandmother had occasionally been during my childhood, coupled with simple duty, dictated my attendance on the sad and dismal scene.

But a telephone conversation from the cafe with my ever-sensible mother convinced me of what I already knew—no waitress in her right mind would attempt three snow-clogged miles in the middle of a blizzard. Especially to attend the death of one whose functional mind had long since gone.

"You stay in town, and enjoy your evening as much as you can, dear," Mother had said. "I'll hold the fort and keep you posted on the developments. Don't let Junior pressure you into doing something rash and dangerous."

And with only a twinge of guilt, I agreed.

A few hours later, Alanna, in a fit of self-interest almost disguised as compassion, suggested that I go home and quietly commune with the spirit of my nearly departed grandmother. That leaving early would also give me a chance to rest up for the midnight brunch never even crossed her mind. I'm almost sure of it.

It crossed *my* mind, however, as I fought the sharp wind and slogged through drifts for three blocks that stretched out like thirty, reflecting that it would take the rest of the evening just to warm up again after breaking a virgin trail down the unplowed main drag.

Even swaddled in multiple scarves, earmuffs, and a hat, bundled in my warmest winter coat and wearing a double layer of Thinsulate gloves and Sorel boots that weighed a ton but were rated for minus 10 degrees, I was cold through to the core. My throat ached from the dry air by the time I finally dragged myself up the trailer steps and stepped into the blessed warmth.

I stood on the throw rug for a moment with my eyes closed to allow the frost on my eyelashes to thaw. I opened them to find that I had interrupted Del and Ian in some sort of intimate moment, stretched out on the living room floor.

Well, not *intimate* exactly, since both were completely dressed (though Del is not a stickler for nudity when it comes to intimacy). They were, however, intently involved with each other in the midst of a cheerful jumble of empty wine bottles and an open Monopoly game that had been my vain holiday attempt to wean Presley away from the Nintendo.

Pulling away with a grin, Ian scrambled to his feet in a hurry. I figured he wanted some more wine, or had to go to the bathroom or something. It took me a moment to realize that he was being polite.

I cannot remember the last time any male stood up when I entered a room, if indeed any had ever done so. As I stomped packed snow off my boots and carefully removed several layers of outerwear, I found myself hoping that Del would hang on to this one a little while. Maybe some of his manners would rub off on the natives.

Unfortunately, it was more likely to be the other way around. A month under the Delphi influence would cure Ian not only of standing in the presence of a woman, but of acknowledging her at all unless he needed another beer.

Del, still lying on the floor, tapped a tiny thimble on the Monopoly board and glared at me.

Ian, with his enchanting English accent, said, "Terribly sorry. We had no idea you'd be back so soon."

I have watched enough John Cleese movies to know that the British have a tendency to preface statements with unnecessary apologies, though I wasn't sure how to respond properly to an extraordinarily handsome man who felt the need to apologize because I'd walked in as he was feeling up my roommate on the living room floor.

"Hey." I shrugged, hanging my coat on the peg by the door. "No problem."

"Why *are* you here anyway?" Del asked. She sat up, cross-legged, and smoothed her hair and sweater down. "I figured you'd be out at the farm by now."

"Yes, we thought you might be with your mother and grandmother," Ian said soberly, which was probably a major achievement considering the number of empty bottles on the floor.

Del can put it away when she's in the mood, but even she could not have drunk one bottle of champagne and three bottles of a nice late harvest Riesling in the last few hours by herself.

My three bottles late harvest Riesling, I belatedly realized. My last three bottles, as a matter of fact.

I shot Del an exasperated look as I went into the kitchen and turned on the hot water and rubbed my frozen fingertips together.

"Would you like me to make you a cup of tea?" Ian followed me into the kitchen. "You look absolutely frozen through."

"Well, um, I'm not having tea," I said as he took the cup from my hand. His fingers brushed mine and he looked directly into my eyes and smiled. "I'm making hot chocolate." I returned the smile, looking back into his deep brown eyes. "Well, not real hot chocolate. Swiss Miss. It's a powder. You just mix it with water . . ."

My voice trailed off. I stood there like an idiot, staring into the wonderfully crinkled eyes of my roommate's blind date.

"I'll make the damn hot chocolate," Del said sharply from behind Ian. I hadn't seen her get up from the living room floor. Or enter the kitchen.

I did, however, see her jaw firmly set in irritation.

"Gimme the cup," she said flatly.

She grabbed it from Ian, and proceeded to dump several heaping tablespoonsful of mix into it and stir furiously. Her movements were the deliberate motions of one who has already had more than enough to drink.

Ian, on the other hand, seemed totally unaffected by alcohol consumption. With his eyes still locked on mine, he gently said, "Ah, but I do so love rescuing a damsel in distress. I shall warm your hands, then."

Before I knew what was happening, he placed his warm hands over my cold ones and rubbed gently.

Increased clinking at the sink brought me back to my senses. It had finally dawned on my poor slow brain that Ian was flirting with me. That thought was so foreign, and the concept so unexpected, that I immediately decided that I must be mistaken.

"This is what my Aunt Featherstonehaugh used to warm me up when I was cold as a lad," he said, taking the steaming cup from Del's hand. "May I?" he asked pointing at the cupboard door.

I nodded, narrowly avoiding the death rays Del beamed in my direction.

He opened the door and pulled out a dusty brandy bottle, poured a healthy dollop into the cup, stirred it smoothly, and handed it to me with a smile. "There, that should do the trick in no time flat."

"Your *Auntie Fanshaw* gave you *booze* when you were a kid?" Del asked, plainly not believing it for a second. She'd believe it even less if she had any notion of how *Fanshaw* was really spelled.

"Yes indeed," Ian said as he deftly wiped the dust off the brandy bottle with a dishtowel before returning it to the shelf. Then he wiped the counter down and swabbed out the sink.

I took a sip. The chocolate warmed the surface and the brandy burned all the way down. It was wonderful.

"See what I mean? Aunt Emily was a wise woman," Ian said, brushing his fingers on my shoulder.

I still wasn't sure whether or not Ian was flirting with me, but he was certainly pissing Del off.

"You were telling us why you are here and not at your grandmother's deathbed, I believe?" she said, leaning dangerously close to me, nastily imitating Ian's phrasing, if not his accent.

I leaned back on the counter, cradling the warm cup in my still cold hands. "The storm isn't over yet." We listened for a moment to the howling wind outside the trailer. "The roads aren't plowed. I would never have been able to make it to the farm anyway. So Mother suggested I stay here and she'd keep me posted."

"Here?" Del asked precisely, locking her beady gaze directly on my eyes. "Does she need to contact you *right here*?"

It finally occurred to me that however pleasant it was to be fed brandy and hot chocolate by a handsome stranger with an intoxicating accent in my own kitchen, the possibility of being stabbed to death in my sleep by my roommate was growing exponentially with every smile.

"Well, no, I don't suppose I have to be *here*, exactly," I said directly to Del. "Mother can get a message to me wherever I am."

"Oh, my. Must you go?" Ian asked, brokenhearted. "I was so enjoying getting to know you. And I'd love to hear more about your charming town." His warm hand settled on my shoulder again.

The homicidal glaze hardened in Del's eyes. "I really must." I said, resisting the urge to tack on an unnecessary apology. I had never realized how contagious an English accent could be. "I think so. Yeah."

I nodded.

Del nodded.

Ian nodded sadly.

"But where shall you go on a night like this? Where can you be safe?"

"That's an easy one," Del said shortly. She reached over and picked up the receiver of the avocado wall phone and punched in a number, and then handed the phone to me with a tight smile.

6

....

Finger Drifts

Okay, so the best possible scenario for New Year's Eve, the one I had carefully planned before my private indiscretions became common knowledge and I was faced with the not entirely unexpected loss of a close relative (and all the complications that death was sure to bring), had just gone down the tubes.

I really would have been more than happy to have spent the evening curled up in a chair alone in the trailer as the wind howled and the house shook on its cement blocks and the pipes slowly froze solid. I would even have been content to take a bucket of ice and a bottle of Southern Comfort and a glass into my bedroom to read and drink while Del and Ian dallied on the living room floor (or on the kitchen table, or wherever else suited them).

But Del's annoyance and Ian's oddly welcoming behavior (well, odd for a man who had only recently been warming his hands under someone else's sweater) made my continued presence superfluous at best.

So though it wasn't on my original agenda for the evening, trudging across the street to Neil's library was the next best solution to an awkward situation. Besides which, he was the only person I could actually talk to about Gina Adler's outburst this afternoon.

On the way across the street, breaking an entirely new trail through drifts that were sometimes waist-high, I pictured a quiet evening spent in Neil's wonderful Victorian house, snug and warm in front of the fireplace, listening to oldies on the stereo, and cracking open at least one bottle of wine (since my stash had come directly from Neil's wine cellar). The more I thought about it, the more I realized that was a far better option than waiting in the trailer for the roof either to blow off or to collapse under the weight of accumulated snow.

I stomped my way into the first floor library foyer after ringing Neil's doorbell. "It's just me," I yelled up the great curved oak staircase that led to Neil's living quarters upstairs as I began to remove once again, multiple layers of outerwear.

The first floor library off the foyer and through the double French doors was dark; bookcases loomed out of the shadows everywhere. But light from upstairs spilled down the stairwell. "Got the wine out yet?"

Neil Pascoe, medium height and solidly built, with more gray hair than anyone almost ten years younger than me should have, leaned over the upstairs railing and shouted back, "Don't take your coat off."

"Why?" I shouted back at him. "Is your furnace out?"

"Nope," he said, loping down the stairs two at a time, shrugging his arms into a brightly colored, down-filled parka. "Furnace is working fine." He wrinkled his glasses up on his nose. "But we're going out."

"*Out,*" I whined. "I don't wanna go out." I stood on the braided rug as snow melted from my boots and puddled on the tile floor. I was not about to let my vision of a warm and quiet evening fade without a fight. "I'm cold and I'm tired. All I want to do is sit here. Besides,

I can't go out in public. You don't know what happened to me today."

"Surely you jest," Neil said, putting on gloves. "Of course I know what happened to you today." He pulled my scarf back up on my head, tucked the ends in, and spun me toward the door. "That's precisely why you have to go out tonight. Stare down the masses. Face that tiger. Climb back on that horse."

"Get eaten alive by a cliché," I said glumly, stepping back out into the cold night. The hairs in my nose immediately froze—a sure sign of below zero temps.

Neil followed me onto the porch and closed the foyer door. He didn't lock it. No one in Delphi locked their doors, not even the lottery-winning millionaire library owner.

"That's the spirit," he said, laughing as he inspected the sky for signs of a break in the storm. "God, I love a blizzard," he shouted at the heavens.

"So exactly where are we going on this lovely night?" I asked, holding my ground, squinting morosely at the same sky that Neil had found so delightful.

"We are going to go and sing karaoke with the rest of the snowbound citizens."

"Uh-uh. No way," I said, heading back toward the door. "I am not about to sit in the bar and let everyone cluck over me."

Neil stood on the step and said quietly, "You're going to have to face them anyway. It might as well be now." He reached for my mittened hand and tugged gently. "Look at it this way, they can't talk about you if you're right there in the room."

"Remind me, how long have you lived here?" I asked, letting him pull me down the stairs and onto the recently shoveled, albeit already snow-covered, sidewalk. Like me, Neil was a Delphi native. And like me, he knew exactly what the hot topic of conversation would be. "You know damn well that my being in the room won't stifle them at all."

"Yeah," he said over his shoulder as he opened his

already idling pickup truck door, "but they'll have to keep the volume down."

Neil had a point. Not one I really wanted to concede, but a point just the same. I was going to have to face them sooner or later. I still would have opted for later, but that option had, evidently, vanished into the snow-filled air.

I climbed up into the passenger side of Neil's truck and arranged myself on the seat as he scraped the windshield. "You sure this beast can make it three whole blocks?"

The question wasn't rhetorical. During major winter storms, ever-moving snow drifts as high as ten feet can, and do, block city streets and county roads. Even navigating the short distance between the library and the bar could be hazardous.

Besides becoming stuck ourselves (a very real possibility, four-wheel drive or not), there was always the chance of running into other stalled vehicles, or over the owners of said vehicles as they struggled to find shelter before succumbing to frostbite. Visibility during a blizzard, even in town, even with halogen high beams, was often reduced to a narrow tunnel of light carved out of a blinding white wall a scant few feet in front of the truck.

With temperatures already below zero, and wind chills even lower, a person could very well die of exposure in less than the time it would take to tromp that far on foot.

"This really isn't a good idea, you know," I said. "We'll probably have the bar to ourselves. No one with any sense would go out on a night like this anyway."

"And how long have *you* lived here?" Neil asked. "Real South Dakotans would never let a little thing like a blizzard get in the way of their New Year's Eve drinking." He patted the dashboard for luck. "Relax, this baby can get us anywhere we need to go tonight. Look at it this way, I'm saving you from having to walk to the cafe by yourself later. All you have to do around midnight is troop across the street and go to work."

I am always amazed at how well informed Neil is about the minutiae of life in Delphi. He stays in his library most of the day, and rarely goes out at night, and yet all of the latest gossip seems to fall right into his lap.

Neil punched a button on the stereo and the Hollies immediately began warbling "Carrie Ann" from their *Greatest Hits* album. Depending on drifts, stalled vehicles, and just plain luck, we could still be negotiating the three-block drive when "He Ain't Heavy, He's My Brother" came up in, say, oh, another twenty minutes.

"Okay, how did you know we were opening up tonight?" I demanded as Neil backed up slowly, wheels bouncing over some of the smaller drifts.

"Your new cook told me," he said, expertly negotiating the driveway backward. We reached the road without getting stuck. "She was my last customer. In fact, she left just as Del called and demanded I take you off her hands for the evening."

"She *told* you? You know sign?" I asked, amazed that Dorothy had found her way to the library on her first day in town. And that Neil had been able to worm useful gossip out of her on such short notice.

"Of course not," Neil said, grinning, as he started down the street.

The snow fell so thickly and the wind whipped it around so thoroughly that we could not see the trailer lights for more than a few seconds before the storm swallowed both it and Neil's three-story home.

"So how did she tell you about Alanna's wonderful revenue-generating idea, then?" I asked, squinting through the windshield in a vain attempt to see further ahead of us. The headlights reflected back a swirling blanket of white, broken here and there in the darkness by amorphous lumps that were either finger drifts in the road, or dead bodies already covered with snow. The dark buildings on either side of the street could just as well have disappeared—we could see nothing of lights, or the bedraggled Christmas decorations that still festooned the business exteriors.

"Your new cook may not be able to speak, Tory, but that doesn't mean she can't write," Neil said, not taking his eyes off the road. "She had a tablet and a pen and she used them both."

I had no idea how he knew we were on the road at all, much less on the right side. I decided not to worry about it. Much.

"And her main topic of conversation was the work schedule at the cafe?" I asked as Graham Nash, et al., segued into "Jennifer Eccles," a song, which in my teens I had been certain was called "Jennifer Echo."

"Nope," Neil swerved to miss the highest portion of a drift that snaked all the way across both lanes from the alley beside Adler's Garage. "She was mostly curious about the operation of the library, and the house."

"Well, she has good taste anyway," I said, bouncing some more. "I think it'll be fun to have her around, if for no other reason than it will irritate the bejesus out of Alanna."

"I got that impression too," Neil said, carefully parking the pickup in front of the cafe. "I expect she can hold her own against our Ms. Luna."

"Well, if she can't, she'll get run over fast," I said, girding up my loins for the trial ahead of me. I was amazed, and more than a little bit dismayed, by the number of other vehicles parked haphazardly up and down the street, and across in front of the bar.

"Either way, it'll be interesting to watch," Neil said, pulling the key from the ignition. "Well, we made it. You ready for this?"

"No," I said flatly. "I wanna go back home."

My home, with Del and Ian engaged in carnal congress, or Neil's home, with a bottle of good wine and even better music. I didn't care which.

"Come on," he said, grinning as he got out. "Where's your sense of adventure?"

"It must be home in my other pants," I said, stepping once more into the snow.

7

....

Delphi, Lodi

There are, in this great country of ours, sensible folk who batten down the hatches when disaster looms. People who, when the authorities recommend the evacuation of homes, towns, and businesses, actually evacuate. Swiftly and peacefully, they move to higher and drier ground with nary an argument, a backward glance, or a second guess.

These are not citizens caught unaware on the sides of no-longer dormant volcanoes. Their children are not swept away in flash floods. Their dogs are not left to wander forlorn among the rubble because no one had the foresight to arrange for kennels in a neighboring town.

These people do not live in Delphi, South Dakota.

Oh, all right, one of them does.

However much she would like to orchestrate Grandma Nillie Osgood's shuffle off this mortal coil, I knew my cousin Junior Deibert would be snug in her farmhouse, carefully watching over her eight-year-old daughter, her three-year-old triplets, her Lutheran minister husband, and however many unborn children she carried in her huge belly, sheltering them all from the storm. She'd stuff rolled-up towels along the windowsills to keep snow from sifting in under the sash. Hot cocoa would steam on the stove to warm chilly little fingers as the wind howled and the drifts grew.

It would drive her crazy not to be able to navigate the four miles between her farm and my mother's. She would forever regret not having been there. She would castigate herself for failing her granddaughterly duty, and she would use any excuse she could find to castigate me for failing mine. But I also knew that she would stay home, safe and sound, because staying in on a night like this was sensible. And Junior always did the sensible thing.

But there is only one Junior, and there are 499 other Delphi citizens.

When faced with imminent disaster, Delphi citizens do what comes naturally to people three generations removed from hardy pioneer stock—they party. And a little thing like a white-out blizzard wasn't going to keep the citizenry home on New Year's Eve.

Not that there were 497 of Delphi's finest in Jackson's Hole when Neil and I opened the door to let a gust of wind and a swirl of snow in with us. A good four-hundred erstwhile citizens had to make do with being there in spirit—spirits being far more able to function than most vehicles during this kind of weather.

But those who could be out and about, were.

And they, unfortunately, were singing.

Not all of them, of course. The current musical interlude was provided by five fairly inebriated guys and three absolutely drunken girls all squeezed together on a small platform near the far end of the bar under the track lights.

Microphones in hand, moving back and forth more or less in time to the insistent back beat provided by an assortment of black boxes and speakers arranged about the platform, the singers squinted through the smoky air at a screen placed dead center on the makeshift stage.

"*Tell me more, tell me more,*" the guys intoned off-key and off-time in possibly the most inept Greaser imitation in the history of the world.

"*Tell me more, tell me more,*" the girls replied Olivia Newton Johnly.

The Japanese will have much to answer for in that final reckoning.

"Thank you so much for browbeating me into coming out tonight," I whispered to Neil as we made our way to one of the few empty tables left in the dark recesses behind the pool table. "I was in dire need of karaoke."

"Honey, we all need karaoke," Neil answered with a laugh as he sat down.

I sat next to him and surveyed the room. The sagging remnants of Christmas garland tinsel, wrapped around everything and stapled everywhere, weakly reflected the few functional bulbs left in the few functional light strings. In the corner, an aluminum Christmas tree with an obvious starboard list twinkled forlornly in the rotating colored light. First blue, then green, then yellow and fading to red and back to blue.

New Year's Eve was the Christmas season's last dying gasp, and decorations, no matter how bedraggled, were left up until the last possible moment to remind customers of that season of giving. Not to mention excessive tips.

Ho ho ho.

Smoke hung heavy and gray over the noisy crowd. In the brief lull between songs and mindless DJ patter, the howling of the wind could be heard. The room was full of drinkers and yakkers and potential singers, many of whom sparkled in cardboard hats and plastic leis. They laughed and blew those annoying noisemakers and roll-up paper things with the feather on the end.

But the holiday party had started long before our arrival, and if there was any residual worry about the

wisdom of getting shit-faced while a terrible storm raged
outside, it was not visible to my naked eye.

My naked sober eye.

"Well, if it isn't our famous rich and single librarian,
come out to slum with the poor folks," Pat Jackson, one
of the owners of Jackson's Hole, said to Neil. She had
what passed for a smile on her normally expressionless
face as she stood, pad in hand, wearing a sweatshirt with
a Santa Claus whose battery-powered nose blinked
redly. Squashed over her permed and dyed short blond
hair was a black plastic top hat with *Happy New Year*
streamers. "What can I get you, sir?"

"Miller Lite, tap," Neil said. I could have sworn that
he was blushing.

"Tory?" Pat asked, pencil to the ready as the original
crooners were replaced by a pair of giggling girls on
stage. Her expression shifted, her smile changed ever so
slightly from genuine to smirk.

I had forgotten that a fair percentage of the witnesses
to this afternoon's debacle with Gina Adler had come
from (and more importantly, returned to) the bar. The
Jacksons' clientele had probably been speculating aloud
as to the nature and timing of my indiscretions all afternoon.

"Black Russian," I said, throwing caution to the wind.
If I had to be on public display, and then go to work
afterward, I might as well make it worth my while.
"Bring two while you're at it."

Pat raised an eyebrow. "Suit yourself." She shrugged
and headed back to the bar.

On stage, the girls launched into one of those inter-
minably soggy sagas by the Judds, barely containing
their giggles as they sang marginally off-key.

"What was Pat talking about?" I leaned over to Neil
and asked. "Which *famous* rich and single librarian?"

"Not a clue," he said, catching Rhonda's eye and waving her over.

"Nonsense," I said, intending to pursue the subject
further, but a movement across the room caught my eye.

From my other side, Rhonda squealed and engulfed me in a large hug, carefully holding her bandaged hand out to avoid accidental contact. "Tory! I can't believe you're here! It's so wonderful that you're out tonight with all of us. It's cool. Just really cool."

Rhonda, in an outfit far too sparkly to be wasted on Delphi, and wearing a glitter tiara that was slightly askew, had evidently opted for liquid anesthetic rather than pharmaceutical. I hugged her back and allowed as how it *was* wonderful to be in a smoky bar on New Year's Eve in the middle of a blizzard getting lung cancer from secondhand smoke. Rhonda laughed and tightened her hug.

I squeezed out from under Rhonda's death grip to see if I had really seen what I thought I had seen before Rhonda grabbed me.

Yup. Gina Adler, no longer wearing her bathrobe and bunny slippers, and more significantly, not carrying a Louisville Slugger, had sauntered into the bar with a small group of laughing and shivering couples.

I instantly forgot Rhonda, and what I had been going to ask Neil. I jabbed him in the ribs with an elbow and inclined my head toward Gina's group. "What do you suppose this means?"

"Uh-oh," Rhonda said, looking over her shoulder at another table nearby. "Ron's over there with a bunch of guys and Brian's mom. He's been here all night and he's pretty drunk already. I hope he doesn't start a fight."

Normally, the notion of Ron Adler engaging in fisticuffs with anyone would have been laughable. But normally the notion of Ron's wife beating the living shit out of his truck with a baseball bat would have been even funnier.

Normal ain't what it used to be in these here parts.

Ron had not spotted his wife yet. He laughed heartily and slopped beer over the edge of his mug as he toasted something or other with another fairly drunk guy while Alanna chuckled and displayed her heroic bosom for the admiring male throng.

Gina, with the vacant smile and empty eyes typical of the inebriated or heavily medicated, scanned the room. Her smile hardened and her eyes narrowed when she spotted her husband and his drinking buddies. Then her eyes went blank again, and she turned to her companions.

"She's ignoring him," Neil said quietly, nodding. "Good. That's better than whacking him upside the head."

"The night's still young," I said, picking up one of the drinks Pat had just set on the table. "There's plenty of time for surprises left."

The buzz in the bar altered slightly as the news that Gina was there made the rounds. Speculative glances bounced between them, but Ron was oblivious and Gina was busy and the crowd very quickly went back to what it was doing. Which was drinking.

And listening to the next batch of singers, who were inadvisably attempting that most unsingable of all disco ditties, "Stayin' Alive."

"Neil," Rhonda said insistently, "you gotta come up and sing with us. We're on the list next. Me and Brian." She turned to me brightly. "You too, Tory."

"Not on your life," I said. "Not if you paid me actual money. No way." And just in case she hadn't gotten the point, I added, "Never."

"Oh please," Rhonda wheedled, draping her bad arm around my shoulders. "We got the perfect song lined up for all of us to sing. Neil's gonna. Aren'tcha Neil?"

"I don't care if Queen Elizabeth is gonna sing it," I said firmly. "I don't care if the Pope is gonna sing it. I am not singing nothing in front of no one."

I didn't care if they produced James Taylor to sing it. The last time I was talked into singing in public, I ended up in the hospital. I was not tempting fate again.

"Can't you make her sing? Rhonda asked Neil.

Neil shrugged. "It took everything I had just to get her to come up here tonight. Let's not press our luck."

"Okay." Rhonda pouted. "But you gotta come up

now, Neil, because we're next." She pulled him out of
his seat and dragged him to the edge of the stage, saying
over her shoulder to me as she left, "You don't know
what you're missing."

I begged to differ with her, but I did settle back to
enjoy the show. Rhonda and Brian closed in on poor
hapless Neil who shot me a *what can you do?* glance
before joining them. They conferred with the DJ, a nice-
looking guy in his mid-thirties, who dangled a cigarette
from his mouth as he consulted a sheaf of papers.

On the other side of the room, Gina Adler tossed back
a straight shot of something at the bar, shuddered briefly,
and then demanded another.

The set of Ron Adler's shoulders alone would have
told me that he'd finally spotted his wife. But if I'd had
any doubt, his wide-eyed, nonblinking stare would have
been a dead giveaway. His mouth was set in a straight
line, that if anything, got even straighter when the bar
door opened and Del and Ian stumbled in, covered with
snow and laughing.

They headed straight for the bar and ordered a round.
Del looked up at Ian with one of those adoring gazes
made so famous by Nancy Reagan. Ian gazed back at
her sweetly, and then settled one arm around her shoulders as they leaned back against the bar to watch the
festivities and sip their drinks.

Gina gazed at both of them, her face unreadable, and
then transferred her attention to the stage.

I sipped my own drink as Neil, Rhonda, and Brian
arranged themselves around the microphone. Instrumen-
tal strains of a CCR intro filled the room and I grinned
to myself, recognizing the song Rhonda had been sure
was perfect for us.

She had been right. Delighted drinkers set their
glasses down and joined in, though, for a change, the
three on the stage were competent singers.

The drunk, the sober, the angry, the happy, the sad,
the rich, the poor, the crazy, the sane, the homicidal, and
the soon to be deceased, not omitting the waitress who

still wished she'd stayed at home, especially since her married ex-boyfriend and his pregnant wife had just come in, all joined in singing at the top of their lungs the most appropriate of songs.

Of course, we changed the words just a bit, but we didn't figure that Mr. Fogarty would mind if just this once we sang "Oh lord, stuck in Delphi again."

8

·······························

The Full Monty Python

It wasn't until I rented *The Full Monty* that I finally understood that Great Britain is much like the United States, with each region having its own vernacular and accent.

I understood it even better after I watched the movie a second time, because I didn't understand one word in ten the first time around.

Before that, to my uneducated ear, all British enunciation fell into two Johns: Lennon or Cleese. Being a reader and not much of a moviegoer (which is just as well, considering that *foreign* movies don't exactly make it to any of my neighborhood multiplexes), I mentally filed all members of the Empire Upon Which the Sun Formerly Never Set under *Mr. Darcy* or *Liverpool*, and let it go at that.

But even a passing familiarity with BBC productions (via cable TV), not to mention the less lofty delights of Benny Hill, did not allow me to narrow down exactly where his aunt illicitly funneled brandy to a cold and underaged Ian O'Hara.

"There's gotta be an Irishman in the family tree," I said. "Featherstonehaugh is strictly English. And O'Hara had to come from somewhere."

It was edging toward midnight as I drained the last of my second round of Black Russians and set the sticky glass on the table with the rest of the empties. I had forgotten to eat supper, and possibly even lunch, and so was not, at the moment, feeling any pain whatsoever.

"You sure it's spelled that way?" Rhonda squinted at the napkin where Neil had written out what we were pronouncing as *Fanshaw*. She rotated the napkin 90 degrees, as if the word would make more sense sideways. "That's an awful lot of letters for just two syllables."

Rhonda was feeling even less pain than me.

"Righto, Cholmondley," Neil said, far more sober than either of us, but still tending toward goofy. He'd been speaking with some sort of English inflection for the last half-hour, ever since we'd started trying to figure out Ian's lineage by deciphering his accent.

Neil had not yet heard the man in question speak and was not entirely enamored with the idea of a handsome stranger cutting a wide swath through the women of Delphi, no matter where he was from. Originally.

"Well, he's not from Sheffield, I can tell you that," I said, remembering the movie.

"Ian can take his clothes off anytime he wants," Rhonda said rolling her eyes at the ceiling. She'd sat in the living room, hooting at the final scene right along with Del and me. "With music, without music. Alone. In a lineup. I don't care."

Rhonda shot a guilty glance over her shoulder at Brian, who was sitting by the stage, helping to shepherd the steady stream of aspiring singers up to the microphone. At the moment some poor guy who was not even Billy Ray Cyrus when sober, was doing even further damage to "Achy Breaky Heart."

"I've been listening to him too, and I don't understand

what he's saying half of the time, but God I just love to listen to Ian talk." Rhonda sighed, turning back to us. "There's something about all those *awnts* and *cawnts* and *shedulls* that just gives me goosebumps."

She shivered with delight.

I knew exactly what Rhonda meant. As politically incorrect as it may seem, I mentally ratcheted upward the estimated IQ of anyone with an English accent. And with the automatic Mensa membership came all the other perks of prejudice: I assumed that all speakers of the Queen's English were kind, trustworthy, and drolly funny.

And when they were as easy on the eye as Ian, I also assumed they were skilled lovers. For a change, living vicariously through Del would be entertaining.

"I don't think he went to Oxford," I declared, though my experience with Oxford grads was nil.

"Why doesn't one of you just go and ask him where he comes from, then," Neil said in his own voice, cutting to the chase.

"Not me," I said, signaling Pat for another round. "I am already on Del's shit list."

I peered through the crowd at Ian and Del, who were standing at the bar laughing. And drinking. Not that I had been keeping strict track, but as far as I could tell, Ian was ahead of Del in the empty glass department by a ratio of three to one.

"I'm just making conversation. Killing time until midnight. Listening to terrible singers singing even worse songs. Waiting for the New Year to begin so I can slog my way across the street and serve scrambled eggs to a bunch of drunk people."

Including myself, possibly.

"I don't care where he came from either," Rhonda declared, though she had been speculating just as avidly as I. Or me, I can never remember. "I just think it's so romantic that Del found love in the personal ads."

"Love is a pretty strong word, don'tcha think?" Neil

asked, handing a still unsmiling Pat Jackson a five and a couple of ones.

Strong it may have been, but Del was gazing up at Ian with one of those puppy-dog gazes that always sent her into gales of laughter when she observed it in others.

"You talking about Little Lord Fauntleroy?" Pat asked, making change for Neil. "Someone should do Del a favor and tell her not to trust that guy."

"Why?"

Pat squinted through the smoke at Ian across the room. "Last time Del went to the can, Master High and Mighty came on to me."

We looked at her, nodding noncommittally with wide-eyed, polite interest, trying to mask a complete and total disbelief that handsome Ian would ever make a pass at Pat Jackson, who in addition to being married and completely humorless, was built like a Green Bay Packer.

The fact that he'd been at least . . . well . . . welcoming . . . to me didn't put a dent in my doubt. I told you I had been drinking.

"Not that Del doesn't deserve a little of her own medicine," Pat mumbled, picking up our empty glasses and trundling back to the bar. "Serve her right if someone cheated on her for a change."

I had noticed that the general attitude toward Del's glee in having snagged Ian through the magic of the free press was, at the very least, resentful.

Gina Adler, whose good cheer was downright ferocious, had been skewering Del with killer looks all evening. When she wasn't glaring at Ron, that is.

Del ignored me completely, which was just as well, considering that I had no desire to relive this afternoon's festivities in front of Stu McKee *and* his wife (who, to give them credit, glared at no one).

Ron spent an equal time glaring at his wife, Del, Stu, me, Neil, the singers and the Pats Jackson (husband *and* wife). In fact the only person he didn't glare at was Alanna, who kept him supplied with drinks on a steady basis and plastered her enormous breasts firmly into his side—a sensation he evidently did not find uncomfortable, since he made no effort to move to a safe distance.

Alanna herself spared Del no courtesy, beaming winning smiles at Ian that hardened into piercing glares whenever he turned away.

I, personally, had no desire to glare at anyone, I just wanted to drink my drinks, avoid Stu and his wife, and then go home and sleep until I woke up with a peaceful hangover.

Unfortunately, that wasn't in the cards for me, so I made do with listening to the music, which had morphed into one of those interminable Mariah Carey inventions that always generated in me the desire to poke the singer in the ass with a cattle prod just to hurry things along. The present singer combined Mariah's unfortunate tendency to embroider every single note with trills without the ability to hit any one of those notes accurately.

While specifically not looking at Stu and his wife as they chatted amiably with a couple of feed store buddies, I spotted Dorothy Gale sitting by herself at a small table near the door, which swung open again, letting in another blast of cold air. She hunched down into her jacket and rubbed her red and chapped hands together to warm them up.

Rhonda caught my glance and said, "We should ask Dorothy over here. Away from the door. She looks like she's freezing."

Neil and I agreed, and dispatched Rhonda with an invitation. And I am sure that Rhonda would have made it to Dorothy's table eventually, but she was waylaid by a few of her old high school chums who had been snowed in and were desperately looking for someone younger than forty to party with.

When we finally realized that Rhonda had been gone overlong (about the time I finished my next to last Black Russian), Dorothy was no longer sitting at her table. But that observation was overshadowed by the amazing sight of Del stepping up to the karaoke microphone.

The urge to watch Del croon Patsy Cline's "Crazy"

to Ian in front of a roomful of woozy Delphinians would have been overwhelming were it not for the fact that Ian was nowhere to be found (a fact that registered on Del's face along about the time she was *crazy for feeling so blue*), and the fact that I had been sitting for several hours, drinking steadily, without even one trip to the bathroom.

Del has a fine singing voice; world weariness and many years of cigarette smoking had deepened it into a husky wonder that was perfectly suited to the song. Under any other circumstances, I would have been more than happy to sit and listen to her sing one of the few country songs I actually liked.

But once I realized that I had to go, I realized that I really had to go.

Immediately.

There was not time for me to collect two hundred dollars, or to listen to my housemate sing as well or better than anyone had so far on this long holiday evening.

I had to go.

I made my excuses to Neil, and threaded my way through the crowd. I was just a bit unsteady, which should not have surprised me considering my generous alcohol intake.

Wasn't it Oscar Wilde who said that the ingestion of a sufficient quantity of alcohol produces all the symptoms of intoxication?

Well, I had ingested a sufficient quantity, which made getting to the bathroom even more of an imperative.

I pushed past the stage, where Del, outwardly calm and crooning, was scanning the crowd with her eyes. I pushed past the bar where Stu stood by himself paying for a drink order. I pushed past the dim lights and the heavy smoke and the noise of the crowd into the semi-dark hallway.

At the far end, the ladies' room door squeaked open sending a spear of bright light into my eyes which momentarily blinded me, but not before I saw the silhouette of a pregnant woman coming out.

Even in a partially befuddled state, my brain recognized instantly that Renee McKee was coming out of the bathroom and heading down the narrow hallway toward me. So in pure panic, and without conscious thought, having not the least desire to confront her sober, much less drunk, I fumbled quickly with a random doorknob and ducked into a side room that was, thank heaven, unlocked.

And ran smack into the two people I would have least expected to find at that moment in time, in that stage of undress, in that particular position.

9

·····························

Wink, Wink, Nudge, Nudge

I gotta wonder whether the guys who write those commercials where beautiful women are driven to shudder-
ing, head-shaking, *yesYesYES* delight by some product
(be it shampoo, ice cream, or fine Corinthian leather)
have any familiarity whatsoever with the female orgasm.

Not that I am an expert, but I have dallied a time or
two in my four-or-so decades, and I am a confirmed fan
of sex as a recreational activity. It burns calories, it
brings a healthy glow to the skin, and it kills time that
might otherwise be spent in ordinary pursuits like fold-
ing underwear or cleaning the cat box. Done properly,
it can, indeed, put a smile on your face that can last for
days.

And done Really Properly, it can induce a certain urge
for vocalization. But not the stuff of movies or TV commercials. No shouting, no wailing. None of the ridiculous high-pitched whooping I'd witnessed, even in
movies with far fewer than 3 X's.

Speaking from my own experience, and vicariously from Del's (trailer house walls are exceptionally thin, after all), the real thing, the Big O, is far more likely to consist, to the casual (and to the not-so-casual) observer as a matter of deep, ragged breaths, an arching of the back, and a low, almost involuntary moan.

Once you've heard that sound (or made it yourself), you recognize it immediately.

Even if you haven't made that sound yourself in far too long.

Even if you wonder when you will ever make that sound again.

Even if you have just stumbled into a dimly lit, for-tuitously unlocked office in order to avoid running into your married ex-boyfriend's pregnant wife.

The light from a small desk lamp was further dimmed by a blouse that had been haphazardly draped over the top. In the split second before I realized exactly what I had interrupted, I had time to register a pair of shoes kicked into the middle of the room, a pair of drinks and a wallet on the desk, and a kneeling man with a pair of hands grasping a pair of ample, naked breasts.

The sound immediately changed frequencies from *moan* to *squeal*, as Gina Adler, who had been leaning back against the desk with her clothes either off, up, or open, desperately scrambled to cover herself. She leaped over the desk and crouched behind it, and then reached up and pulled her blouse from the lampshade, which threw the room into full light.

By then I knew what was happening, and I did not need full light to recognize who was smoothing his hair as he rose unsteadily from the floor, where he had been kneeling in front of Gina.

Shocked, surprised, incredibly embarrassed, worried that I'd back out the door and run smack into Renee, and maybe even a little jealous (that had been some moan, after all), I stammered, "Um . . . ah, sorry, I didn't realize . . ." to Ian O'Hara and fumbled back into the hallway, hoping that the whole exchange had happened too fast for either of them to recognize me.

The hallway, thank God, was empty. I rushed down to the bathroom, pushed my way into the bright light, stumbled into one of the two stalls, and locked the door, breathing heavily.

Before I could even process what I'd just seen, and the possible consequences that could arise therefrom, the narrow bathroom filled with a gaggle of gigglers. One immediately went into the stall next to mine. Another pounded on my door.

"Hey, you in there, hurry up," she said, laughing and dancing a little. "I gotta pee."

"Just a minute," I answered, remembering why I'd come down the hallway in the first place. "I'll be right out."

"Tory? Tory is that you in there?" Rhonda asked from the stall on the other side of me.

I peeked down at the floor under the divider, and sure enough, there were Rhonda's shoes. "Yeah, it's me," I said quietly, blowing all my air out.

Not especially wanting to face her in the bright light, but having no choice, I opened the door to find several obviously impatient, inebriated girls, all doing the bathroom shuffle.

"About damn time," one said, pushing past me into the stall.

Rhonda flushed and emerged, to the relief of the next one in line.

We squeezed together at the stained sink. I washed my hands and dried them on the roller towel. She dipped her uninjured hand under the faucet and then wiped it on the seat of her jeans. She then pulled a makeup bag from her shoulder purse.

I avoided eye contact, suddenly fascinated with the chipped blue paint that was flaking from the sewer pipe that ran up the corner.

Rhonda peered at me in the mirror, frowning as she expertly applied her lipstick. "Something wrong with you? You look awful."

I reluctantly squinted at the mirror and had to admit that I had looked better. My face was pale except for two bright circles of red on my cheeks. My hair was in its usual nonstyle, only worse. My makeup faded to nothing in the harsh light from the bulb hanging overhead. My eyes were bleary. I was a sad specimen. I halfheartedly fluffed at my hair and tried to figure out what to do next.

However newsworthy the events of the last few minutes, I would not have told Rhonda what I'd just seen, even if we'd been alone in the can. I assumed that Gina would put herself together and head back to the bar (or if I was lucky, out the door and home), pretending it never happened. I fervently hoped that Ian would nonchalantly reappear in time to hear the last of Del's song, and then quietly disappear from her life.

If I could get by with it, I would never tell anyone what I had just seen (well, maybe I'd tell Neil, but even that retelling would have to wait for privacy and full sobriety).

"Rhonda's right, you don't look so hot, Tory," another of the girls said, peering over my shoulder into the small mirror to adjust her perfect hair and to light another cigarette.

"Just a little too much to drink," I said, forcing a smile. "A dose of caffeine and I'll be fine."

What I really needed was a retreat from reality.

Unfortunately, the only place I was going was back into the real world. The one where roomates' hearts were about to be broken in seventeen places.

Without looking at Rhonda directly as she primped, I asked innocently, "Anyone in the hallway when you came down?"

"Nope," she said, reapplying blush. "Why?" She exchanged a worried glance with one of the other girls.

"No reason," I lied.

I mumbled a good-bye, took a deep breath, and pushed through the swinging door back into the hall.

The empty hall.

I scurried past the darkened office doorway, under which no light shone, and ducked back into the bar just as Del was finishing her encore, a rousing rendition of Sade's "Smooth Operator," a tune far more relevant than she knew.

I hurried through the crowd, looking neither right nor left as I made my way back to Neil, who was sitting at our table with Dorothy Gale. She'd evidently found her way there without Rhonda's help.

"You all right?" he asked, peering at me in the dim light. "You don't look so good."

"I been hearing that a lot," I said, risking a quick sideways glance that netted me the location of Stu and Renee, safely across the room. They were again ensconced in a lively conversation with some feed store people. "I'm just tired, that's all."

I surreptitiously scanned the rest of the crowd. Del was cooing again with Ian, who shot an inscrutable glance at me over his shoulder. I had no idea what was going on behind that handsome, slightly flushed face, but he didn't look like a man who'd just been caught *in flagrante delicto*. In fact he looked like a man who was having a wonderful time, a man who was toasting the New Year with obvious enthusiasm.

In short, he looked a lot like Del when she has just pulled off a narrow escape.

Maybe they *were* suited for each other.

It took a while longer to find Gina Adler, but that's because she was in the place where I would have least expected to find her (excepting of course, the last place I had found her, which won all the prizes for Least Expectations). She stood, outwardly smooth and calm, put back together reasonably well, on the stage, laughing with the karaoke DJ. Her face showed no traces of the encounter I'd just interrupted.

For some reason, I remembered Eric Idle, of Monty Python fame, and his salacious little sketch where he would elbow the guy next to him and ask, with a wink, if his wife was a *goer*.

Judging by the fact that Gina conversed comfortably with the DJ as she got ready to sing, I'd guess that Ron Adler's wife was, indeed, a *goer*.

And from what I'd heard in the office a few minutes earlier, I knew for damn sure that she was also a *comer*.

Amazing the things you find out about people you've known your whole life.

"Tory," Neil said, snapping his fingers in front of my face as Gina started singing "Leaving on a Jet Plane" reasonably well. "Are you sure you're all right?"

For some reason, Gina's song touched a chord with the other inebriated celebrants in the bar because everyone in the place joined in singing.

Everyone that is, except Ron Adler, who was deep in conversation at his table with Alanna Luna. And Dorothy, who couldn't sing. And Neil, who looked at me peculiarly. And me. I couldn't have sung at that moment to save my life.

"I'm fine, really," I said to him, over the chorus, casting about for a logical explanation for my weird mood. I would tell Neil what I'd witnessed eventually, but I couldn't do it in the crowded bar and with all of the participants, not to mention Dorothy, in possible earshot. "I think I just need to get some air."

I consulted my watch; it was several minutes before midnight. "Maybe I'll head over to the cafe and get started. I want to get out of this smoke for a while anyway."

Dorothy, whose hearing was not impaired at all, gestured that she'd come along and help, but I waved her off. I needed some time alone, and could handle the early prep work by myself.

"You stay and enjoy the rest of the singing," I said to her, resisting the urge to shout. As I said, she could hear just fine. "I'll see you in an hour or so."

Dorothy nodded and turned back to watch Gina with a smile.

"You really have to go now?" Neil asked, searching my face carefully. He really was worried about me.

"Yeah, I should," I said, forcing a nearly genuine smile. "It's going to be busy over there tonight, and there is a lot to do."

"I'll walk you across then," Neil said, putting his coat on.

"You don't have to walk me to the cafe, Neil. For crying out loud, it's only across the street," I said, putting my own coat on and wrapping the scarf back around my head.

He tossed a couple of bills on the table and took my arm. "I'm not *walking you across the street*," he said, parroting my inflection. "I am going to start my truck so that the sucker doesn't freeze solid while it's parked out there in the open."

Allowing vehicles exposed to the bitter cold and wind, not to mention blown in snow, to idle for fifteen minutes every couple of hours was good insurance against stalls, and service calls. It was standard operating practice in the winter here. In fact, Neil had started his truck once during the evening already.

"Well in that case"—I took his arm—"I will be pleased to have you accompany me as far as your vehicle."

I didn't look back at Gina who was still belting it out on stage, but I swear I could feel her relief as I walked out with Neil. I did catch a quizzical glance from Ian and a puzzled one from Del, who noticed Ian's expression, though neither interrupted their singing. Renee sang along merrily and probably didn't see me at all. Stu, who did not sing, watched us with a contemplative expression as we threaded our way through the crowd to the door.

Neil hunched down into his coat as he held the door for me. I stepped into the newly drifted snow in front of the doorway. Any tracks that had been there earlier had been blown completely smooth.

The crowd back in the smoky warmth finished singing as we stood for a moment peering into the wall of white in front of us, trying to adjust to the sudden and drastic temperature change.

The wind had settled a bit, and it had briefly stopped snowing. But it was bitterly cold, the kind of below-zero temps that can freeze exposed flesh in minutes, and kill within an hour.

"Shall we?" Neil asked, taking a deep breath.

"Might just as well," I said, stepping into the street.

We waded through knee-high drifts and around some finger drifts that were almost waist-high. It took us a couple of minutes to make our way over to Neil's truck.

Amazingly enough, I was mostly sober by the time he dug his keys out of his pocket. I guess fear, surprise, sub-zero air, and physical exertion are a powerful combo.

"You coming over later for breakfast? I'll serve you one on the house," I said. He'd brought me uptown and had already offered to stick around and take me back home. It was the least I could do.

"Yeah." Neil opened the driver's side door, reached in, and inserted the key in the ignition and turned it. The truck started immediately and began to idle smoothly. Up and down the street, other parked vehicles were running with their windows frosted solid and exhaust steaming from their tailpipes.

"I'll hang out over there until the bar closes and then I'll come over and help you," he said, closing the pickup door.

"You don't have to help," I said, stepping closer to give him a swift hug. "But you're more than welcome to sit and keep me company."

Neil cocked his head to the side; his glasses had already begun to accumulate frost around the edges. "Listen," he said, quietly.

Faintly from across the street, I heard the beginning of a countdown. "Ten . . . nine . . . eight . . ." the excited voices chanted from inside the bar.

"It's New Year's Eve," he said softly.

". . . seven . . . six . . . five . . ."

"Thank God this year is over," I said, looking into his warm brown eyes. "It's been one for the record books."

"I've had better," Neil agreed quietly, smoothing hair back from my forehead.

". . . four . . . three . . . two . . ." the voices continued.

"Too bad we didn't remember to bring some champagne," I said.

". . . one . . ." From inside the bar came a muffled whooping and cheering and a very loud, very badly sung rendition of "Auld Lang Syne."

"We can celebrate later," he said, and then he added so quietly that I could barely hear him over the wind and the music from across the street, "Happy New Year, Tory."

And since it was the normal, traditional, noncommittal, friendly thing to do, I stood on my tiptoes in a snow drift, shivering slightly in the bitter cold, and kissed my best friend Neil Pascoe. It was a soft, sweet, friendly kiss on the lips that only lasted for about . . .

. . . two seconds . . .

Or was it two hours . . . Or maybe it was two years . . .

Somewhere in the middle of that kiss, I thought about pulling back and apologizing. I thought about explaining that I had only meant for it to be a quick peck. I thought about explaining that we weren't really starting anything here.

That I wasn't ready to start anything. That I hadn't yet finished the thing that was already supposed to be over, the one that *had* to be finished before I could even think about starting something else.

I considered all that as Neil's fingers traced my cheek and his other arm drew me in.

I knew what I had to do. I had to explain, to disclaim, to hold back, to protect both myself and Neil. To turn back the clock before we jeopardized the one really good thing in my life by taking such an idiotic risk with our friendship.

I had to stop.

But my traitor arms tightened around him and my traitor brain ignored the sensible interior voice.

And my traitor heart beat wildly as the wind howled and the snow swirled around us.

10

....

Unexpected Treats

It isn't exactly news that there are no guarantees in life.

I mean, you can be comfortably settled, relatively content with your lot and situation, and the doorbell rings. Your kid gets up and opens the door to find Ed McMahon standing outside with balloons and lights and cameras and an oversize check in hand.

Or you can be out strolling, minding your own business, gazing at the birdies or humming along with the tunes playing in your head, step off the curb, and get hit by a bus.

Life can change from dull and predictable to interesting and exciting (in any sense of those words) in an instant.

Let's say you just spent a perfectly awful day, one in a long string of less than wonderful days, where every decision was the absolute wrong one, with each of those wrong-headed choices coming back to haunt you spectacularly and publicly. At the end of that long and awful day, which incidentally rounded out a long and awful year, you gave your best friend what started out to be a friendly peck, the kind you'd bestow on any casual acquaintance on such an occasion.

You might then find yourself, in the middle of the cafe you half-own, grinning like an idiot.

Or you might find yourself in the middle of the cafe you half-own, still a little drunk and completely at sea—not knowing whether to be happy or terrified.

Or you could find your brain in such a jumble that you don't know what the fuck to think or feel.

But you know what you remember.

At least I do.

While still standing beside his idling truck, Neil had gently tilted my chin up in order to search my eyes for . . . something . . . which I think he found because he nodded to himself before leaning down to kiss me softly on the forehead.

As he pulled away, his eyes locked on mine again, a small and wonderful smile playing at the corners of his mouth.

"Neil . . ." I said softly, and then hesitated, not knowing what else to say.

He put his gloved finger to his lips and said, "Shhh. We'll talk later."

And with that he turned and headed back across the street into the snow, jumping over the low drifts and plowing through the higher ones. Halfway to the bar, he turned around and stood for just a moment.

We looked at each other through the snow, smiling though it was so cold that the outside of my nose was beginning to freeze just like the inside.

Smiling though it was time for both of us to go inside.

Which, after a small, shy wave, we both did.

I wandered into the dark and familiar cafe that was more home to me than my own home. I sat in one of the window booths and did my best not to think of anything at all.

For a few minutes I watched the outside of Jackson's Hole kitty-corner across the street, seeing but not registering the folks who came in and out. I specifically ignored the fact that the cafe would soon be overrun with drunken patrons who would want to eat *before* they started fighting and throwing up all over the bathroom.

I cradled my head on my arms, replaying that kiss and deliberately not thinking about anything else. I must have dozed off because suddenly the cafe was flooded in light.

"Tory, what in the hell are you doing?" Alanna demanded. "We got hungry folks comin' over any minute and here you are lollygaggin'."

Her accent was in high gear, so I knew that she was putting on a show for someone. Someone of the male persuasion, most likely.

I sat up bleary-eyed. "What time is it?"

"It's breakfast time," Ron Adler slurred, blinking drunkenly. "Come on you women, rustle me up something to eat." In addition to being drunk, he was obviously in a bad mood. He glared at me sullenly.

It was also obvious that Ron, who was always the first one in line at the cafe in the morning, didn't know that it was no longer politic to order me around. He plainly didn't know what I knew about his wife.

And I knew that he wasn't going to know what I knew about his wife. At least he wasn't going to hear it from me.

I stood up and stretched. "Yeah, yeah, yeah," I said. "You have to remember that I'm not used to staying up this late."

Or drinking this much, I added silently.

Or being kissed in the snow.

But that was neither here nor there. As Alanna said, we had a passel of hungry drunks heading out any minute to ford the wild drifts and demand food at least as impatiently and crabbily as Ron had.

"I'll start cracking eggs and you can get the tables ready," I said to Alanna. Once Dorothy arrived and got the kitchen well in hand, I would venture back out to wait on tables, since it would be just the three of us working.

But for right now, my job was to get the grill fired up and the bacon precooked and the pancake batter ready.

As I poured water into the mix, the cafe door swung open. I peeked around the stainless steel counter that divided the kitchen from the cafe to see Dorothy stomp in, shaking snow off her head and shoulders. Her eyelashes were coated with frost and her cheeks and nose were alarmingly white.

"Good lord, Dorothy, get in here before you get frostbite," I said, concerned as she stepped into the kitchen. "This is no weather for a midnight stroll."

Dorothy shrugged with a tight smile as she took her coat off and hung it on the hook over by the long butcher block table against the wall.

She turned to me, rubbing her very red fingers together. I reached out, and placed my warm hands on her cheeks. The flesh beneath my palms was cold and raw but I could feel the warmth passing from my hands to her skin. When I pulled my hands away, the color slowly returned to her face.

"You gotta be careful in weather like this," I said sternly. "You're not in Kansas anymore. This shit'll kill you if you don't watch out."

She nodded sheepishly and gestured toward the grill.

I nodded back to her and we worked silently together, getting ready for the crowd. Alanna bustled around between the booths and tables, clinking silverware and setting out small copies of the very limited menu we would be serving that night, and clucking over an unsmiling Ron who was more than mildly drunk and in dire need of food and coffee.

At about twelve-fifty, an hour and some before the

bar was scheduled to close, the first of the revelers stumbled into the cafe.

By one-fifty A.M. on this brand-new day in a brand-new year, haphazardly removed boots and coats draped on the backs of chairs, not to mention soggy mittens scattered everywhere, made walking between the filled booths and tables nearly impossible.

"I really shouldn't be eating all this," Rhonda said, surveying her plate, which was heaped with scrambled eggs, a short stack, bacon, and hash browns. She tried to spread the two small scoops of butter on her pancakes with her uninjured left hand and gave up. Gingerly with her right, she poured hot syrup over everything. "I'm going to have to exercise all day tomorrow to work this off," she said with a full mouth.

"No shit," agreed one of her friends as each of the girls sitting at the table dug into about one thousand calories' worth of midnight snack.

I didn't think they were going to have to worry about retaining those particular calories because judging by their level of inebriation, that food would be making a return trip real soon.

"So where's Brian?" I asked Rhonda as I picked up dirty plates from the booth next to her where Ron had been sitting and blinking the whole time we'd been open. He held his ground after he'd eaten, and assorted friends had joined him to order their breakfasts in turn.

"Brian's waiting for the bar to close in order to help the DJ pack up," she said, waving a forkful of syrup-covered eggs in the general direction of the bar. "They've gotta get all that equipment back in his van tonight."

"Why? He's not going to be able to leave town," I said, peering through the window at the blowing snow. "What difference does it make if it doesn't get loaded until morning?"

Rhonda shrugged. "I think he's worried about people stealing stuff or something."

That didn't seem like a big concern—even if someone

stole all of the DJ's audio equipment, they weren't going to get anywhere with it.

Judging by the drifts, it didn't look like anyone with any sense would try to leave Delphi at all.

A bell tinkled from the kitchen—Dorothy's signal that more breakfasts were ready.

"Gotta run," I said to Rhonda, who continued to eat enthusiastically with her friends.

The commotion in the cafe was incredible. The crowd laughed and smoked and ate and demanded more food and jostled each other good-naturedly. After having spent the last few hours shouting to be heard over the music at the bar, no one saw any reason to turn down the volume.

I had never heard it so loud in there, not a single person could hear the James Taylor tape I'd plugged in. "Don't Let Me Be Lonely Tonight" played inaudibly to all ears but mine from the portable stereo that sat on the far counter.

I had never seen it so busy.

Or watched Alanna having such a good time.

She waited tables, laughing and flirting and cajoling huge tips from grinning husbands whose tired wives were becoming increasingly crabby.

In the months since we'd reluctantly begun our partnership, I had forgotten that, as a former stripper and nightclub worker, she was used to working a late-night, booze-addled crowd.

With the exception of keeping her clothes firmly in place, she was obviously in her element, and she made sure that I understood that opening late had been a good decision. She beamed triumphant smiles my way every time she caught my eye.

And judging by the number of people in the cafe and the ringing of the till and the number of times Dorothy had banged her little domed bell, Alanna was right.

The take for this night would be astounding.

That was the good news.

The bad news was that Alanna would want to do this on a regular basis.

And the further bad news was that I would have to agree to her scheme if we wanted to stay in business.

Dorothy's bell dinged again. She smiled apologetically as she slid three more plates out through the opening. She was certainly a competent cook, and we'd had no complaints about either the food or the service so far this evening.

I signaled an "atta girl" at her, blew my bangs back off my forehead, and picked up the plates and delivered them to the appreciative folks at the table on Rhonda's other side.

"Can I have some more syrup, Tory?" someone asked from behind me.

"Sure," I replied, leaning over another table to grab an extra pitcher that had somehow ended up there, turned and ran straight into Del.

Her coat and mittens were covered with a fine dusting of snow. She was cold and she was sober.

And she was plainly upset.

With no preamble she demanded quietly, "Have you seen Ian?"

"No," I said, going around her. There were people standing at the till ready to be checked out. "He hasn't been here."

I went behind the counter and automatically rang out two couples, pocketing a generous gratuity. Alanna had been on to something when she said that alcohol loosened the purse strings.

"Are you sure?" Del repeated.

"Yes I am sure," I said, shortly, picking up several more full plates. "I've been out here since the place filled up and I would have seen him come in."

Del, looking uncharacteristically vulnerable, chewed her lip and stood uncertainly in the middle of the aisle, blocking traffic.

I delivered the breakfasts to other hungry partiers, and then took Del by the shoulder and steered her to an empty chair and sat her down. The cafe was starting to clear out a little. Drunk and tired citizens wearily waited to be rung out, and open spots were not refilling immediately. With any luck, we could go home in about an hour and collapse.

"I don't know where he is." Instead of staying put out of the way, Del got up and followed me to the counter. "He was with me over at Jackson's, right there the whole time. And then he was gone."

Explaining to Del that Ian was most likely dallying without her was not going to improve my evening. Or hers.

So I didn't.

"He has to be over there," I said, lying. "There isn't anywhere else for him to be. He can't leave town and he isn't here."

I was not about to add that he may have found refuge in the arms and bedrooms of any number of the easily seduced women of Delphi. She would figure that one out soon enough by herself.

"Maybe he's at the trailer already," I said after a brief brainstorm. "Waiting for you with an open bottle of champagne."

Del brightened. "Yeah. You're probably right. I'll bet he's there right now."

"Are you talking about Ian?" Rhonda interrupted. We had been standing next to her booth. And evidently she had been eavesdropping.

Or we had been talking louder than we had realized.

Del nodded distractedly.

"Well," Rhonda said, swabbing the last bit of syrup off her plate with the last crumb of pancake, "I saw him talking to Gina Adler earlier tonight."

Several of Rhonda's companions chorused an agreement.

"Yeah, I saw them together too. They were over by the door talking and laughing," one of them said. "Boy, I love to listen to him talk. That Scotch accent is sooooooo sexy. He sounds just like that guy who used to play James Bond."

"Ooooh God," another moaned. "And he is *so* hot."

None of this was welcome news to Del, whose mouth tightened into a straight line.

I patted her on the shoulder and was going to say something comforting and entirely false about Ian talking and laughing companionably with everyone in the bar, male and female, but the cafe door swung open and Neil strode in.

With a quick smile for me, he went to Del and pulled her aside.

"Pat Jackson just got a call at the bar," he said urgently. "Presley, John Adler, and Mardelle are stranded out in the storm. I guess they were trying to get home from a party at a farm north of here and they ran off one of the gravel roads into the ditch."

Del paled. Her maternal instincts were minimal, to say the least, but she knew, as did everyone who was in hearing range, that in weather like this, stranded motorists were in severe danger.

They sometimes froze to death, either in their cars or from mistakenly thinking they could safely walk the quarter-mile to the next farm. Or they suffocated from the monoxide fumes that flooded the interior of any vehicle left running while stuck in a snow drift.

This was a serious situation and everyone knew it.

"Oh my God," Del said quietly. "We have to get to them. Where are they?"

Neil placed a comforting arm around her shoulders. "Luckily, Mardelle had her dad's cell phone and it was charged up. They were able to tell us their location. The wind has gone down some and there hasn't been any new snow for about an hour now. We know where they are, and we should be able to go out and get them."

"I'm going with you," Del said firmly.

Seeing that it would do no good to argue with her, he nodded and then turned to Ron in the booth next to her. "Is your winch truck functional?"

"No," Ron said. His voice was clipped and tight.

I would have been amazed if it had been, since that vehicle was the object of Gina's wrath this afternoon.

Ron didn't look directly at Del or me. Or Alanna, who hovered nearby. He spoke only to Neil. "But I have another winch we could anchor to the front bumper of your pickup. Give me ten minutes to get things together at the garage and we can leave."

Neil looked Ron up and down, taking stock of his lack of sobriety. "Okay," he said finally. "We need to get going. I'll drive."

Ron, still slightly unsteady, his mouth pale and tight, slipped back into his coat and then out the door.

Neil then turned to the cafe at large and said loudly, "We need at least two more men and a four-wheel-drive pickup to rescue some kids stranded in the storm. Another cell phone would help too."

We all knew that there would be no use in calling the police. No help would be able to get to Delphi, even if the storm ended. The roads would be impassable, and if the wind started blowing again, there was every chance that the rescuers themselves would become stranded.

This could be a life-or-death situation for everyone involved.

"Neil," I said, placing a hand on his arm. But then I hesitated. There was nothing I could say to him in front of the people who were left in the cafe.

He looked back at me with a small and very private smile. "We'll be all right. I'll be back in an hour with some cold kids who should be grounded for life. I'll pick you up here."

"Okay," I said quietly, trying not to wonder exactly what that might mean.

Del, all thoughts of Ian obviously driven from her mind by the imminent danger to her only son, stood next to Neil wringing her hands.

Neil, calm and in charge, called out orders to the people milling around him. He looked back one more time, winked at me, and then opened the door.

Stu McKee came into the cafe, alone and obviously cold.

He eyed Neil and the assembled crowd, sensing immediately that something was wrong. "What's up?" he asked.

"Presley, John Adler, and Mardelle Jackson are stranded in the storm," Del said shortly, naming the kids' location. "We're going to get them."

A Delphi native, Stu knew exactly what was at stake in a situation like this. "The wind has gone down," he said softly. "You should be able to get out and back without much trouble. You need more help?"

That last he addressed to Neil directly.

Neil and Stu stood, looking at each other, faces completely unreadable, for a moment.

"I think we have enough men and trucks to get them," Neil finally said.

Then there was another long pause, or at least it seemed long to me, standing there in the nearly empty cafe sensing the tension between the two men.

"Okay," Stu said, nodding. "I'll wait here. If you need anything, or run into trouble, call the cafe and I'll bring more help."

Neil glanced back at me, I nodded imperceptibly, and he nodded at Stu one more time.

And then they were out the door and into the storm, leaving me in the nearly empty cafe with Stu.

11

....

The Luck of the Draw

I've never been a big fan of the late great Frank Sinatra.

I do not deny that mellow voice, and certainly anyone who can survive the celebrity mill long enough to die relatively peacefully at a good old age deserves respect.

But I cut my musical teeth on the British Invasion. I was in high school during Summer of Love. I spent my twenties *boogie oogie oogieing* (not that I am especially proud of that, but it remains the truth). By my thirties I was already looking back fondly on the music of my youth, and now that I am in my forties, I am fairly convinced that when it comes to popular music, very little worth mentioning was made either before or after John Lennon.

I'm too young for Elvis, for crying out loud, much less a crooner who got his start setting the big band ballrooms on fire.

So why had my brain supplied me with Ol' Blue Eyes' voice *doobie doobie dooin* away about it being quarter to three and no one in the joint except Stu and me?

Because my brain has a warped sense of humor, that's why.

Or maybe it was God's wacky irony to closet me alone with Stuart McKee for the first time since our breakup, on the very day that I was pretty sure that I was done with him forever.

Ah, but God or whoever has the last laugh. Here in Delphi, there is no way you can ever be *done* with anyone. The town is too small, the community too inbred, the history too intertwined. And the dining selection too limited.

If Stu wanted to eat out during the rest of his residency in Delphi, he had no choice but to come here.

And since I was now half-owner of this cafe, I had no choice but to wait on him.

Not that he was interested in eating.

"Coffee is fine," he said, leaning back in the booth. "Full strength. I may need the jolt." He cocked his head and watched me get the pot of regular from the big Bunn behind the counter.

With slightly receding sandy-brown hair and green eyes that crinkled when he smiled, he was still no one's definition of gorgeous. But he was Prairie Handsome, with weathered skin and strong arms and a quiet sense of humor that showed up in the oddest places.

Like in bed.

I shook that thought from my head as I filled his cup.

I'd turned the *Open* sign around after the last of the sleepy customers had wandered out into the snow about a half hour earlier. After Dorothy put the kitchen to rights, she left with my blessing and an agreement to open again in a few hours. With an apology for the unreasonable shifts, I gave her the extra set of keys and waved good night as she left.

Alanna, annoyed for some reason, had schlumped around the cafe, halfheartedly rearranging the napkin holders and filling ketchup bottles. Even counting the big take didn't excite her, which was odd considering how delighted she'd been with the haul.

A thick wad of newly acquired fives and tens, along with a few twenties and one memorable hundred, were loosely banded together in the blue zipper pouch on the counter by the till.

"Oh my." Alanna yawned theatrically, stretching her arms high over her head, getting in one last mammary display for the one last male in the vicinity. "I am so very, very tired."

Stu rolled his eyes and then sipped his coffee.

I looked around the cafe. Most of the work was done, and I was wide awake and had to wait for Neil and the rest of the rescuers to return anyway. Alanna's conversational ability was limited on most days to complaints about the weather and chest flexing. Keeping her here would only make her crabby, or increase the strutting, neither of which I felt like dealing with.

"Why don't you go on home, Alanna. It's been a long night and a busy one. I can handle what is left. There is no sense in both of us staying up all night if we don't have to."

Plainly the option she had been angling for, Alanna brightened, then looked immediately downcast. "Do you have to stay here too, Stuart?" she cooed at him.

"I'd better," Stu said seriously. "I told Neil I'd stick around in case they needed more help."

Alanna peered anxiously out the window. "I don't understand why they all had to go out into this terrible weather anyway. It's just so silly."

"They went because the kids could die if they don't," I said, exasperated.

Winter virgins were a pain in the ass sometimes.

"But can't y'all survive in this kind of cold sometimes? I thought you were hardy. I mean the pioneers and the Indians did it for hundreds of years."

Getting into the Indian/pioneer timeline with Alanna was probably more trouble than it was worth at the moment, so I concentrated on her question instead. "Yes, people can survive this kind of cold if they stay out of the wind and keep their wits about them and they are lucky. But this is two thirteen-year-old boys and a sixteen-year-old girl. If they'd had any sense, they wouldn't have been out in the storm at all. So we can't count on their ability to stay safe for the rest of the night on their own."

Alanna chewed her lip. "Oh, I suppose y'all are right about that. Kids tend to let their hormones run ahead of them far too often and we all know what that—"

The rest of her little homily was cut short by the ringing of the pay phone by the door. She was the closest so she picked up the receiver.

"Hello?" she asked. Then she listened for a minute and nodded her head and said, "Okay." Then she nodded her head a little more and said, "She's taking care of Stuart McKee right now. Yes, he's still here."

I headed for the phone, certain that it was Neil on the other end. I was also fairly certain that Neil knew that I was not *taking care* of Stuart McKee in any but the most waitressly sense, but I wanted to assure him of that anyway.

But before I could get there, she nodded once or twice more and said, "Well, that's good news. Drive safely then." And then she hung up.

"That was Ronnie Adler," Alanna said to us with a grin. "They got to the kids all right but it's gonna take them a little longer than they thought to get back into town. However, he says that the roads are clearer than they'd expected and that they shouldn't have any trouble getting back into town in about an hour or so."

I was thrilled that Pres, John, and Mardelle, not to mention the assorted rescuers (who had been partying pretty seriously themselves earlier in the evening), were safe and on their way back into town. But I was also terribly disappointed that it would take another hour for them to get here.

"Well, since everyone is all safe and sound, Stuart," Alanna said, pouring on her most seductive accent, "perhaps you'd just as soon go home yourself."

Not trusting her motives, but applauding the senti-
ment, I added, "Yeah, Stu. I can take care of things here.
I'll just sit and wait for them to get back."

"Nah," he said with a smile. "I told Neil I would wait
in case there was any more trouble. But thank *y'all* for
the thought."

Alanna shrugged and then narrowed her eyes at us
with an evil little grin as she donned multiple layers of
outerwear. "Of course, you said you would wait and you
have to wait. I would never try to talk a man out of
doing his duty."

With that, she headed out the door, leaving us alone
in the midst of a most awkward silence.

Or it was awkward until Stu laughed and then I had
to laugh too.

"Sit down," he said. "You've done everything that
needs doing and all we have to do is wait."

"I wish I'd told Neil that I was just going to go home
and he could..." I hesitated remembering to whom I
was speaking and tried to regroup. "...just go home
and I'd talk to him tomorrow."

From the way Stu raised an eyebrow at me, I could
tell that the backpedal had not been successful. "Why
don't you call him now and tell him that you're going
home," he said gently. "That way he wouldn't worry."

"I'd love to," I said, pouring myself a glass of Diet
Coke. I sat down wearily in the booth, opposite Stu.
"But he doesn't have his cell phone with him and I don't
know any of the other numbers."

Any other time in my relationship with Neil, I would
simply have done the logical, sensible thing and gone
home. I would have trusted him to figure out what I had
done. And why. I would never have worried about the
fallout.

But things were different between Neil and me now.
Logic and sense no longer had the upper hand. I had
said that I was going to wait at the cafe for him. It would
take a major emergency to get me to budge.

Stu evidently saw that. Or he saw enough to let the subject drop. We sat in almost companionable silence for a bit. He stared down at his coffee cup, and I looked out the window at the darkness across the street and the swirling snow.

Rogue memories of stolen afternoons with him slipped in and out of my mind, not whole scenes, just wisps: a kiss here, a laugh there, a warm moment somewhere else. I did my best to banish them.

Other people learn how to have a purely social relationship with former lovers. I would have to too.

Of course, learning how to be comfortable with a man I once knew naked was something I'd had no practice in. The first naked man in my life had died on me, and the second was most assuredly still alive, sitting in an empty cafe in the middle of the night, staring sadly into his coffee cup.

"How are you?" I asked quietly. "Are things okay now?" There was no sense pretending that we did not have a history.

"I don't know, Tory," he said, looking up at me. "Bits and pieces are fine, and the whole thing looks good from the outside. But the simple truth is that I don't know."

I stared into those green eyes and for just a moment I was on the brink again. I remembered a jumble of arms and eyes and lips and other assorted body parts. I remembered warmth and laughter and the overwhelming marvel of being wanted.

And then I remembered sneaking and secrecy and the terror of being caught out in a lie. I remembered the shame of Gina's revelations.

And finally I remembered warm brown eyes. And a soft kiss in the cold snow.

I blinked twice, surprised at my inability to concentrate.

I started to say something, though I don't know what. Luckily the phone rang.

Thinking it was Neil, and about goddam time too, I

answered the phone happily and was horrified to hear only heavy sobbing.

"Yes?" I said tentatively into the phone, instantly terrified by the confusion coming from the other end of the line. "You have to calm down. I can't understand a word you're saying."

The tone of my voice, and probably the expression on my face, alarmed Stu. He jumped up from the booth and rushed over to me.

"Tory, Tory is that you?" the voice said.

It was my cousin Junior, weeping and wailing.

I'd heard Junior on a rampage before, but I'd never heard her like this—out of control and on the verge of hysteria.

"Yes, Junior, it's me," I said into the phone, breathing heavily and alarmed. "What's wrong? Are you and the kids all right?"

Junior was always firmly in charge of herself and every other detail in her life. This loss of control struck terror into my very heart. It would take no less than the death of her husband or one of her children to produce this sort of reaction.

"Junior, take a deep breath and tell me what happened," I said as soothingly as my own wildly beating heart would allow.

"It's Grandma," she said, sobbing.

A huge relief flooded through me. The death of our mutual grandmother was not only long expected, but had been predicted for this very night. She'd lapsed into a coma from which she was not expected to recover.

"Yes, Junior, it's Grandma," I said, relief making me dizzy. "We all knew she was going to die soon. It's hard for us, but it's also a blessing."

"You jackass!" Junior shouted, suddenly furious. "I know damn well that Grandma is dying and it will be a blessing when she goes. But did you think that she'd go without one last hurrah?"

Junior's voice faded and another started talking.

"Tory, Tory is that you?" Clay Deibert asked. Clay

was Junior's husband, her eminently sensible husband. There was no outright panic in his voice but there was deep concern and some anxiety.

"Yes, it's me, Clay," I said. "What's going on?"

Stu hovered nearby, with a comforting hand on my shoulder.

"Juanita called a few minutes ago," Clay said softly.

Juanita was Junior's mother, my mother's younger sister.

"Fernice had just called her," Clay continued when I didn't say anything, "and told her that Nillie was having a bad time of it. But before she could get all the details straight the phone line went dead and we haven't been able to get through to the farm since then. Whatever is going on, I think Fernice needs immediate help. Someone needs to go out there tonight. Juanita thought she should go."

"To the farm?" I asked, incredulous. There were miles of snow-packed roads between Aunt Juanita's house and my mother's farm. "Aunt Juanita could never get to the farm in her little Toyota."

I did not add that Uncle Albert would never let her try. Junior had learned her world domination gig at her mother's knee, but Uncle Albert still held the upper hand once in a while. When it came to knowing that no Toyota ever built was equal to country roads in the middle of a blizzard, Uncle Albert would prevail.

"You're right. Albert, Junior, and I all agree that she shouldn't attempt the drive," Clay said wearily.

"So Junior wants to go to Mother's farm instead, right?"

"Yes," Clay answered, and then he covered the phone because I heard some muffled conversation going on in the background. He came back to the receiver. "But I simply cannot let her try to travel tonight in this storm."

"Well, of course you can't," I said, exasperated. "She's pregnant and you have small children. I know she feels it's her duty to be there for Grandma Nillie's death and to help Mother however she can, but this is ridiculous."

"Unfortunately, it's not as ridiculous as you think, Tory." Clay lowered his voice to a whisper and continued. "Junior is beside herself and not reacting rationally. She's obsessing on the fact that Fernice is out there at the farm, all by herself in a blizzard and that she needs help immediately. She's convinced that Nillie is going into convulsions and that your mother can't possibly handle the situation alone. And unfortunately, I think she may be right."

"Oh lord," I said, sighing, nightmare visions of my mother wrestling with the convulsing body of my frail looking but deceptively strong grandmother dancing in my head.

"Yes," Clay said sadly. "I know that Fernice didn't want you to be bothered with this, but Juanita called here begging us to go."

It was the Delphi version of the jungle grapevine— Mother called Juanita. Juanita called Junior. And Junior, of course, called me.

"It goes without saying that I would never let Junior go," Clay continued. "Though I would try to get there myself if I could. But we are completely snowed in. We can't get to the farm by any route. We can't even get out of the driveway."

"And Junior thought that I might be able to get to the farm from town," I said, finally realizing the obvious. "Do you agree with her?"

"Unfortunately, yes," Clay said in a normal voice. "We tried calling at the trailer but there was no answer at your house so we figured that you and Neil Pascoe might still be at the cafe since there was no answer at the library either. Is he there with you? The last I heard, the road from Delphi was relatively clear. I wouldn't even suggest such a foolish and dangerous thing, but I think things at the farm are seriously out of control and the two of you together could be of real help to your mom. You know that the emergency crew can't make it into Delphi tonight."

"Neil is out with a bunch of guys trying to bring some stranded kids back into town," I said, and then explained the situation to Clay. "But Stu McKee is here, and I think he has a functional four-wheel-drive pickup."

Stu, who had caught on to the situation, nodded solemnly and took the phone from me. "Stu here, what do you need?" he said.

He listened for a moment and then nodded and hung up.

"The wind has gone down almost completely and the snow has stopped; we can make it to your Grandma's farm in a little over a half-hour, I think," he said calmly.

The instinct to hurry to my mother's side warred with the fact that I had promised Neil that I would wait at the cafe for him.

It was dangerous to go, though less dangerous than I had thought, considering that Neil and the others had made it safely to Presley, John, and Mardelle.

And it was impossible to stay.

Though I would perhaps have discounted Junior's hysteria, I was far more frightened by Clay's calm concern. He would never have asked if he had not thought it vital for someone, anyone, to get to the farm immediately.

I looked directly into Stu's eyes and saw only concern and a desire to help someone who desperately needed it. If it had been anyone else in the cafe with me, anyone with a four-wheel-drive pickup and snow tires, I would not have hesitated at all.

It was just the luck of the draw that I was considering venturing out into a killer storm with Stu.

"But Neil . . ." I said softly.

"Neil has waited this long for you," said Stu, whose intelligence I had routinely underestimated. "Another night isn't going to matter."

I looked at him once more, searching his eyes for anything awful, anything selfish, anything beside an overriding concern for me and my family.

We locked eyes for a long moment. Then I nodded.

"If we go now, we can get there before the next storm front hits," he said.

"Let me just write a note for Neil, then," I said quietly. "So he'll know not to worry."

12

······························

Dashing Through the Snow

The word *blizzard* is bandied about far too often these days.

Youngsters and newbies, and those with short memories, often paste that label on a measly six inches. Meteorologists, especially those from warmer climes, tend to wax rhapsodic over even a pissy amount, like a foot of new snow.

But a blizzard, as old-timers and middle-aged natives will tell you, is not just an accumulation of snow. Nor is it the major inconvenience experienced from even a heavy snowfall.

A blizzard is a combination of snow *and* wind.

Snow by itself, even three feet of snow, is only cold and pretty.

Wind by itself here in northeastern South Dakota is par for the course.

But wind and snow together, now that's what it takes to make a blizzard.

It doesn't even have to be falling snow. Wind combined with any accumulation of preexisting powder can turn a perfectly clear day into an instant ground blizzard.

But when the Weather Gods throw freshly falling snow and high arctic winds into the mix with below-zero temperatures, you not only have a blizzard, but you have one for the record books.

This one looked to be a keeper.

The wind had howled throughout the snowfall, so it was difficult to gauge the actual accumulation of snow. There were spots on the road, and in fields with no wind-break, that were blown dry, right down to pavement or stubble.

That relocated snow, as fine and dry as powdered sugar, accumulated around anything that constituted even a small barrier, including other piles of snow. Ever growing drifts could bury houses, or block roads completely with a slow-moving dance of pure white dunes that inched their way out of the fence lines and from between trees.

It's hard enough to navigate through the aftereffects of such a storm in the daylight, with the sunlight glittering off the frozen landscape.

In the pitch-black darkness on the first day of the new year, it was a deadly serious business.

I'd taped a note to the window on the cafe door explaining to Neil where we'd gone and the route we'd taken. I had my Sorel boots at the cafe and enough layers of outerwear to keep me comfortable on the short drive, though the cab of Stu's burgundy Chevy was barely warm, even with the heater cranked up full blast.

There is only so much that General Motors can do against Mother Nature and a wind chill of minus 37.

I was too anxious for much conversation on the bumpy ride. Visibility in the dark was limited to no more than five or six feet in front of the truck. It had seemed almost calm in town with the buildings and houses forming a perfect windbreak, but out in the open, even low winds stirred up the top layer of snow into an impenetrable swirling, hypnotic curtain.

Just staying on the road, much less on our own side, was difficult. I only hoped that Stu could tell by instinct where the road ended and the ditch began.

We bumped over a low drift on what I assumed was our side of the road. "Not such a good idea, huh?" I said ruefully to Stu, hanging on to the door handle for support.

"Nah," he said, peering straight ahead, concentrating on the road. "Where's your sense of adventure?"

Seems like someone else had asked me that already tonight. Or last night, to be precise.

"I don't have one anymore," I said, trying to make out if the murky shapes looming outside the passenger window were trees or drifts. Or neither of the above. Just being alone in Stu's pickup again was more adventure than I had bargained for. "I think I used up all of my *adventure* in the war."

Stu took his eyes off the road to look at me. He reached over and patted my shoulder gently with a gloved hand. "Hang in there, kiddo. I know you're worried, but we'll get you to your mom's safe and sound in no time."

He smiled at me encouragingly, turned back to take the wheel with both hands again, swore sharply, and swerved left to miss a drift that loomed suddenly out of the darkness. It was easily six feet high at the center, which was exactly where we were aimed.

The sudden turn sent the truck around the far edge of the drift, but the tires caught a rut in the snow. We followed the rut bouncing off the edge of the pavement and ended nose first into the deep snow in the ditch on the wrong side of the road.

Even wearing a seatbelt and shoulder harness I had managed to whack my head solidly on the door frame. We were sitting at a low angle with the pickup hood deep in the snow.

"Jesus Christ!" Stu said shakily. "Are you all right?"

I took my glove off and felt my head gingerly but only found a small lump and no blood at all.

"Yeah, I think so," I said. "How about you?"

"I'm fine," he said, still breathing heavily. "But we need to get the truck out of this ditch right now, or we'll be stuck here the rest of the night."

He didn't have to tell me that. I knew immediately that we were in trouble. In fact, it was probably already too late. Even if we could get the truck back out of the ditch ourselves, a doubtful proposition in any case, the motor was probably now packed with snow and would not run long enough to get us to Mother's farm.

Stu threw the truck into reverse and tried to back up. We moved about four inches before the wheels started to spin.

I moaned inwardly. This was not a good sign.

He gently tried to pull forward, but we didn't even go a half a foot before spinning again.

For several minutes, he rocked up and back, though we both knew that he was most likely digging us in deeper and more solidly. At this angle, and with no traction, there was no way that we could back the truck out the way we came in. And with easily four feet of snow in the deepest part of the ditch in front of us, there was no way to go forward.

Working together, we might have been able to dig ourselves out before any serious frostbite set in, as long as Stu carried a shovel in the back of the truck.

"Do you mind if I say some very bad words?" Stu asked, with a small, nearly humorless laugh.

"No shovel, huh?" I asked.

"Dad took it this morning to clean the sidewalk in front of the store and left it standing by the door. He was supposed to put it back in the truck box, but it was still there when I went home last night."

"Yeah, well, you didn't think you were going to be joyriding in the middle of the night in a blizzard," I said softly. "This is all my fault. I am so sorry."

"*Your* fault?" he said, incredulous. "I'm the one who

took my eyes off the fucking road. We wouldn't be in the ditch if I had been paying attention." He rubbed his face with a gloved hand.

His very real despair made me want to comfort him.

"We'd have been in trouble no matter what," I said instead. "If we'd hit that drift the truck would have been heavily damaged and we could have been hurt."

Despite the mobile nature of snow drifts and their feather-light components, they have all the cushioning properties of a concrete wall. Even at our low speed, hitting one dead on would have rendered the truck, and probably us, nonfunctional.

"We're all right. All we have to do is call someone and let them know we're stuck, and then just sit tight until the rescue," I said, looking on the bright side.

Stu looked at me guiltily. "We can't call anyone, Tory. I don't have my cell phone with me."

"You don't have a cell phone with you!" I said, probably a little more forcefully than necessary. A cell phone was an even more important piece of survival equipment than a shovel in a South Dakotan winter.

He sat, with both hands on the steering wheel, his breath blowing white in front of him. It was already getting colder in the cab. "I left the phone with Renee because she was afraid there would be a power outage and she didn't want to be cut off completely," he said without looking at me.

"Oh," I said.

We sat in the silence, listening to each other breathe.

Stu's wife, Renee, was pregnant, and they had a small son. Of course he'd left his cell phone with her in case of emergency.

"Listen, I'm sorry for snapping," I said. "We'll be all right. Clay knew the route we were taking and what time we left. When Neil gets to the cafe, he'll call Mother, and when she tells him that we didn't make it, they'll just head out here and use Ron's winch to pull us out of this ditch."

"And in the meantime, we're here for the duration," Stu said, looking at me with a sigh.

The wind had picked up again, buffeting the truck. But even if it had been completely calm, it would have been too cold to attempt walking anywhere. There were no nearby farms on this stretch of road, no way to signal anyone. And there would be no passing motorists who just happened to have been going our way.

The possibility of freezing to death if we spent more than an hour outside was damn near 100 percent. Even if the cold wasn't of the killing variety, the chance of stumbling off the road and getting lost was too real to discount. Every year people who should have known better died in winter storms because they made stupid, panicked decisions.

We did not want to become another statistic for the rest of the town to cluck over as they drank their coffee in Alanna's Cafe.

There was no formal discussion on staying put in the increasingly colder truck cab. It was simply our best chance for coming out of this with our fingers and toes, not to mention everything else, intact.

I punched Stu softly on the shoulder. "Where's your sense of adventure? We can turn this into something to tell the great-grandchildren."

I wanted to take those words back as soon as they were out of my mouth. It was impolitic at best to remind either of us that we would have no great-grandchildren in common. "Well," I said, trying to cover up my faux pas, "you know what I mean."

Instead of laughing, he turned to me and said softly, "I wish I had found you back in high school."

I reached out a gloved hand and touched his cheek, my eyes filling with sudden tears. "It was too late even then, Stu," I said, telling the truth. "I was in love with Nicky before I ever knew who you were."

He leaned his cheek into my hand.

I swallowed and continued. "It *was* wonderful. But . . ."

He sat up with a small smile. "There's always that *but*, isn't there? God, I hate that word."

"Hey," I said softly, "we'll always have Webster."

And there was nothing to do after that but laugh. So we did.

And talk, which we did also. Not about old times, no reminiscences or ex-lovers' confidences. Just conversation, the kind we never bothered with when we spent every minute alone together naked. It was conversation about inconsequentialities that kept us awake and our minds off the ever-increasing cold.

We were both Cold Winter Natives. We knew, without having to discuss the fact, that no matter how tired we were, no matter that I had been up for going on twenty-four hours already, staying awake was the surest method of staying alive.

Sleep can equal death in a situation like this.

The mindless chatter also kept me from brooding about Mother, from being overwhelmed by visions of how terrible it must be for her out at the farm alone with my dying grandmother.

Stu didn't have to be told that I was preoccupied. He just kept up the cheerful banter and the optimistic predictions that we would be rescued soon.

I think I came to know, and like, Stuart McKee better during those hours than all the others combined.

As the night waned and we became friends, it got colder and colder in the cab of the truck. Stu was able to run the engine and heater for ten minutes or so every hour. We had to conserve both gas and battery power since neither one of us actually said out loud what we both knew to be a possibility—that we might not be rescued immediately.

And neither one of us dared to speak the thing that was truly frightening, that we might not be rescued in time at all.

Instead, we talked, breath pluming out in great puffs, and during those intervals while the engine ran, we plugged tapes into the stereo and listened to the odd assortment of music Stu carried around with him.

We heard some of *Abraxas* during one warming session, realizing that dashboard light was the only way to listen to Santana. We decided that "Black Magic Woman" was supreme makeout music, though neither of us was tempted to put it to the test.

Not much anyway.

During another heater run, I discovered James Taylor's *Hourglass* in the cubbyhole.

Long ago, Stu had bought an assortment of JT music for my benefit, but this particular album had come out after our breakup. Stu was not a great fan of Sweet Baby James, generally preferring more twang to his music. I raised a questioning eyebrow at him.

He shrugged. "It makes me think of you," he said simply, plugging it in.

And as always, that sweet nasal voice carried me along.

But despite Stu's periodic efforts to keep the cab warm, frost formed on the inside of the truck windows. Though the interior temperature was easily forty degrees warmer than the exterior temps, even without the wind chill factored in, it was still bitterly cold.

Our breath had at first fogged over the glass, and as time passed, the fog turned to an ever-thickening coat of ice and frost.

Ah well, it was dark and we didn't need to see outside anyway.

Though Stu did not have a shovel, and he also didn't have a formal blizzard kit (which South Dakotans are encouraged to carry at all times during the winter), he did find a smelly old wool army blanket stuffed under the seat. He spread it over me.

"This is ridiculous," I said from my side of the seat, near the door. "There is no reason for you to freeze to death while I am snug over here."

Neither of us was at the shivering stage yet, but we were both becoming seriously cold, and there was no doubt that we should conserve body heat by sharing the blanket.

"Get over here," I ordered, lifting up a corner of the blanket.

He knew as well as I did that by wrapping ourselves in together, our chances of survival increased dramatically.

But we both felt guilty about it.

Which was silly.

"Now," I said. This was not flirtation, this was survival.

And so he did. We arranged ourselves under the blanket, sitting as close as possible, with Stu's arms around me, snuggled in as much as our bulky outer clothing would allow. We did our best to tuck the blanket ends over our feet.

We talked less and less as we became increasingly colder. At regular intervals we took our gloves off and held hands, hoping that skin-to-skin contact would ease the painful cold.

When that didn't work, we vigorously rubbed each other's hands, face, back, and legs.

"We're going to be in big trouble if we keep this up, you know," Stu said, laughing quietly.

"Stuart McKee, if you can think about sex while we are freezing to death, then you are truly depraved," I laughed back.

"Tory Bauer, what better time is there to think about sex?" he asked with a grin. "But thinking is as far as I would get, I'm afraid. I doubt I'll ever function normally again."

"Hah," I said, and was about to continue a conversation that could become dangerous and foolish, when I thought I heard something outside. The wind had gone down again and the sun was beginning to send exploratory pink fingers over the horizon. Visibility had returned, at least in a limited fashion.

I turned around and scraped a tiny hole in the thick ice that coated the back window to look out at the road and saw a short string of headlights less than a quarter mile away. The honking continued.

"The cavalry to the rescue," Stu said. "Thank God." He disentangled himself from me and the blanket, moved back to the steering wheel, pulled his gloves on, and turned the key in the ignition.

The engine turned over sluggishly, distinctly unhappy about a night spent in the cold snow of a country ditch. But the motor caught and Stu was able to turn on his lights and flashers and honk back, signaling that we were at least alive.

The lead truck in the small convoy flashed its lights back, indicating that they had seen us.

Stu tried to open his door but the snow was packed in too tightly. It wouldn't budge. We would have to be dug out before either of us could get out of the cab.

"I guess you're stuck with me for a few more minutes," Stu said softly, taking my hand. "I can't think of anyone I'd rather be stranded with."

I couldn't say exactly the same thing, but I could agree that there were less pleasant people to be stuck with all night in a freezing pickup truck in the middle of a blizzard in the middle of nowhere.

I had to allow that all things considered, it had been almost fun. Not an experience I'd care to repeat, but we had survived, and I think we had come to a new peace. A new understanding of ourselves and the relationship that we'd had.

At least I had.

Stu had his life. And his wife and his children.

If he was unhappy with any of those factors, there was nothing I could do about it.

I had my life.

And I was ready to move on.

For just an instant, I considered leaning over and giving Stu one last kiss, one last moment that was ours and ours alone. But the trucks pulled up on the road beside the drift that had caused our adventure, and the moment died. Which was just as well.

Ron Adler and some others jumped out and bounded to us through the snow.

Neil stepped out of his truck slowly and deliberately.

Ron made it to us first. He pounded on my window, which I rolled down.

"You two all right in there?" he shouted, pale and blinking wildly.

"Ron," Stu laughed. "We're cold, not deaf. Yes, we're fine."

Ron shouted the news over his shoulder at the assembled crew.

"Did you get the kids in all right?" I asked him. Though Stu and I had been talking lightly and laughing all night, whistling in the dark, so to speak, my fear for the stranded young ones was never far beneath the surface.

Nor had my concern for my mother and grandmother lessened during our ordeal.

"And out at the farm? Is everything all right there?" I asked Neil, who'd finally made it to my window.

"No," he said. "Phone service is erratic, but we were able to find out that your grandmother died an hour ago and your mother is still alone at the farm with her now."

There was no smile on his face. There was no smile in his voice.

There was no echoing of the happiness I felt in just seeing him.

"Neil," I said, desperately wishing he would look me in the eye.

But his attention was caught by something behind the truck.

Already a couple of the guys had shoveled snow away from the driver's side door. Stu was able to push his door open far enough in the snow to slip out, though he gave my hand a brief squeeze before going.

He stepped out into the deep snow and stretched mightily.

Then someone opened my door, and I slid out, my bones and joints aching and popping audibly.

It felt so good to stand up, to breathe the cold morning air, to know I was safe and would soon be warm.

"McKee, come here," Neil said sharply. He was bent over the trunk of the box, feverishly brushing snow away from something.

I looked at Stu across the nose of the pickup. If Neil had found a shovel back there and we could have rescued ourselves hours ago, I was going to be royally pissed.

Stu shrugged and went back to look.

"Do you always drive around with one of these?" Neil asked Stu quietly, pointing to whatever he'd uncovered in the truck box.

In the frigid early morning sunlight, already beginning to shiver, I leaned over Ron Adler's shoulder to see what had caught Neil's attention.

It was a human hand.

Which was unmistakably attached to an entire human body.

13

....

Cold Front

Our 360-degree horizon, our endless miles of gently rolling prairie, our dearth of lakes and navigable waterways and native forests, our unfriendly climate and low population base have already convinced the rest of the country that South Dakota is an alien landscape.

We can see it in the tourists' eyes as they squint into the far distance. They look up, bewildered, and maybe a little intimidated, by the sheer volume of sky above us. They glance sideways, dismayed by what seems to be the largest empty lot in the world.

They examine us as though we were specimens under a microscope, unable to understand exactly why we stay in this godforsaken place.

The larger world only notices us when some disaster has focused the national eye our way.

Or in the dry brown fall when the grass has died and millionaire hunters pilot their Lear jets into our regional airports with their eyes peeled only for the increasingly elusive ringneck pheasant and coed barmaids.

Or in the heart of the summer, when the fierce sun has already parched the few hardy plants down to nothing and the air swims like a mirage in the distance, as they scurry from their air-conditioned RVs searching in vain for a recognizable franchise in which to eat their lunch so they can continue on.

Only the natives see the gentle green of spring or the wondrous renewal of the thaw or the spectacular blaze of the sunset every single day, so I guess the outsiders can be forgiven for missing the stark beauty in the open plains. The endless expanse of flat earth that never fails to remind us of how insignificant we really are.

We know this land; it is etched in our hearts and minds and in the backs of our eyes. We can see one-quarter of land and know the whole. We can find our way in the dark. We know this place, and we recognize it immediately.

That is, unless six feet of snow have fallen in the last twenty-four hours.

In which case, the place looks like an alien landscape to us too.

In the brilliant early morning sunshine, the whole world looked to have been coated with a thick layer of down. Our land of sharp planes and angles had been transformed into an endless vista of softly mounded white.

Along the roadside, only the top few inches of fenceposts peeked above the snow; the fences themselves were covered completely. Between the trees, drifts grew to fifteen feet or higher. The gravel ribbon of road was intersected every quarter-mile or so by long fingers of white that snaked from the ditch.

The windbreak trees were plastered on one side with a layer of snow compacted by the fierce winds, while the other side had been blown clean.

In the far distance, smoke from a farmhouse chimney floated up into the early morning sky. From our vantage, the house and outbuildings were white-on-white lumps, barely distinguishable from the surrounding fields.

The frigid air had crystallized every last particle of moisture, turning the world into a Christmas card that sparkled as though each surface had been sprinkled with glitter.

It truly was a spectacular sight. One that few are privileged to see.

But no one in my immediate vicinity paid the least bit of attention to nature's fierce beauty because blizzards and their aftermath could be witnessed once or twice every single winter.

While the frozen body of Ian O'Hara lying facedown in the box of Stuart McKee's burgundy Chevy truck was a once in a lifetime sight.

"Jesus Christ!" Stu said vehemently under his breath, his arms wrapped around himself for warmth.

He looked at me in bewildered shock.

I mirrored both the expression and the emotion, and then glanced at the men circled around the truck box. They shuffled uncomfortably, whispering to one another quietly.

"I take it you had no idea that he was back here?" Neil asked Stu, his voice tightly controlled. He ignored me completely. "Is there any way he could have crawled up here during the night?"

"For God's sake, no," Stu said, annoyed and frowning, looking to me for conformation. "Of *course* not."

"Like *they* would have noticed," one of the guys snickered.

I fixed the joker with a stare that should have frozen him completely. It had no effect whatsoever.

"Yeah, just how did you two stay warm enough last night anyway?" another asked, to the vast amusement of nearly everyone assembled. "You know what they say about generating body heat."

To my outright horror, the assembled men burst into guffaws, except for a pale Ron Adler, who chuckled weakly while avoiding my gaze.

And Neil, who stood stone-faced looking down at Ian's body.

Now somewhere in the back of my brain, I knew that the jokes about Stu and me were a way of avoiding the terrible fact of a dead body in our midst. Clinical observation would have showed me that underneath the lewd banter was a very real thread of fear and unease, an inability to process the information in front of their very eyes.

But I wasn't being clinical at that particular moment. I was furious.

On the very morning when my relationship with Stu had matured into something we could both put behind us, or at the very least live with relatively comfortably— on the day after the start of something that could be entirely wonderful with Neil—I was forced to deal with public snickering about what had been over and done with a long time ago.

And all because of Gina Adler and her breakdown.

Without her, it would not have been general knowledge, on this of all days, that my affair with Stu had begun before his wife left.

If I had been fair, I would have had to admit, to myself anyway, that Gina had only been the messenger of that particular piece of news. The message had been written, unfortunately, by Stu and me months before, though it had taken an awful long time for the news to get to the general populace.

Breathing heavily, perhaps to avoid thinking about the poor man lying in front of me too, I focused instead on a white-hot, useless anger.

I knew that neither Stu nor I had done anything for which we needed to feel any guilt at all.

At least not while we were stranded in the blizzard.

But none of the assembled would ever believe that. In fact, denials would only cement their certainty that we had survived the night by running our own internal combustion engines.

And once that story, with its attendant speculations,

got out, no one else would believe in our innocence either.

Well, no one except Neil.

I looked at him, expecting, needing, an indication that he understood that nothing had happened between Stu and me during that long cold night. That he knew that Ian's presence in the back of the truck had been a complete and unwelcome surprise to us.

And most importantly, that last night's wonderful beginning was not the end of the story.

But he stood straight and stiff and unsmiling, his breath pluming out whitely in front of him. I could not see his eyes through the glare of the sun reflected from his glasses.

"Neil," I said quietly, but he turned away to confer with Ron Adler, who blinked wildly, casting suspicious glances over his shoulder at both Stu and me.

"Well, it seems mighty strange for this English guy to end up dead in the back of McKee's pickup," someone said. "Dontcha think?"

"It sorta looks like foul play to me," added another.

"You s'pose he crawled up there and committed suicide by freezing?" asked another wit.

That comment sent the assembled group into gales of nervous laughter once again.

All except Neil, who took a cell phone from one of the guys.

Grim-faced, he punched in 911 and waited for the dispatcher to answer.

The rest of the group quieted down, though they still continued to snicker quietly as Neil explained the situation into the phone.

"Okay," Neil said, craning his neck to look over the edge of the truck box. "As far as I can tell, no trauma is visible at all. No blood, no injuries, no sign of a struggle." He listened a moment and then said, "He'd only just come into town the night before, so I couldn't say."

Neil covered the phone and turned to me. "Tory, you talked to him more than the rest of us, did Mr. O'Hara mention anything about any diseases to you—diabetes, allergies . . ."

"Terminal cancer . . . death wish . . . a deep-seated need to freeze his balls off . . ." someone said in the background before being shushed.

I shook my head no.

Ignoring the others, Neil listened to the dispatcher again and then asked me, "Did he say anything about where he came from or give you any information about his life?"

I realized that my brief exposure to Ian, coupled with my now permanent connection to his death, would serve to make me a reigning expert on the man. But there was nothing I could add to the pool of knowledge.

"Not a word," I said softly to Neil, searching his face in vain for any indication of friendship or warmth.

"I'll check his ID," Ron Adler said, jumping into the back of the pickup. "That'll tell them something." He'd reached Ian's body and had gingerly patted the back pants pocket, and carefully checked the sheepskin coat pockets before anyone could stop him.

"No," Neil said forcefully after listening to the phone again for a moment. "No, no no! Ron, stop. We're to leave the body as it is, and the truck box as it is, and bring both into town right now and put them into an unheated garage until the sheriff can arrive."

Ron shrugged. "Nothing in the pockets anyway." He jumped out of the truck box with a look of relief on his face. "No wallet, no ID, no nothing. At least not that I could tell."

The idea of Ron Adler going through the pockets of the man who had been dallying with his wife less than twelve hours before was too unreal to contemplate. I rubbed my face and wished mightily that I was in bed and that this had all been a dream.

Neil said something else into the phone and then hung up.

He turned to face the group. "You heard what we have to do. Let's get this truck back into town and wait for the plows to open the highway so the sheriff can take over."

He quietly called out orders to the assortment of helpers, who seemed glad of something specific to do. Stu joined the rest of the guys, who were now quietly somber.

The humor of the situation had worn off. The sexual joking had only been a buffer between them and the dead body lying less than five feet away.

While the winch was set up and the hook attached to Stu's bumper, Neil finally turned to me.

"Do you want to go home?" he asked, not looking at me directly. "Or do you want someone to take you out to your mother's farm?"

"I suppose that depends on what Mother thinks," I said, the chill in Neil's voice settling around me like another blanket of ice. "And whether or not she needs me now. Can I use the phone for a second?"

Neil handed it to me without a word.

I squinted up at him. "Do the police want me in Delphi? Do I need to go there to make a statement?"

He shrugged. "They'll want to talk to you eventually I suppose. But since you didn't kill Ian O'Hara, I don't think you have too much to worry about."

He looked at me directly; this time I could see his eyes, and I didn't like what I saw at all. "You *didn't* kill Ian O'Hara, did you? With Stuart McKee or without him?"

The venom in his voice shocked me to the core.

And it pissed me off.

"No, I did not fucking kill Ian O'Hara," I said to him, enunciating every single word carefully. "And I didn't do anything else either. With or without Stuart McKee."

"Yeah, well," he said, glancing to the side. "That's one of those things I'm going to have to take on faith, isn't it?"

"You damn right you better take it on faith, buster," I said through clenched teeth. "I froze my ass off all night, worried about my mother, worried about my grandmother, worried about Presley and Mardelle. And worried about you."

"Do you think you had a monopoly on worry?" he asked fiercely, his face contorted with anger. "Do you think I didn't spend this whole goddamn night frightened out of my wits that I was going to find you dead? Frozen as solid as our friend over there?"

"I'm sorry you were scared. We were all scared. But I didn't have a choice. Mother needed me and I had to go. Ron said that the roads weren't as bad as you'd expected them to be. I figured I'd be out at the farm and Stu would make it back to town safely, and everything would be hunky-dory."

"Well, maybe it'd be a good idea to get your story straight with your mother then," Neil continued, his voice loud enough to cause a few wary glances over shoulders from the vicinity of the pickup.

"And what the hell is that supposed to mean?" I asked.

I must have been shouting, because several more men, including Stu, stopped what they were doing and looked my way for a moment before going back to their tasks.

"Not long after you left last night, Junior called me at the cafe in hysterics," I said, lowering my voice. "She demanded that I go out to the farm immediately to help Mother because she was alone with Grandma, and Grandma was having convulsions."

"And do you always jump when Junior calls?" Neil asked, almost sweetly.

I wasn't fooled.

"Clay said that things were terrible at the farm and he asked that I find a way to get there to be with Mother. You *know* that Clay is sensible. You know I would never even have considered such a cockamamie idea if he hadn't asked me to. I thought I had to."

"Well, you might be surprised to hear your mother's version of the events," Neil said, hunching down into his coat for warmth. "Go ahead and call. If you can get through, I think you'll be interested in what she has to say. Then when you decide what you want to do, let one of these guys know and they'll take you wherever you want to go."

With that, he turned away and tromped over to a knot of men who were busy shoveling snow away from the truck tires.

I watched his back for a moment.

I was angry. Resentful. Tired. Cold.

And incredibly confused.

Then I dialed the phone.

14

....

The $64,000 Question

They say that the road to hell is paved with good intentions.

I'll certainly agree that many a wrongheaded idea was formed for all the right reasons.

And I can admit that a fair percentage of individuals do bad while only, and entirely, trying to do good.

So there is some truth to the old cliché.

But I think that they have it backward.

Far more often than not, the road to good intentions runs directly through hell.

With a stopover in Delphi.

A static-filled phone call to my mother as the men dislodged Stu's pickup, confirmed that Grandma Nillie had revived from her coma enough to go into convulsions. And most assuredly superintending her death, alone in a blizzard, was a less than jolly experience.

I even discovered that Mother had mentioned in passing to Juanita over the phone just before the line went dead the first time, and Grandma went into the worst, and last, of her convulsive episodes, that she would prefer to have some company during the ordeal.

But never once did Mother suggest to Juanita, or anyone else, that I should attempt the snow-packed country roads to join her vigil in the middle of the blizzard.

That little embroidery had come from Aunt Juanita, and it had been embellished by the hysterical, pregnant Junior, who had alarmed her generally calm and steady husband enough to pressure me into making the trip.

"Good heavens, dear, why in the world would I want to subject you to something terrible like that?" Mother had asked sensibly.

There was, of course, no logical answer to that question.

But I hadn't been operating on logic last night.

I had been tired, and still a little drunk.

And I had been frightened.

Unfortunately, all those ingredients, mixed with a large dollop of good intentions, put me squarely in the position that I least wanted to occupy: back in the Delphi spotlight with a dead body.

The line died again just as Mother had added an admonition to go home and sleep, that there was nothing for me to do at the farm, that there was, indeed, nothing for her to do at the farm until the roads were plowed and an ambulance was able to pick up Grandma Nillie's body.

Seeing the wisdom in her advice, I opted to ride back into town, squished in the front seat of a beat-up pickup, with a smoker on one side, and a pale, and probably hung over, Ron Adler on the other.

I suppose I could have ridden back into town with Stu, but that idea hadn't appealed to me at all. And after the scene earlier, I was not about to ask Neil for a ride.

He probably wouldn't have given me one anyway. After being informed of my decision to ride back to Delphi, his only comment was that I should go and sit in one of the vehicles and try to warm up while they finished dislodging Stu's truck.

Too tired to play with the Testosterone Rescue Brigade, and too cold to function on any level beyond instinct, I took his advice and climbed into one of the idling pickups and tried not to think.

The skin on my fingers and face was red and raw and painfully cold, but I saw no telltale white spots when I examined myself in the rearview mirror.

My toes were numb, but I had been wearing heavy-duty winter boots, so it was almost safe to assume that I would have no permanent physical damage from last night's adventure.

The psychological and emotional damage had yet to be cataloged.

"So what was it like out there?" the driver asked me on the slow ride back to town.

He was a grizzled, local farmer who occasionally made it into the cafe on rainy days, though he usually spent his off time camped in the bar. I'd waited on him here and there for years, but my brain was so fogged at the moment that I couldn't remember his name. But he'd offered his truck as a taxi and he had the heater running full blast and the forced air was finally making a dent in my bone-deep cold, so he deserved an answer.

"It was cold," I said, shrugging, and shivering a little. "Real cold."

On the other hand, I wasn't interested in talking about either Stu or Ian O'Hara's dead body, which severely limited the conversational opportunities.

The road had not yet been plowed, but the wind had done us a favor by rearranging a few of the worst drifts. We drove at the head of a convoy of pickups. Stu's truck, bearing its unexpected cargo, brought up the rear.

We had been able to drive on nearly dry pavement for most of the way, swerving carefully around the drifts that still snaked past the center of the road.

The driver rolled his window down a couple of inches and flicked a still-burning cigarette out into the snow.

"It had to be scary some," he said with a sideways glance at me. "I mean, not knowing if you were going to die out there in the snow."

Evidently I was going to have to pay for my rescue, and subsequent free ride, by giving him and Ron, who hadn't spoken a word for the entire trip, an exclusive on My Night in the Blizzard.

I suppressed a sigh and decided that talking was better than thinking anyway.

I chattered mindlessly about the wind and the snow and hitting my head on the door frame of Stu's truck. I talked about conserving battery power and not worrying about starving to death in that short period of time.

"Well you was lucky," the driver said, squinting into the brilliant white landscape, "that you weren't alone. They say that two people have a better chance of surviving the cold together than they would apart. Something about body heat and stuff like that."

This time I didn't suppress the sigh. I knew what he was driving at. He wanted an answer to the Big Question, the one that was on the minds of each and every one of the rescuers, including, to my complete dismay, Neil Pascoe. It would be on the minds of every Delphi citizen as they heard and repeated the story.

I was going to have to face it sooner or later. I opted for sooner.

"Listen," I said, rubbing my face. "Stuart McKee and I did not have sex in the cab of his pickup truck last night in order to keep from freezing to death. Stuart McKee and I did not do anything last night except talk and listen to the stereo and wait for daylight to come and for you guys to find us.

"You might not have noticed," I continued, not giving either one time to inject further questions or commentary, "but I'm a fat girl. Fat is an insulator. It helps keep us chubbies warm in the winter. Even if I had been alone, I would have been in no danger of freezing to death because I was dressed warmly and out of the wind.

Stu and I both had enough sense to stay put until morning.

"*That* is why we are alive to tell the tale. It was cold. It was frightening. It was a very, very long night. And neither of us had any fun at all." I fixed the driver with an eagle eye. "Got it?"

Judging by his guilty grin, I'd say he got it.

I turned to Ron on my other side to catch him in the same gimlet stare. "You got it too, Ron?"

Ron, however, had been staring out the passenger window, and probably had not heard a word of my declaration.

"Yeah, sure," he mumbled, blinking miserably. "No problem."

While I had been busy damming up the holes in my reputation, I had forgotten about what the last twenty-four hours had done to Ron Adler's domestic life.

Though I imagine that their marriage had never been the smooth combination of Competent Wife/Mother and Business Owner/Luster After Delphine Bauer that it seemed to be from the outside, they had still managed to get by without any major cracks visible to the general public.

Gina's middle-of-the-street breakdown yesterday had shattered a carefully crafted illusion.

Or maybe it hadn't been an illusion. Maybe they'd had a precariously balanced relationship that had simply been far more fragile than either they, or anyone else, had realized.

In all the years I had known Gina, I had never sniffed even a hint of a rumor of an interest in any man other than Ron.

So either she had been the craftiest woman ever to grace our fair town, or she had truly gone off the deep end yesterday. Her dalliance with Ian, aborted by my unfortunate interruption, told me that the breakage was no surface disturbance.

Gina was not the kind of girl who could indulge in a guilt-free one-nighter. For her to have broken her marriage vows, she had to have been deeply disturbed.

Of course, Ron didn't know anything about that yet.

And Gina had been pretty drunk, and sometimes unhappy drunk people do really stupid things that have long-term repercussions.

I just hoped in the course of the investigation into Ian's death, that I would not have to tell anyone what I had seen last night.

Ron continued to stare glumly out the passenger side window.

"So what do you think he died from?" the driver asked, undaunted. We were just pulling into Delphi. He'd lit another cigarette and was puffing happily away. Either he was determined to suck every piece of information that he could out of me, or he was the most clueless man in South Dakota. "You know, that English guy, I mean."

"Oh, him," I said, deciding that the scales were weighted toward *clueless*. "I don't suppose we'll know for sure until the medical examiner gets through with him. I assume he froze to death."

"Well, he was an interesting fella. With some interesting friends," the driver said.

Ian had garnered more than his share of notice during his small residency in Delphi. I assumed the driver had been out and about last night and had observed Ian's way with the ladies.

There wasn't much I could say in reply, considering that the husband of one of Ian's *interesting friends* was sitting right next to me.

Though I probably could have said anything I wanted since Ron looked out the window and paid no attention to the conversation.

Ron's somber mood was contagious. Or maybe we were all just too tired to talk anymore. We sat in silence for the remainder of the trip. The driver pulled over in front of the trailer without being told which one it was.

Delphi is a small town and it is possible that he already knew where I lived, even though I still could not pry his name from my frozen memory banks.

However, it was more likely that he knew where I lived because he'd been inside the trailer on some earlier occasion.

With Del.

As I gathered up my mittens and scarves, the other trucks drove past us as slow and solemn as a funeral procession, which I suppose it was.

They all turned right at the corner just before the cafe. It had been decided by a general consensus, and another phone call, that Stu's truck would be parked as-is in the unheated garage that my Uncle Albert Engebretson's insurance agency shared with the cafe.

Neither business used the garage, so everything inside would remain undisturbed until the authorities arrived and did whatever investigating they could considering that the site had been thoroughly trampled, and was not a crime scene anyway.

At least in the garage, Ian was unlikely to thaw before the medical examiner and ambulance arrived.

I shook that disturbing thought from my head and saw that the driver was still waiting for some parting words.

"Thanks for the ride," I said earnestly. "This has been a pretty awful experience. It was bad enough being stranded, but finding a body in the truck, was . . . well." I thought I could let the commentary dangle there. But I could see he wanted some sort of conclusion, a summing up of the whole experience. I did my best to please him; after all, he had performed a service for which I would be grateful as soon as I warmed up.

"I think that Ian O'Hara froze to death," I said slowly. "He'd had a lot to drink and maybe he became disoriented and climbed up into the box of Stu's pickup while it was still parked in front of the bar. And then he passed out and died. I think it was just bad luck and terrible timing."

For him, and for us.

The driver nodded, satisfied.

Ron nodded too.

I even nodded.

Up until that very moment, I had not formulated the possible whys and wherefores of Ian's unexpected demise.

But my off-the-cuff theory made sense to me.

Which is just as well, because I expected to have to repeat it an endless number of times over the next day or so.

15

....

Show Me the Money

Despite the notion that there is nothing for single small-town females of a certain age to do except stumble over dead bodies, I am doing my best not to grow up and become Jessica Fletcher.

Though my personal body count keeps rising, our differences still far outweigh our similarities.

Ol' Jess got to leave her rustic seaside town on occasion (which was a good thing considering that Cabot Cove was on the brink of decimation until she widened her social circle), while I am stuck here in Delphi, a town whose population was dwindling even before I became the official discoverer of the recently deceased.

I don't ever remember an episode where La Fletcher's sex life had any bearing on the murder (or the solution, come to think of it).

I can't recall her experiencing any sort of financial difficulties.

And it's far too late to produce a slew of obliging

nephews to lead me into, or out of, adventures.

But probably the biggest difference between Jessica and me is that when I am presented with a dead body in even slightly mysterious circumstances, my first reaction is not to investigate, but to run screaming in the other direction.

That is also my second and third reaction.

And it would have been my reaction now too, but I had been up for more than twenty-four hours and I was too cold and tired to run anywhere, much less scream.

But I had no intention of investigating anything.

It was not quite eight A.M. when I finally tiptoed into the trailer. The snow on the steps had been trampled, so I knew that either Del or Presley had already been up and out.

I hoped they were still out because the last thing I wanted to do was talk to anyone.

I dropped the boots and gloves and scarves that had kept me warm during the previous night in a haphazard pile on the living room floor, shivering.

My bravura pronouncement on the warming qualities of body fat had been at least partially hot air. Yes, my own mass kept me warmer than, say, your average supermodel would have been under the same circumstances.

But cold is cold, and cold fat is *really* cold.

I had been truly grateful for that smelly army blanket. And I had been doubly grateful for Stuart McKee's company and body heat. I would have survived the night without those things, but the combo had made the long night bearable.

Though I was not about to admit that in public.

I was not about to go in public at all, with or without admissions.

I stood in the living room, still wearing the clothes I had on last night, waffling over which had the greater appeal: a long hot shower or some hot chocolate (laced with brandy as per Ian's Auntie Featherstonehaugh). After a moment of contemplation during which no decision had been made, I added the option of shit-canning everything and heading for bed.

Shower, chocolate, bed. Shower, chocolate, brandy, bed. Shower, James Taylor, chocolate, brandy, bed.

Bed won.

I stumbled through the kitchen and into my bedroom, closing the door firmly behind me.

I peeled off my damp socks and crawled under the covers, lay there a minute realizing that my feet were like lumps of ice, got up and put on a clean, dry pair of socks, and crawled back into bed and closed my eyes and settled into the growing warmth.

The door to my room banged open suddenly, startling the bejabbers out of me.

"Arrgh . . ." I said, pulling the covers over my head without bothering to identify the interloper. "Go away."

"Get up," said Del. "I need to talk to you."

"No you don't," I said, my head stuffed into the pillow. It was warm in there. Deliciously warm. "I don't want to talk to anyone."

"Tough shit," Del said, pulling on the covers.

I hung on to the top blanket, but Del was stronger and more determined.

A rush of cold air raised goosebumps on my arms.

I reached for the covers, with my eyes still closed, and tried to pull them back over my head. "I just got here. I haven't even been to sleep yet. Whatever it is can wait."

"Just got here, my ass," Del said sharply. "It's noon and you've been sacked out for about four hours already."

"Noon?" I asked, disbelieving. I cracked open the eye that was closest to my alarm clock, mostly in order to prove to Del that she couldn't possibly be right about the time, but the clock face was black and blank.

I reached out and tapped the top of the clock. Nothing happened. I picked it up and shook it.

"Won't do you any good to do that," Del said matter-of-factly, sitting down on the edge of the bed. "Power's been out for about an hour."

I groaned and covered my head and said several very bad words loud enough for anyone in the trailer to hear. But Del held her ground.

"That's why I'm here," Del said. "At home, I mean. No power, no reason to keep the cafe open. I went in to work this morning, but things were hairy what with . . . well, you know . . ."

I finally focused on Del's face and saw that despite her expert makeup job, her eyes were red-rimmed. She looked worn and haggard, every bit her age.

Staring at the ceiling, I wondered why it was that Del's heart had been touched by the one guy whose sweet stories she should have discounted completely.

I struggled to sit up, my bones creaking and muscles protesting.

"I'm sorry," I said, reaching out to touch her shoulder gently. Del was not a huggable woman. "Were you at the cafe when you heard about Ian?"

She nodded miserably, her eyes filling with tears again.

I reached over and grabbed a Kleenex from the box on the nightstand and handed it to her.

Del took the tissue and dabbed at her eyes carefully. "Yeah, well, it wasn't that busy at first. Most of the early morning crowd was still snowed in, and the in-town ones were still sleeping last night off.

"But we were still busy enough for Alanna to call Brian in to cook. Rhonda was no help, with her hand burned. So Alanna and I worked the floor and Brian was doing fine in the kitchen, keeping up with the crowd—"

"Wait a second," I interrupted her. "Brian was cooking? Where was Dorothy?"

"Dorothy?" Del asked, blowing her nose delicately. "Dorothy wasn't going to work this morning. You were supposed to, but we knew that you couldn't, what with being out in the snow with Stu all night and all."

I sat up fully. "Dorothy was too supposed to work. She agreed to open this morning. We confirmed it last night before she left the cafe."

"Well, she didn't show up," Del said firmly. "It would have made a hell of a difference if she had. Things got really crazy after they brought . . . you know . . . the body back into town."

"Yeah," I said, chewing my lip. "I suppose it did."

I could see the cafe, filling up with very cold, very tired, at least partially hung-over rescuers, all bursting to tell their version of what they had seen and heard out in the snow.

"Yeah, well, we'd heard the news already anyway," Del said, sniffing. Her eyes were dry again. "Presley and John Adler caught it on the scanner and they ran to the cafe to warn us first."

"Pres was up already?" I asked. "I figured he'd be in bed all day after last night."

"Shit," Del said, disgusted. "He thinks last night was an adventure. He's ready to do it again." Her lips tightened.

Del was no one's definition of a good mother, but she had been genuinely frightened for the safety of her only son last night. I thought that Presley might find himself in more trouble than he'd expected over this little *adventure*.

"I'll speak to him too," I said, hugging my knees.

Now that I was sitting up, I could feel that the temperature in the trailer had dropped a good twenty degrees. With no power, the gas furnace had no fan, and without a fan, we had no heat. With no heat, the inside temps would fall rapidly. Within a day, the interior of the trailer would be literally freezing. And shortly after that, the frozen pipes would burst.

Our best hope was for the power to be restored as quickly as possible.

"I'll remind him that joyriding in the middle of a blizzard is a dangerous pastime," I continued. He sometimes listened to me when he wouldn't even hear Del.

"Well," Del said, looking over her shoulder at the open doorway. "I wouldn't say much of anything to him right now, if I were you."

Presley shuffled past my door wearing a hooded sweatshirt and carrying a bag of potato chips. He didn't look my way at all.

I raised an eyebrow at Del.

"He's pretty pissed," Del said simply, looking me straight in the eye. "You broke his heart. He thought that I was the only one who boffed married men. Evidently he could live with my betrayal of womankind. But you, he had on a pedestal."

There was real bitterness in her voice.

I remembered Presley's hurt and bewildered face yesterday out in the street after Gina's shouted revelation.

Knowing that I had begun my affair with Stu before his wife had left him had probably shattered his version of an orderly world.

"Fuck," I said, lying back down and covering my face again.

"Succinctly put," Del said, examining her fingernails. "He'll get over it. They all get over it eventually."

I peeled the covers back again. "I'd better go talk to him. Try to explain."

"Explain what?" Del asked. "Explain your sterling reasons for sleeping with Stuart McKee when you both knew that he was married? That'll go over big, I can tell you."

I groaned.

"Besides, you can't talk to him right now. John Adler is here. He was out with Presley and Mardelle in the snow too. He spent the rest of the night here."

"Gina let him come here instead of going straight home?" I asked, surprised.

Gina was a good mother. She would have been beside herself with worry over John's safety.

"Last night Ron whacked him alongside the head and told him to go home with Presley rather than waking up his mother and scaring her," Del said, squinting to remember the sequence of events. "He figured the kid could face the music today."

"Makes sense, I guess," I said, thinking it through. Ron knew that John was safe, and he could tell Gina the news when he got home.

Outside, we heard the unmistakable sound of someone stomping snow off their boots just inside the porch door.

Del and I both rolled our eyes at the ceiling.

"Whoever it is, I'm not here," I said, covering my head one last time.

Bang-bang-banging echoed throughout the house.

"Move over, I'm coming in with you," Del said, with the first smile I'd seen today.

Presley opened the door and we heard mumbled conversation, and then he said very clearly, "She's in her bedroom. It's just off the kitchen there."

"Nooooooo," I moaned. "Please noooooo."

The footsteps pounded closer.

"There you are!" Alanna shouted from the doorway. She was bundled up and too bright for the naked eye.

I can't even begin to imagine where she'd found an electric-green snowmobile suit. With matching boots, gloves, and goggles.

"Where the hell have you been?" she continued, coming into my bedroom, her beady eyes taking in every detail.

It would do no good to hide my head. She already knew I was here, so I sat up.

Del excused herself politely and tried to squeeze by Alanna.

"Not so fast, honey chile," Alanna said, freezing Del in her tracks. "We all got somethin' to talk about right here and now."

"Can't it wait? I just spent a harrowing night," I said to Alanna patiently.

I would never have used a word like *harrowing* in general conversation, but I wanted to impress her with the severity of the situation.

I might just as well have thrown *excruciating* at her,

not to mention *grueling* and *agonizing,* for all the good
it did.

"I don't care what kind of night you just spent with
your old sweetie," Alanna said. "You have my heartiest
congratulations. Or my deepest regrets, whichever is the
most appropriate in the given situation."

Del and I glanced at each other in confusion. I had
no idea where Alanna was headed with this conversation, but she was plainly upset enough to have poured
herself into her good dress coveralls and confront us.
Or, to be more specific, me.

"I, personally, don't care in the least," she continued
before either of us could interrupt. "All I want to know
is, where is the money?"

"What do you mean, where is the money?" I asked,
even more confused than before.

"Cain't y'all understand English? I want to know
where the money from last night is."

Alanna's eyes narrowed dangerously.

I spotted a moving shadow outside the bedroom door,
so I knew that Presley was hovering outside, eavesdropping.

I wanted him to know that while I may have been an
adulteress, I most certainly was not a thief, so I said
loudly and very clearly, "The money from last night is
in the blue bag. Right where we always put the money."

"I assumed that," Alanna said sharply. "Just tell me
where the blue bag is, and I'll let you get back to your
beauty sleep."

Her insinuation that I *needed* beauty sleep whizzed
past too fast to register any outrage. Besides, she was
right.

"The blue bag is on the counter by the till. At least
that's where I saw it last. It was there when I left the
cafe," I said.

Del turned to look at me too, an odd expression on
her face.

"You left a couple thousand bucks on the counter last
night? You didn't even lock it up?"

"Yes, I left it there," I said defensively. The thought of putting the bag away had not even occurred to me. "I was scared and in a hurry, and I forgot."

I looked at Alanna and Del, who were exchanging incredulous glances in an unusual show of solidarity.

"It was only a few hours until time to open again, and the banks are closed today anyway," I said to both of them. "Besides Dorothy was going to come in and open this morning. I assumed she'd put the money under the counter until you got there."

Alanna shot a triumphant look at Del and another at me.

I didn't like either one.

"Well, I assume that *your* Dorothy did put the money somewhere," Alanna said with an entirely phony smile, placing an undue emphasis on the word *your*. "Because no one has seen either one of them today."

16

....

There's No Place Like Home

Little towns like Delphi don't have their own road crews. The tax base is too small to underwrite full-time employees, and having to stay sober, alert, and on call keeps the few part-timers who could actually do the job from wanting it.

So each year, bids are taken for park and cemetery maintenance, road grading, street sweeping, and, of course, snow removal, with the contract being awarded to the crew submitting the lowest offer (or having the closest personal relationship with the city council).

Some years, the plow boys twiddled their thumbs during early Christmas thaws and even earlier spring rains. In others, the city budget was depleted by November. During those winters, the guys were run ragged because contracts stipulated that snow accumulations over six inches on the roads had to be removed or bladed as soon as physically possible—holidays, overtime, or hangovers notwithstanding.

So even though the county and state plows had not yet made it near Delphi, the fellas who'd won the in-town snow removal bid were busy because they actually lived in town. Once the general consensus agreed that the snowfall was at least temporarily over, the plows had been out in full force.

And in Delphi, *full force* consisted of two guys happily counting future paychecks, two gravel trucks with adjustable blades, one dump truck with a hoist, and a front end loader. Together, they slowly but surely made the roadways of Delphi navigable again.

Down the main drag, one gravel truck would noisily and none too evenly scrape the snow in a single swath away from the curb. The second truck would follow shortly behind and about eight feet to the left, scraping that windrow up with another swath of snow and depositing it toward the middle of the street.

They would continue in like fashion up and down both sides of the road until all of the snow, or as much as they could scrape from the frozen roadway, was piled in one very tall, muddy, lumpy, solid wall of snow running the length of the town.

While this frozen divider was in place, no one could get from one side of the street, not to mention town, to the other, since the snow was sometimes piled twelve feet high right through the intersections.

Luckily for me, I had no desire to cross the street.

I could hear Neil's snow blower running from the trailer steps and knew that he was cleaning the library sidewalks. After this morning, I had no desire to climb over the snow pile to say hello. I had no desire to be outside at all.

My only desire was to crawl back into my rapidly cooling bed, but Alanna had demanded that I tromp up to the cafe to show her exactly where I'd left the money bag.

And while I had no need for a refresher course in the minute details of after-blizzard snow removal, I had to admit to a certain desire to see for myself that the blue bag, and the money, were really gone.

"You didn't see it at all?" I asked Alanna's electric-green back.

We were walking single-file down the sidewalk, which had a pathway of exactly one shovel-width cleared down its length.

The plow boys had switched equipment. One now drove a dump truck, whose box the other methodically filled with snow using a front end loader. They started in the intersections, clearing them for nonexistent cross traffic.

"Not a stitch," Alanna said, not bothering to look back. Her breath trailed behind her like a steam train. Alanna was a big woman, but she was spry. Even in boots and coveralls, she covered ground at a pretty good clip.

I had to hurry to keep up with her, so I kept my questions short as I panted in the dry, sub-zero air.

"It wasn't laying by the till, then?" I asked, waving at the driver of the dump truck as he pulled away with a full load that he would deposit along the banks of the James River, or at least as close to the banks as he could get considering road conditions. The spring thaw would take care of the excess moisture.

"I already told you—" Alanna said, stopping so abruptly that I ran into her. "Oof, watch where you're goin'."

I had been looking down at the sidewalk in order to avoid the slippery spots and had not noticed the teenager with the snow blower. He simultaneously ogled Alanna and sprayed snow in a high white powdery arc right over where we would have been if her testosterone radar had not been instantly aware of his admiring gaze.

I assume she smiled sweetly at the boy because his face flushed a deep red that had nothing to do with wind chills. Then she continued on, swinging her hips.

"I unlocked the door this morning and found the cafe empty and dark. It didn't even occur to me to wonder about the money." She turned around and fixed me with a stern glare. "We were too busy to worry about things like that, bein' short-handed and all."

If she thought I'd feel guilty about sleeping while she toiled, she was sorely mistaken. "Why didn't you just call Dorothy in?" I asked, stepping off the curb at the end of the block to cross the street.

Right then the remaining snow pack was pristine, but a day or so of traffic would break it up and give it the texture and color of brown sugar.

Alanna stopped abruptly again, but I saw her in time. "Exactly how was I to call her?" she turned around and demanded sharply. "You were in such a god-awful hurry to hire her yesterday that we didn't get a current address or phone number. We're lucky we got anything out of her at all."

She turned around and stomped off again.

"Dorothy didn't write down her address?" I asked, confused. Our employment application form had a spot for addresses and phone numbers and all that routine stuff. It never occurred to me to make sure she'd filled in every blank. "Why not?"

"Oh for heaven's sake," Alanna said, digging the cafe keys out of her coverall pocket. "If I knew the answer to that, we'd probably still have our money."

I was too cold and too tired to follow her reasoning, so I just followed her into the cafe. I flipped the light switch up and down a couple times, confused as to why the room stayed dark.

"The power is out, Tory," Alanna said. "Remember?"

"Oh, yeah," I said, embarrassed. Or I would have been if I hadn't been so confused. "But I still don't understand what you're saying. How would knowing Dorothy's address have kept the money from disappearing?"

Though it was warmer inside the cafe than out, it was still cold enough that I was not tempted to take off my coat. Or hat. Or gloves. After peering at the empty spot next to the till for a moment, I sat in a window booth where the light was good.

Alanna rummaged behind the long counter and pulled a ledger and some papers out and then piled them on the table in front of me.

"Shall I spell it out for you?" She sat down opposite in the booth.

"Yes, please do," I said wearily.

Across the street, the scowling road crew worked around an old van and a beat-up pickup that blocked their progress. As a rule, vehicles left parked along the roadways after heavy snowfalls were ticketed and towed at owner expense, usually by Ron Adler with his handy winch truck, long before the plows made an appearance.

But evidently Ron's winch truck was still nonfunctional. And perhaps Ron Adler himself was too nonfunctional to use his portable winch on some other 4WD vehicle.

Like too many of us, he'd been up all night too, and perhaps he'd made up with Gina and was sleeping off the excitement of the last twenty-four hours.

"And so you see what I mean finally?" Alanna asked sweetly.

She'd been droning along and her drawl had been hypnotic and the action out the window interesting enough that I hadn't heard a single word she'd said.

"Uh, yeah, right," I said, trying to cover for myself, trying but failing to recall any part of her current commentary.

She eyed me warily. "So you agree that Dorothy probably stole the money then?"

That time I heard her.

"What?"

"See, I knew you weren't listening to me. Who else could have done it, if not Dorothy?"

"Well." I racked my brain, which was not firing on any cylinders at the moment. "Every single person in here last night knew we were raking in the money hand over fist. Any one of them could have broken in and taken it. Besides which, we still don't know that the money was stolen. Maybe it just got misplaced."

Across the street Presley and John Adler stomped their way into the bar. Probably going to see Mardelle in the upstairs living quarters she shared with her parents, the better to rehash their New Year's Eve adventure. Or think up entirely new ways to rapidly age the grown-ups in town.

"There was no evidence of the cafe being broken into," Alanna said patiently. "I unlocked the door just like always and there wasn't a single thing out of place inside."

"And the money bag wasn't on the counter, huh?" I asked, rubbing my forehead.

I could see that however the money disappeared, the loss was going to be laid at my doorstep. I had been the one to leave a large amount of badly needed cash out in the open.

"Nope," Alanna said, digging through the papers. She pulled one out and handed it to me. "See there? No address, no phone number."

"You know, just because some money disappeared, doesn't mean she took it," I said. "It's unfair of us even to suspect her. For all we know, she may have been out in the snow all night herself."

Alanna looked at me wide-eyed.

"Do you think she might be dead?"

"No, of course not," I said. Until the words popped out of my mouth, the idea of Dorothy lying frozen in the snow had not even occurred to me.

And now, despite my assurance to Alanna, the picture would not leave my mind.

"Has *anyone* seen her today?" I asked.

"Not that I know of," Alanna said quietly.

"Well, she was here last night," I said. "Right here in the cafe. She went home just before you did."

Yup, she'd left the cafe just after I'd handed her the extra set of keys. No need to break in if you can just unlock the door. Nosiree.

It finally sank in that none of us had a notion of where "home" was to Dorothy. I looked down at her employment application, at the blank lines where her present and previous addresses should have been filled in. "Why didn't she write it down?" I asked myself out loud.

"Because she didn't want to be traced, that's why," Alanna said triumphantly.

"Well," I said, looking out the window at the sparse traffic in the street and the few hardy souls who braved the cold on foot, "we're still snowed in. It's a sure bet that anyone who was in town last night is still here somewhere. Someone has to have seen her. She can't have disappeared completely."

"Well, I am so glad to hear you say that," Alanna said, gathering up the papers. "You better get started right away then."

"Get started doing what?" I asked, though I knew I was going to be sorry as soon as I heard the answer.

"Why, investigating Dorothy's whereabouts, of course. You yourself said that she has to be here in Delphi still. She can't get away until the plows come, and once the plows and the police get here, she'll be able to scoot with our money."

17

....

Locked Town

The situation reminded me a little of those Golden Age mysteries that are pure puzzle. Forgetting about character development and nuance, not to mention lyrical prose, the writer would gather a motley assortment of principals together in workmanlike fashion and sequester them in a room, or a spooky country house, or on a deserted island where no one else could get in, and no one could get out.

In due time (usually by the end of the first chapter) one of the characters was cleverly bumped off, usually a bad guy and usually in a nearly impossible fashion. It was then left to the sleuth to sort through the living and breathing (whose number tended to diminish rapidly as a rule) until the culprit was uncovered, by process of elimination if nothing else.

Delphi wasn't on a deserted island. Nor was it a spooky house. And though we most assuredly had a body, no one was even hinting out loud that Ian O'Hara had done anything other than accidentally freeze himself to death.

But we did have a locked room of sorts. Or more specifically, a locked town.

Since the onset of the blizzard, no one who was not already in town could get in.

And as Stu and I proved so thoroughly, the heavy snowfall made certain that no one could have gotten out.

And we did have a mystery—about two grand in missing, untraceable cash.

And we had a mysterious, and also missing, mute cook.

I've mentioned already that my first, second, and third reactions to bodies and mysteries was to cover my ears and sing *la la la* very loudly.

But occasionally, and unfortunately, my fourth reaction included wading in with both feet.

Though I was nowhere near as convinced as Alanna that Dorothy had taken the cash, I did remember that she was one of the few people who actually knew where the money bag was. It had been on the counter by the till as she left for the night.

Right after I had given her the extra set of cafe keys.

And it was absolutely certain that no one could have gotten out of Delphi last night, in a vehicle, or on foot.

Ergo, Dorothy was here somewhere.

And the money was here somewhere too.

So I decided to find out if they were, by some strange coincidence, together.

But where?

And how?

After a bit of thought along the lines of "what would Miss Marple do?" I decided that it would be easier to find one Dorothy than several hundred low-denomination loose bills. If nothing else, she would be easier to spot and considerably harder to divide up and stuff into hidey-holes in various locations.

I stalled on that morbid thought for a bit, watching the activity outside in the blinding afternoon sunshine. I suppose the power outage kept most of the in-town people at home in the aftermath of the major storm. But still, there were a few hardy souls out and about.

More than a few of them stepped into Jackson's Hole down and across the street. And since they did not step right back out again, I had to assume that Pat and Pat Jackson were, lack of electricity notwithstanding, open for business.

And since Pat Jackson herself had seen Dorothy in the bar last night, talking to her would probably be a good idea. And having a drink was an even better idea.

But first, I needed to make a few calls.

Sighing, I got up and unlocked the cash register and then flipped the release under the cash drawer. It slid open easily (who needs electricity anyway?) to reveal that the thief had at least left us our small change, which was a good thing. I needed quarters for the pay phone in the corner by the bathroom.

Making a mental note to talk to Alanna about putting a regular phone in the kitchen, I plugged a quarter in the slot and dialed her number.

"Yeah," I said when she answered. "It's Tory."

I rolled my eyes at the ceiling as she asked the inevitable.

"No, of course I haven't found her yet," I said, tiredly. "Or the money. But I need to talk to Rhonda or Brian, if either of them are there."

"Sure," she said, and then she covered the phone in an imperfect muffle because I heard her say, "Hon, will you go and see if Rhonda or Brian can come to the phone?" And then she turned back to the receiver. "Why?"

"Well, I want to talk to everyone who talked to Dorothy yesterday. Maybe they caught something that we missed."

"Sounds good," Alanna said. "Say, how long are the lights going to be off anyway?"

"How should I know? Do I look like a lineman?" I asked, closing my eyes and shaking my head.

"Some days, yes," Alanna said sharply. "I just thought since y'all have been through more winters than I have, that you might *know* something."

"Well, all I *know* is that they'll get the power back on as soon as they can. They usually manage to do it before all the pipes freeze and burst and the vents clog with ice and people die of sewer gas poisoning in their beds and ordinary citizens are forced to use the burners on their gas stoves to keep their toes and fingers from turning black with frostbite."

She had asked a legitimate question and I had snapped for no reason.

Actually I had a reason. Several of them in fact. I was tired. I was cold. I was worried about my relationship with Neil. I was worried about my relationship with Presley. I was worried about the financial standing of the cafe. I was distressed because I had once again been put in the path of a dead body. I was pissed that my oversight had cost us a good two thousand dollars. I hated the déjà vu feeling I get every time I start making phone calls and asking snoopy questions.

But mostly I snapped because Alanna Luna usually annoys the living hell out of me.

None of which were good enough reasons for incivility. I mumbled an apology.

She sniffed and gave the phone to Rhonda without another word.

"What's up, Tory?" Rhonda chirped, not sounding like a woman who had been partying seriously only eight hours before.

"Sorry to bother you on your holiday," I said, wishing for the speedy recovery of youth. "I need to know if you talked to Dorothy last night at the bar, or here at the cafe. She must still be in town, and I'm trying to get a lead on her whereabouts."

Rhonda lowered her voice. "Do you think she took the money too?"

Alanna must have been hovering nearby.

"Not really," I said, meaning it mostly. "We still don't

even know if the money was actually taken or if it was just misplaced."

"I've never misplaced that much money," Rhonda said, laughing.

"Unfortunately, I have," I said glumly. "And I'd like to get it back, and she's as good a place to start as any. Anything about her seem odd or unusual to you?"

"You mean besides the fact that she had a cell phone?"

That stopped me short. What would a mute woman need with a cell phone?

"A cell phone?"

"Yeah, I saw her with it last night. She was just closing it up as she came through the door at the bar."

I thought about that for a minute. "Well, they have regular phones for people who can't hear and talk, I suppose there must be hand-held portable versions too."

"That's gotta be it," Rhonda said. "I mean, she didn't do anything, she just held it to her ear and then she folded it back up and stuck it in her coat pocket."

"I suppose there are places that you can call that give information just by punching the right combo of numbers. I mean, she could hear just fine, she just couldn't talk."

"Sure. I do stuff like that all the time. You know, like voting on MTV for your favorite video. And you can get credit card stuff and never say a word."

"And weather info," I said, mulling that one over.

"See, it makes perfect sense," Rhonda said. "But other than that, I don't know anything. We only just talked about easy stuff, you know, the kind of things that you don't need words for. Like, well, she could tell right away that . . ." Rhonda paused, her voice trailing off.

Evidently she'd changed her mind about what she wanted to say because her next sentence was on a different track altogether. "And she made it very clear that she thought Ian was handsome, too." Rhonda paused again. "Oh shit, I forgot. He's dead isn't he?"

"Yeah," I said.

I kept forgetting that little fact.

"And you had to find him," Rhonda said mournfully. "And you spent the night with Stu. Oh Tory."

Oh Tory indeed.

Beyond that, Rhonda didn't have anything else to add to the Dorothy queries, and I didn't want to dwell on either Ian's dead body or spending the night with Stu.

Unfortunately, I wasn't going to get away from either subject with my next call.

I stared at the phone for a while willing it not to work during power outages so I could go home and crawl into bed with an almost clear conscience.

But the power stayed out and the phone continued to function. I slipped another quarter in the slot and dialed a familiar number and rubbed my cold hands together as the phone rang.

"Library," Neil said quietly.

I'd meant to sound normal, chirpy if I could manage it, but my voice died in my throat.

"Hello?" he said.

"Hi," I said finally.

The pause was on his end this time.

"Hi," he said neutrally.

I had never known that *neutral* could hurt so much.

"Listen," I said in a rush, partly to keep from apologizing. "I won't keep you."

Neil was mad at me, and with a good enough reason.

For the second time, he'd made a move, and for the second time Stuart McKee had gotten in the way.

But I was mad at him, with an even better reason.

I understood why he was upset, but he'd hit me with an unreasonable accusation, whether he really meant it or not.

And I was not about to apologize first. At least not this soon.

I continued even faster. "There's been a robbery maybe at the cafe and I need to ask you a couple of questions about Dorothy."

"What do you mean, *a robbery maybe*? And what does that have to do with Dorothy?"

He sounded interested, which was a whole lot better than neutral.

I told him the sorry tale about the money bag and Dorothy's serendipitous absence from the premises.

"Hmm," he said. "You know she was here yesterday afternoon, late. She asked for a full tour of the house."

"And did she get the full tour?"

"Of course. I live to serve." Neil laughed, forgetting that he was mad for just a moment. A lovely moment. But the laughter stopped abruptly. "Just a second."

I heard him put the phone down and open a drawer. He must have been sitting at his big oak desk on the main floor of the library.

He rummaged and moved papers around for a full minute, then I heard several other drawers open and close, the rummaging got louder and a little more agitated.

"Well, I'll be damned," he said into the phone again.

"What? What is it?"

"The petty cash," he said, voice bewildered. "It's gone."

"Gone?"

"Gone," he said. "Kaput. Vamoosed. Vanished. The money has exited the building."

I asked him how much petty cash he usually kept on hand.

"Not that much, a few hundred in small bills and coins, mostly to make change for the pop machine, or to pay for C.O.D. deliveries, to give as rewards to the kids who read a lot. You know."

"Pretty strange that money should disappear from the library *and* the cafe on the same exact day," I said slowly.

"It's stranger than that," Neil said even more slowly.

"How so?"

"The last time I got into that money, the last time I

took it out of the drawer and made change, guess who was standing right beside me, looking over my shoulder?"

"Dorothy Gale," we said together.

18

....

WWMMD?

It's not like I pattern my daily life after fictional detectives or anything.

But sometimes, in some situations, it's handy to know how, say, Myron Bolitar or Leo Waterman, not to mention Tamara Hayle or Stephanie Plum, might go about investigating a case.

Not that I had a case, and not that big-city gumshoes would have the slightest idea what to do in a burg like Delphi. But I was pretty sure if any of that crew was handed a coincidence like the one Neil and I had just discovered, that they'd at least continue poking around.

"Maybe Alanna's on the right track after all," I said, wincing in advance. Her crowing would be absolutely unbearable.

I was still in the cafe, getting colder and colder, talking to Neil on the pay phone by the till.

"Probably too soon to be jumping to conclusions," Neil said. "Wait a minute. I'll be right back." I could hear him walking through the rooms of the first floor library, opening doors and drawers. "Everything looks fine down here," he said when he picked up the phone again. "There wasn't anything to steal except that little bit of money."

"And about six zillion books and a quarter of a million CDs," I said.

Neil laughed. "Yeah, well, it's hard to abscond with that sort of loot on foot. In the dark. In a blizzard. I have all the classics, but I don't have any limited editions or signed firsts or anything a book thief would value. I wouldn't expect a felonious collector to bother with a couple hundred in small change."

"Unless they wanted to add it to the 2K from the cafe and buy a Gutenberg Bible," I said, thinking out loud.

"Gonna take a whole lot of New Year's Eve bashes to pay for one of those," Neil said. He set the receiver down. I could hear him going upstairs.

"Why would anyone take that small amount of money anyway?" I asked when he picked up again. "It's not enough to do anything with. I mean, you can't even go to the Bahamas on it. It's barely enough to get you through one evening at the casino. Who would risk a jail term over something so little?"

"Lots of people, Tory," Neil said. There was more rummaging in the background. "Burglars aren't always smart, you know. It was probably a combo of opportunity and whim."

"Yeah, and when did this opportunity occur, anyway? Assuming for the moment that Dorothy took the money, she sure didn't take it while you were standing there watching her."

More rattling. Silverware this time.

"Well, you and I left the library together," Neil said quietly.

Oh yeah, I thought.

"And the library was empty for the rest of the night," he continued softly. "I didn't get home until after daylight. Whoever wanted to get in had plenty of opportunity. Everyone knows that I never lock the place."

He opened another door. "Aha," Neil said suddenly.

"What? What?"

"Someone *has* been in here," he said, voice tight. "Damn."

"What's gone?"

"I don't know yet," he said sharply. "But someone's been in my mother's jewelry box. Everything has been moved around, it's all out of place."

He was breathing heavily. Angry and upset.

"Your jewelry missing?" I asked.

"I don't have any jewelry. I'm not a gold chain kind of guy," Neil said. "But a ring of my mother's is gone. Her wedding band."

Neil's parents had been killed in a car accident shortly after he'd won the Iowa State Lottery. He never talked about them or the accident, but I knew that the few mementos he kept were stored in that jewelry box in his bedroom.

For all his money, Neil lived very simply. That ring had meant a lot to him.

"Oh, I am so sorry," I said. "I'll let you go so that you can call the police. I have to too—Alanna hasn't reported the missing cash either."

"Yeah," he said, obviously distracted.

"If Dorothy did this," I said firmly, trying to reassure him, "she has to be here still because everyone is here."

"And if she didn't do it?" Neil asked.

"Same thing applies," I said. "*Everyone* who was here last night is still here. And *everything* that was here last night is still here somewhere too. We just have to play like Miss Marple and figure out who and where."

"So WWMMD?" Neil asked.

I said, "We should start selling T-shirts and fridge magnets. We'd make a fortune."

It was nice to laugh with Neil again. It made me hope that last night hadn't been both the beginning and the end of . . . well, whatever it was anyway.

We finished the conversation with a list of the storm

rescuers, including Joe Marlow, the inquisitive farmer whose name had escaped my tired frozen brain this morning.

There was no need to set up a rescuer timetable (WWMMD notwithstanding) because all of them had gathered in front of the bar at roughly the same time. They left together and stayed together. All night. Not a single one of them could have robbed Neil's library in the ten-minute window allowed while Ron gathered the equipment he needed from his garage.

"Del joined us a little late," Neil said. "But we can pretty well cross her off the list of suspects too."

Del has any number of sins laid against her, but I would have bet everything that petty theft was not one of them. "I can ask her if she saw anything at least," I said.

"I imagine all she saw was Ron. They came in together," Neil said.

"Together? That's interesting. And what were they doing together?"

Ten minutes seemed a little speedy for a below-zero quickie in the middle of a blizzard, but I suppose it could be managed.

"Arguing, what else do they ever do these days?" Neil said.

"I guess you're right. I think their quickie days are over," I said.

We hung up amiably, though without making any specific arrangements to get together later.

We both knew we'd have to talk this one out. And we were, evidently, both content to leave it at that.

Intending to gather whatever info I could for the police, I picked up Dorothy's employment application and sat in the window booth again. It was the only spot in the dim cafe with enough light to read by.

Dorothy had filled in at least a few of the blanks. There were a couple of references listed. All were in Nebraska. She'd also written in a Social Security number.

There were at least a few leads for the sheriff if he wanted them, and a few more for Neil when the power came back on and he could use his computer to do an Internet search for anything pertaining to our missing cook using the scant info she *had* provided.

Directly across the street, Eldon McKee had already clumsily but cheerfully cleaned the sidewalk in front of the Feed and Seed Store, and was tackling the St. John's Lutheran walk with the shovel that should have been in the back of Stu's pickup.

I resisted the urge to curse him—last night's events had been put into motion long before the snow began.

As if hearing my thoughts, Eldon stood up and waved at me from across the street. He pulled a flask out of his pocket and gestured at it and then at me.

He may have had a stroke but there was nothing wrong with his eyesight.

Or his instincts.

I waved back but sadly declined his offer of a drink.

He shrugged and offered the flask to the next passerby, who also declined and tromped past the post office, which was on the feed store's other side.

The sidewalks were a hive of movement, with Presley and Mardelle throwing as much snow at each other as they scooped from in front of Jackson's Hole.

On the corner of the next block, John Adler far more glumly hand-shoveled a drift from the big double doors of his father's garage. He stopped for a moment and watched Pres and Mardelle frolicking, blinking just like his father. Then he scowled a little more and bent back to his task.

In the cold clear air, the snow sparkled brilliantly. The sunlight shining through the dirty cafe window was warm. Or at least it was warmer than the air outside, and inside.

I sat in a sunbeam, mindlessly watching the activity outside and enjoying the uncharacteristic quiet inside the cafe. The power outage had forced a closure in the middle of what surely would have been a profitable afternoon. But it also gave me a chance to sit in peace for a change.

My thoughts wandered idly from Alanna to Del to Ian to Gina to Ron and then, because of the similarity in their names I suppose, to Rhonda. Thinking about Rhonda brought me back to Dorothy.

Without putting too much effort into it, I pondered why Dorothy had come to Delphi in the first place.

Why Delphi?

Why the cafe?

Why on New Year's Eve in the middle of a blizzard? I thought so much that my eyes drooped closed.

And then I thought some more, with my chin propped on a hand.

And for a second, I thought I saw something in my mind's eye.

Something that provided a key to the questions I had just been lazily asking myself.

But the phone rang, clanging sharply in the stillness of the cafe. It startled the hell out of me, driving whatever it was out of my head.

I jumped up, embarrassed that I had been nearly dozing when I should have been working.

"Yes," I said into the phone. "Um . . . I mean, Delphi Cafe."

"I'd like to speak to Tory Bauer please," a slightly nasal feminine voice said.

"Speaking," I said, shaking my head to get the cobwebs out. I needed some caffeine. A lot of it. Fast.

"Ms. Bauer, this is the Spink County Sheriff's Office," the voice said.

Not pausing to wonder why the police had called me, I said, "Oh, good. I needed to talk to you anyway. There's been a possible burglary at the cafe here in Delphi."

Or was it a robbery? I'd read hundreds of P.I. books and police procedurals, and still I wasn't up on the proper lingo.

I started to tell the dispatcher what had happened—

about the missing money and the missing and mysterious mute cook.

But she interrupted me.

"Yes," she said, drawing out that syllable unpleasantly. "We can get all of that information when the officers arrive in Delphi as soon as the roads are plowed."

"You don't want to write it down now?" I asked, confused. "But I need to report a possible crime." I thought about that for a second, and then amended the statement. "A probable crime."

"Yes," she said again, in exactly the same irritating tone of voice. "I am certain that the deputy will want to get all of the details from you a little later. But right now we are swamped with rescue calls, and stranded citizens in danger, and complications from the storm that could mean life and death to any number of people."

I pulled the phone away from my ear and peered at it suspiciously, as if that would help me to understand a police officer who was uninterested in a crime report.

I put the receiver back up to my ear. "If that's the case, why did you call me? No life or death situations here."

"Well, that's not exactly the case, now is it, Ms. Bauer?"

"Huh?" I was completely confused.

"Well, you seem to have been involved in a death, haven't you?" she said.

"No," I said sharply. "I *haven't* been involved in a death. I just happened, by a stroke of bad luck, to be around when a death was discovered."

"Ah, yes, well, that's why we called. I need to take your statement about that incident," she said. "And the deputy will want to talk to you personally as soon as he gets to Delphi."

I was flabbergasted.

I was at least marginally prepared for snickering about my night in Stu McKee's pickup truck.

I was not prepared to be treated like a suspect in a questionable death.

"You think *I* had something to do with Ian O'Hara freezing?" My voice rose with each word. "You think *I* was responsible?"

"I didn't say that, Ms. Bauer," the dispatcher said patiently. "We just need to get your version of events recorded now. And you need to be available for the deputy whenever he gets to Delphi."

"Are you telling me not to leave town?" I asked, incredulous.

"Well, that would be redundant at the moment," she said, snorting. "But we do need a statement immediately. And we would definitely like to do a follow-up interview as soon as possible."

"Certainly," I said, closing my eyes and rubbing my forehead.

It would do no good to rail at the system. The only way to prove that I had not been involved in Ian's death was to tell my whole story.

And nothing but my story.

"It would be my pleasure to do whatever I can to help your investigation," I said into the phone with a sigh.

A few minutes earlier, I had been wishing for caffeine and wondering WWMMD.

As I recounted last night's adventures to an annoyingly polite dispatcher, I decided instead to do what any self-respecting P.I. would do in the same situation.

19

The Fifth Reaction

So what is it about middle-aged single women and crime detection?

Is it a figment of the collective writers' imaginations, or does all that inherent snoopiness mask something else? Something deeper and darker.

Like an inability to deal with life as it is on the surface?

A deeply seated need to control others?

A sublimation of sexual urges?

Taking Miss Marple as an example, there seems to be something to the theory. Here was an elderly lady, a spinster, who I would have bet was also a virgin.

What was her favorite, nay only, excitement in life?

She loved her garden and she enjoyed her knitting and she doted on her convenient nephews.

But it was observation and gossip and deduction that tripped her trigger.

Tea parties were for the other old ladies. Miss Marple

only really came alive after being confronted with another of the ever-increasing number of dead bodies in St. Mary Mead.

I was beginning to think that Miss Marple was a lousy role model.

Besides, after yesterday's ruckus in the middle of the street, there was no one in Delphi who could, with a straight face, accuse me of being a chaste widow, much less a spinster virgin.

And in my present mood, a tea party just wasn't going to cut it.

My fourth reaction to a puzzle may have been to investigate.

But my *fifth*, especially after having been accused of being a part of the mystery instead of an innocent bystander, was to drink.

Fuck tea. I wanted whiskey.

"My, aren't we in a jolly mood," Pat Jackson said as she sat my Windsor and Coke tall on the bar in front of me. She looked calm and collected for a mother whose daughter had spent a fair portion of the night stuck in a blizzard with a couple of juvenile boys.

I dug in my coat pocket for the twenty I'd borrowed from the till and tucked in there, along with Dorothy's employment application form to give to Neil later.

"Been one of those days, I guess," I said, making an effort to smile in motherly, or at least *blizzardly* solidarity. "Right?"

Pat took my money with a grunt that could have been an agreement. Or it could have been disagreement. I couldn't tell.

She turned to make change. Their regular till was electronic too, but an old chrome mechanical cash register had been pressed into service. She punched the numbers in and pulled the handle and the drawer popped open with a musical clang.

Always dim, the interior of Jackson's was even more impenetrable than usual. Cheap scented pillar candles flickered on every table and Coleman lanterns were evenly spaced along the bar. Placed strategically here and there about the floor were small kerosene heaters that kept the air at least marginally warm.

The Christmas lights, of course, wouldn't work without power. The resultant soft lighting, not to mention the odd mix of vanilla, peppermint, and kerosene odors, made for a sophisticated sort of ambiance in a place where just using the word *ambiance* could get you tossed out on your ear.

The lantern by the register flickered as Pat bent down to see, and count, my change, which she slapped unceremoniously down next to my glass. Which was already half-empty.

There were probably twenty hardy souls, mostly men, scattered at assorted tables and along the bar. Some were talking quietly with one another or playing cards in the candlelight. But most sat alone, nursing a single drink and a cigarette, staring at their own hands. They were part of the regular afternoon bar crowd, the folks for whom a blizzard, and the resultant power outage, would never get in the way of getting drunk every day.

"The fire marshal's gotta love this kind of situation," I said to Pat in an attempt at being conversational, pointing at all the open flames, on her next walk through.

"By the time the fire marshal gets here, the power'll be back on," she said, with a ghost of a smile. "Besides, I think it looks kinda pretty."

"It is," I said, swiveling around on the bar stool to look at the bar instead of my own murky and unhappy reflection in the mirror behind the bar. "Makes the whole place look different. Like the cafe just now. All quiet and empty, it doesn't look the same as when everything is happening at once."

"Well, quiet I don't mind," Pat said, making me another drink. She poured whiskey with one hand and filled the glass with pop from the canister hand spigot. "But empty is another story. We can't afford to close down in the afternoon. Not like you."

"What do you mean, *not like me?*" I said, at least mildly amused.

It was common knowledge that parsimonious Pat Jackson, who kept the family and business purse strings away from her jollier, free-spending husband, had more money than most of us.

She certainly had more than Alanna and me *and* the cafe. "Things are so tough at the cafe that I don't know if we're going to make it," I said. I was being indiscreet, but making the financial situation at the cafe public knowledge would take the spotlight off my personal life for a while.

"Oh?" Pat said, raising an eyebrow, something I would not have thought possible considering that hers melded together somewhere over the middle of her nose. "From what that Presley of yours says, money is just flowing through the cafe."

"That Presley isn't mine," I said, though most days it felt like he was. "And what would he know about the money situation at the cafe, anyway?"

"Well, he was flashing a couple of twenties earlier," Pat said, leaning her elbows on the counter. "Wanting change for the pool table since the pinball machines are outta commission. Said Miss Take Your Clothes Off and Get Us All Arrested paid him for cleaning her side-walks."

I swiveled back around on the stool. "Alanna *paid* Presley to shovel?"

I couldn't picture Alanna paying anyone to do anything. She was far too used to cajoling and sweet-talking men into doing her work for her.

And I certainly couldn't picture Presley hiring himself out for anything so lowly as manual labor. What he had been doing with Mardelle in the snow in front of the bar had plainly been a combination of goofing around and adolescent foreplay. He'd been flirting, something that had obviously irritated John Adler, who *had* been working for his father, and probably for free.

"Well, that's weird," I said, mostly to myself.

"Not as weird as the cafe having money troubles," Pat said, swabbing the bar with a damp rag. She didn't look up.

Actually, she had a point. Aphrodite had made the cafe profitable all by herself. Alanna and I together couldn't make a go of the place.

I was about to say something companionable and self-deprecating along those lines, but Pat continued. "What with help from Neil, I figured you'd be rolling in the dough."

I set my drink down abruptly. "*What?*"

She smiled slyly. "Well, I just assumed our local rich and single millionaire librarian *looooved* to help out area businesses with his money. And since you two are like this"—she held up her hand and crossed her fingers— "I figured you were first in line for a handout."

"What in the world gave you that idea?" I asked sharply, not knowing which was more insulting: the notion that Neil would offer me money, or that I would take it.

"The paper," she said, still smiling almost sweetly. "The *Argus Leader*, two weeks ago. Big spread on Neil and his lottery and his library and his charities. Pictures. Charities. House. Didn't he tell you?"

No, he hadn't told me, but that wasn't unusual. Neil was not a spotlight hound. He would never have sought out a profile in the Sioux Falls paper, which was, by the way, the largest daily in the state. And it was entirely typical that when an article had been done, he had told no one.

Sioux Falls was two hundred miles away, and their paper was not stocked in the local grocery store.

But Pat had seen the article. And she had been needling him about it.

In fact, she'd said something to him about slumming with the poor folk last night, but Neil had brushed it over.

"What are *you* doing getting the *Argus*?" I asked. I would not have expected either of the Jacksons to have

been avid newspaper readers. Unless you counted the
National Enquirer.

Pat shrugged. "Mardelle needed it for research for
some kind of school paper. We've been getting it in the
mail. Costs a fortune, though, and the subscription is
gonna run out pretty soon. I figure we'll just let it go
when the time comes. But it's been handy. We found
the DJ for the karaoke last night in it. And he was pretty
good."

I was saved the necessity of giving her an answer, or
even a grunt, because Joe Marlow, the inquisitive farmer
whose name I could not recall this morning, slid onto
the stool next to me.

Pat transferred her attention to Joe.

"Warmed up yet?" he asked me conversationally. He
paused to cup his hand over a cigarette and light it. "I'll
take another for me, and set one up for the pretty lady
too."

Pat nodded and turned to making the drinks.

"Thanks, Joe," I said, grateful that I had finally remembered his name. "I'm getting there. But it's hard to
get warm with no power."

"Yup," he said, agreeing with a smile. "Things ain't
so bad out at the farm. I talked to Ma out there and she
said that she's had power all along. It's just in town here,
and east that lost all the juice."

Ma, of course was Joe's wife, not his mother. I
couldn't remember her name either.

"That's nice," I said, swirling the few melting ice
cubes around in my glass. "You going to get home today?"

Though I hadn't remembered seeing him, Joe had obviously been in the bar last night or he wouldn't have
been recruited for the rescue team.

And just as obviously, if he'd been here last night,
then he was still here today, because everyone was still
here today.

Joe shrugged. "Maybe, maybe not. Doesn't matter. I
been in town two nights already. I can sleep on the

couch over to my daughter's house again if need be. And Ma will survive another night on her own. She's a tough old bird."

I allowed as how that was probably so with a shrug of my own.

"Things is more interesting in town anyway," he said, lowering his voice and tilting his head toward me. "Whaddya think of the dead guy. That Ian whatshisname?"

I sipped a little of my drink and thought that one over. He'd been amusing and I loved listening to him talk. He certainly was handsome. He'd charmed the shit out of Del, and who knows how many other women. He'd also been very fast to take advantage of Gina Adler, despite the fact that he'd been on a date with another woman.

"I think I didn't know him well enough to come to any conclusions," I said.

"Well, it's obvious he liked to live dangerously," Joe paused as Pat walked out from behind the bar to take orders from a couple of tables. "And his taste in women left something to be desired."

Since I was pretty sure that some time or other, Joe had dallied with Del himself, I thought that was pretty ungracious. I just raised an eyebrow at him.

He indicated Pat over his shoulder. "You imagine any man in his right mind with Delphine by his side wanting *her*?"

"Pat, you mean?" I asked, relieved that Joe was repeating Pat's gossip from the night before. For some reason I had been ready to defend Del's universal desirability. "She told you that too, huh?"

"Hon, she told *everybody* that," Joe said, chuckling. "Not that one person in ten believed her."

I know I hadn't believed her.

I doubt that Del would have believed that Ian O'Hara had made a pass at Pat Jackson either, though she would have wiped the floor with Pat just for making the suggestion. A furious Del was more than a match for the forty-pound difference in their weights.

And then I wondered why it was so hard to fathom Ian making a pass at Pat. After all, he'd made one (or at least come close) at me. And I was no beauty queen.

And surely he'd made some sort of advance to Gina, who was pretty enough for a plump middle-aged woman, but not a stunner.

"Well, we know that whether he found all the women attractive or not, all the women found him attractive anyway," I said, looking at Joe.

"Not all the women," he said. "Ol' Pat over there wasn't all that thrilled with him taking liberties. And then just before I went over to the cafe last night, I saw him arguin' with another. Leastways, they was discussing something pretty seriously, and neither one of 'em looked to be happy about it."

"Oh yeah?" I asked. He had my full attention now. "Who?"

"That pretty little thing with a helluva swing," he said, smiling. "You know, the one with the baseball bat."

20

·····························

Black and White
and Read All Over

Isolation is not a new concept to a citizenry accustomed to a population density of less than 0.5 person per square mile. People who are overwhelmed by the vast and empty silence of the open plains don't stick around long enough to get lonely.

Those of us who do stay (by choice or otherwise) have not only our own vain stoicism to carry us through, we also have repeated comparisons to pioneers who managed to survive a far more hostile and unpopulated environment without the aid of sports utility vehicles, compact discs, and the Weather Channel.

In our day-to-day life, the notion of being alone is neither foreign nor frightening. But every once in a while Mother Nature reminds us in a big way exactly how far we are from real civilization, and from those amenities we take for granted.

Like timely deliveries from the USPS.

"There wouldn't have been any mail today anyway," Del said, in answer to my grousing, "even if they'd been able to get through the snow. It's a holiday. Remember? Happy New Year?"

She twirled a finger in the air and mimed excitement.

"Oh," I said, disappointed. "Yeah. Damn."

I'd spent the entire frigid slog home from the bar in anticipation of a new *Newsweek*. Or at least *People*, since a trip to the library for new books was currently impolitic.

"What were you gonna read 'em by anyway?" Del asked. She indicated the shadows lengthening in the trailer house living room.

It was late afternoon. Without power, the whole town would shortly be plunged into darkness.

"I would have given candles a shot," I said. "The pioneers did it, we can."

"Yeah, well, the pioneers pulled their own teeth with pliers too," Del said. "And they weren't apt to burn themselves out of house and home just to read about Brad Pitt's new girlfriend."

She was fairly grumpy herself. There seemed no point in continuing a crabby tally of exactly what we could not do on this holiday afternoon, cut off as we were from the twentieth century, not to mention most of Delphi.

Unfortunately, without the gentle aid of Northwestern Public Service, there wasn't much we could do except talk and listen to the wind as the pipes slowly froze.

Problem was, there wasn't much to talk about except Ian, and we'd already exhausted that subject. And I definitely did not want to discuss my night in the snow with Stu or its possible effect on my relationship with Neil.

I might have enjoyed talking about Gina Adler and her "Laugh With Ian One Minute and Fight With Him the Next" personality disorder (at least according to the differing reports of Rhonda and Joe Marlow), but since I could not mention her equally intriguing "Be Caught With Ian in a Compromising Position in a Public Place" syndrome, that subject was completely off-limits.

I not only didn't want to talk. I didn't want to think. Given the circumstances, there was only one nonthinking, nontalking alternative open.

"I'm going to take a long, hot bath," I announced, thanking providence that gas water heaters, and not electric, were standard-issue in trailer houses. Besides which, running water through the pipes would help to keep them from freezing.

Crystal Singman at the store had gotten in an assortment of aromatherapy candles with touchy-feely names at the store a while back. I had been waiting for a special occasion to light my Happy Heart votive. I had a feeling that this was as *special* as my life was going to get, though expecting one small candle (which mostly smelled like orange sherbet) to overcome the combined effects of no power, no boyfriend, no money, and a surfeit of dead bodies was a bit of a stretch.

"Good luck," Del said sourly, tucking her hands into her armpits. She'd put on another sweatshirt over the two she already wore. This one had a teddy bear on it. "Presley and John Adler have been hogging the bathroom all afternoon."

"John Adler? What the heck is he still doing here?"

I knew that he'd spent the rest of the night with Presley after being rescued from the storm. But instead of going to his own house after reluctantly shoveling snow from in front of his father's garage, he'd come back here?

"You got me," Del said, flipping halfheartedly through the pages of an old magazine, one she'd read and declared useless a month ago. "The bigger question is what the hell are they doing in the bathroom for hours on end?"

"You don't really want to know," I said absentmindedly. "I can't figure out why Gina hasn't ordered him home."

Though as soon as I said that, I realized that Gina Adler might have a dozen good reasons for wanting to hash things out with Ron privately. If Presley had been upset to learn about my dalliance with a married man (and he'd been more than upset, he'd been crushed), how much more would it affect a boy whose nice, normal nuclear family had at least maintained the image of being calm and happy?

The big question, now that I thought about it, was: Would Gina Adler ever want her son to come home?

I hoped so. If nothing else, I would like to take a bath eventually.

My sympathy for Gina was real, but it was also tempered by the complications that her irrational outburst were going to have on my everyday life.

Which led right back to a whole slew of subjects I couldn't, or didn't want to discuss.

"Does she even know he's here?" I asked Del, mostly just to keep from saying anything else.

"Last I heard, she told him flat-out to stay put," Del said. She was up and pacing now, restless and unhappy. "Pres said that John called her from the garage and she told him that he should stay where there was a gas stove rather than come home where there were only electric appliances."

Gina was not in Junior's league when it came to overprotecting her children, but under no circumstances would the Gina I had known for over twenty-five years tell her son to stay away during a storm because her stove wasn't functional at the moment.

Then again, the Gina Adler I knew would not have bashed the shit out of her husband's pickup truck either.

I was beginning to realize that I didn't know Gina Adler very well at all.

"So I guess that means we're cooking for four tonight," I said, sighing.

The cafe was closed, but I could make supper at the trailer as long as I worked out a menu that didn't need a microwave. Or a blender. Or an electric can opener.

At least the stove would generate a little heat.

"Make that five," Del said from the kitchen. "Mardelle Jackson is here with the boys."

"Good grief. Has she been in the bathroom all afternoon too?"

"I don't know," Del said distractedly. She was sitting slumped at the table, with Ian's letters spread out in front of her. She selected one and began reading it out loud again, mostly from memory since the light was too dim to see clearly.

I'd heard each of his letters more times than I wanted to *before* Ian had arrived in Delphi. I was not interested in hearing them again, though there seemed to be no way to derail Del's despondency.

And truly, her grief for a relationship that could have been was every bit as honorable as mine for a relationship that had just ended.

More so, perhaps, because in Del's case, neither one had been married.

Or so we'd thought.

I interrupted Del. "Did you send your letters directly to his house, or did he have a post office box?"

"Huh?" She frowned.

"Your letters to Ian," I repeated. "Did you mail them to him directly, or did he use a letter drop?"

"It wasn't a *letter drop*," she said sarcastically. "The newspaper has a service where people who take out personal ads can have the replies sent through them. Then they get the mail and the people pick it up. It's free and it keeps the weirdos from finding your house."

Actually, I knew how it worked, but had forgotten. Last month when we'd run an ad looking for a new cook in the Sioux Falls paper, we'd been offered the mail drop option too but declined. There was no sense in keeping the location of the cafe secret since prospective employees would have to take that into consideration before applying.

"So he gave you his address after you'd written a couple of letters back and forth and got to know each other a bit?" I asked, pulling a big kettle out of the low cupboard by the stove.

Lighting in the kitchen was poor under the best of

circumstances. Today, with the early sundown and no electricity, it was hard to tell if the pan I'd placed in the sink under the running faucet was full yet.

"Not exactly," Del said sharply. "After I answered his ad, he wrote here, and I just sent letters back through the paper." She shrugged. "It didn't seem to matter. Mail from Sioux Falls gets here overnight anyway. If I wrote on Monday, I'd hear back on Wednesday. He got my letters. That's all that matters."

"Hmm," I said noncommittally, setting the pan on the stove and salting the water heavily. I dropped a glob of hamburger into a frying pan and turned up the heat.

I rummaged in the cupboard for the spaghetti and a jar of sauce as an excuse not to say anything to Del, who was already defensive. It had to have occurred to her that Ian may have had a good reason for not giving her his home address.

A reason that involved a wife and maybe a few English-accented kiddies.

Or at least a few more correspondents as enchanted with his Auntie Featherstonehaugh as we all had been.

Ian had not, in our brief acquaintance, impressed me with his enduring faithfulness.

Though I doubted that she knew exactly why I had my suspicions (she may have heard and discounted Pat Jackson's tale, but she surely knew nothing about Ian and Gina's interrupted rendezvous), she knew exactly where I was going with my questions.

"Listen," she said, stuffing several envelopes back into her pants pocket, "Ian may not have been as classy as *your* boyfriends, but that doesn't mean he was hiding anything."

In the several decades of our friendship, I had never pegged Del to be the Last to Know, but I also knew that the heart can convince the brain of just about anything it wants.

And since I had nothing more than a hunch to back up the notion that Ian was married, and no proof that anything other than concern about possible stalkers caused him to use the newspaper mail drop, I let the subject go.

Del was tired and sad, and like everyone else in town, cold. Agitating her would do no good whatsoever and it would, in turn, make my life more miserable.

In truth, wasting time concentrating on Ian was just that—a waste of time.

The fact that he'd been covered with snow all night in the back of Stu's pickup told me that Ian had nothing to do with the missing money at the cafe or our missing cook, both of which were, or should have been, my priorities.

And once I had the rest of Delphi's problems sorted, it wouldn't hurt to spend a little serious synapse time working on my own garbled social life.

But first I had to cook supper in the dark and feed three hungry kids and a couple of tired and rapidly aging adults.

Oh yeah, and there was that little problem of how to survive another night without freezing to death ourselves.

21

....

The Little Trailer House on the Prairie

The logistics of cold weather survival are pretty basic and mostly reactive. In fact the only proactive thing you can do about winter is move to warmer climes.

Since that isn't an option for most of us, and since the season comes around regularly in these here parts, it's a good idea to review periodically the rules that allow us hearty midwestern types to make it through a full twelve months with all of our extremities intact.

The simplest and most important rule is: When it's cold outside, stay inside.

If for some reason (due to circumstances beyond your control or, perhaps, unchecked stupidity) you find yourself outside and unprotected, seek shelter. If you have shelter (defined as any place out of the wind: inside a car or barn, behind a haystack, under a blanket next to a warm naked human being), stay there.

Even the most bitter cold will not kill you if you stay covered, stay put, stay sober, stay together (if you are fortunate enough to have a companion in your adventure), and use a modicum of common sense.

It also helps to have a cell phone, a shovel, some candles, and a candy bar or two.

But Stu and I had proven that strict adherence to the most important rules marked the difference between survival and the unpleasant alternative.

Unlike poor Ian, who had ventured out into the frigid night, more than likely drunk, and stumbled into his last sleep in the open box of a pickup truck.

I suppose the English, even those currently residing in Sioux Falls, South Dakota, are not sufficiently drilled in the dangers of wandering alone into that great, dark snowy night.

It was hard enough sometimes to keep ones who should certainly have known better, ones who *had* been drilled since infancy, safely indoors.

"Sure," Del said absently. "Why not?"

She sat at the kitchen table in the flickering candlelight, poking disconsolately at the rapidly cooling spaghetti plate. I thought she hadn't heard her son correctly.

"Are you out of your mind?" I asked her sweetly. I'd have added a colorful Anglo-Saxon gerund to the question, but there were minors present at the table. Three of them, all gazing hopefully at Del. "After half the town risked their necks to rescue these idiots last night, you're going to let them go out again?"

"Oh ho," Presley hooted, mouth full of spaghetti. "Look who's talking. Like we were the only ones who needed rescuing."

He had not forgiven me for my indiscretions, but he'd implemented a tentative truce. At least in front of company.

"There's no comparison between what happened to me last night and what happened to you," I said severely, my breath pluming in the candlelight.

It wasn't literally freezing in the trailer, but it was cold. Damn cold.

And dark, except for the candles scattered here and there. It would have been pretty, maybe even romantic, if not for the general circumstances.

And the bad moods of those assembled.

"Yeah," Presley said, voice hard. "None of *us* is married."

So much for fragile truces.

"I wouldn't have gone *anywhere* last night," I said, not entirely sure why I was arguing the point with a surly thirteen-year-old whose uncharacteristic nastiness was likely caused by the twin evils of puberty and deeply disappointed expectations, not to mention chilly hands and feet. "But my grandmother was dying. And the rest of the men were out in the country doing their best to keep some other people from freezing to death."

No one had anything to say to that.

The wind had gone down. Except for the slow but steady trickle of the kitchen faucet, turned on to forestall freezing, there was a creaking silence both inside and outside the trailer as everyone concentrated awkwardly on the shadows cast by the flickering candlelight, or spun lengths of pasta around fork tines. Or warmed their hands over the meager flames.

"Yes, and we're so glad they did too," Mardelle said diplomatically. "It was really stupid of me to suggest going to that party in the first place. I should have known better than to drag these little kids out into the country on a night like that."

John Adler opened his mouth to protest but stopped suddenly. Presley probably kicked him under the table. His mouth closed with a snap.

Mardelle was sixteen and looked nothing like either of her parents. She was smart and she was pretty and she had a bustline like no sixteen-year-old girls had when I was sixteen. Presley had an enormous crush on her.

But Presley had an enormous crush on every marginally attractive breathing female, and like all of his Bauer blood relations, he had a hypnotic effect on members of the opposite sex.

Which probably explained why a pretty sixteen-year-old girl would choose to spend time with a couple of boys whose voices had not yet fully changed.

On the other hand, they'd been close friends since early childhood, and Mardelle had dragged the boys along on her jaunts before.

Until last night, we'd had no cause to mistrust her judgment.

"You're not leaving town, right?" Del asked.

I hadn't thought she'd been listening to the conversation. She'd sat staring off into the distance while we ate. Once in a while she poked the handle of her spoon into the melted wax that pooled on the top of my aromatherapy candle, which burned bravely from a saucer in the middle of the table.

Presley wheedled, I argued uselessly, Mardelle tried to conciliate, and John mostly kept his mouth shut.

Through it all, Del was in her own little world. I still didn't think she was grasping the subject matter clearly.

She just stirred the wax. Every time she did, it gave off a faint, orangy odor.

"I thought he was grounded," I reminded Del quietly. "For the rest of his life. For scaring the wits out of you."

"It doesn't do any good to ground the kid when he can't go anywhere anyway," Del said.

"That doesn't make any sense," I said, arguing as if the boys and their co-conspirator weren't sitting right there at the table with us. "They *want* to go somewhere. They want to go up to the bar, for crying out loud."

I didn't remind her that she'd just given permission for them to do it. I was hoping I could get her to change her mind.

"Come on, Tory," Pres said, batting his eyelashes at me. "The DJ is only staying this one extra night. We'll be good. I promise."

The sarcastic teenage act hadn't gotten him anywhere

with me, so I guess he was unleashing the big guns.

They didn't work either.

There wasn't enough time in the world to explain to a thirteen-year-old boy, who'd been far closer than he imagined to his own death not twenty-four hours ago, that allowing him to spend time in a bar with his other teenage friends was a silly idea.

"It's okay with Mom and Dad," Mardelle said quietly. "I already called them to make sure. There's no way that the DJ they hired for last night can get back to Sioux Falls tonight, so they figured that he might as well work as sit around. They're going to try something new, a cappella karaoke. All acoustic, all night." She smiled weakly.

"Problem is, if not enough people show up at the bar and spend the minimum tonight, then they'll have to come up with the rest of his fee out of their own pockets." She looked down and pushed what was left of her spaghetti around. "We all earned a little money this afternoon shoveling sidewalks, we might as well spend it on a good cause, right?"

She cast a sidelong glance at the boys, who nodded enthusiastically.

I sighed at the notion that we would be doing a good deed by allowing the underaged to spend time in an establishment that served alcohol.

If it had been my choice, I would have said no. And I'd have held fast to the decision no matter how much the kids whined and wheedled.

But Presley was Del's son. And, for whatever reason, she'd already given her permission for them to venture out into the night.

The storm itself was over and our in-town roads were mostly clear. But the thermometer still registered far below zero, and we still had no electricity.

The whole idea was incredibly stupid.

Which, I suppose, is why it attracted them so.

"Well, there's another mother to take into consideration," I said, smiling wickedly. "John, what does Gina say about this excursion?"

In the cold and near dark, John swallowed. "I'm sure it'll be okay with her," he said bravely. "As long as either you or Presley's mom calls her for permission."

Del snorted at the notion of applying to Gina Adler for anything.

Presley understood the nature of his mother's snort. "Well, Tory could call the Adlers then, couldn't you, Tory?"

Given what we all knew had happened yesterday out in front of the cafe, in addition to what I alone knew had happened last night in the storeroom of the bar, I rather doubted that Gina would want to talk to me either.

"Nope," I said, rubbing my hands together to warm them. "You want to go out, you get your own permission."

John sat quietly and didn't say anything, his face miserably solemn.

I felt a twinge of sympathy for him. His home life had come crashing down around his ears in the space of one day. No wonder he'd rather do just about anything to avoid facing his mother and father.

But that sympathy didn't extend to helping him to do something that I thought was foolish.

"Oh for crying out loud," Presley said, disgusted. "*I'll* call his mom."

He stomped over to the phone and dialed John's number and waited for it to ring.

I'm assuming that it must have rung, and that someone answered on the other end, because Pres opened his mouth to speak. But he listened for a moment and then stood there with his mouth open.

He pulled the receiver away from his ear and frowned at it, and then handed the phone to me, miming confusion.

I took the phone from him and held it gingerly to my ear, not sure what I expected.

Whatever I'd expected didn't hold a candle to what I actually heard.

I heard Gina Adler giggling wildly, telling someone to stop his little boy silliness right this instant and hand her the phone or she was going to spank him.

22

....

Cabin Fever

Fable and fiction are filled to the brim with horror stories of what can happen when people are closeted together over a long and unrelenting winter.

While it sounds romantic, enforced intimacy often serves to bring out the worst in everyone. Or at least what we come to see as the worst.

As Matt Groening, by way of Stephen King and Stanley Kubrick, so amply proved: *All work and no beer makes Homer go crazy.*

Whether you're in a luxury hotel in the upper reaches of the Colorado Rockies, or stuck in a one-horse town in the middle of the Great Flat Empty, no good can come from long periods in a severely restricted social circle.

You'd be amazed how quickly honey bunch's tics, the ones you formerly found endearing, have you reaching for the ball peen hammer or *The Donner Party Cookbook.*

It just usually takes more than twenty-four hours before people head down that long and winding road.

On the other hand, Gina Adler had traveled at least halfway there before the big storm even began.

Had we but known that her performance with the Louisville Slugger was just a warm up for the entertainment to follow, we could have made some popcorn and enjoyed the show.

Though I was pleased that she and Ron had patched things up (and were now evidently at the *Giddy Make-Up Sex* stage), I wasn't sure what to say to the giggling Gina who had wrested the phone from her boyish tormenter. After all, I hadn't intended to talk to her, and we had a few unresolved issues of our own that would have to be dealt with eventually in private.

"Yes?" she said, a little breathless, still laughing.

I looked over at Del for help, but she was off in her own little world again, her face sad and tired in the flickering candlelight. Presley looked pleased to have forced me into doing what I had declared I would not do. Mardelle was interested, and John was wary.

I, personally, was confused. What the hell was I going to say to Gina? Hanging up without speaking was always an option, but in this day of Caller ID and the services of Star 69, anonymous phone calls were less apt to stay anonymous, and therefore not nearly as much fun as they used to be.

"Hello?" Gina said again. Not giggling now, but not concerned either.

Whether I said anything or not, she was probably going to find out that the call had originated from the trailer.

"Um . . . hello Gina," I said, frantically trying to figure out what should come next. "This is Tory Bauer." Before she could assume I was making a social call, I hastened to add, "I'm calling about John."

"Oh," she said, all hilarity gone. If I hadn't known better, I'd have said that she sounded nervous. "Listen, I'm sorry for dumping him on you without warning, but it's not a good idea for him to come home right now."

She paused for a moment and then continued, "What with the storm and no power and all."

I'd expected a furtherance of yesterday's hostility. Or at least the cold shoulder, given what I'd seen in the Jackson's Hole storeroom. The tone of anxiety, which completely replaced her earlier hilarity, was doubly confusing.

Especially since she seemed mostly anxious that John stay exactly where he was.

Three pairs of young eyes squinted at me, full of hope in the dark. Del continued to stare off into the distance.

"Well, yeah, that's why I called," I said, though of course *I* hadn't called at all. "About John, that is."

I wanted her to understand absolutely that I wasn't calling to ask her why she'd seen fit to announce to the whole town that I'd been sleeping with Stu long before his wife left him.

I also wanted her to understand subliminally that I wasn't about to return the favor by revealing her indiscretions to all and sundry, though an evil voice inside me prompted me to do just that.

"Well, thanks so much for calling," Gina said brightly and falsely. "You do whatever you think is best. I'm sure you'll take good care of him. Tell him that I'll see him tomorrow."

That made so little sense that I held the receiver away from my ear and stared at it.

It finally occurred to me that Gina might be speaking in code, that she was unwilling or unable to carry on a conversation at the moment.

"Are you all right?" I asked quietly.

Suddenly I had a vision of Gina being held hostage. Maybe Ian's death wasn't just the inevitable combination of winter, ignorance, and too much alcohol. Maybe Dorothy Gale had not vanished into the night voluntarily.

Maybe there was a crazy person loose among us.

Someone far crazier than Gina Adler.

I turned my back to the kids, not wanting John to overhear and be frightened.

"Do you need help Gina?" I whispered. "Are you in some kind of trouble?"

I wished there was some kind of universal secret signal that was easily recognized, something she could use now to let me know that the situation was dire without bringing undue attention to the conversation.

"Help?" She laughed. "You think *I* need help?"

It was not the forced laugh of someone with a knife to the throat.

It was a real laugh.

A cackle.

A guffaw.

"Help? Honey, I'm not the one who needs help," she said, giggling.

And then she hung up.

I wanted to scream in frustration, and maybe embarrassment, for once again leaping to a spectacularly wrong conclusion.

Instead, I sighed and hung the phone back on the wall.

All three kids spoke up at the same time.

"Well?" Presley asked.

"What did she say?" John asked.

"Can they go out?" Mardelle asked.

I was not the mother of any of the assembled adolescents. And their mothers had either already given permission or abdicated responsibility. The one set of grown-ups who might have had legal reservations had already signed off on the idea (knowing, I suppose that no ticket-bearing officials would darken the door looking for underage partiers).

What could I do?

I threw my hands into the air and shrugged. "Seems like everyone in town has lost their mind," I said.

"Wahoo!" Pres said, high-fiving John. He planted a large and wet kiss on my forehead. "You're an angel, Tory. What can we do to make this up to you?"

"You can start with the dishes," I said. "It's too early to go anywhere yet anyway."

He looked at me with narrowed eyes.

I looked back equally narrowly. I figured I should press what small advantage I had. I couldn't keep them in, but I could at least make them work for their privileges. And while they were busy, I could sneak into the bathroom with a battery-powered tape player and some James Taylor for a little quiet time in the warm.

Just me and my orange sherbet Happy Heart candle.

Presley capitulated with a grin, understanding that he'd won the skirmish. Maybe even the war. "Okay, fair enough. Come on guys, let's get this mess cleaned up."

John was less enthused about the housework-for-excursions trade, but he set to scraping congealed spaghetti off the plates anyway. Mardelle shot me a speculative glance and then started piling glasses and gathering silverware.

Del had wandered into the living room and was sitting on the couch. Her cigarette glowed in the dark.

In my concern for Gina Adler's state of mind, I had dismissed Del's uncharacteristic pensiveness as just a result of cold and fatigue and disappointed expectations.

I was starting to wonder now if the events of the last day hadn't plunged her into an unexpected but deep, and real, depression.

While the kids bustled around the dark kitchen making a game of doing dishes by candlelight, I covered Del up with an afghan and sat down next to her.

"Are you okay?" I asked quietly.

"Not really," she said shakily. "I've been thinking about last night."

I slung an arm around her shoulders and gave her a swift hug, though hugging Del was a prickly proposition. She did not go for the sisterhood routine.

"Yeah, it's been on my mind too," I said.

I expect it was on everyone's mind.

Or at least everyone who mattered in my universe.

"There's stuff," she said, inhaling deeply on the cigarette.

I waited for her to continue, but she just blew smoke out in a tired puff.

"What stuff?" I asked, though I already knew *what stuff*.

Del had lusted far and wide. She indulged in dalliances both legal and illegal, wise and unwise. She broke hearts right and left.

But she rarely offered her own.

For some reason, Ian had touched her, and she'd allowed herself to hope for that elusive Happily Ever After.

That Ian was decidedly not worth her fragile gift was beside the point.

He was gone and all of those delicious possibilities were also gone, in a flash.

Del was not one of those women who could be comforted with platitudes. I tried to think of something concrete to say that would help her, but the phone rang.

"Yeah?" Presley said into the phone, wiping his sudsy hands on his shirt. "Sure, just a minute." He turned to me. "For you. It's Neil."

Another Delphi citizen for whom the last twenty-four hours had brought a few unexpected surprises.

It was a veritable epidemic.

I left Del to her thoughts and took the wet phone from Presley.

"What are you doing tonight?" Neil asked without a preamble.

I knew that he wasn't angling for a date—we'd have to work long and hard to find our way back to the last happy moment we'd spent together. If that was even possible.

But I knew that something was up.

Something that was going to take precedence over any plans I'd made.

"Not a thing," I said, visions of my lovely quiet, warm (and long overdue) bath vanishing into the cold night air.

23

....

The Domino Effect

Like the interlocking countries in Southeast Asia, the downfall of one small and poorly run dictatorship usually leads to a regional instability that eventually precipitates the toppling of all the neighboring fiefdoms.

Closely knit countries depend on one another not only for supplies and material goods, but for the kind of spiritual and cultural continuity necessary for community survival.

Take away the rainfall in one region and the crops fail, putting an undue strain on the next, which in turn places a terrible burden on the one farther out to maintain the status quo.

So it goes in small towns.

No matter what the local chambers of commerce would have you believe, the survival of a community in an isolated area depends far more on the comfort of keeping things the same than it ever does on marching toward the future.

Even small changes can have an unexpected rippling effect.

One divorce triggers feelings of discontent in six other marriages, three of which eventually split and spread the contagion.

Happily ever afters rarely occur in real life. Happy endings are pretty much nonexistent.

Even happy beginnings can trigger surprising consequences.

Especially when the relationship in question wasn't a good idea in the first place.

Take my affair with Stuart McKee. Please.

I knew he was married.

He certainly knew he was married.

We got together anyway, trying desperately to keep the whole shebang (so to speak) quiet.

Of course that didn't work.

A couple of the folks who knew about our affair, namely Del and Ron Adler, were unsettled enough by my fall from good girl status to attempt their own long-desired affair.

Which was an unmitigated disaster, which in turn caused the ending of their mostly celibate friendship, though of course they occasionally tried again, usually with the same disastrous results.

The ending of Del and Ron's brief fling also led to Del's pining away for a tall, blonde Englishman she'd never met, which resulted, in a roundabout way, in his death.

Ron's reaction to the ending of their fizzled affair was every bit as damaging, though not quite as fatal. His confession to Gina, which for some reason contained the corollary info on the beginning of my affair, evidently triggered Gina's astonishing stunt the day before.

The consequences of which have yet to be fully tallied.

It's entirely possible that the events and upheavals of this week were set in place last June when I mistook a pair of contact lenses for sparkling green eyes.

The concentric dramas that resulted from that little miscalculation were still playing themselves out, sometimes in front of my eyes.

My tired eyes.

"Tell me again why we're here," I said.

"Buck up, kiddo," Neil said, cuffing me on the shoulder. "We're on a reconnaissance mission, scoping out dastardly deeds and sniffing out wrongdoers. We got us a felony or two to deal with. Not to mention mysterious disappearances and even more mysterious arrivals."

He was amazingly jolly, considering.

"That I know," I said, not nearly so jolly myself. "But why are we *here*? And why now?"

I waved my hand at the interior of the bar, which was dark as usual, and smoky as usual, though the smoke was nearly overpowered by kerosene fumes from the assorted Coleman lanterns set on tables and along the bar.

It was also crowded—a whole lot more crowded than I would have expected since it was a national holiday and we'd just weathered the worst blizzard in ten years. Oh yeah, and we still had no power.

"Because it all revolves around the bar somehow," Neil said. "I have a feeling that everything started here."

Since I had just been thinking that the whole mess had started with me, Neil's declaration came as something of a relief.

We were sitting at a corner table, as far away from the bar and the makeshift karaoke stage as possible, though there were no karaoke-ers in sight. Or any DJ.

Or really, any of the major players from last night's minidramas. Stu and Renee were not among the revelers, thank goodness. Giddy and giggling Gina Adler was also a no-show. She was probably at home with her bad-boy husband. Alanna, Rhonda, and Brian were conspicuous by their absence. Ian, as we all knew, would not be celebrating this or any other New Year's Day. And Dorothy Gale, whose significance I still dismissed, was probably somewhere over the rainbow by now.

Presley, John, and Mardelle, however, were huddled at another corner table as far away from us as they could possibly get. They had not been delighted when I announced that we were meeting Neil at the bar, but they were making the best of things, buying pops for themselves and moaning over the fact that the pinball machines wouldn't work. They made do by flashing their cash at the pool table instead, challenging each other, and anyone they could entice, into a little eight-ball, buck a game.

Del had also been less than enthused when I'd declared that she was coming along whether she liked it or not. I thought that she might be teetering on the brink of a real depression and was unwilling to leave her home by herself. Neil stepped in and wisely pointed out that the bar would be warmer than the trailer, and that we could all go to his house afterward, where the fireplace would keep us from freezing during the night.

Del reluctantly agreed to accompany us. But she didn't agree to pretend that she was having fun.

So until it was time to recess to the comfortable warmth of Neil's upstairs living room, we sat in the bar, sorting out the origins of yesterday's mysteries.

"What makes you think it started here?" I asked, sipping my lukewarm Black Russian. Just because it was cold inside, and far colder outside, didn't mean that the ice machine was working. Or the refrigerators. Pat had used up her small store of ice on the afternoon customers.

"It *had* to have started with them." He indicated Pat and Pat Jackson, who stood behind the bar, still wearing their flashing Santa sweatshirts, soberly inspecting the clientele and their money in the glowing red light of their own battery-operated clothing.

I raised an eyebrow and sipped again. Del sat back in her chair, arms crossed, pretending to stare off into the distance, but I knew that she was listening to Neil.

"They got the newspaper," Neil said triumphantly.

When he didn't continue on his own, I asked, just like I was supposed to, "What newspaper?"

Though as soon as the words left my mouth, I realized what he was talking about.

"The *Sioux Falls Argus Leader*," we said together.

"Yup," Neil said, leaning forward on his elbows. "It began with the *Argus*."

"The article about you, the one where your big money and civic charitable works were all mentioned in bold type, when did it come out?" I asked, leaning forward myself.

"About a month ago," Neil said, grinning from ear to ear. His glasses reflected the candlelight from the peppermint-scented pillar lit at our table.

"Don't tell me," I said, not meaning it. "The Jacksons subscribed to the *Argus* temporarily for Mardelle's school project. Then when she was done, they let everyone else read it."

That was how Del met Ian in the first place. Through his ad in that paper.

"But not before they read it themselves," Neil said. "Which is where and how they found our intrepid DJ for the karaoke."

He'd driven all the way to Delphi in a blizzard to perform, which was confusing since there were easily several hundred bars in between where his services would have been welcome. And probably better paid to boot. "Who comes to Delphi when they have someplace better to go?"

"That was my thought exactly," said Neil. "So I called the Jacksons this afternoon and asked them about him. Seems like our DJ had an unexpected cancellation in his schedule and could just happen to fit us in for a New Year's Eve extravaganza."

Neil sat back in his chair and signaled Pat for another round, though I had not finished my warm drink yet, and Del was still nursing her first beer.

She lit a cigarette, the match flaring to show her tired face, and then continued to listen to us.

Maybe it was the assorted bodies in the bar, combined with the heat of all the candles and the lanterns that raised the BTU level, but we were finally warming up a little.

Or maybe it was those half-finished drinks.

Or maybe we were beginning to get heated up by our own half-baked notions.

"And you wanna know *why* he had a cancellation in his schedule that just coincidentally made it possible for him to drive to Delphi on New Year's Eve, which is the one evening you'd expect even an incompetent DJ to have booked months in advance?"

"Does the Pope have lips?" I asked.

Does a Delphite love gossip?

"Do you two really enjoy this shit?" Del asked.

We ignored her.

"His schedule just happened to be open on that most overbooked of nights because he'd recently gotten himself arrested for robbing at least one house in Beresford after his performance." He sat back and sipped his beer triumphantly.

Pat Jackson set another round on the table abruptly.

Neil handed her a five and a couple of ones. He was feeling generous, I guess.

"Nah," Pat said, waving her hand dismissively. "This one is on the house."

We all stopped for a moment, awed—Pat Jackson was giving out free drinks. Something completely unheard of in all of Delphi history.

She seemed to understand our surprise, and smiled a bit herself.

"Consider it our thanks for providing the boom boxes." She nodded at the stage, where there were several portable CD players scattered on the floor around the microphones. "*And* the batteries. Thanks to you we'll have *real* music tonight." Her face reverted to its usual frown. "That is if the dumbshit DJ ever shows up."

"You haven't heard from him today?" Neil asked, sipping innocently.

"Nope," Pat said, gathering up empty glasses and damp napkins. "Last night at closing he said he'd be back here tonight by seven-thirty. That was the last I saw him."

"Well, he can't have gone far," I said, thinking that no one could have gone far, given the road conditions.

"He's around somewhere. And he'd better hustle his ass down here quick," Pat said ominously as she left the table.

As soon as Pat was out of earshot again, I said, "But, if he'd been caught burglarizing homes, why did the Jacksons hire him? Not even for New Year's Eve would they court the loss of hard-earned cash."

Another thought struck me. "Are the Jacksons missing money too?"

Presley made a bank shot at the pool table and whooped loudly. John frowned and handed over a small wad of bills to him. Mardelle grinned and patted both boys on the shoulder, and then picked up a cue herself.

"Mardelle didn't say anything about a robbery," I said, watching the kids play. "Neither did Pat when I was in here earlier today." Though she *had* mentioned money. Neil's money. "At least not to me. Did you hear anything?"

"Not a thing," Del said. She stubbed one cigarette out and lit another one almost immediately, coughing delicately between drags.

"I don't think any money was missing from here," Neil said. "Pat would certainly have mentioned it." He was being kind. Pat would have blown a gasket if money had come up missing. "However, they didn't know that there was a reason for caution. I doubt they knew that he'd been arrested."

"But you did," I said triumphantly. "That's what you've been doing this afternoon. On the computer and the phone, checking out the DJ, right?"

"No computer," Neil said. "My generator isn't reliable enough to bet my computer against a surge or another outage. But I was able to run the fax machine for a few minutes. And I was able to call around for info."

"And we're uptown, just after a blizzard with no power, in order to keep an eye on the DJ," I said, finally realizing where Neil was headed.

"That is if he shows up," Neil said. "No one has seen *him* today either."

"Very interesting," I said. "The DJ was here, and then he was gone."

"The money was here, and then the money was gone."

"Quite a coincidence," I said. "But there's no real reason to think that the DJ had anything to do with our missing money. Or yours either, for that matter."

"Maybe, maybe not," Neil said, lowering his voice. "But, during one of the interludes when I had the generator fired up, it occurred to me to check my answering machine for last night. I'd gotten several hang-up calls between about ten P.M. and one A.M."

"Yeah?" I said. "No message, no heavy breathing. Just a hang up?"

"The caller evidently waited long enough for my message to play and then disconnected."

"What makes you think those calls had anything to do with the DJ?" I asked.

"Or the bar," Del asked, "since you are so certain that everything centers here?"

She was becoming less and less patient with our speculations.

"Because I have Caller ID on my machine. Most of those calls originated right here. From Jackson's Hole."

We all sat back and thought about that for a minute.

Neil himself had been quite visible at the bar during most of those hours last night. He'd even spent some time on stage in front of the rest of the crowd.

And yet someone inside the bar had used the phone to call the library several times and listen to the canned recording, but left no messages of their own.

"That doesn't make any sense," I said finally.

"Well, it does if you take into consideration that the person calling didn't know if my house was empty. It was obvious that I was here, but that didn't mean that the library was deserted."

"Did you see him use the phone?" I asked. "Either of you?"

"Not exactly," Del said. "He was over by that corner of the bar a few times during breaks, and he could have made some calls. On the other hand, you two've been having so much fun chasing down wild geese that you missed a couple of obvious suspects right under your noses."

She drained her beer and set the glass down heavily. "I'll tell you who I did see using the phone last night. Several times, in fact."

We waited.

"Alanna Luna," she said theatrically.

"Alanna made phone calls?" Neil asked.

"Who would she have been calling?" I asked at the same time.

We had all been assembled at the bar last night. Alanna's co-owner and co-workers and employees were there. Her son was at the bar. Who the hell had she been calling?

"That's not the most important question," Del said, smiling. She blew out a smoke ring and crossed her arms.

"So what's the most important question, then?" I asked. One of us had to—she wasn't going to give up her information unless we paid the price. Besides, I genuinely wanted to know where she was going with this line of logic.

"The most important question is: *Who lost the most money?*" Del said slowly. "And that's followed by the next most important question: *Who needed the money the most?*"

Neil and I exchanged a quick and disbelieving glance.

"You think Alanna would have robbed her own cafe?" I asked, incredulous. "That's absolutely ridiculous."

Alanna had bored me to tears with get-rich-quick-at-the-cafe schemes for the last month. Every single day she came up with some new harebrained way to make money. The notion that she would rob herself was ridiculous.

"Nonsense," I said, just to emphasize the point. "She wants to make the cafe work. It's all she ever talks about."

"Well, you wouldn't expect her to talk about her own money problems, would you?" Del asked nastily. "You know she came here with some baggage. Remember?"

I had to admit that Del had a point. Alanna most assuredly had a shady past, a car far out of her price range, and possible problems with the law in Oklahoma involving extortion and bookkeeping that didn't tally.

But the notion that she would take her own money, blame it on someone else, and then . . . "You think she burgled the library in order to cover up the robbery at the cafe?" I asked, finishing my thought out loud.

"Makes sense to me," Del said sweetly.

"Well, it doesn't make sense to me," I said, shaking my head.

I wasn't fond of Alanna, but I'd far rather suspect an unknown quantity like an itinerant DJ with felony charges leveled against him already than the woman I'd worked alongside for the last two months.

If she'd stolen from the cafe, she'd stolen from me too.

"Nonsense," I said again.

"Well, either way, it wouldn't hurt to call her," Neil said.

"Why?" I asked, surprised. I hadn't thought that Neil would put any stock in Del's theory.

"Well, if nothing else, Brian may know where the DJ is right now, since they were together last night."

"And no one's heard from Alanna for the past few hours," I said, suddenly thinking up excuses to call her too—if for no other reason than to let her phony Southern accent convince me once again that everything was normal.

Though when you boiled it down, normal for Alanna

consisted of failed businesses and brushes with illegality.

"She's not used to winter," I said reluctantly. "Not real winter. She may not know how to deal with having no electricity. I suppose we'd better make sure that she's safe."

Neil pulled out a cell phone and dialed her number and waited.

And waited.

Finally, he closed the phone.

"No answer. Maybe you better go over there, Tory, and check it out."

"Me?" I asked. "Why me?"

Intriguing speculations notwithstanding, I was cold, I was tired, I was unwashed, and I most assuredly did not want to slog over to Alanna's house through the snow to make sure that she was okay, whether she had robbed the cafe or not.

"We wouldn't want it on our conscience if something happened to her, now would we?" Neil asked with a laugh.

"Who's this *we* you're talking about?" I asked sourly. "Why the hell don't you go?"

"Because I have to stay here and sweet-talk Pat Jackson into giving me the rest of the scoop on our nefarious DJ, that's why."

24

....

A Bathroom on the Right

It is a universally known and accepted fact that bladder activation in small children is triggered by the combination of bitter winter weather and the number of layers of insulated outerwear worn at any given moment.

Unwary, and perhaps inexperienced mothers can be lulled by vehement assurances, and even direct observation, into thinking that no offspring could possibly need the facilities for the next half-hour at least. Comforted by the notion of peace and quiet for the duration, she bundles the child in layer after layer of clothing specifically designed to allow the fragile human body to survive sub-zero temps without losing one or more extremity to frostbite.

Long johns, and overalls, and mittens with Thinsulate liners, and sweaters, and jackets and parkas, and earmuffs and mufflers and face masks and multiple pairs of socks inside boots with removable felt liners—all zipped and wrapped and tucked and snugged down and patted into place. When the child is finally ready, wearing enough layers to render width roughly equal to height, when the exhausted mother has finally closed the door and collapsed in hopes of a quiet interlude . . .

The kid realizes it's time to go again.

I don't know if it is the weight of the clothes, or the sudden change between interior warmth and frigid exterior, or if it is purely mental—but it happens every time.

Unfortunately, it works the same way for adults. Especially when you factor in a couple of Black Russians.

It hadn't been all that warm inside at Jackson's Hole, but it had been one whole helluva lot warmer than outside, where the temps hovered in that minus 10 range— cold enough to freeze the hairs inside your nose, but not enough to frost your eyelashes together.

Unlike most kiddies with overprotective mommas, I wore the minimum of heavy outerwear: a sweater, a coat, gloves with liners, arctic boots, earmuffs, and a scarf. It was enough to keep me warm without restricting movement (my width already being roughly equal to my height). But it was still enough to make going to the bathroom without disrobing almost completely a total pain.

Besides which, I was already a block from the bar, tromping along mostly shoveled sidewalks in the frigid night air, having been sent on a wild-goose chase by Neil Pascoe.

There were no Porta-Pottys in sight.

There were houses, however, each of which was equipped with a functional bathroom (unless the pipes had frozen), taunting me in the cold night air.

I could see candles flickering in the windows of several otherwise unlit homes, and the vague shadows of people hovering around fireplaces for warmth, bundled in blankets and afghans.

I hunkered down into my coat and shoved my hands deeper into my pockets and muttered to myself as I walked.

It was dark out, but the sky was clear and the moon was rising. I had a flashlight, but it stayed in my pocket. With a full moon and a soft blanket of pure white snow, the landscape looked much like daytime viewed through a smoky lens.

Without the usual noise and bustle that accompanies even a small-town evening, Delphi was unnaturally still and quiet. No cars traveled the roads honking and revving engines. No kids hollered and shouted friendly obscenities at each other. No steroidal sound systems blasted alienated music designed to drive the grown-ups batty from upstairs teenage bedrooms, no faint echoes of *Wheel of Fortune* floated into the street from living rooms where fathers drank their beers and mothers flipped through the latest issue of *People* magazine.

No random conversations on the streets wafted softly into the air.

What sound there was carried oddly in the extreme cold. Even two blocks away, I could hear just faintly the muffled sounds from inside the raucous bar. Every once in a while I heard the faint and rhythmic metallic zing of shovel on sidewalk from the other side of town.

I would have enjoyed the chance to walk through my own town, seeing and hearing it in a whole new way. But I was still cold. And vaguely crabby. And extremely tired. And certain that I was on a wild-goose chase.

Not to mention that I had to go to the bathroom.

Really bad.

The only people I really knew on this block were the Adlers, and I was not about to interrupt their joyful reunion to ask if I could use the facilities even though their front door suddenly opened, spilling a tightly focused beam from a hand-held halogen flashlight onto the sidewalk a few houses down and across the street from me.

In the light of the newly risen moon, I could vaguely make out Gina Adler, wrapped in what looked to be the bathrobe she'd worn on the street yesterday while bashing Ron's truck. With the door open, she kissed her heavily swaddled husband on the front steps as I walked past.

They both saw me. Gina waved halfheartedly and ducked immediately back into the house and closed the door with a bang. I suppose that love can keep you warm for only just so long (not nearly as long as unbridled anger—she'd been outside dressed very much the same yesterday, for a whole lot longer time and didn't even raise a goose bump).

Forgoing the salutation and friendly wave, Ron shut off his flashlight and hustled around the corner of the house, and tromped off kitty-corner through the neighbor's snowy yard and across the alley. I assumed he was heading toward his garage.

Or the bar.

Both establishments were in that general direction. But I lost sight of him long before I turned the corner onto Alanna's street.

Knowing I'd never make it all the way back to the bar without a pit stop, I vowed to use her bathroom with or without her permission. Whether the pipes were frozen or not.

The houses on this street were even less lit. A few of the homes had candles in the window, but most were dark, including Alanna's.

Though unless her timing was perfect, and she'd taken a route that had avoided me completely (as unused to winter, and unfamiliar with Delphi's streets as Alanna was, that seemed highly unlikely), I was pretty sure that she had no choice but to be at home. I pictured her hunkering down in the dark, cursing the South Dakotan winter and co-owners sloppy enough to leave large amounts of money lying on counters.

Unless Del was right, in which case she was rubbing her hands together in glee, having committed the almost-perfect crime.

I turned up her front sidewalk and then angled around to the back door, squinting at the windows of the little

house that had once belonged to Aphrodite Ferguson,
looking for any sign of life inside.

From the outside anyway, the house was silent and
dark.

I stomped up onto the creaky back porch, making as
much noise as possible in the stillness. I figured that if
Alanna was sitting and shivering inside in the total
blackness, she'd hear me and come to the door.

No sound came from inside.

I banged on the door and shouted, and then cocked
my head toward the house.

I thought I heard a small muffled noise but decided
that it was just another door opening down the block.

I stood there for a minute more, thinking through my
options.

I could turn around and sprint, in full winter gear,
back to the bar and hope I made it without wetting my
pants.

I could bang on the door one more time, shouting and
making a lot more noise in the hope that Alanna really
was home and had just not heard me the first time.

Or I could use the key (if it was still hidden in Aphrodite's old hidey-hole) to let myself in and use the bathroom.

If I was caught, I could always explain that I had been
deeply worried that our Sweet Southern Flower would
freeze into one very large-busted block of ice in the aftermath of that mean old South Dakota blizzard.

Checking on your neighbors and co-workers during
any of the myriad meteorological emergencies regularly
visited upon us by the Weather Gods was one of the
prairie duties instilled in us from birth anyway.

Besides which, Alanna didn't know a damn thing
about real winter survival. I figured she was the kind of
woman who would pour hot water on an icy car windshield. She might actually be in danger by herself in an
unheated house if the power stayed off much longer.

Annoyed at my own civic-minded do-gooding, I

vowed to drag Alanna over to Neil's and certain warmth if I found her shivering and cold inside.

With no more arguments against myself to offer, I reached around the porch support and grabbed the key that was still there, and with one last loud bang and an accompanying holler, I opened Alanna's back door and stepped into the kitchen.

Once inside the familiar, dark kitchen, I yelled once again, thinking that if I hurried, I could use the bathroom and be back at the bar in fifteen minutes, with or without Alanna.

I stomped the snow off my boots and stumbled through into the living room.

"Damn. Ouch," I said, tripping over a footstool that was in the middle of the floor. "Alanna! Brian! Anyone!" I shouted loudly. "This is Tory. I'm just checking to make sure you're all right. In the cold. What with no power. And all."

I didn't figure she was actually there, but I wanted to be safe if she happened to walk in the back door while I was exploring her dark house.

"Alanna," I sing-songed, shuffling my feet in case there were any other invisible obstacles in the way. "Oh Alanna. Wherefore art thou?"

I made my way through the remainder of the living room unstubbed, heading toward the bathroom. I'd already unwound my scarf and removed my mittens.

I unzipped my coat, ready to make a mad dash for the toilet.

Which I would have done had I not stepped right on Alanna and Ron Adler, huddled silently in the dark on the floor, with their *delictos flagranted* all over the place.

25

....

Is That a Wallet
in Your Pocket...

I am a grown woman. Fully grown. Overgrown perhaps.

In any case, I reached my majority about half a life-time ago, and as such I assumed that I understood sexual attraction as well as almost any consenting adult. I truly thought that I could no longer be flabbergasted by the endless variations on a theme attempted by the carbon-based bipeds with which I share a small town on this swiftly tilting planet.

Silly me.

Just living with Del should have prepared me for a life of sexual surprises.

Hell, my own questionable choices should have paved the way for a permanent state of wonderment and per-plexity.

Be that as it may, there was probably no one more surprised than me when I stumbled, literally, onto Ron Adler and Alanna Luna in the dark.

On the floor.

In the buff.

In the act.

Except maybe Ron and Alanna themselves.

"Eeek!" I said, though that is a particularly stupid sound to make under any circumstances, and especially so in this one. Somehow I'd gotten the flashlight out of my pocket and turned on before I fully realized that illuminating the situation wasn't exactly a good idea.

"Eeek!" Alanna echoed, scrambling out of the pool of light to cover herself with an afghan.

I fumbled with the flashlight, trying to turn it off, though of course that was like closing the barn door after the horse escaped. I'd already seen far more than I ever wanted to.

I gave up trying to turn the flashlight off. As awkward as it was to be holding the only light source in the room, it would be even more awkward to turn it off and then stand in the darkness, trying to make conversation after permanently imprinting my retinas with the vision of Ron Adler's narrow and surprisingly hairy naked butt scooting behind the couch.

I stood frozen, with the flashlight pooling in the dark, my original mission forgotten. A hand snaked out blindly from behind the couch, felt around a bit, and finally snagged a shirt sleeve and dragged it back into the dark recesses. My brain repeating only one thought: *. . . but he can't even grow a mustache.*

No one said anything.

Not that I didn't want to, mind you, but the whole notion of Ron and Alanna together in the biblical sense was mind-boggling.

The only sounds came from the steady drip of the kitchen faucet, and the soft and frantic noise of clothes being hastily donned in the dark.

Alanna recovered first. She stood up, brushed herself off, and perched nonchalantly on the arm of the worn couch. The one Ron was hiding behind.

She cleared her throat, then smoothed her mussed

hair, and then finally said, "Did you need something specific, Tory?"

It was a partial recovery at best.

"Well, um . . ." I said, trying to figure out how to respond. "Mostly, I dropped by to make sure you were okay," I said. I didn't add that I'd needed to use the bathroom or that Del suspected her of robbing her own place of business. "There's no power you know," I said stupidly, pointing the flashlight at the dark ceiling, "and no heat either. I was worried . . . well, Neil was worried . . . we *all* were worried that you might be freezing to death in an unheated house . . ."

I had to stop right there because it was painfully obvious that while we had been busy worrying (with varying degrees of intensity) about whether or not Alanna was equipped to survive the terrible cold and lack of amenities, she and Ron had been making like the Eskimos and raising their body temps the old-fashioned way.

". . . And that's why I came in when you didn't answer . . ." More awkward pauses ensued. ". . . anyway, I'm supposed to take you back to the bar with me, and from there to Neil's house for the night. He has a fireplace and it'll be warm enough even if the power doesn't come on until tomorrow. Which is probably the case since it's dark now. And there's no power yet . . ."

My small supply of perkiness was exhausted by the strain of maintaining the fiction that nothing weird was going on.

"Well, that's nice of you and Neil," Alanna said carefully. Her accent hadn't returned completely yet, and her voice cracked just a bit.

It was a small consolation to know that she felt every bit as awkward me. I could only guess what Ron felt about the situation since he was still ensconced behind the couch.

I did my best to keep the flashlight beam away from faces, and still partially unclothed bodies, but the visibility was still better than I needed. I caught a glimpse of a hand again, this time reaching over the top of the couch, patting, searching for something.

Ron said something but it was mumbled and I couldn't understand.

He'd evidently not spoken in their private lovers' language because Alanna, while keeping a steely eye on me, leaned back on the arm and asked airily, "What was that?"

The mumbling came again, a little more insistent but not a whole lot more intelligible.

"*Mumee my panns*," he said again. I could hear his teeth clenching.

Alanna shot a tight agonized smile in my direction and then turned around completely, leaned down, and repeated her question over the back of the couch.

"Pants," came the clipped voice from behind the couch. The very annoyed clipped voice from behind the couch. "I need my *pants*."

"Oooh," Alanna said, nodding her head. "Of course."

She looked down at the floor by the couch, and though there were other feminine items too intimate to describe, there were no jeans. She glanced around in the general area, but came up empty.

Only thinking to help (though obviously not thinking too clearly), I flashed the beam around the room and spotted a pair of blue jeans in the far living room corner, draped over the back of an overstuffed chair. They were right next to a lacy pink underwire bra with cups big enough to hold bowling balls.

"There they are," I said, hoping that Ron at least had his underwear with him.

I grabbed the jeans and picked them up (leaving the bra for its owner to retrieve) and gave them an underarm toss in Alanna's general direction, but they were heavier than I'd expected and they landed with a thunk less than half the distance across the room.

Frowning, I walked over and picked the jeans up and something soft fell on my foot from a back pocket.

Tucking the jeans under my arm, I bent down to pick up what had fallen.

I knew what it was right away, it was a wallet. A dark brown, well worn, ordinary man's leather wallet, thick with bits of paper and clippings sticking out of it.

And I knew it wasn't Ron's.

From long years of waiting on the man and watching him pay for his morning and afternoon coffees, I knew very well that Ron carried a black leather trifold wallet that he kept tucked in the inside pocket of his jacket, never in the back pocket of his pants.

That's why I had been surprised by the extra weight of his jeans and misjudged my throw. I had not expected there to be anything more than a little loose change, and possibly an empty condom wrapper, in the front pockets.

I frowned.

"You changing your style this late in the game, Ron?" I asked, looking at the wallet and turning it over in my hand, shining the flashlight first on it and then toward the couch.

The wallet looked familiar.

"Could I please have my pants now?" Ron asked.

He'd stood up behind the couch. The back was tall enough and his shirt long enough to save me, mercifully, from knowing for sure whether he'd found his underwear.

"Yeah," I said distractedly.

Without looking, I tossed the jeans directly to him. They hit their mark this time.

Ron bent over and put them on, standing back up to snap and zip.

"I was gonna turn that in," he said quickly, without preamble. "But things was so busy today that I didn't get a chance."

I barely heard Ron.

I'd seen the wallet at the bar last night, I was certain, and was trying to bring the memory into focus. It was an ordinary wallet. Just a plain brown, used wallet. But there was something . . .

Ron blinked at Alanna, who shrugged in return.

"Besides," he said, chuckling weakly, "there wasn't anyone to turn it over to anyway."

Something about bras draped over furniture. Unexpected bras draped over unexpected furniture . . .

I looked up at Ron, who looked back at me, now wide-eyed and flushed. Bright red circles outlined his cheeks.

Alanna looked at Ron and then at me, plainly confused.

"What's the matter? Whose wallet is that anyway?" Her accent had returned. So had her petulance. She was not the center of attention, and that annoyed her.

I knew where I'd seen that wallet before.

And I knew whose picture I'd see when I looked inside.

"What difference does it make whose wallet that is?" Alanna demanded.

"I guess that depends," I said, with a small hard smile, tossing the wallet in a little one-handed juggle, "on exactly how this ended up in Ron's back pocket."

26

....

... Or Are You Just Happy
to See Me?

We are all at the mercy of the Fickle Finger of Fate.

Seemingly random events place us where we do not want to be, in order to see and hear things we'd just as soon avoid so that we will eventually be able to comprehend the incomprehensible when it is before our very eyes.

Well, maybe *comprehend* is too strong a term.

I doubt I'll ever fully understand exactly what I had seen in the last couple of days, from the destruction of one pickup to a body frozen solid in the box of another to the unexpected coupling of two people who I'd thought would have had better taste, if not sense.

But fate, or a Higher Power with a deeply quirky sense of humor, had seen fit to plop me smack dab in the middle of some mighty inexplicable situations over the last day and a half, none of which had seemed to be related in any way, and all of which I would have skipped happily.

But since mere mortals aren't in charge of that cosmic interaction stuff, I'd dutifully tucked away a whole string of useless and random information because in life, sometimes there actually is a test later.

Who knew that one of the answers would involve recognizing the most inexplicable object of all, when it landed, literally, at my feet?

"How'd you say you got this?" I asked Ron. I was not being confrontational. I was truly confused, and absolutely interested in what he'd say. I focused the flashlight beam directly on him, curious to see as well as to hear his answer.

"I found it," he said, smoothing his thinning hair back with both hands, blinking in the bright light. He walked stiffly from behind the couch and sat on the end, as far from Alanna as he could get and still be on the same piece of furniture. "I saw it lying on the sidewalk outside the bar last night after we all got back into town."

The flashlight beam was wide and bright enough that I didn't have to miss Ron's movements to keep them both in sight.

Alanna looked at Ron first, confused, and then at me. "I don't understand what's goin' on here," she said, her accent in full force. She slid down the couch toward Ron, who shrank further into the arm. "It's a wallet, for God's sake. What difference does it make where or how he got it?"

"In most cases it wouldn't matter at all," I agreed softly. "But I do think that people, possibly even the authorities, are going to wonder just how a dead man's wallet ended up in Ron's possession."

Alanna's eyes widened sharply. She looked at Ron, totally confused, and then back at me. She even forgot to tilt her head attractively and wet her lips.

If she had been anyone else, I would have taken her expression for the real thing. I would have assumed that

Ron Adler's possession of Ian O'Hara's wallet was as big a surprise to her as it was to me.

On the other hand, any woman who'd spent years taking her clothes off for roomfuls of men, managing to convince each one simultaneously that she was performing for him and him alone, had to be an Oscar-worthy actress.

"A *dead* man?" Alanna asked, wavering her attention between Ron and me. "I don't understand."

"I don't either," I said, sitting on the nearest chair, the one that happened to have Alanna's bra still draped over the back. "Maybe Ron can enlighten us both."

I smiled at Ron.

It was a gentle, encouraging smile. One guaranteed to worm information out of the most reluctant person.

Like most of the world, Ron was resistant to my charms.

"As I said," he repeated, wide-eyed. "I found it on the sidewalk last night. I glanced at it and saw the picture and just figured I'd give it back to him, or you or Del . . ." Ron's eyes flickered sideways when he said Del's name but Alanna kept her steely, innocent façade. ". . . and you guys could give it back to him. I didn't know it was going to be . . . um . . . impossible to give it back . . ." Ron's voice trailed off into nothing and he looked down at his bare feet.

"Ah," I said, noncommittally, my brain already wrestling with something that didn't make any sense. Well, one of the many things that didn't make sense in this situation.

"See," Alanna crowed. "Nothing mysterious, nothing out of line. He found the wallet and didn't have a chance to give it back to the owner."

"Yeah," Ron agreed, voice more firm and resolute. "I only glanced inside to see whose it was . . . and I want you to know that there was no money in that wallet when I found it. He either spent it all, or someone else stole the wallet and the money and then threw it down on the sidewalk." Ron paused for a second, gaining enough strength to repeat himself. "Which is what I think happened. I think someone stole that wallet and took the money out and then dropped it where I found it."

I sat, mulling that over.

"Well, aren't you going to say anything?" Ron demanded.

"Yeah," I said, "put some socks on. Both of you. You make me cold just looking at you."

I was buying time, trying to work out one inconsistency that I could see, and grasp hold of another that was dancing just out of my reach. And trying to figure out whether to wait and consult with Neil before saying anything to Ron about either.

Ron and Alanna took me at my word and scrambled for socks and shoes. And sweaters and mufflers. No one made a grab for the bra, whose satin-covered underwires poked me in the ear every time I leaned back in the chair.

They ignored me, rubbing their hands together and shivering as they finished dressing. They didn't talk to each other either but I caught some very significant looks that passed between them.

It was not a comfortable situation for any of us. Emotionally or physically.

It wasn't literally freezing in the house yet, but it was cold enough for everyone's breath to be visible in great foggy puffs.

Cold enough that I couldn't figure out why they'd been fooling around on the drafty floor rather than snug under covers in a bed.

If they'd been dallying where intelligent adulterous people dally, I'd never have stumbled over them at all. I would have flashed the beam around the room, used the bathroom, written a hasty note with Neil's invitation, and left none the wiser and a whole lot happier.

Of course, if they'd interrupted themselves to answer the phone when Neil called in the first place, I'd never have left the bar.

But then I would not have seen Ian's wallet in Ron's possession.

The wallet he said he'd picked up *on the sidewalk in front of the bar last night.*

But if he'd had the wallet since the night before, why did he jump into the back of Stu's pickup this morning and pat Ian's dead body down for ID? And why did he come up empty?

We had a major discrepancy here.

Either Ron was lying about when he'd come into possession of the wallet or he'd searched Ian's body looking for something entirely different.

Neither scenario made a bit of sense to me.

I watched him as he pulled his boots on.

There were always plenty of good reasons to lie, but in this case I thought he was probably protecting someone.

I didn't for an instant think that Ron had taken any money from Ian or anyone else.

But some thought that Alanna was capable of stealing.

And Ron was here, fooling around with Alanna.

Maybe he was protecting her.

But then again, Gina had been fooling around with Ian.

Maybe Ron knew that and was protecting her instead.

Would faithful and honest Gina take Ian's wallet?

Would faithful and honest Gina smash the shit out of Ron's truck with a baseball bat?

That other inconsistency, the one I couldn't quite see, danced into view for just a moment.

"Uh, Tory," Alanna said softly, interrupting. "I . . . um . . . know that we don't always get along and all . . ." She stopped and shot an entirely readable glance at Ron, who shrugged. ". . . but we'd appreciate . . . I mean Ron here and me . . . Well . . ."

Her voice died in the quiet.

I knew what she was asking, but I doubted I could keep to it. There were far too many facets that demanded discussion. Far too many people who would be deeply interested.

But since everyone else seemed to be so adept at lying, I decided to play too.

"Sure," I said, mentally crossing my fingers. "I understand. I won't tell anyone."

"Thanks," she said, plainly relieved and taking me at my word. "We really appreciate it."

Ron mumbled something that I couldn't understand.

"And if that invitation is still open, I'm sure we'd love to go over to Neil's and get warm," Alanna continued.

"Uh . . ." I hesitated, stalling. The invitation had been for Alanna and Brian, and possibly Rhonda if she was around.

It would be an understatement to say that I had not expected to find Ron Adler on the premises. If I showed up with him in tow, not only would everyone be instantly suspicious, Del would be livid.

On the other hand, it would be outright rude to exclude him from certain warmth.

I wondered if Emily Post had any etiquette rules to cover invitations involving possibly larcenous business partners and their new, married boyfriends.

"Well . . ." I said, hesitating. To avoid having to look Ron in the eye, I idly flipped opened the wallet and pretended to inspect the contents.

"I can't make it," Ron, no dummy, said quickly. "Thanks and all, and I do want to stop by the bar for a bit later, but I have to go home first and check on—"

Before he could say his wife's name out loud, the other discrepancy popped into my head.

But before I had a chance to sort out those new permutations, I saw, I mean really saw, what lay open in my hand.

27

....

Can You Dig It?

Blame it on exhaustion.

I was tired. I was cold. I was unwashed. I was hungry.

And I still had to go to the bathroom.

My brain, when it had functioned at all, had been a sieve—information poured in and then flowed right back out at the same speed.

Any self-respecting mystery reader (of which I had formerly considered myself) would have seen long ago that there were strange doings on the prairie.

Here in snowbound Delphi, in the space of one day we'd been visited by three strangers of varying degrees of mysteriousness during which time the whole town had been closeted in what was, in effect, the hoariest of mystery conventions: a locked room.

One stranger had a shady past.

One missing stranger may or may not have absconded with a lot of money.

And one handsome stranger was most assuredly dead.

That's at least two too many strangers and five or six
more conundrums than necessary on the ordinary South
Dakota winter holiday.

Amateur (or professional) literary sleuths would have
been summarily bounced from the publishing world long
ago for committing the unpardonable mystery-book sin
of not even realizing that they had a mystery on their
hands until page 219.

All I can say is that it's a good thing that this is real
life and not fiction.

"Houston, I think we have a mystery," Neil said quietly after I handed him the wallet.

I'd somehow managed to keep a straight face as I
slipped the wallet into my coat pocket. Both Alanna and
Ron were still scurrying around getting ready to leave
when I airily told them that I'd meet them back at the
bar.

I imagine I was back with Neil before they even realized I'd gone.

"No shit," I said to him. "This sorta changes everything, doesn't it?"

I'd hustled him to a candlelit booth, back behind the
pool table. Del was still staring morosely into her beer.
I don't think it even registered that we'd left her alone.

The DJ had returned from who-knows-where, and
with the help of Neil's assorted boom boxes and evidently inexhaustible supply of D batteries, was putting
on a relatively good show for a fairly large crowd that
had opted to be cold together uptown, wearing tattered
leftover New Year's hats, rather than cold alone at home.
He didn't have a microphone, and neither did any of the
singers, and they all had to wing it as far as lyrics went,
but everyone made up in enthusiastic volume what they
lacked in electronic enhancement. At least we were
saved from innumerable acoustic versions of "Kum-
bayah."

Most of the regulars were in attendance, though Ron
and Alanna had yet to make their separate entrances.
Brian and Rhonda, basking in their own glow, were

helping the DJ, drinking beer and laughing. I would have expected Rhonda to be spectacularly hung over, but she looked radiant.

Gina Adler sat on a barstool and stared at her own reflection in the back bar mirror. Even in the lantern light, she looked haggard, a good ten years older than last week, which is not especially surprising. Most of the patrons gave her a wide berth, as befitted a woman who had been violently and publicly insane only a day earlier.

Joe Marlow, whose *ma* had not yet made it into town, sat hunched with a couple of other rumpled farmers down at the other end of the bar. They shot surreptitious glances now and again at Gina, who was oblivious.

I had worried about the community reaction to Gina's revelation about the beginning of my affair with Stu (and no doubt that there would be more fallout on that particular point), but I had forgotten that the messenger in this case was so much more fascinating than the message. People were going to remember that Louisville Slugger a whole lot longer than they were going to remember exactly when Renee McKee moved back to Minnesota.

Especially since she was back in Delphi now, and the whole point was moot.

But for now, it served my present purposes to go unnoticed. In fact, if not for Pat Jackson, who could smell a tip in the dark, bringing drinks, and the occasional exasperated looks from Presley and John Adler, I could well have been invisible.

Which was handy, since I wanted to talk to Neil privately, and keep an eye on everyone else at the same time.

"Yeah," I said, sighing. "It changes things, but I'm not sure how."

"Well, for one thing," Neil said, pushing his glasses up on his nose and leaning closer to the candle to inspect the Nebraska driver's license he'd removed from the wallet. "We don't have to wonder why he called himself

Ian." He looked up and smiled at me. "I mean, wouldn't you if your name really was Oscar Z. Diggs?"

"Actually," I said, keeping my voice as low as possible, "we don't know if his name was really Oscar either. That's obviously him in the picture, but these days it's not so hard to fake identification."

Neil sat back in his chair. "You're right. And that name seems familiar somehow. But whoever he was, this shows that he was here in Delphi under false pretenses." He waved the license.

I took a drink and thought for a minute. "Maybe it doesn't mean all that much. Maybe he was just married and sneaking around and trying not to get caught."

I'd already had adequate personal and anecdotal proof that he wasn't above smooching more than one girl at a time.

"And maybe he was here scoping out the joint for other purposes," Neil said, thoughtfully.

"Like what?"

"Well, you're missing a bunch of money at the cafe, aren't you?" Neil asked, holding up one finger. "And I'm missing a little cash and a diamond ring myself." He held up another finger. "And who knows what else in town might be missing?"

Three fingers.

"Yeah, but he can't have taken the cafe money," I said, thinking through last night's events. "The bag was still on the counter when I left the cafe with . . ."

Oh that's right. I'd gone off with Stu McKee in his truck and gotten stuck alone with him all night, which had pissed Neil off royally.

It was not a subject I particularly wanted to discuss so I backpedaled.

". . . he had to have been in the back of . . . the pickup already by the time I left town," I said carefully, cupping my hands around my glass and not looking Neil in the eye. "Because he was there in the morning and the money had to have been taken from the cafe during the night. Ditto with your stuff."

For just an instant, Neil's lips tightened and then relaxed. "You're right. He couldn't have robbed anyone. At least not here last night." He leaned forward again, excited, "But he could have had help."

"An accomplice?" I asked. "But Ian was a stranger. He didn't know anyone here."

"Didn't he?" Neil asked quietly, eyeing the stage. "How do we know that? Just because *we* didn't know *him* doesn't mean that *he* didn't know anyone else."

Neil's line of reasoning led directly to the karaoke DJ.

"You mean they might have done it together?" I asked, eyeing the DJ myself.

I hadn't paid much attention to him before. He was a youngish, handsome-ish, affable-seeming guy who was pretty good at crowd control and karaoke. But considering his record, and his sudden availability to work in Delphi, it seemed as though his burglary skills weren't exactly up to par.

"What's his name anyway?" I asked, watching as a couple of guys tried to do Garth Brooks proud. "Allegedly?"

"Wayne," Neil said, squinting at the stage suspiciously. "Wayne DePaul. Of Sioux Falls, South Dakota. At least according to Pat Jackson. And the police report I found."

Sioux Falls. Everything seemed to center around Sioux Falls.

"For what it's worth, Del found 'Ian' in the Sioux Falls paper," I said.

"And just coincidentally, me and my millions were profiled in the Sioux Falls paper too," Neil said bitterly.

He wasn't an unhappy rich guy, but his money hadn't brightened his life either. In fact, it often caused more problems than it solved.

And it did, on occasion, attract all the wrong kinds of attention.

"Damn," I said, exhaling sharply.

Maybe we were getting somewhere.

Maybe Ian (it was easier to continue to call him that—

he just didn't look like an Oscar) and Wayne had come to Delphi jointly to relieve the sap librarian of some of his unearned moola.

And maybe I was really tired and not thinking straight.

"I think we're missing a whole lot here," I said, leaning forward myself. "Whatever Ian and Wayne were doing here, jointly or separately, it doesn't explain why Ron Adler had his wallet."

Right on cue, Ron sashayed through the bar door, letting in a gust of wind that blew out three of the nearest candles. He'd evidently gone home and changed his clothes.

And taken a shower—his still-wet hair sparkled with frost.

Gina saw him in the mirror and swiveled away, the better to ignore him completely.

Over at our former table, Del looked up from her intense contemplation of the initials carved into the table to watch Ron as he walked over to the far end of the bar. Her face was flat and unreadable. She glanced over at me, still with no expression, and then back down at the table.

John Adler, who'd studiously ignored his mother at the bar for the past hour, shot his father a completely murderous glare comprised of equal parts adolescent hatred and blinks.

Presley and Mardelle didn't glare at anyone, but they did exchange glances with each other, and then they each sent a guilty peek my way.

The bar door opened again and Alanna clomped in, wrapped to the gills in coats and sweaters and boots and mittens.

In fact, if I hadn't recognized most of the outerwear, I wouldn't have known it was her at all. Her nose was red and her eyes were frost-rimmed; she rubbed her mittened hands together and shivered.

I guessed that she intended to keep all of her clothes

on for the duration, which would disappoint a fair share of the males gathered.

She also intended to maintain an innocent façade, as she waltzed past Ron at the bar without even a second glance.

It was a good ploy, one that might have worked had Ron not followed her with his wide and unblinking stare as she greeted Brian and Rhonda with big hugs.

Which reminded me that in the excitement of handing over the wallet, I'd forgotten to tell Neil about finding Ron and Alanna together.

Gina watched Alanna with narrowed and dangerous eyes, and I thought that somehow she knew that her husband and the ex-stripper had been together.

Which was when the other discrepancy, the one I couldn't quite grasp at Alanna's, danced directly into view.

If Ron had been with Alanna, who the hell had Gina kissed at her own front door?

28

....

Gobi Gred

When it comes to interstate rivalries, the minor irritations between South Dakota and our neighbors to the south are easily ignored, or swept away in the larger annoyances that stem from our eastern and northern borders.

There's no doubt that a certain enmity exists between Minnesotans who look down on us as rubes and hicks just because they have a couple of largish cities and a big honkin' mall, and the rubes and hicks who return the favor by thinking of Minnesota as Snob Central.

It did our bitter little hearts no small amount of good to watch the nation chuckle when the weird, and mostly inexplicable, *Fargo* hit the national consciousness. We knew that no one in the state actually talked that way, but it didn't bother us one whit to have the rest of the country think so.

And North Dakota, exporters of such cultural treasures as Lawrence Welk and Angie Dickinson, has the temerity to feel superior because we can boast of only Catherine Bach and Cheryl Ladd.

In truth, there is as little difference between ourselves and our various geographies as there is between the average neighboring Balkan nations, and about as much respect. Though we do tend to leave the bazookas at home.

That said, Nebraska is mostly neutral territory.

Outside of what seems to us to be an obsessional enthusiasm for the Cornhuskers, and a tendency to run the shouted words "Go Big Red!" together when large numbers of natives are assembled, Nebraskans are only a little different in ways that don't really count.

The state is mostly like South Dakota, with just a shade more humidity and a few of those weird land formations that others immediately recognize as hills. And like us, the people are generally affable and easygoing.

So why, when we get along so well, Nebraska decided to inflict its most unlikely of citizens, Oscar Z. Diggs (AKA Ian Douglas O'Hara), on us, is beyond me.

"Funny, he didn't sound Nebraskan," I said, looking at the address on the driver's license and trying to remember my geography. "South Sioux City, huh?"

"Yeah, right across the border from Sioux City," Neil said. He always could read my mind.

"South Dakota or Iowa?"

"Iowa. North Sioux City is in South Dakota, remember?"

"That's right," I said, rubbing my head. "None of them are all that far from Sioux Falls, are they?"

They couldn't be, since Del had said that Ian had answered her letters almost immediately, which meant that he'd picked them up at the drop in Sioux Falls probably every day.

"About eighty miles," Neil said. "No big deal."

It wasn't a big deal—a one-hundred-sixty-mile round trip in country where traffic was a non-issue lasted exactly as long as it took to drive one hundred sixty miles without getting stopped for a speeding ticket.

"So he drove up from Nebraska to pick up letters from his sweetie . . ." Neil said.

"Or sweeties, plural," I interrupted. "We have no way of knowing how many women he was stringing along with his phony accent and name."

Well, I didn't really know if the accent was phony or not. In fact, I'd have bet the farm that it was authentic. And not only did it seem authentic, but it had been intoxicating to listen to, if a little hard to understand.

Then I remembered, that good or bad, real or phony, the guy was literally stone cold, and this wasn't a game.

He was dead and I was out two thousand bucks.

All serious shit.

"So where do we go from here?" I asked Neil wearily.

We'd already hashed over the amazing union of Alanna and Ron and run out of guesses as to why he had the wallet, and how. We'd gone over and over the puzzling mystery of Gina's new sweetie, all the while sitting in the same back booth.

In fact, we'd been at it for the last hour, and it was long past time to rejoin Del, if for no other reason than that she looked vulnerable sitting alone at our rear table.

No one had joined her, no one had bought her a drink. No one had propositioned her with the near certainty of being accepted. Her son played pool without paying his mother a bit of attention. Her former boyfriend (well, all of them, there were several in the room) ignored her completely. For the first time in her life, she wasn't the object of anyone's lust, and I don't think she cared.

In fact, I don't think I'd ever seen her as downcast. Ian's death was an unexpectedly heavy blow for her.

I did not relish telling her the rest of what we knew for sure, never mind surmised, about the man she'd allowed into her heart, however briefly.

The rest of the bar was noisy and busy, if slightly subdued. Candle and kerosene flames were undeniably romantic, and they even gave off a little heat, but no amount of alcohol or soft lighting was going to make up for the fact that you needed a flashlight to find your way down the long hall to the bathroom.

Or that even a relatively tropical 40 or so degrees was still not exactly comfortable.

Most of the people in the bar looked as used and bedraggled as I felt. No one was very clean, no one looked rested, and no one was particularly happy about being served their drinks neat. Their New Year's finery was wilted and beginning to sag.

The fumes from the lanterns and candles intermixed with cigarette smoke, making the atmosphere even more fetid than usual. Without the help of ceiling and exhaust fans and the occasional circulation of frigid but fresh air to move things around, the interior smog drifted down and lay along the floor like mist.

There was singing and laughter. Patrons young and old lined up for their turn on stage so that they too could sing the wrong lyrics to country standards. They drank and they laughed, and they smoked a whole helluva lot. But the red and drippy noses were real and the chapped hands were sore, and the worry that lingered behind all of the eyes, that this wasn't just a temporary power outage, that we were going to have to live like this for a long time, never quite went away.

They laughed all right, but the hilarity was forced—as though no one would have been here if they'd had any better place to be.

The problem was, I had a better place to be.

Neil not only had a working fireplace, but he had a small generator, which meant that at least a few of his lights, if not major appliances, would be working.

At Neil's I could soak in a big deep tub and listen to James Taylor on a portable CD player.

At Neil's I could hunker down under a big blanket and get warm. Finally.

At Neil's, there would be . . . well . . . Neil . . . which was the best of all. The tension between us temporarily dissolved in our joint search for answers to the assorted mysteries we'd been handed.

I hoped that would last.

But it would be a while before I would get to find out, because instead of saying, "Let's chuck this shit and go home" (not that I really expected him to say such a thing), Neil answered my mostly rhetorical question thusly: "I think you should go and talk to Del and Gina, and maybe even Alanna. I'm going to see if I can track down Ian's landlord and ask a few questions."

"Alanna, I can see," I said slowly. "I'm curious to find out what she says about Ron and the wallet too. That is, if I can get her to say anything. We're not exactly friends, you know."

"Yeah, I know," Neil said, smiling.

"But can't talking to her wait until we're back at your house? She's coming with us." I said that sadly.

"But she won't talk freely in front of Del, and Del's coming too," Neil said, pushing his glasses up on his nose. "And Del won't talk in front of Alanna either. My house is not big enough for those two to get far enough apart to talk to them privately. And none of us will be able to get a word in edgewise with the kids around."

He pointed at the pool table where Presley, John, and Mardelle had been joined by a young and mostly drunk farmer who was insisting on upping the ante to five bucks a game.

Presley, who was both sober and a good pool player, laid a five-dollar bill on the table and the game began.

"Don't you think that Mardelle will *stay* home, and that John will *go* home?" I asked.

Mardelle lived in the apartment above the bar with her parents. And John's parents, while very busy not acknowledging each other, were both in the bar.

"I wouldn't count on it," Neil said. "Where would you rather be?"

He had a point.

In fact, I'd do pretty much anything if it would get me out of the bar and keep me from having to deal with the Adlers. Alone or together.

Unfortunately, that option wasn't available.

And the only way I was ever going to get away was by carrying out my part of the assignment.

Despite what Neil said about not being able to talk to Del privately, I knew that I could finagle a few moments with her later if necessary.

And whether Alanna wanted to talk with Del in close proximity or not, I was going to get some answers from her (if there were answers to be gotten) whether she liked it or not.

But the only opportunity I'd have to talk to Gina Adler, that is, in-person, real-time, not-on-the-telephone opportunity, was right now.

I doubted she'd talk to me though.

There was only one way to find out.

While Neil dialed his cell phone, I sighed and ferried our empty glasses up to the bar as an excuse to get close enough to Gina to try some noncommittal small talk, though the notion of making chit-chat with the woman who'd announced my deepest secret to the whole world just yesterday was more than a bit ridiculous.

As it was, I didn't have to worry about starting the conversation.

29

....

Joe Blow

You know what they say about the best laid plans of cold, dirty, and tired waitresses, never mind the mice, don't you?

It's not like I was looking forward to tackling Gina Adler. Asking her questions that I knew she wouldn't want to answer and making both of us uncomfortable at best (and downright angry at worst) wasn't exactly on my priority list at the moment.

Given her performance yesterday, I had as good a reason as anyone to want to keep Gina happy.

Or at least away from blunt instruments.

But as tired as I was, and as much as I wanted to go home and forget the whole mess, I knew that Neil's idea was sound.

However it had happened (and I'd be lying if I said I wasn't intensely curious as to exactly how it came about), Gina had known Ian better than anyone in Delphi, save Del. I'm not sure that even Del got to quite as many bases as Gina had in the storeroom of the bar last night.

But that was last night.

Today Ian is dead.

Today we know that he came to Delphi using a false name which we had to assume he adopted for nefarious purposes.

And today Gina was in the bar and this was my only chance to corner her for a heart-to-heart about our mutual deceased acquaintance.

Problem was, I had not a clue as to how to go about broaching such a touchy subject with a woman who was pretty damn touchy herself.

On the long walk up to the bar, I'd formulated a strategy that combined a heartfelt, and almost genuine, empathy combined with a little bit of passive/aggressive guilt (Gina couldn't very well refuse to talk to me if I was willing to talk to her, now could she?).

I scrapped that notion almost immediately in favor of a bold frontal attack. I'd just ask her flat out what the hell she was doing with Ian in the first place and see what she said.

Knowing immediately that I lacked the courage, I replaced that loony-tunes idea with the far more workable (albeit far less apt to succeed) program of standing next to her innocently and waiting for her to bring the subject up.

But like the many flowers that wither away unseen (or however the hell that poem goes), my varied plans died aborning because the minute I set our glasses on the bar, Joe Marlow ambled drunkenly away from his companions over to us.

He stood between Gina and me, slung his arms around us both, and said very carefully, in the way of the truly inebriated, "Well, well, well, I'd be willing to bet that you two have a lot to talk about, right?"

Neither of us answered him.

Gina looked at him with undisguised contempt,

though for just a second; before it was squashed, I could swear I saw a spark of panic in there.

I was too busy watching Gina to peek at Joe, though peeking wasn't exactly necessary because he'd moved in even closer and was now directly between us.

Joe was one of those grizzled farmers of whose weathered skin and thinning, graying hair gave no definitive clue as to his age. I thought he looked to be in his mid-fifties, which probably meant that he was younger than me.

He carried himself with all the dignity of a good ol' boy who realized that he'd had plenty to drink and no access to a toothbrush for the last couple of days, but who nevertheless had something of importance to discuss.

"I say," he said, doing an uncanny Foghorn Leghorn, "I say, you two must have a whole helluva lot to talk about."

"Not really," Gina said coldly before turning back to the mirror. She fidgeted nervously with her own hands. There was no doubt that she'd bear no real regret if both Joe Marlow and I suddenly disappeared from the face of the earth.

This wasn't exactly the opening I'd been looking for, but it was already obvious that my favored plan (the one where I stood by quietly and waited for Gina to speak first) was destined to failure. So I jumped in with a non-committal "What do you mean, Joe?"

"Well, ain't it obvious?" he asked loudly.

A whole lot more loudly than necessary. A few heads in the vicinity turned away from the stage to see what the commotion was.

"Not really," I said, still trying to figure out how to lead from Joe to Ian. That is if we could get rid of Joe.

Which didn't seem likely. His hands tightened around our shoulders, and I became painfully aware that he'd been away from deodorant for the duration too.

"Well, on the one hand," he said, patting me solidly on the top of the head, "we got the lil' lady who spent the night with a dead guy in the back of her old boy-friend's pickup box out in the snow."

That was not one of those facts of which I needed reminding.

Gina either, by the disgusted look on her face.

"And on the other hand," Joe continued, giving Gina a hearty squeeze, "we got us a little woman with a mean swing who was arguing her pretty little head off with the dead guy before he got so mysteriously dead."

Joe stepped back and held his hands out to both of us. "Seems like several ripe topics for conversation, don't you think?"

Joe had mentioned to me earlier that he'd seen Gina arguing with Ian last night, though I'd heard no confirmation of that from anyone else.

The last time I saw them together, they weren't exactly having a dispute.

I wondered if Joe's memory was as fuzzy as his breath, or if Gina's relationship with Ian had turned from romantic (if a quickie in a bar storeroom could be called a romance), to stormy in the space of a couple of hours.

Joe's insinuation made me wonder if their relationship had gotten to be more than stormy very quickly indeed.

Because that's certainly where he was leading.

I believe that he was implying that a woman who could demolish an inanimate object with a baseball bat might also be capable of personal violence if pushed hard enough.

It was an interesting notion, shot down immediately by the obvious frozen serenity of Ian's poor stiff corpse.

Whatever had happened to him, he had not been done in with the proverbial blunt object.

I don't know if Gina was following Joe's line of reasoning, but she was perfectly ready to squash his speculation.

"I don't know what you're talking about," she said. Her voice held a deathly calm and an icy assurance. "I didn't even know the man. Now I don't want to be rude, but I'd appreciate it if everyone would just go away and leave me alone."

She pinned Joe with a steely glare, daring him to contradict her.

"Hah," Joe said, triumphant. "You can pretend all you want, but you two was arguing in front of this bar last night, and nothing you say will change that."

Gina didn't even bother responding to him. She just waved Pat Jackson over.

Mr. Pat Jackson.

"Pat, will you kindly suggest to *this man*"—she said the words as though they were a substitute for something purely disgusting, like *snot ball*—"that I'd like some peace and quiet?"

She said it softly, but there was a strength and force behind her words that surprised me.

It must have surprised Pat and Joe too, because when Pat raised an eyebrow at Joe, he backed off, waving his hands.

"No offense, missus," he said, grinning. "Just passing the time of night with you, that's all."

He ambled back to his cronies, who'd all watched the preceding conversation with great interest.

Gina may have gotten rid of Joe, but the speculation would continue.

"You okay now?" Pat asked Gina quietly.

I caught Gina's eye in the mirror and looked at her steadily, wondering if she'd have Pat move me along too.

The defiance died in her eyes and she slumped at the bar. "Yeah, I'm fine. Thanks."

I sat on the bar stool beside Gina and looked down at my own hands, which were chapped, red, and cold.

She continued to rub her own hands, especially her left hand.

Especially the ringless third finger of her left hand.

"Wanna talk?" I asked softly, looking straight ahead.

"No," she said, sighing. "But I suppose you won't go away until I confess, right?"

"Confess?" I asked, surprised.

Maybe Gina was going to solve the entire mystery for me right here and now so that I could go home and still have time for a bath.

"Well, I don't suppose *confession* is the right word," she said. "But it won't do any good to deny that I knew him, will it?"

"No," I said, with a small shrug.

"I was hoping that the light was too low, or maybe you'd had too much to drink to recognize me," she said sadly. "You must think I've lost my mind completely."

She ran her fingers through her bedraggled hair.

There was really no resemblance between the Gina Adler I'd known most of my life and the tired and miserable woman who sat next to me on a bar stool in the cold candlelight.

She was younger than me, but I don't think anyone would have guessed it at the moment.

"And I suppose you hate me now," she said.

This time she looked me right in the eye.

I shrugged, not entirely sure how I felt about her.

"It would have come out eventually anyway," I said finally.

It was the truth. Delphi was also too small a town for secrets to stay secret.

"I could have used a little warning, but I suppose you had more on your mind than me," I said.

Gina laughed a bitter little laugh. "No shit. I thought that Ronnie had taken up with Delphine again. I mean, I'd lived with his *fascination* for our whole married life and I thought I'd made my peace with it. I loved him, he wanted her. Not an optimum situation, but livable. He was a good enough husband and a good enough father. We got by without the kind of trouble most couples have. I used to pride myself that at least my marriage wasn't as bad as yours."

She looked at me apologetically, and then down at her bare hand, hurt etched in every line of her face.

"And when it finally ended between them, I thought

that maybe my time had come. I deserved it. I'd paid my dues. It was my turn."

She leaned back on the stool a little bit, oblivious of everything that was going on around her.

The singers still sang off-key, and the DJ still DJ'ed, though I caught him watching us with a speculative glance once or twice—probably wondering what he was doing wrong that two sad-looking ladies could sit by themselves, immune to his charming patter.

Joe and his friends shot glances our way, and then hunched together like a flock of hens.

Gina closed her eyes and inhaled. "Things seemed to be going well. Then he was gone a whole night. I figured he was with *her* and that it was starting up all over again. I sat up all night waiting for him to sneak back in, but he didn't. Then I waited for him to come home for lunch, but he didn't.

"I waited and I waited, and finally I decided that twenty-five years was more than enough waiting for him to pay attention to me."

"Well, you got his attention," I said quietly. "I doubt he'll ignore you now."

That was an understatement. No one in Delphi would ever ignore Gina Adler again.

"Lotta good it did me," she said. "It was bad enough thinking he'd been with Del, but when you said she couldn't have been with Ronnie, I really snapped."

I thought about her fine distinction between snapping and *really* snapping, and decided I didn't need another demonstration.

"I didn't want to believe you and I didn't want to hear any more." Gina inhaled sharply. "So I shut you up."

That she had. And very well indeed.

"I'm sorry, you know," she said quietly. "I wish I hadn't said it. I wish I could take it back. I wish I could take back everything." She paused. "Everything."

"I know the feeling," I said, amazed that I was feeling sorry for her. "What's done is done," I said, knowing it was true.

It didn't matter how sorry we all were, the horse was out of the barn and the milk was spilled and the goose was cooked.

"We'll get over it. A new scandal will come along and everyone will forget about you and me," I said.

"Yeah, and the new scandal will be that when Ronnie finally got over Delphine, instead of coming back to me, he found another woman right away." She looked me right in the eye. "Did you know that he spent the night with Alanna?"

Despite the recent nastiness, Gina and I had formed a Cheated Spouse Bond, and in honor of that, she deserved honesty, however much it hurt.

"I don't know about last night. But I knew he was with her today," I said.

She snorted. "No not last night, I mean the night before. When I thought he was with Del, he'd really been with Alanna. When I found that out—"

"You mean they were *already* seeing each other?" I interrupted, surprised.

I'd noticed that Alanna had been paying attention to Ron, but it didn't seem to be any more than the attention she paid to any breathing male.

And Ron had certainly noticed Alanna, but I had dismissed that mostly as a male fascination with her bustline combined with a desire to make Del as jealous and miserable as possible.

It had never occurred to me that they were fooling around before I stumbled on them.

In fact I had assumed that their affair began specifically to assuage Ron's wounded pride after Gina's public display of ire.

"That little weasel," I said.

I was furious with Ron.

Actually, I was furious with Stu too, for being married, even though I had known it from the start.

I was furious with my charming but philandering late husband, who was, luckily for him, long dead.

I was instantly furious with all cheating men.

Which included Ian Douglas O'Hara.

Ian, who'd somehow gained Del's trust, only to betray her.

"So when Ian made a pass at you, you took him up on it," I said, finally understanding.

"I was tired of being a good girl," Gina said.

"And I interrupted you," I said.

"It's just as well, he wasn't a very nice guy anyway," Gina said, understating the obvious. "We smooched a bit and then I didn't see him again."

"At all?" I asked, contemplating Gina's definition of *smooching a bit.*

Joe Marlow had been pretty insistent about seeing them argue later.

Was he mistaken or was Gina lying now?

Had she been lying all along?

Honestly, I didn't know.

I did know that her bad girl act hadn't ended with Ian's death, since I'd also seen her smooching someone else at her own front door, just a few hours earlier.

And since I still didn't know who that mystery man was, or where he fit into this puzzle, I decided to tread softly.

"Nope," she said, swiveling herself around on the stool and standing up. "I made a stupid mistake, but I never saw the man alive again. Never."

Once she'd emphasized that point with another nod, she gathered up her change from the bar. It was plain that she wanted to get as far away from me as possible.

"You'll have to excuse me, Tory," she said without eye contact. "I need to visit the little girls' room. And I'm too tired to talk any more."

She hurried away before I had a chance to respond.

I sat on the stool watching her, knowing absolutely that she'd just lied to me.

But for the life of me, I couldn't figure out why.

30

....

Georgie Porgie

There is a body of anecdotal and documentary evidence
from the time when isolated communities were *really*
isolated, both by geography and culture, proving that the
proverbial handsome stranger was sometimes welcomed
into the village with open arms.

Literal open arms.

I suspect that even before the principles of heredity
were even formulated, much less understood, *Homo er-
ectus* knew instinctively that the gene pool would stag-
nate without an occasional out-of-town infusion.

Unfortunately for some of the wanderers, humans
were humans no matter what time or place. And given
that, I assume that not all of them made it successfully
out of Dodge after having spread cheer among the stag-
nated ladies.

After all, they'd done the ultimate favor for the village's succeeding generations, there was no reason why
they shouldn't also make the ultimate sacrifice.

Maybe there's a lingering genetic predisposition that renders visible and audible *otherness* completely irresistible to a certain percentage of females who still reside in isolated villages.

How else to explain the wide swath cut in just one night by one good-looking guy with an English accent.

Del, who never trusted anyone, had trusted Ian.

And Gina, whom I would have sworn was a one-man woman, had thrown over her vows with just a couple of sweet, if mostly unintelligible, words.

I had even found myself a tad intrigued by his Featherstonehaugh stories and his warm hands.

Was it just a matter of opposites attracting, or did the fact that he'd more than likely be gone in the morning (one way or another) tip the scale?

That was a question for the ages.

I was more intrigued by a question that could be answered right now, by one of the few village women who'd managed to resist sacrificing herself for the good of the communal gene pool.

"Weren't you even tempted?" I asked Pat Jackson as she set another glass in front of me on the bar.

I'd ordered a Diet Coke. My thinking was fuzzy enough without adding more undiluted vodka and Kahlua to the mix. I wanted to know why she had found Ian so eminently resistible, if that could be put into words. And I wanted to be able to remember her answer in the morning.

Pat shrugged.

"I've seen his type before," she said, adjusting the wick on the Coleman lantern that sat on the bar beside me. "You get guys like him in bars all the time—thinking they're God's gift to women. I outgrew that kind of nonsense a long time ago."

I was about to agree noncommittally when she continued.

"Besides, he talked funny."

Ah, xenophobia rears its ugly head.

Some village people are drawn by unfamiliarity.

Others want to stamp it out.

"He flashed money all over the place, big bills too. I saw a couple of hundreds. But he didn't tip worth a shit."

Finally we were down to the crux of the matter.

Neither Ian's ne'er-do-well ways, nor his foreignness had as much to do with Pat's enmity as the fact that he wasn't willing to share his wealth with her.

"I guess he thought asking about business was some kind of sweet talk," Pat said, shaking her head at the wonder of it all.

"He asked you a lot of questions? About the business?"

"He was trying to be sneaky like," Pat answered, "but I knew what he was doing. He was checking the place out."

"Did anything come up missing this morning?" I asked.

The bar was a thriving business, and Pat was notoriously tight. I always figured there was a safe somewhere on the premises stuffed full of cash.

"Nope," Pat said. "I made sure to tell Monty Python that we always let a Rottweiler loose to guard the bar at night." She grinned widely at her own ingenious falsehood. "It was amazing how fast he found someone else to schmooze."

"Anyone I know?"

Bar owners, like waitresses, have seen it all. Most of the time they remember it. And they're willing to talk.

"Yeah." Pat nodded in the general direction of the hallway at the end of the bar. "I saw him talking to Miss Baseball for a while. And he also spent a little time with your business partner."

"Alanna?" I asked, surprised. "What would he have to talk to her about?"

"Well, if your business is as poor as what you been saying, I doubt if they had anything at all to talk about," Pat said grimly. "But for what little time they talked, it looked like they was both enjoying themselves."

Someone down at the end of the bar called Pat. I sat on my stool, holding my hands near the lantern for warmth and thought about what she'd just said.

Ian had had money and wasn't afraid to spend it (I personally saw him pay for several rounds of drinks at the bar last night). And yet he'd left no tips for the barmaid, which was unusual. Money showoffs like to lord it up by spreading the largesse around to the little people.

They especially like to impress waitresses with big tips because they know our minimum-wage lives are so bleak and empty.

If sober guys act like that in cafes, it must be even worse in bars with the inebriated.

Could Ian have spent all of that cash he liked to flash early in the evening, before it was time to tally up with Pat?

Before he lost his wallet?

Or before his wallet was stolen?

Ron had made a specific point of mentioning that the wallet had been empty when he'd found it.

But he'd said nothing at all of Ian's *other* name, which he surely would have noticed if he'd actually looked inside the damn thing.

And when exactly did it come into his possession?

I hadn't been paying strict attention, but I would have sworn that he had not palmed a wallet while frisking Ian's corpse this morning.

The whole scenario gave me a headache. I had a feeling that I was overlooking something pretty obvious. Something I would probably have been able to see if my brain had been functioning properly.

Which, tired and cold as I was, seemed unlikely to happen any time soon.

"Here," Pat said, breaking in on my reverie. I must have been frowning because she added, "You look like you need it."

She sat another Black Russian down on the bar in front of me.

"But I didn't order this," I said, frowning some more.

"I know," Pat said, pointing toward the door. "They did."

Down at the end of the bar, Joe Marlow and his cohort smiled and waved me over.

"Oh," I said, hoping one or more of them wasn't gearing up to make a pass at me. Unfortunately, they looked to be a crowd who'd be willing to take a go at a cold, fat, unwashed waitress.

"Yeah," Pat said grinning evilly, following my train of thought. "You have fun now, ya hear."

She trundled off, and there was nothing left for me but to gather up my drink and go see what Joe wanted.

"Hey, fellas, thanks for the drink," I said, smoothing my hair back until I realized that might seem a tad coquettish. I sighed and stuck my hand firmly in my pocket. "Just what I need before slogging on home." I wanted to squash any notions that I'd be going anywhere with any of them.

"Our pleasure," Joe said expansively. Joe had evidently been elected spokesman for the group. The others nodded sagely in agreement but said nothing as he continued. "We just wanted to talk a minute before you went back to your fella over there."

"My fella?" I asked, confused. For a split second I thought he meant Stu. I even got so far as to wondering why I hadn't noticed him in the bar myself, before I realized who Joe was talking about. And for another split second, I basked in the glow of that particular notion. "Oh. Well, he's not my fella. We're just friends, but that's okay. I do need to get back pretty quick anyway."

"Whatever." Joe winked broadly. The guys behind him chuckled in agreement. "But no one who got as riled as he did this morning is anyone's *friend*." He emphasized the word. "Anyhoo, I just wanted to tell you that I wasn't lying about nothing. I did see young Missus arguing with the dead guy right outside the bar here. Right on that sidewalk." He pointed toward the door with his cigarette. "Last night before we lit out to save those asses from getting froze to death." He leaned over and said confidentially, "And it weren't no little argument neither. They was really fighting. Though he was so drunk he could hardly stand."

"I believe you," I said, to Joe.

I added that factoid to everything else that didn't add up so far.

It was a long list.

"And I think she was putting on for her husband," Joe said.

"But he was as drunk as Ian was last night," I said, remembering Ron in the bar. He had been so slurry that Neil had not wanted him to drive while rescuing his own son. "And he was doing his level best to ignore her completely."

That much I did remember. The Adlers had acted as though neither existed, frostily excluding each other from their respective universes.

"Not last night," Joe said gently. "I mean right now. She was putting on for him, not wanting him to know that she'd had anything to do with the dead fella."

"What do you mean?" I asked confused. "She wasn't talking to Ron, she was talking to us."

"Yeah, but he was hovering by, wandering back and forth almost natural like he wasn't listening in. But I could tell he heard every single word. At least everything that was said while I was there, while she was denyin' the hell outta knowing that guy. After that he sorta ranged in and out."

Some Miss Marple I was. I hadn't noticed Ron at all. I'd been too busy watching Gina watch herself in the mirror, and avoiding Joe's breath.

"What's he doing now?" I asked, not wanting to turn around, just in case Ron was orbiting like a lost moon, eavesdropping.

"Beats the hell outta me," Joe said, laughing. "Not too long after she got down from her high horse, he took off like a bat."

"Took off?"

"Left. Vamoosed. Exited stage left," Joe said, doing one of those *away she goes* moves made famous by both Jackie Gleason and Snagglepuss.

"Left?"

I had no idea what Joe was talking about.

"Left the building. He rushed outta here so fast, I thought his pants was on fire."

31

....

Phone Tag

Personally, I vote for the cell phone as the world's most irritating necessity, even though I may be the only person in North America without one.

The much-touted, life-saving possibilities of cell phone ownership pale in comparison to the annoyance caused by idiots who conduct business meetings three rows behind you at a movie theater.

Or the danger you court every time you try to pass fools who actually think they can drive and talk at the same time.

Sure, a cell phone probably saved Presley, John, and Mardelle's lives as they were stuck in the blizzard in the middle of the night since the rescuers would not have known where to find them otherwise.

But if the kids had applied a little common sense, they could have avoided the situation altogether by staying home.

And there are definitely times when a functioning cell

phone is downright inconvenient, when it interferes with the comfort of a well-ordered life.

And I'm not just talking about supper being interrupted by dipshits who try to sell you magazine subscriptions.

Neil had left his phone home last night, and look where that had gotten me.

And if he'd done it again tonight, or if he'd conveniently let the battery run down, we could have been back at his relatively warm house, sitting in comfortable chairs, maybe even figuring out what was going to happen next in our relationship in between placing calls on an ordinary wall phone.

Unfortunately, Neil had learned his lesson. And he was far too efficient to allow his batteries to run down. Besides which, he was way too rich to use substandard products, which meant that his equipment (so to speak) was in good working order. And since I reluctantly agreed that keeping an eye on the assembled motley crew was a good idea—especially considering Joe Marlow and Pat Jackson's new additions to the canon—we were still stuck in a smoky, cold, dark bar as the wind howled outside, while inside, the red-nosed merrymakers became progressively drunk.

I'd returned to our original table brimming with news and speculation to share, but Neil, with a phone to his ear, had smiled and held up his hand as he listened intently.

He had to shout to make himself heard, and listening to the replies was made more difficult by an ill-advised attempt by several young men to sing an a cappella version of *Bohemian Rhapsody*.

A loud a cappella version, roundly cheered by everyone in the bar old enough to remember Queen or young enough to appreciate Garth and Wayne.

Well, almost everyone.

I tried to listen in on Neil's end of the conversation, but gave it up as hopeless.

And Del sat there, staring into her warm beer.

It was as good an opportunity to talk to her as any, given that Alanna was across the room and Neil was still blocking outside noise so that he could hear.

"Are you going to be okay?" I asked her softly. It was a stupid question, one she probably couldn't answer honestly.

Instead of answering me, she looked at the jolly singers and just shook her head.

I'd kept an eye on her while I was up at the bar. I assumed she'd noticed Ron and Alanna's deliberate and obvious avoidance of each other. Of course, Del was likely way ahead of me on the Adler-Luna curve, having known out there in the street yesterday that if she hadn't been with Ron all night, then *someone* surely had.

And there were only so many *someones* in Delphi.

"Things change," Del said simply.

I'd never heard her so down. So sad.

"That they do," I said. I'd discovered that painful little truth a while back.

"And they don't ever change back, do they?"

It was a mostly rhetorical question asked with a small, cynical smile.

I took a sip of my iceless drink before answering. "Nope."

"That's what I thought," she said, still watching Alanna who watched the door, waiting, presumably, for Ron to reappear.

Del's face was sad but calm.

"You know what they say about one door closing and all that . . ." I let my voice trail off.

"Well, this door isn't closed completely yet," Del said, draining her glass.

She wasn't in the mood to be cheered up, and truly, I wasn't in the mood to do any cheering.

It had been a miserable twenty-four hours, which had been preceded by a mostly miserable year. I knew better than to make wild assumptions, but I had to hope the new year would be easier, if not better, than last year. For all of us.

We listened to the bad music for a while. Neil continued to talk. He looked excited. We sat quietly through a few more ditties, thinking our own morose thoughts.

"Ian may have taken the cafe money, you know," Del finally said, out of nowhere.

Well, maybe not out of nowhere—I assume she'd been dwelling on Ian, and nothing else, all day.

"I thought you thought that Alanna did it," I said, watching Alanna myself, not sure whether I believed that she was actually capable of robbing her own business.

Del shrugged. "She could have. I wouldn't put it past her. But at the trailer last night, Ian asked a lot of questions about the cafe. I didn't think about it much at the time, but he was really curious about everything. Especially where we kept the money. I told him everything. Something about that voice was hypnotic. Like I had no choice but to answer."

"It was the accent," I said. "That John Cleese meets *Masterpiece Theater* stuff—us hick Americans were putty in his hands. But he couldn't have taken the money. He was already long dead by the time it was gone."

I told her what Neil and I knew, and surmised, about Ian.

She sighed, not nearly as surprised as I'd expected her to be.

"He made a couple of phone calls from the trailer while I was in the bathroom. He tried to be quiet, but I heard him talking. And I think he got beeped once or twice too. But that's not all. Did you realize that he insisted on washing dishes last night before leaving the trailer?"

"You're kidding."

I'd overlook philandering and aliases and mysterious phone calls for a guy who voluntarily did dishes.

"He absolutely insisted on drying," Del said. "He made me wash."

I couldn't find any particular significance in that, so I waited for her to continue.

"He dried the glasses thoroughly. Very thoroughly."

"I'm not following you," I said.

"He polished each and every piece perfectly, and then held it up to the light before putting it back in the cupboard." She mimed the action in the candlelight, turning an imaginary glass around and around in her hand. "It wasn't until just now that I realized that he didn't touch the glasses with his bare hands while he was drying them. He wrapped the towel around his hand first. And when we were done, he wiped down the cupboard, and the sink, and the faucets." She gave a small, humorless chuckle. "I thought he was just being thorough."

"He wiped *everything* down?" I asked. Something niggled at the back of my brain.

"Yeah, shined it up, clean as a whistle," Del said. She looked at me significantly, waiting for me to catch on.

Which I did. Finally.

I inhaled sharply.

"He was wiping his fingerprints off, wasn't he?"

Last night, he'd poured brandy into my cup, then carefully taken the dishtowel and wiped off the dusty bottle before replacing it in the cupboard.

I'd thought he was just being overly neat when what he really had been doing was removing all traces of himself.

I sat, openmouthed.

And then I remembered a salient fact.

"But he was dead before the cafe money disappeared," I said. "And probably before the library was robbed."

We still didn't have a timeline for that break-in, if walking in through an unlocked front door can be called a break-in. It could have happened any time during the evening or night.

"He had an accomplice," Del said simply. "Those phone calls were to someone, you know." She stared hard at the DJ, who was just getting ready to take a break. "Ian wasn't the only one here from Sioux Falls yesterday."

I looked at the DJ too.

The DJ who'd been arrested for burglary and who just happened to be free to come to Delphi on New Year's Eve.

It was all interesting. Very interesting.

Maybe sitting in the cold, dank bar for a while longer wasn't such a bad idea after all.

32

....

Capital T That Rhymes with P

I suppose the world would be a far easier place in which to survive if we reproduced asexually.

I doubt amoebas experience anywhere near our agony and heartbreak, not to mention the pure complications that ensue when we attempt the mating dance.

I mean, would any part of this entire situation have happened if not for sex?

Well, we'd still be cut off from civilization, stuck in a pure white winter world with no power.

But outside of those immutable facts, every other occurrence of significance in the last two days revolved directly around the horizontal polka.

Del would not have been pining after a mysterious pen pal had she not finally discovered that she could not have what she wanted most.

Ron Adler would not have taken up with Alanna had he not discovered, to everyone's sorrow, that familiarity truly did breed contempt. And that getting what you want is not exactly the same as wanting what you get.

If not for that discovery, Gina Adler may well have left the baseball bat in the closet where it belonged. And there's no doubt that she would not have attempted that little encounter in the storeroom, not to mention the front-door smoochies I'd seen.

And of course, if I'd been a bit better at reining in my own errant desires, she'd have had no weapon with which to whomp my life to bits.

If Presley and Mardelle, not to mention John Adler, had not been drawn in by the twin demons of hormones and alcohol, they would not have gotten stuck in the snow, and Neil would have been waiting to take me home from the cafe at closing time.

In which case, I would have been far away from Stuart McKee, and even farther from Ian Douglas O'Hara's frozen corpse when it was finally uncovered.

But I didn't make the rules.

And, truth be known, I'd not have it otherwise, even with all the complications.

Complications that were still unfolding as we sat.

Neil finally flipped his phone shut and tucked it in his pocket and smiled.

"Now *that* was an interesting call," he said, the candlelight reflecting in his glasses.

"Which one?" I asked. He'd made at least three while I'd talked to Del, and who knows how many while I was up at the bar with Gina.

"All of 'em, actually," Neil said, waving Pat over for another round. "I think we're on the brink of a breakthrough."

Del didn't lean forward, and she didn't ask questions, but she was listening to every word Neil said, which was a major change from her usual dismissive stance whenever we thought we'd uncovered a mystery.

"Well, first of all, there've been a rash of small home and business burglaries in North Sioux City and neighboring environs," Neil said. I knew he was just getting warmed up, that there was juicier stuff to follow.

"Anything major taken?" I asked. At least from our sampling, the losses were small enough not to be noticed immediately. They were not the kind of crimes that got much coverage even on the local news.

"Nope, nothing worth more than a few hundred tops. And the cash was all small bills, twenties or less," Neil said, ticking off on his fingers. "A little jewelry here, a small valuable there. Whoever was doing it concentrated mostly on piddly stuff, minor break-ins. No vandalism, no damage, no big insurance losses to deal with. No one was ever hurt, or even frightened. It's like a band of really polite robbers would move into a town for a day or so, take a few things, and then disappear again without a trace."

"Gee, sorta sounds familiar," I said. "Anything tying the DJ in directly to any of the break-ins? Or to Ian, for that matter? Or to anything that happened here?"

"Just the stuff we talked about already—small losses, bits and pieces gone. No one has any descriptions of anyone, except in the case where Wayne DePaul was specifically charged. And there he was stupid enough to get caught in the act."

"Wish we'd have been so lucky," I said, thinking that the 2K loss at the cafe was the only one large enough to draw real attention. It didn't seem to fit in with any of the other robberies.

Over in the corner, Presley evidently won another pool game. The young guy he'd been playing against angrily threw a five down on the table and stomped off.

Pres picked up the five and a couple more that had been left on the bumper, and kissed them soundly. He made a great show of tucking them into his shirt pocket, to the vast amusement and approval of Mardelle Jackson. John watched solemnly, blinking just like his father as he leaned against his cue. He shot a glance toward us and then turned away quickly, as if embarrassed to have been caught looking.

The kid had been acting strangely all evening. Usually

he was as loud and obnoxious as Pres, but I had not seen him smile all day.

Which I guess was understandable—there is no good age for one's parents' marriage to disintegrate in public. And thirteen is probably a spectacularly bad age for that sort of upheaval, considering that he was probably going through an upheaval or two of his own.

I wondered if his parents, wrapped up as they were in their own problems, even realized how miserable their son was.

But Ron was still among the missing, and Gina was taking an especially long time in the bathroom. Both seem to have abdicated parental duties to Del and me.

Unfortunately for John, I wasn't equipped to take on another lost adolescent, and Del had her hands full with her own kid, who whipped out one of his newly garnered fives and handed it to Pat Jackson as she tried to slide past him with a tray full of drinks.

Pat took the money, but she shook her head *no* as she tucked the bill into her apron.

I suppose he'd been trying to buy beer, a ploy that might actually have worked if we hadn't been here too.

"You'd better watch that kid," Pat said, almost laughing. She set a pitcher of beer on the table and clean glasses for Neil and Del. She sat another Black Russian down in front of me. I had lost track of how many drinks I'd had, which was not a good sign.

"He's got way too much charm," she said, making change for me, "and a shitload more money than any kid his age needs. You guys are paying him way too well to shovel."

"Huh?" None of us had paid him to do anything. "I figured *you* must have paid him," I said to Pat.

I'd seen him fooling around with Mardelle in front of the bar earlier. They'd supposedly been shoveling, though I caught the subtle signals of a pubescent mating dance in the making. Money alone would not have tempted him to commit acts of manual labor.

"Me?" Pat snorted. "I don't pay no one to do nothing."

Which was an understatement.

"He said earlier that the stripper over there"—Pat pointed over her shoulder at Alanna, who was talking to Brian and Rhonda and the DJ, by the stage—"was paying him for errands and shoveling and stuff."

Pat had mentioned that earlier.

It hadn't made sense then, and it didn't now.

Alanna never paid males to do anything. She just batted her eyelids and they begged to serve her every whim.

All of my present and future ready cash had disappeared in the Great New Year's Cafe Robbery.

"Not us," I said firmly. "Maybe Ron paid them to shovel his place."

I'd seen John shoveling too, in front of his dad's garage, though he'd obviously not been having nearly as good a time in the snow as Pres and Mardelle.

"Could be." Pat shrugged. "Either way, they shouldn't be flashing so much cash around. Never know what's going to happen around here. Strange doings going on, you know."

We knew.

I told her to keep the change and she almost smiled.

"What do you make of that?" I asked Del and Neil after Pat left the table.

"Nothing to make of it," Del said, sharply. "The kid works small jobs all the time. For us, for Rhonda. Probably for Steel Magnolia too. He always has money."

"Why, what do you think?" Neil asked, peering at me intently.

"Nothing, I guess," I said, dismissing some sudden unwelcome, and certainly unpleasant, thoughts that had just surfaced in my eminently suspicious mind. "Nothing at all."

I shook my head and took a sip of my warm drink and sat up straight. "So what else did you learn?" I asked Neil brightly, changing the subject.

His eyes narrowed at me suspiciously for just a moment, and then he smiled too.

"Well, I talked to Oscar Z. Diggs's landlord, for one. And I learned a couple of things that are pretty damn interesting."

He sat back and waited for the response, so I tried not to disappoint him.

But Del was no longer listening to us. She was too busy watching Presley and John.

33

....

Me Gotta Go

Rock and roll as an industry has had more than its share of tempests in teapots, which is not surprising really, considering that one of its raisons d'être is to shock the shit out of the grown-ups.

That was a goal back in the fifties when Elvis and Chuck Berry ruled the roost and the one-eyed jack was peeping in the seafood store.

It was the goal in the sixties when *doing it in the road,* and *making it with you* meant exactly what the oldsters were afraid it meant.

It was the goal in the seventies when Lady Marmalade urged everyone to getcha getcha ya-ya here, and Lindsey Buckingham co-opted the USC Trojan marching band to honor his morning boner.

The eighties, well, eighties music might have been more about cocaine than sex, but drugs are also efficient disturbers of the adult equilibrium, especially if the adults in question have conveniently forgotten their own participation in upsetting assorted apple carts.

And the nineties—*whoo doggie*, any decade that produces both Mariah Carey and Marilyn Manson has already earned its own private circle in hell.

Which is exactly how it ought to be.

Kids are supposed to be shocking.

Grown-ups are supposed to be shocked.

That's why it's especially fun once in a while to knock the socks off the youngsters with ancient music whose lyrics they'd never quite grasped until that very moment, in a cold dark bar, played on a portable boom box.

While I'd been ready to brand our newest suspect a cohort, a felon, and a robber, I hadn't quite pegged him as being a musical subversive.

Wayne DePaul, who would always be the DJ to me, had already thanked us very much several times, said that we were a great crowd, and that he'd be back shortly with even more fun and games before plugging in a tape to tide the music-deprived over during his break.

For two nights running, he'd enthusiastically played the standard mix of country and pop standards for anyone who worked up the courage to belt an off-key ditty in front of the hometown crowd (with or without microphones).

But tonight, given the opportunity to play anything in the world he wanted, he'd plugged in the Broadway cast recording of *Hair,* which has just as much power to offend now as it did in 1969.

Not that Presley, who had been halfheartedly playing a solo game of lantern-light eightball, had ever really listened to the lyrics, even though I'd played my own copy at home enough times for him to recognize the tunes.

For some reason, the words sank in this time.

Maybe he'd lately learned the definition of *cunnilingus.*

Whatever the reason for his newfound understanding, he shot a protective look at his mother, who wasn't listening to the music anyway (and who had discovered the definition of that particular word, and most of the others on the album, when she was not a whole lot older than Pres anyway), and an annoyed look at me, as though it was somehow all my fault.

Hey, I mimed back. *Don't blame me, I didn't write the stuff.*

He set his pool cue down and wandered over to our table, rubbing his cold hands together.

I could tell that he had not completely forgiven me. I'd let him down by being a shade more human than comfortable.

But I could tell also that he wasn't going to hold his grudge forever. There were already cracks in his disapproving demeanor.

And since I'd made an exception in my standard All Thirteen-Year-Olds Are the Spawn of the Devil and Should Be Killed Immediately policy, I was glad to know that his frostiness wouldn't last.

"And you guys complain about my music," he said, flopping down on a chair he'd pulled up between Del and me.

"That's nothing," I said, grinning. "If you want to hear a really dirty song, go listen to 'Louie Louie.' That one's so nasty they convened a Senate hearing just to figure out what to do about it."

"No kidding?" he asked, trying not to look intrigued. "I thought it was just nonsense words."

"Cross my heart," I said solemnly. "Right, Neil?"

Neil was bursting with news of his own, which would have to wait until Presley left the table. In the meantime, he decided to play along. "Tory wouldn't kid you about something that important," he said.

Or maybe he decided to use the opportunity to fish for information too.

"Must be a booming business shoveling these days," Neil said offhandedly.

Neil had also heard two and two and added it up to

a whole lot of cash for a couple of boys who were usually flat broke, no matter what Del said.

Presley grinned.

"Yup," he said, not looking a bit guilty. "We got us a gig that'll keep us in the ready money for a while." He rubbed his fingers together avidly. "Not only is Brian's mom paying us to keep her sidewalks clean, but John's dad gave him a whole lot in advance for us to keep the driveway shoveled at the garage too. Sort of a retainer, like."

Del frowned at us over Presley's head as he talked. She'd understood exactly what Neil was driving at and she wasn't pleased.

Pres leaned in confidentially and said, "A *big* retainer. I'm not supposed to tell anyone, but he gave us a whole hundred dollars. A hundred-dollar bill!"

He sat back and crossed his arms, satisfied with himself and his entire world. A world in which one hundred dollars split two (or was it three?) ways was an incredible fortune.

I didn't actually think that the boys had stolen any money, and they certainly could not have taken the cafe money anyway—but they *had* been flashing bills willy nilly in the bar.

Flashing them often, and obnoxiously enough for Pat Jackson to take note.

Flashing them often enough for me to notice, and for Del to become defensive.

Problem was, I still didn't believe that Alanna was actually going to pay them to do anything.

I suspected that she was running her own little scam on the boys.

And if that was the case, she'd have both Del and me to deal with.

Not to mention Gina Adler, if she ever got her head out of her own problems to notice exactly how miserable her son was.

And I definitely wondered what the hell Ron Adler was doing handing out large bills to young boys for work that had yet to be completed. He had a longstanding policy of not paying kids to work for him. As his son, John was expected to contribute labor to the family business.

I wondered why the turnabout. And why having so much unexpected cash hadn't tickled John the way it had Presley.

Instead of spending money and basking in the glow, John sat listlessly in a chair pulled up to the pool table, idly batting the balls with his hand, rebounding them off the cushions.

There were no more dollars on the table and evidently no one wanted to challenge John or take possession of the game.

Most of the older guys were clustered around the bar buying each other drinks and warming their hands over candles, or ogling Alanna, who always blossomed under male attention, though she still kept an eagle eye on the door. Rhonda and Brian stood talking and laughing with the DJ, who didn't look felonious in the least.

Though neither had Ian, so that shot my observational powers right out of the water.

Mardelle stood up at the bar, talking to her parents.

"I'll bet John's mom is happy that he'll be working for his dad," Neil said carefully. "I'm sure she was really worried about him last night."

It was a terrible segue, but Neil wasn't experienced in conducting a smooth undercover interrogation.

Presley shrugged carefully. "I don't think John's talked to his mom today much. Outside of her telling him to stay with us, that is."

Pres shot a worried look at his friend, and then scanned the rest of the bar.

"I can't imagine she was thrilled when you guys decided to leave town last night," Neil said, still prodding. "She had to have been a little annoyed when you took off early."

I didn't know where Neil was leading, so I sat back and listened.

"We *didn't* leave early," Pres said, shooting a side-ways look at his own mother. "It was after midnight when we took off. Mardelle knew where there was a party, and when we realized that we had enough money to . . ."

His voice trailed off. I think he'd just decided that discretion was the better part of valor.

Or at least survival.

Pres looked around the bar. "Where *is* John's mom anyway?" he asked innocently.

I'd wondered that myself, though I was far more in-terested to hear exactly how the boys had come across enough money after midnight that they could suddenly consider attending a pay-your-own-way kegger.

It didn't seem likely that an inebriated Ron had cor-nered them late last night and secured their future shov-eling services.

And Alanna had been far too busy to care about charming adolescents into free work.

Pres must have finally noticed that he had Neil's and my, and more importantly his mother's, undivided at-tention.

"I haven't seen her for a while," Pres said quickly. "John's mom, I mean." He stood up, obviously intending a hasty retreat, having already said far more than he should have to any set of adults, not to mention the functioning and biological parental units. "I'd better go. If you do see her, tell her that John wants to talk."

He smiled and said something noncommittal about catching us back at the library and was gone before any of us could say anything else.

Or perhaps more importantly, before he could say anything else to us.

"Gina disappeared down the hall toward the bathroom a while back," Del said quietly. "I saw her take the flash-light and go in that direction. And she hasn't come back out."

I frowned. It'd been at least a half-hour since she'd flounced off her bar stool. That was a long time to spend

in a pitch black, unheated bathroom, even with a Mag-
Lite to show you the way to the toilet paper.

"You think someone should check on her?" I asked,
scanning the room for obviously missing males.

Maybe Gina was making a habit of storeroom trysts.

"I have to pee anyway," Del said, standing up. She
was suddenly in a hurry to leave the table. Maybe she
was beating a hasty retreat too. "I'll check the can while
I'm there." She turned to me. "You still got your flashlight?"

I nodded and fished in my coat pocket for it and was
surprised to find a folded piece of paper down at the
very bottom.

I handed Del the flashlight, and then stared at the paper for a minute before remembering what it was.

34

....

Digging Up Dirt

These days, forensics is an exact and precise science.

Investigations are conducted by specially trained technicians and specialists. Evidence is gathered, sometimes in portions too small to be seen by the naked eye, and examined microscopically using every tool at mankind's disposal.

Crime scenes are dissected and inspected and protected against contamination so that the whole process can be repeated if necessary at a later date.

The results are tabulated and correlated and compared and analyzed by experts who routinely employ computers more powerful than what NASA used to send men to the moon.

And by these methods, crimes are solved, bad guys are apprehended, and justice is made to prevail.

But in order to use the equipment and the expertise, you must have access to same.

In the ordinary course of events, we might have actually been granted the use of such investigatory marvels.

Or at least we might have been able to stand by and watch as our home-grown experts bottled and bagged specimens and sent them off to laboratories better equipped than our own, for examination.

But at the moment, we were in a meteorological lockdown.

Examiners and detectives could not get in.

And innocent and guilty alike were held in close quarters, firmly imprisoned by a vast and impenetrable wall of white.

No one could get in or out of town, not even the dead guy, whose untimely accidental death, and coincidental stranding in the garage out behind the cafe, allowed us to realize, without the benefit of modern technology, that he had been inextricably involved in the crimes that had taken place over the last day.

Whether he'd worked alone or not remained to be seen.

But what we'd uncovered, we'd uncovered the old-fashioned way.

We'd been lucky.

And we'd asked questions.

Well, Neil had asked questions. I had just eavesdropped and accidentally bumped into people, and had the obvious pointed out to me on several occasions.

I watched Del stop by the pool table and pull Presley aside for a brief but private talk before shining the flashlight beam down the hallway and disappearing into the bathroom.

"What do you make of that?" I asked Neil.

"I don't know," he said, frowning. "Something's up, that's for sure."

"Yeah. One or both of them is lying you know. Unless Ron had a stroke, you know he wouldn't hand out money to kids, especially in advance. And Alanna didn't mention putting anyone on the payroll."

"Which one is the culprit you think?" Neil asked,

pushing his glasses up on his nose and leaning his elbows on the table. "Presley didn't look like he was lying. Or at least the only thing that made him uncomfortable was letting his mother know that he'd left town last night."

"Which she knew already," I said. "And therefore had no business being surprised about. However, looking innocent is a Bauer specialty—he was born with the ability. I've never caught him in big lies, but that just means he's good at it. I have no doubt that he's capable."

"But is he capable of stealing?" Neil asked.

That was the hard question, the one I'd been wondering myself.

"Those two are swimming in cash. They got it somewhere."

John banked the eight ball, which went in the corner pocket. Followed immediately by the cue ball. Even in the lantern light he looked dejected as he handed over another bill to a crowing Presley.

"And Pres says that Ron gave them the money," Neil said. "As much as it pains me to admit that a close personal acquaintance is indulging in untruths, it's obvious that one of them is."

"And as reluctant as I am to admit it, I can't think of a single reason for Ron to give them money. I've seen their shoveling. The two of them aren't worth fifty cents, much less fifty dollars," I said. "Especially paid in advance."

"I wonder if Gina could shed any light on the situation," Neil said, eyeing the empty hallway. Neither Del nor Gina had emerged from the dark.

"I kinda doubt it. I don't think she's spoken to Ron since yesterday afternoon out in the street. I'd assumed that they were together this afternoon, but it turns out I was wrong about that," I said, still amazed at the individual Adler infidelities. "And even if they did talk, I think they'd have more important things to worry about than sidewalk shoveling."

"No shit," Neil said softly. "What a mess."

"It's worse than that," I said. I filled Neil in on my conversations, both with Gina and with Joe Marlow.

Then we discussed Del and her odd behavior.

Which brought us back to Ian, of course.

"At least there are some things we do know about our English interloper," Neil said, smiling. "Thanks to this"—he waved Ian's wallet. "And this"—he pointed to the phone in his shirt pocket.

"So tell," I commanded.

"What do you want to know first?" he teased. "That Oscar Z. Diggs's landlord confirms that a guy who talked funny for Nebraska and who looked a whole lot like Ian did indeed rent an apartment from him for the last four months?"

"That'll do for a start. Continue."

"Maybe you'd like to know that the tenant of that particular apartment disappeared suddenly a day or so ago. Moved out lock, stock, and barrel."

"Good, good," I said.

"It may interest you also to know that said tenant left with a portion of his rent in arrears, while at the same time managing to leave behind a goodly assortment of empty bottles that formerly contained several kinds of alcoholic beverages."

"Considering the number of wine bottles he and Del emptied at the trailer last night, I'm not surprised. Tell me, was the apartment eerily clean and the empties wiped down?"

"How did you know that?" Neil stopped and eyed me curiously.

"I'll tell you in a minute, just continue," I said, smiling.

"Well, Miss Smarty, I'll bet you don't know that the man who came to dinner wasn't exactly living alone at his apartment."

"That's Mrs. Smarty to you," I said before Neil's last declaration sank in. Then I sat for a minute just looking at him while he grinned. "He had a roommate?"

"Yup."

"Don't tell me," I said. "Okay, tell me. It was the DJ, right?"

That would solve all our problems in one fell swoop—we'd understand the mystery of Ian's appearance, place our errant music monger under a citizen's arrest, and then sit back and wait for the snowplows to come.

"Of course not," Neil said, laughing. "What do you think this is, TV? Endings around here are never that neat and tidy."

"Well, who then?"

"I don't know for sure," Neil said. "The landlord didn't talk to her very much and her name wasn't on the lease agreement."

He sat back and waited again.

He didn't have to wait long this time.

"Her? That son of a bitch was married? I knew that he was sneaking around. There was no other reason in the world for him to be using a Sioux Falls address drop if everything was on the up and up in Nebraska."

"Not to mention using aliases," Neil said. "Though there's something about that Oscar Z name that bothers me too. Something about it doesn't ring true."

"Well, lots of names are odd," I said, thinking of a few right here in Delphi. "And if my name was Oscar, and I was hoping to impress honeys to whom I wasn't married, I'd change my moniker too."

"Especially if he wanted to keep Mrs. Diggs from finding out."

"Mrs.?" I asked, my voice rising. "You know for sure they were married?"

"Well, the landlord assumed they were married. They moved in together and they lived together in the apartment."

"Which you don't need to be married to do," I said. "But married or not, he was with someone female, and writing to Del at the same time."

Not to mention seeing Del and simultaneously making an incomplete pass at Pat Jackson, and finding rather more success with Gina.

"We got a name for this mystery woman?" I asked.

"Not really. The landlord never really talked to her. Said she was the quiet type. But he thought her name was Emily or Emma or something like that."

"Emily Diggs, huh?" I tried the name out, but didn't like it much. "Emily O'Hara sounds much better."

"Maybe old Oscar thought so too," Neil said, laughing.

It was the first time he'd looked genuinely happy since last night in the snow outside the cafe.

His warm brown eyes sparkled behind his glasses. Our knees touched under the table and I didn't move away.

And neither did he.

My hand itched to reach out and touch his face, but I held back, strangely reluctant to break the spell.

This moment was so calm, so peaceful.

So filled with promise that I hated to take a chance by saying or doing the wrong thing.

For just a moment, I forgot the cold and the snow and the dark, smelly bar, and the assorted complications of everyone around us, alive and dead.

I wanted to bask forever in the candlelight and the warmth of Neil's smile.

Which is why no one should be surprised that his phone chose that exact moment to ring.

35

·······························

Cleaning Out the Garage

If this was a made-for-TV movie, our intrepid sleuth would be happily on the way to solving the assorted mysteries in assorted clever ways by now, and the rest of us would just be waiting for a commercial so we could go to the bathroom and replenish the ice in our drinks, satisfied that we could all do a better job of investigating given the opportunity.

No fictional mystery would ever get away with dragging the suspense out so painfully. No literary detective would be forgiven for taking so damn long to see that we got trouble in River City. No author would be allowed to bore readers to tears with page after page describing blizzards and overshoes, when sunny climes and bikinis are so much more entertaining.

High-concept stories don't bother their little best-selling heads with the small details, the everyday stuff.

Americans want a big bang for their buck.

They want life and death.

They want car chases and skinny chicks in low-cut dresses.

That's why most Americans don't live in South Dakota.

At least in the winter.

Those of us who do live here are usually willing to settle for such excitement as we get, often wishing that things were even more boring than they really are.

Personally, I'd have been delighted for this New Year's Day to have been like all of my forty-plus New Year's Days—long, cold and uneventful.

But I was shit outta luck.

At least on the *uneventful* part.

And my day was getting less uneventful by the minute.

"Yeah?" Neil said into his phone.

I think he was too tired for normal phone etiquette.

Or maybe he was annoyed by the interruption too.

He rolled his eyes.

Then he listened intently, and then sat up straight.

"How much?"

He listened some more.

"When do you think?"

Another pause.

"Any sign of forced entry?"

I didn't know who he was talking to, but I assumed we had another burglary on our hands.

I shot a look at the DJ, who was still laughing with Rhonda and Brian up at the bar. Even Pat Jackson was smiling.

Evidently he was a good tipper, and probably he believed in large mythical guard dogs, which was all that mattered in Pat's universe.

So far, we didn't have a single lead on Wayne De-Paul's whereabouts last night. After the bar closed, he could have been anywhere in Delphi, doing anything.

Including robbing various establishments owned and operated by Delphi citizens while they participated in blizzard rescues.

Or were in dire need of rescuing themselves.

In fact, the theft from the cafe could not have taken place any earlier than two A.M., since that's when I left the building with Stu.

Of course, the suspect list need not have been comprised only of out-of-towners, but it was so much easier to accuse (and to blame) those we did not know.

Maybe I had a touch of xenophobia myself.

"There's not much point in that," Neil said into the phone. He raised an eyebrow at me. "Why don't you just lock up and come back here? But first you should call it in. I expect the plows will make it through tomorrow sometime, and I imagine the County Mounties will be right on their tail." He listened for another moment. "Well, if you really feel that way, then we'll see you tomorrow." Pause . . . "Yeah, sure we'll tell her."

He flipped his phone closed and shook his head.

"Ron?" I asked.

There really wasn't anyone else who would have called Neil with the news of a robbery. He must have overheard me talking with Pat Jackson about our suspicions and rushed out to check the garage.

Neil nodded. "He discovered about two hundred in loose change and cash missing from the lock box he keeps in the bottom drawer of his desk."

"The lock box he never locks?" I asked. It was common Delphi knowledge that Ron took cash for changing tires and small tow calls and kept the proceeds in his desk, away from the ledger books and theoretically away from the IRS.

"The one and the same," Neil said, sighing. "He's pretty upset. So upset that he's going to sit at the garage all night with a flashlight and a shotgun in order to catch the perp."

"But the perp already got away with the loot, why would he come back?" I asked.

"Ron says they only took about half the cash. He figures they'll come back for the rest. Personally, I doubt that gentleman burglars make repeat appearances, but it'll make Ron feel good to sit there. I just hope no one surprises him at the garage with a legit visit tonight. They might get a twelve-gauge surprise of their own."

"Sheesh," I said. And I meant it too.

"And that's not all, we're supposed to relay the information to Alanna as soon as possible." Neil sighed.

I sighed.

"What's up?" Del asked, back from the bathroom. She set my flashlight on the table. "You two look like you just got an unexpected arithmetic assignment."

Which is pretty much what it felt like—an unwelcome complication in an already full schedule.

"Ron Adler's garage was broken into and some of his cash was stolen," I said to her. Then I turned to Neil. "The garage *was* broken into, wasn't it?"

Neil shrugged. "He didn't say there were any specific signs. But money is definitely missing and he's not exactly happy about it. That's all he cares about. That and making sure it doesn't happen again tonight."

"Yeah," I said, "don't go sneaking into the garage or you might get a load of buckshot. He's itching to deter some bad guys."

Del snorted. "Just like Ron. Always the big man when it doesn't matter anymore."

She sounded genuinely bitter.

I think the events of the past couple of days had finally pushed her past her inexplicable infatuation with Ron. For decades she used and dismissed him. Then one night she decided to reward his patience and ended up smitten herself. Whereupon he immediately realized that he didn't really want her after all.

Tensions between them had been high ever since.

Which reminded me of something that Neil had said earlier today.

"What were you two fighting about last night?" I asked Del bluntly.

"Who?" Del asked. "Me?"

She seemed genuinely baffled at first, and then she shook her head. "Oh, that. As I was walking over from the cafe to the garage last night, I ran into him heading that way too. He looked pretty awful and I said something about it."

Ron *had* looked awful.

I had expected him to make a lunge for the bathroom before he left the cafe for the rescue run—he'd been pale and sweaty even then.

"And then he made some snotty remark about not keeping track of my own kid and endangering the whole town with his stupidity." She looked directly at me. "And you know I couldn't let that go. Especially considering that John was out there with Pres and Mardelle."

Which explained the argument completely. Del had taken a pot shot at Ron, and Ron had retaliated with an even nastier jab. And they'd both ended up doing what they did best lately.

Out of bed anyway.

I imagine between-the-sheets activity between them was now out of the question, a development I could only greet with a sigh of relief. A truce of any sort would alleviate some of the tension in the air.

"He was acting weird last night," Neil said thoughtfully.

"It's not surprising," I said. "He was really drunk, and he'd started a new affair that he wanted to keep secret . . ." I shot a sideways glance at Del, whose lips tightened dangerously.

"And he was delayed and running behind schedule," Neil said. "He had to take time to throw up in the alley."

"Eeew," I said, thinking ahead to the thaw. "Too bad he couldn't make it to the garage first."

"You know," Del said, leaning forward, "Ian asked me about the garage too."

36

....

Caller ID

Telephone companies never seem to believe that there are customers who can be satisfied with *less* service.

I often detect a smug assurance in the perky and helpful voices of the communications representatives who have just interrupted my supper. So certain are they that their amazing offer of Call Waiting, or Universal Caller ID, or a Teen Line, will be accepted that they get several sentences into the rest of their spiel before they realize that I turned them down flat.

They just can't understand that I rarely want to talk to the person I am talking to, or that the notion of interrupting one boring call in order to answer another simply doesn't interest me.

I prefer to employ the old fashioned method of call waiting: If someone calls me and the line is busy, they can wait.

If someone has good news, I'll be that much more excited when I finally get the call.

If it's bad news, then ignorance is bliss.

That is not to say that I don't appreciate modern technological marvels when others employ them, especially when it suits my purposes.

"Did you get any calls from the trailer last night?" I asked Neil.

"There are always calls from the trailer," Neil said. "We always leave messages for each other."

"Yeah, but were there calls last night that originated from the trailer? Hang-up calls? While we were up at the bar?"

Del's announcement that Ian had pumped her for garage info had triggered a brainstorm.

"You know, there were," Neil said, amazed. "But I didn't think anything of it—I just saw your number flash by on the screen and didn't process the ramifications. All of the recorded calls and hang-ups came while we were up at the bar, or over at the cafe, or out on rescues during the night."

"So, there were calls logged in from the trailer when you and I were both uptown," I said to Neil. Then I turned to Del. "I assume you didn't make the calls yourself, right?"

Del snorted by way of answer.

"Ergo, Ian must have made the calls from the trailer while Del was in the bathroom," I said triumphantly.

"Wait a second," Del said, tapping ash off her cigarette. "Were there messages left? From the trailer calls, I mean? Because I thought all of Neil's messages were hang-ups. And I definitely heard Ian talking while I was in the can."

Neil squinted in concentration. "Nope, no messages. In fact I didn't get any spoken messages at all except for a couple of calls from Clay Deibert way late in the night apologizing for asking if I'd try to drive Tory out to the farm."

I winced at his brief, pained expression. It was obvious even in the candlelight.

Del looked back and forth between us, raising an eyebrow.

"Just because he didn't leave a message at the library, doesn't mean he didn't also call his accomplice and *talk* to him," I said quickly, to smooth the moment over. "The phone rang on and off at the bar all night. And since you got calls from the bar too, there's no reason to think that the accomplice didn't call from there."

"But why?" Del asked. "Why call the library when Neil was obviously not home."

"To make sure that the place was really empty," I said.

"Maybe they were worried that I had a girlfriend staying with me who had a headache last night," Neil said simply.

I shot a hard look at him and he laughed.

"It *is* possible, you know," he said. "I am not completely without charm."

I knew. That was why I shot him the look.

Del's eyes narrowed. She was not in the mood for whatever it was that Neil and I were doing.

I wasn't so sure myself, though to an outside observer, it might have looked like flirting.

Which was too silly to contemplate.

"And there were unlogged calls, right?" I asked Neil. "Ones without numbers?"

"Yeah, there are gizmos that can disrupt the call tracing mechanism so that no number will be left. Also cell phones can't be traced that way. Telemarketers mask their numbers too."

"You think a telemarketer was calling the library in the middle of the night?" Del asked sarcastically. "On New Year's Eve?"

"It wasn't the middle of the night, or New Year's Eve, in Taiwan," Neil said simply.

"You get telemarketing calls from overseas?" I asked, amazed.

"You'd be amazed," Neil said solemnly.

Which caused us both to laugh out loud.

And Del to frown.

"So you got hang-up calls last night. Some from here, some from the trailer, and some from God knows where. Does that actually mean anything?"

"It wouldn't under ordinary circumstances," I said. "But since the library was robbed, and the cafe was robbed, and Adler's Garage was robbed—and the owners of each were all away last night—I think there's a connection. A real connection."

"I do too," Neil said. "And I think Ian was in on the robberies. Or at least I think he coordinated them, kept people otherwise occupied, scoped out the joints, asked pertinent questions, and relayed information."

"To whom?" Del asked. "Exactly who do you suspect of being Ian's accomplice?"

She knew the answer already. She even agreed with us. But I guess she wanted us to say it out loud.

Neil and I looked at each other and then both pointed across the room.

"Him."

37

....

Behind the Eight Ball

There's a fine line between just plain snoopiness and real investigation, however slapdash the operation might be.

When inquiring minds no longer want, but *need*, to know.

When speculation becomes a fascinating exercise in futility.

No matter how you try to avoid it, there comes a time when inaction is no longer an option.

When an amateur sleuth has to do *something* to earn the title.

Of course, I'd have put the whole confrontation scenario off for a bit longer, especially considering that I've never aspired to sleuthdom, but the decision had already been made for me when Neil and I simultaneously, and unanimously, declared a suspect.

"So Tommy and Tuppence have decided that the big bad DJ is a thief, huh?" Del asked, with a small smile that was only a tiny bit cynical.

I looked at Neil. His eyes behind his glasses were unreadable. He shrugged.

"Yeah, I guess we have," I said, peeking over at the DJ, who was getting ready to start playing music again. "The facts seem to add up, and the conclusions are logical."

Or at least they had seemed logical until we'd said them out loud.

But I have nothing if not the courage of my convictions, so I nodded bravely in affirmation of my own declaration.

Del lit another cigarette and inhaled deeply and looked at us.

"Well what are you going to do about it then?"

"Do?" I asked, voice rising. "What do you mean do? I wasn't planning on doing anything." I turned to Neil. "Was I?"

"Well . . ." Neil said.

"Oh come on now, why me?" I asked. "How come I have to do all the dirty work? We all think the same thing." I was pleading. "You know we do."

"Sorry," said Neil, grinning. "But I agree with Del. You're the obvious person to carry out the rest of the covert operation. You blend in so very well with your mild-mannered-waitress disguise."

I assumed he meant my tired, crabby, dirty, going-bankrupt-in-a-hurry waitress disguise—the one that never fooled anyone for a minute.

"So what am I supposed to do?"

There was no point in fighting Neil and Del. They agreed so seldom that their combined power could not be thwarted by mere weary mortals.

"Well, actually talking to the guy might help," Del said, innocently.

"Yeah, right. I'm supposed to go up to him and just ask him if he stole a bunch of money from everyone, huh?"

"Well, that'd save a lot of time," Neil said, laughing. "But I suppose a little more subtlety is in order. It'd be nice if we could just get a handle on the guy and a notion of where he was last night. He can't have been robbing the joints outside all night or most of his extremities would be gone by now. It was pretty damn cold, if you remember."

I remembered.

"Well, he seems to be getting along with Rhonda and Brian pretty well. And Brian was supposed to help him load equipment after closing last night. Maybe they know something," I said, warming up to the task a little.

"Maybe Brian helped him do more than load equipment," Del said nastily.

I looked at Brian, young, handsome, gazing at Rhonda in the lamplight with puppy dog eyes.

"Nah, Brian didn't have anything to do with it. Besides which, I am pretty sure he has a good alibi."

I'd talked to Rhonda at Alanna's earlier, which meant that Rhonda had spent a snowbound night in town too. Judging by the looks she gave Brian, I doubt he spent the night in the cold practicing his B&E skills.

"Like mother, like son," Del said simply.

I glanced at Presley, who was soundly beating John at another game of flashlight pool, to the vast delight of a circle of onlookers. I decided that was not a particularly comforting philosophy.

"Well, Alanna hasn't been convicted of anything," I said lamely.

"Yet," Del said darkly.

"You can ask Rhonda about Ian too," Neil said, changing the subject. "She'll tell you more than she'd ever tell me."

I doubted that Rhonda had any insider info on Ian, but that would give me a conversation opener, not that I really needed one. All you had to do was stand near Rhonda and she'd reward you with a big hug and her life story.

And if she'd been drinking beer, a squeal or two.

She'd been drinking beer, so questioning her would

be the easy part. Getting coherent answers would be something else entirely.

"And don't forget that you're supposed to tell Alanna that Ron will not be returning this evening," Neil added.

Del growled into her beer. "Yeah, and find out if *Oscar Z. Diggs* put the moves on her too." She said the name with contempt.

Considering Alanna's new, and inexplicable, infatuation with Ron, and the fact that Oscar/Ian would have to have been one fast-working English dude to have gotten around to Alanna also in his allotted time, I assumed that we'd draw a blank there. But I was curious.

"Why?"

"Because if he did, I can be even happier that he's dead," Del said bluntly.

"You know, that name still sounds odd," Neil said thoughtfully. "There's something about it that doesn't ring true. I wish to hell I could remember why it sounds so familiar."

"You mean *Ian*?" Del asked. "I thought it was strange that his name was exactly the same as my favorite English name."

Which was news to me. I had thought her favorite name in any language was Delphine.

Shows you what I know.

"Huh?"

"Well when we first started writing, he didn't use any name at all. No one gives out personal information right away. He didn't tell me that his name was Ian until after I said that I loved the name." She shook her head at her own gullibility. "I should have known."

"Not just Ian," Neil said, mostly ignoring Del. A sound policy. "Something about Oscar Z. rings odd too." He shook his head. "But it'll come to me eventually. In the meantime, you go Jessica Fletcher the hell outta them there suspects." He patted me on the shoulder in a comradely manner.

"Gee thanks," I said slowly. "I think. "What else should I be looking for?"

I had a few ideas of my own, but it didn't hurt to collaborate.

It also put off having to leave our calm little corner a few minutes longer.

"Find out why the son of a bitch was such a jerk," Del said. She hadn't eaten much supper and I think the beers were getting to her. She was becoming maudlin. And crabby. "And why he lied to me."

I didn't know which son of a bitch she was talking about, Ron or Ian, but I doubted I'd get the answer in twenty-five words or less.

"If you can, find out whether anyone else saw Gina and Ian arguing last night besides Joe Marlow. Everyone who is here now was here last night too."

"And in your spare time, figure out where the fuck Gina is right now," Del commanded, finishing her beer.

As little as I wanted to go and interrogate anyone, it would be more pleasant than sitting there with a surly Del.

I sighed and stood up and stretched and rubbed my cold hands together, almost ready to make my second trek up to the bar for investigative purposes, when cheering erupted at the pool table.

Presley had evidently won another game. He crowed, raising his cue in the air triumphantly.

Which was why he was completely unprepared, and totally off-balance, when John Adler landed a very well-aimed, thirteen-year-old fist, right on his nose.

38

....

Right on the Old Bazoo

Now when I was a kid, minors could not only legally spend time in establishments whose primary commercial function was to serve alcohol, but as long as a parent or guardian was there (and doing the actual ordering and buying), they could drink legally at any age.

Not that it was officially recognized as legal underage drinking, but for all of my youth (and for a good long time past my early bloom) it was legal for parents to make decisions about their children's behavior and welfare that were at odds with state and federal mandates.

The authorities didn't particularly like it, but they figured that if the parents decided it was okay for the kid to drink, then there was nothing much that they could do about it.

It was sorta like the old official attitude toward men who enjoyed smacking their wives around—the powers-that-be were really sorry but it was a family matter and what was a government gonna do?

Not that *my* mother cottoned to such nonsense.

There was never a time when it was okay with her if I drank, especially in her presence (not that it stopped me—I just didn't get to enjoy the distinctly South Dakotan privilege of sitting in a bar at age sixteen, savoring a leisurely Tom Collins alongside good ol' Mom without the worry of being busted).

These days, of course, the government thinks nothing of stepping between a parent and a child (in most cases, this is a good idea), and it is therefore no longer legal for parents to encourage public delinquency in a minor child. Theirs or anyone else's.

In fact, minors are no longer allowed to loiter in alcohol-serving establishments, with or without parental presence.

And underage consumption of mind-altering substances is taboo under all circumstances.

But here in Delphi, immediately after a paralyzing blizzard, with the power still out and the populace unwashed, undercover agents for the state were not apt to be skulking about, taking names and numbers for future prosecution.

If it had been a normal day, Presley and John Adler would not have been allowed to spend time in the bar at all. If nothing else, the serious drinkers, the ones who consistently paid Pat's bills, would have complained loudly about the disruption to their quiet drinking time, and Pat (knowing which side her dollar was buttered on), would have ejected them forthwith.

But tonight, in the aftermath of a rather inconvenient storm, when stray bucks were a rarity, the Jacksons had welcomed the teens with open arms and cash registers.

I don't think they'd been drinking—even Pat would be leery of serving a minor while some of the parental units were in full view at least some of the time. But she was more than happy to overcharge the boys for Cokes and to rake in a steady stream of quarters at the dilapidated pool table. Especially since the jukebox was temporarily nonfunctional.

She tolerated them gladly. At least until the fisticuffs broke out, then all bets were off.

But since altercations of a physical nature were usually caused, or complicated, by alcohol consumption (especially when mixed with stressful situations), no one had paid any attention to the boys' pool playing except me.

And I hadn't been watching all that close.

So none of us saw it coming.

Especially Presley, who stood frozen for one long second with his eyes wide and surprised, mouth open, breathing heavily. His free hand tentatively reached for his nose.

He seemed surprised to find wetness there; he pulled his hand away, and stared at what seemed to be, in the lantern light, dark brown liquid on his fingertips.

We all stood frozen, shocked by the suddenness of the attack. Surprised into inaction by the trickle of blood running down to Presley's lip.

Which was unfortunate. If we'd been a little more alert, we could have grabbed both of the boys and stopped them right then and there.

But Presley was a whole lot younger than the rest of us. And a whole lot more sober. Which meant that his reaction time was a whole lot faster.

Before anyone could move, he threw his cue aside and lunged at John.

"You ass wipe!"

He tackled John, knocking him to the floor. And before anyone could stop them, they were rolling together, throwing and landing punches and knocking chairs over on top of themselves, all of which had to have been less painful than the insults they hurled at each other.

"Dip wad!"

"Butt cheese!"

They continued hurling thirteen-year-old invective, which led, inevitably, to "Motherfucker!"

At which point the battle degenerated into a true brawl, with fists and blood, torn shirts and probably broken noses. Not to mention more commentary in the your-mother-wears-army-boots vein.

By then, Neil and the DJ had waded into the middle, and with the help of Brian Hunt, managed to separate the whirling dervishes, who continued to shout furiously at each other.

I was still standing by the pool table, finally ready to lend a hand if it proved necessary, so I had a good view of the boys on the floor, and everyone else staring, open-mouthed, at all that pubescent fury.

I also had a great view of the dimly lit hallway that led to the bathroom.

And an even better view of the storeroom door, which opened a crack as the shouting escalated, though I couldn't see inside.

"Loser! If your mother didn't fuck every man in town every chance she got, things would be a whole lot better for everyone," John shouted, spraying saliva and blood in Presley's general direction.

I looked back at Del, who still sat, rooted in her chair, stricken.

"*My* mother!" Pres shouted, indignant, enraged, struggling against Neil, who held him back. "My mother wasn't outside like *your* crazy mother, screaming about wedding rings with total strangers who weren't even her date!"

Neil did his best to calm Presley down and Brian tried to lead John over to the bar, out of fist range, and maybe out of earshot.

They wanted to end this fight before it got even nastier. Already there was a great deal of uncomfortable shuffling among the spectators.

It was one thing to watch adults make a mess of their lives.

It was another thing entirely to watch a couple of kids, whose lives had been thoroughly messed up by adults, go at it in public.

"Well, if your mother would of stayed away from my father, none of it would have happened!" John said over his shoulder as he was being led away. He wasn't screaming now, he was speaking in a calm and terrible voice that was even worse than the screams.

"Well," Presley answered in kind, "if your father woulda kept it in his pants, your mom wouldn't have had to play batting practice with his pickup truck just to get his attention. I think you're gonna need a new bat, John. And maybe we better make sure his new girlfriend has one too. She'll need it sooner or later."

The nastiness of their comments was surpassed only by the truth of every one of them.

Not a single person in the bar was oblivious to the naked pain on display in front of us, not even Alanna, who actually hung her head in shame.

Not a single person there was unaware that boys on the edge of puberty, that children of any age, should never have to trade, or hear, mostly accurate insults about the moral characters of their parents, especially not a shattered Del, whose heart was broken, and whose past could not be undone.

And not a single person, except maybe me, saw Gina Adler, tears running down her miserable face, swing the door wide and step out of the storeroom and into the hallway.

39

....

Errant Parents

I've always figured that there were two sets of people about whose sex lives, believe me, you just don't wanna know.

You can cluck, or crow, at the assorted predicaments and peccadilloes of your siblings and friends, you can speculate over your neighbor's sleeping habits, you can wonder long and hard about your boss's strong attachment to his Dalmatian, but it's best if you avert your eyes and cover your ears when the conversation turns to the generations just before and after your own.

In the case of your children, there's nothing you can do about it anyway, and sometimes ignorance is true bliss. Tell me, do you *really* want the details of what happened after the prom in the backseat of someone's mother's Plymouth? Let me remind you that there was probably an abundance of alcohol and a lack of readily available birth control devices.

That's what I thought.

Ditto with your parents at the neighbor's barbecue.

If there are skeletons in their dim and dark sexual closets, you will be ever so much better off if you don't go poking and prying around.

Nasty secrets have no half-life.

And the acid burns the innocent just as surely as the guilty.

Which was obvious as we watched a pair of boys, whose sexual knowledge stemmed pretty much from un-settling dreams and shampoo commercials, trade insults about each other's parents.

And it was even more obvious by the looks on their mothers' faces.

Del still hadn't moved from our table in the back, though she'd certainly heard and seen everything.

Even Alanna looked as though she'd been slapped, and *her* son hadn't participated in the mother bashing.

Gina emerged from the hallway into the lantern light and took a tentative step toward her son, who turned away angrily.

Neil had an arm around Presley's shoulders.

I should have gone to Gina and oh-so-gently ques-tioned her. It would have been the perfect opportunity. She was sad, she was unguarded and vulnerable, she would likely have told me everything, if there was, in-deed, an *everything* to tell.

I could even have cornered Alanna and Rhonda for their interpretation of last night's events in their proper sequence. They would have enjoyed rehashing it, and my conscience would have been clear.

But Del was plainly incapacitated, unable to do what was right. And Pres was hurt.

I knew where I belonged.

"Can't let you out in public at all, can we?" I asked gently, handing a napkin to Pres so he could swab his bloody nose.

He tried to smile in return, but winced.

The kid was going to have a shiner or two and a fat lip. But it looked like his teeth were still firmly seated and his nose was without those twists and bends common in prize fighters.

"I don't know what happened," he said, bewildered. "John's been acting weird since last night, but I thought he was going to be okay. I mean . . . his mom and dad . . . well . . . you know . . ."

I nodded.

Pres continued. "And mostly we were playing and, like, having fun, but he was crabby anyway, and even Mardelle couldn't get him to laugh." He shook his head in amazement. "And then out of the blue, he hit me. And even then I wouldn'ta done anything, but he'd been saying little things about Mom all night long. And . . . well . . . you know . . . I hadda do something."

Judge Wapner would probably have argued against the existence of fightin' words. But Judge Wapner wasn't thirteen anymore.

And *his* mother had not been maligned.

Likely Presley had heard those same comments year in and year out from kids at school. To hear them from his best friend must have been intolerable.

If he'd been older, maybe he could have resisted the bait.

Then again, considering the behavior of the adults around him, I kinda doubt it.

The three of us sat down at the nearest table. Over by the bar, John had allowed his mother to come closer, but he still stood apart, like a small wounded animal, tense and ready to spring again. Rhonda tried to soothe him, and Mardelle hovered helplessly nearby.

The DJ, who may have been a thief but was also no dummy, sensed the tension in the chilly room and began playing music again, to the vast relief of almost everyone gathered.

A bar fight can be fun, but this time around it was too hard to choose sides.

"When did John start acting weird?" I asked, after making sure no one was standing close enough to overhear us.

Presley sniffed and then swallowed, grimacing. "He was mostly okay last night early, even after what happened out in the street. In the afternoon, I mean. And I don't blame him for getting upset. I mean I would of if I'd seen that too."

He inspected the bloody napkin and then stuffed it in his pants pocket. Saving it for later, I guess.

"Was John in the street yesterday too?"

I guess I shouldn't be surprised that I hadn't noticed him.

"Not right then. He'd been working for his dad. And he'd been complaining that his dad never paid him and just made him work like a damn slave all the time. So he was uptown, but the whole thing was almost over by the time he got outside."

Presley sighed. "But that didn't matter. Everyone told him everything right away anyway. You know how it is."

I allowed that I did.

He continued. "Well, last night we were farting around his house, trying to figure out what to do. I mean it was New Year's Eve and it was past midnight, and neither of us wanted to sit around like dumbshits. Then Mardelle called and said she'd take us to this party she knew about in the country but we had to pay for . . ." He peered at me warily.

"Yeah, yeah, yeah," I said. "I got it."

"Well, neither of us had any money, but John thought maybe we could sweet-talk his mom into giving him some. So we walked from John's house up to the bar."

"John was upset with his mom, but still he'd let her give him money, huh?"

"Of course," Pres said. "Like who wouldn't?"

I sighed. "And then what?"

He rubbed his nose with his hand and checked it again for blood. Then he touched his eye gingerly and squinted at me. "We came around the corner and saw his mom out in front here." Pres peeked over at Gina, who was talking quietly with John at the bar. "But she was with that English guy. You know, Mom's date."

"Oh," I said. No wonder that John had been upset. It had discombobulated me to find them together, and I was neither thirteen, nor her son.

Pres shook his head vehemently. "No," he said, disgusted, "they weren't doing anything like that. They were arguing."

I looked at Neil. Here was the confirmation we'd been looking for.

"Wait a minute," Neil interrupted. "You were still in town after midnight? I thought you'd left for the party early in the evening."

That's what we'd assumed anyway. That the three kids had made it to the party, and gotten worried about the weather (and/or parental disapproval) and decided to come back into town, sober but alert.

We'd thought that they had run off the road and into the drift and gotten stuck on the way *back* home.

"Well," Pres said sheepishly, "we knew that we were going to be in trouble anyway, we thought it would look better if you all thought we hadn't waited until so late to leave town."

I guess that passed for logical thinking in a thirteen-year-old.

"So what did Gina do when she saw you?" I asked.

"Jeez, Tory. What do you think we are, idiots?" Pres asked, rolling his eyes. "We didn't let her see us. We hid around the edge of the building. But we could hear them."

"Oh?" I said innocently. "What were they fighting about?"

"It didn't make any sense. She was shouting about her ring and how he'd taken it or something like that."

I'd seen Gina restlessly massaging her ring finger earlier in the evening.

Her ringless ring finger.

"What did Ian do?" Neil asked.

"He just laughed," Pres said, confused. "He was hard to understand, but I think he said he didn't take jewelry from pretty ladies. But he'd be happy to buy her another ring anyway." In an aside, Pres added, "He was pretty drunk, you know. He was weaving around a little."

"Go on," I said, resisting the urge to shout at him to hurry it up.

"Well, he got his wallet out and was going to open it, when Mrs. Adler said something like, *'I already got enough from you, you thief!'* and slapped it out of his hand. That sucker flew something like fifteen feet."

There was no small amount of admiration in Presley's voice.

That Gina Adler was a woman of surprising talents.

"Then she said some bad words at him and turned around and went back into the bar. One of the old geezers had just come out the door, and she almost ran him down. But he was pretty drunk too."

So that's where Joe Marlow had come into the story. He'd seen the end of the fight, and then embroidered the rest.

It was a skill born to most Delphi natives.

"And then?"

"The English guy looked at his watch and said something out loud. I kinda thought he was talking to someone but he was turned around with his back to us. Maybe he had a phone or something. Then he just sorta walked off down the street. I never saw him again.

"After that John and me stood there around the corner and looked at each other for a minute and didn't move, even though we were freezing. I didn't know what to say to him. It had been his *mother* out there after all. Fighting with a guy who wasn't his father, and after what happened earlier . . . Well, it was too weird. So we didn't say anything. Then John ran out into the street and picked up that wallet. I asked him what he was going to do with the damn thing, but he didn't answer."

"Did he look in it?" Neil asked gently.

What he was really asking was: *Did John take Ian's money?*

We'd thought it was odd for a man with lots of ready

cash to have been found dead with no wallet.

And we'd thought it was odder still for Ron Adler to have possession of said wallet.

And even stranger yet for that wallet to be empty when it finally did come to light. Though this at least explained why he hadn't tipped Pat Jackson.

"I don't know, because while John was in the street, his dad came out of the bar and started walking across to the cafe," Presley continued.

I had the timeline now—I'd been snoozing in the dark, warm cafe, dreaming of kisses in the snow when Ron had come to the cafe from the bar.

With Alanna.

"He wasn't alone, was he?" I asked.

Presley winced again. "No. He was with . . . Well, you know who he was with. I thought John was gonna come unglued. He was so mad."

For Presley's sake, I wanted to pretend that Ron and Alanna had just been friends. This was too much adultery for two boys to absorb in such a short time. "Maybe they were just walking over at the same time," I said lamely.

"She kissed him for chrissakes, Tory. And not a cute little kiss either. It was a big honkin' smack on the lips."

Presley shuddered.

"Oh," I said, trying to imagine what it must have been like for John Adler to see his mother go crazy in public, and then fight with a man she'd obviously done *something* immoral with, and then minutes later catch his father being kissed by an overblown ex-stripper.

My mind fairly boggled.

Which is probably why John did what he did next.

"So you hid some more, right?"

It's a wonder they weren't frostbitten, what with all that standing outside in the sub-zero temps, skulking around corners.

"No, that was the weird thing. John didn't even try to hide. He just ran over to his dad and talked to him for a minute. His dad looked kinda funny but he talked to

him sorta normal. It was all pretty weird. I just hoped I
could get John out of town. I figured it'd be a good idea
for him to stop thinking about all that stuff. You can't
change any of it anyway, so there's no point in going
crazy," he said matter-of-factly.

And if there was anyone who would know that fact
intimately, it was Presley Bauer.

"So John gave the wallet to his dad, and then his dad
gave you a bunch of money, and you left town, right?"

That at least explained *how* Ron had come into possession of the wallet, but not why he'd lied about it. Or
why he'd said that he would never pay any kids to work
for him.

"I guess," Pres said.

"What do you mean, *you guess*?"

"Well," Pres said, as though we were particularly
dense for not figuring it out for ourselves. "While he
was talking to his dad, John looked over his shoulder at
me and gave me the okay signal, and sort of motioned
for me to go into the bar. I knew that meant that he got
some money, so I ran in and found Mardelle and we
waited out back for John to come. When he got there,
he gave me a shitload of money and said we had a job
working for his dad, and then we left town." He
shrugged. "You know the rest."

Which was not quite the case.

But we were getting closer.

40

···

Ring Around the Rosy

I was beginning to think that not only did it start with Gina Adler, but it ended with her too.

Gina set the whole sorry mess in motion with her trusty Louisville Slugger, and kept it moving along briskly via her storeroom encounter with Ian Douglas O'Hara (AKA whoever he really was), and continued the motion by arguing with him and batting his wallet into the street for her son to find.

I was starting to wonder if she hadn't somehow arranged for him to fall gently to sleep in the box of Stu McKee's pickup, just so we could find an Iancicle the next morning and continue the merry chase.

That budding theory wasn't as far-fetched as it sounded.

No authorities, medical or legal, had yet examined Ian's body.

Though we had seen no obvious trauma, that did not mean that grave bodily harm had not been done to our handsome, genial, felonious, horny, drunken English visitor.

And though I would never have believed it before, I now knew that Gina was perfectly capable of wreaking physical and emotional havoc on everyone around her.

I'd been willing to forgive (or at least overlook) what she'd done to me in the street because we both knew what it was like to be married to louts.

But even in Nicky's heyday, when he'd been sniffing after every breathing female like a puppy dog, I had never felt the urge to harm his property (though that may have been because I'd paid for all of it), or his person.

And when he'd died, my grief had been no less for his infidelities.

In fact, I still did not wish him dead, though I was glad not to be going through the continual upheavals our marriage had provided.

Not that our present upheavals were any less entertaining or engrossing.

Presley, making the kind of recovery that youth is most famous for, perked up almost immediately after unburdening himself to Neil and me. The heavy weight of guilt was off his shoulders, and after a restorative jolt of caffeine and a promise to behave, he'd returned to the pool table to whack balls around by himself. He wasn't carefree, but he wasn't full of smoldering resentment either.

The DJ had done his best to draw attention to himself and the music. The cold and tired crowd mostly gathered around him, though I thought that some people had left, maybe preferring their own dark homes to the bar where anything, and everything, could happen.

As a group, we just didn't have the energy for any more excitement.

John, his pressure-cooker tension evidently, and I hoped not just temporarily, relieved by public outburst (he was his mother's son, after all), broke free of Gina's hovering and pretended to listen to the music. He pretended to be wandering aimlessly, but in actuality he was gravitating back toward the pool table with Mardelle, who talked to him continually as if nothing had happened.

We watched the boys for a minute. Beneath their bravado, they were both still little boys, and my heart ached for them as they eyed each other surreptitiously, pretending to ignore each other's existence.

"Oh Lord, are they going to go at it again?" I asked Neil.

We were still sitting at the table where we'd interrogated Presley.

"I don't think so," Neil said, smiling. "Watch."

John nonchalantly leaned on the pool table bumper and watched the DJ, moving slightly to the music, even though someone was singing "Lyin' Eyes," and I knew full well that both of the boys thought that the Eagles sucked big time.

Then Presley tapped his foot to the music a little.

John looked over his shoulder and said something that caused Presley to burst out laughing. It must have been dirty because they both looked at us guiltily.

"I'll be damned," I said, marveling. "How do guys do that? When women fight, they pout and sulk for months before speaking to each other again. And then they have to cry a good long time before things get back to normal."

"Chalk it up to the restorative powers of testosterone," Neil said, laughing. "It's magic stuff."

"Yup, break each other's noses and then fifteen minutes later go buy a boat, right?" I said, laughing too.

"You got it babe," he said.

"Isn't that the sweetest thing in the world?" Rhonda said over my shoulder.

I hadn't seen her coming up behind me. I think she may have been talking to Del, who sat forlornly at our old table.

I would have gone over there myself, but I am not as brave, or as young, as Rhonda. I knew that Del would have to work through this on her own, and that she was apt to bite anyone who got in the way.

"Well, if you call physical violence and split-second attention spans, not to mention complete and utter unpredictability, sweet, then I guess you're right," I said.

Rhonda sat down and examined her dirty bandage. It looked a little ragged after the last day's worth of activities. "You know, those boys are just sublimating their sexual energy in the only way they can. Puberty is a time of vast mood swings and great energy bursts. Without normal release, they have no choice but to use that seething energy elsewhere."

Rhonda was taking psychology in college.

"Amazingly enough, I did know that, Dr. Freud," I said. "But the fact of the matter remains that if our seething, pubescent holy terrors feel like rolling around on the floor again, they'd better seriously consider taking it to the street or Pat will sublimate all of their energy for them permanently."

"What will Pat do?" Pat Jackson asked.

It was my day not to see people coming up behind me.

"Pat will get us another round of drinks on me for starters," Neil said. "I think I need one. Get one for yourself while you're at it."

"And I thank you kindly sir," Pat said, almost coquettishly. "I'll be right back."

She headed back toward the bar, pausing briefly to glare briefly at Presley and John, who had the grace to look abashed.

The DJ obligingly played Celine Dion's latest overwrought movie-theme ballad—the one that aired approximately fifteen times an hour. Every single hour. Every single day.

Rhonda sighed. "I love that song. Wayne is such a good DJ—did you notice how he controlled the crowd right after the fight? They teach them how to do that in DJ school."

Neil and I exchanged glances. Talkaboutcher great openings.

Which I blew entirely.

"There is such a thing as DJ school?" I asked incredulously. "With a degree and everything?"

Doctor of Discology? Sounded like something Dr. Demento invented.

"Of course there is," Rhonda said, indignant. "There are schools for everything. But it happens that Wayne went to a Vo-Tech in Sioux Falls, and one of the elective courses was in Crowd Control Via Electronic Medium. He got all A's."

"With a minor in Single Dwelling Burglary," I said, mouth running ahead of my brain.

"Oh, you heard about that, huh?" Rhonda said, disappointed in us for some reason. "You know it was a trumped up charge, don't you?"

"No, we didn't know that," Neil said gently. "But we'd like to."

"Well," Rhonda leaned forward, delighted to be dishing dirt, even on her friend. She was a Delphi native, after all. "He told Brian that he was seeing this lady who happened to be married to a guy who worked the night shift at John Morrell. And one night, you see, the husband came home early and caught him just as he was leaving the house."

"Go on," I encouraged. It was a good story anyway.

"Well, the husband was a real bastard and liked to smack her around, and Wayne didn't want him to beat her up, so he let the guy think he'd been robbing the house to keep him from knowing what was really going on."

"The DJ took a fall to save the lady's reputation?" I asked, incredulous.

"He was a real mean guy, Tory," Rhonda said earnestly. "Wayne had to or the guy woulda killed her."

"What a prince," I said absentmindedly.

"So he told Brian all this?" Neil asked.

"Yeah, well, they talked a lot last night," Rhonda said.

"The DJ spent the night with you and Brian at Alanna's?"

Boy, oh boy, that shot our favorite theory all to shit.

Rhonda looked a little abashed. "Not exactly. Mr. Adler was over at our house." She blushed. "I mean, Alanna's house, and there wasn't room for anyone else."

"Why am I the last to know these things?" I demanded of Rhonda. "You knew that Ron and Alanna were together, Gina knew they were together, Del knew they were together. Even Presley and John knew they were together last night."

"Don't forget Dorothy Gale," Rhonda said.

"What do you mean, *don't forget Dorothy Gale?*"

"Well, I thought you were ticking off people who realized that Ron and Alanna were fooling around. Dorothy figured it out right away."

"What, she was with you last night too?"

I hadn't even bothered to formulate a theory on Dorothy's whereabouts. But if I had, it wouldn't have been with Ronda.

"No," Rhonda said, laughing. "But when we were in the bar last night, after you left with Neil . . ." She shot a sly look at Neil. That Rhonda doesn't miss much. "We sat and talked for awhile."

"She *talked* to you. She can talk?"

I was beginning to feel like the odd man out on everything.

"Not *talk* talk, but she could make herself understood," Rhonda said matter-of-factly. "She's the one who pointed out to me that Wayne was paying attention to Gina Adler."

"What?"

This was all too much. My head was spinning.

"Dorothy pointed out that Wayne was watching Gina. I told Brian, and we decided that since Ron"—her voice dripped disgust—"was busy, that it wouldn't hurt things if Gina had a little fun too. We figured that, number one, he wouldn't come home, and number two, he couldn't beat up anyone anyway."

Yeah, Gina had custody of the bat.

"So Gina spent the night with the DJ?"

Rhonda nodded.

I had a headache.

"All night?"

"I think so," Rhonda said. "I know they were still together this afternoon."

Which meant that Wayne DePaul, Self-Admitted Burglar and Gallant Fella, was Gina's slap-and-tickle man on the phone.

Which put me back to square one.

Almost.

"But," I said, trying in vain to sort all of this out, "why did Gina even consider going with the DJ, *another* strange man, after her terrible day yesterday? It makes no sense. You'd have thought she would have learned her lesson about strangers with Ian and the missing wedding ring."

"What missing wedding ring?" Pat Jackson asked, setting a tray of drinks down on the table.

"Uh," I said, not sure that Gina would want the story broadcast all around town, even though the boys had already rendered some of it public domain. "Well, Gina Adler lost her wedding ring last night," I finished lamely.

"Is that so?" Pat said, grinning widely. It wasn't a pretty sight.

She dug deep into her pants pocket and pulled out a ring with a smallish diamond solitaire.

"I found this on the floor in my storeroom this morning. You suppose it might be hers?"

41

....

My Beautiful Balloon

Amazing how things work sometimes, isn't it?

You look up and down and in all the wrong places.

You draw conclusions and make a fool of yourself.

You change your mind a dozen times and still find out that you're barking up the wrong tree.

You get ready to give up, to concede defeat, to throw in the towel.

And then, with no warning whatsoever, the key falls right into your lap.

Well, not necessarily in your lap, but close.

Pat stood with a smile, bouncing the ring up and down in her hand innocently. "*Her* wedding ring? No wonder I caught her snooping around the storeroom tonight. Twice."

"Maybe," I said cautiously

It could have been someone else's wedding ring.

It could have belonged to any of the dozen women Ian had evidently wooed in the last few hours of his life.

But probably it belonged to Gina Adler.

"Well, since you get along with her so well, *you* give it back to her then," Pat said, flipping the ring into the middle of the table. "I have enough to do with controlling juvenile delinquents and keeping this rowdy crowd happy to worry about lost jewelry."

She wandered away frowning at her many burdens, pocketing Neil's ten-dollar bill. Then she stopped and turned around. "But if it turns out not to be hers, I get it back. Okay?"

"Sure," I said, reluctantly, figuring the odds of that at about a zillion to one.

"What do I do now?" I asked Rhonda and Neil.

"Well, I guess you give it back to her and see what she says," Neil said softly. Neither of us was sure exactly what Gina Adler would do anymore.

"And you're the absolute right person to do it too," Rhonda said encouragingly. She patted me on the back with her good hand. "You always know what to say and how to make people feel better."

I thought she was practicing more Psychology 101 on me.

Unfortunately, most of the errant notions had been mine, and it really was up to me to continue on, right or wrong.

I looked at them both and sighed.

"Wish me luck," I said airily. "And if you see her pulling out a bat, give me a signal. Wave wildly or something."

"Will do, tiger," Neil said, patting me encouragingly on the rear end.

I inhaled deeply, filling my lungs with dank, smoke-filled air and headed single-mindedly toward the bar as the DJ played "What the World Needs Now."

Love sweet love, bah humbug.

"Tory." Alanna grabbed my arm on the way past her.

She looked as cold and miserable as I felt. Her usually perfect hair was blowsy and straggling. Her nose was red and her eyes were rimmed with runny mascara. I had never seen her look so completely unsexual, so human, so normal.

I doubted she'd be taking her clothes off for anyone tonight.

Including Ron Adler.

"Tory, I need to talk to you," she said with almost no accent.

"Can it wait, Alanna?" I asked wearily. I had no time for more of her get-rich-quick schemes. I had no energy for rehashing the cafe burglary. I had no desire to talk to her at all.

"No, it really shouldn't wait," Alanna said. "It's important."

I was desperate to avoid a heart-to-heart with Alanna. Whatever it was, it could wait until the lights came back on and the roads were plowed.

At the very least it would keep until the banks reopened.

I hit on a way to get rid of her. Or at least to divert her attention. "You know, I was supposed to give you a message a long time ago. Ron called and he's over at his garage. Seems that it got robbed last night too. Probably by the same person who stole our money. The one who took the stuff from the library."

She bit her lip and frowned. "Money missing from the garage?"

"Yeah, and I think Ron wants you to go over there with him."

"Oh," she said, voice trailing off. She wasn't nearly as excited about the tie-in to our two robberies as I'd expected. "Well then I'd better go to him."

There she was, a statuesque blond who was considered desirable in many circles—chasing after Ron Adler, whose attraction was a complete and total mystery to me.

"Be sure to make a lot of noise on the way in," I said.

"What?" she asked over her shoulder.

"Just don't sneak up on him," I said. "In fact you'd better call first so he knows you're coming."

"Oh, okay."

I'm not sure she believed me.

Over Alanna's shoulder I could see that Gina was gathering her stuff together dejectedly and heading toward the door. I had no idea if the DJ was going to spend another night with her, but just in case, I had to talk to her before she left the bar.

I figured Alanna could take care of herself.

"Gina," I said, hurrying after her. "Just a minute."

She turned around warily. "What?"

Without looking around to see if anyone was nearby, I held out her ring.

Her eyes widened.

She inhaled sharply.

"How did you get that?" she asked, suddenly pale.

I nodded at the bar. "Pat found it on the floor in the storeroom. She asked me if I knew whose it was."

"It was in the storeroom all this time?" Gina's voice wavered.

I thought maybe she was going to faint.

I shrugged. "I think so. She said she found it there this morning."

Gina sat down in the nearest chair. "Oh my god. I thought *he'd* taken it."

I knew she was talking about Ian. That she'd accused him of stealing her wedding ring.

And we both knew now that she'd been wrong.

"Do you know what I said to him? What I called him?" she asked me, eyes wide.

"Sort of," I said. I'd heard enough of the narrative to fill in the blanks myself.

"Jesus," she said softly.

"No kidding."

A hand touched my shoulder.

I turned around to find Del standing behind me.

To say I was surprised would be to understate the case just a bit.

Del and Gina hated each other.

Del and Gina would sometimes be in the same public

place at the same time because there was occasionally
no choice in the matter, but they never acknowledged
each other's existence directly.

And they never spoke to each other.

"Can you excuse us for a minute, Tory?" Del asked
me softly. "I have to talk to Gina for a minute. I have
to . . ." She paused.

I had no idea what she was going to say as the DJ
led the crowd in a group sing of "Up, Up and Away."

Del swallowed. She looked at the floor, and then directly at Gina. "I have to apologize."

Of all the things Del could have said at that minute,
nothing could have surprised me nearly as much.

Except what she said next.

"Besides, I think Neil wants to talk to you, Tory. He's
been waving frantically ever since this song started."

42

Pay No Attention to the Man Behind the Curtain

I knew immediately that Neil was not telling me that Gina had pulled a weapon, if for no other reason than I could see both of her hands.

They were clenched on the table as she stood looking at her husband's former lover, who was about to do what no one who knew Del would have ever imagined.

As much as I would like to have listened in on that particular conversation, Neil was indeed waving me frantically over.

I made some sort of lame excuse to Del and Gina who didn't even hear me, and worked my way toward Neil, who met me halfway.

"I got it! I got it! I got it!" he said excitedly, doing a little victory dance. "I got it!"

I was fairly sure he hadn't gotten drunk in the ten minutes I'd been gone, and I sincerely hoped he hadn't had a stroke.

But I definitely didn't know what the hell he was talking about and I sincerely wondered about his sanity.

"Listen to the song," he commanded, humming along.

"Yeah, yeah, up in the air, beautiful balloon, we can fly. I know the song. I like the song. I worship the Fifth Dimension," I said, raising an eyebrow at him. "I'm so happy that you're so happy."

"Not the song, doofus," he said cuffing me lightly on the shoulder. "Well, yes the song. But what the song made me remember."

He was making even less sense than before.

I put a hand on his forehead.

"Are you feeling okay?" I asked.

"I am feeling absolutely wonderful," he crowed. "I know why Oscar Z. Diggs sounded so fucking familiar."

"You gonna let me in on it?" I asked.

"Think for a minute," he said, laughing. "Think of balloons. Think of stories. Think of the initials."

"Initials?" I was still confused.

"Oscar Z," Neil said slowly. "O-Z."

"Oz," I said, breathing deeply and remembering finally. "Oscar Z."

Together we said, "Oscar Zoroaster Phadrig Issac Norman Henkle Emmanuel Ambroise Diggs."

It was an old refrain. We both loved the books. Neil had the whole set, though not first editions. Nothing valuable. Nothing any book collectors would want to steal. Just wonderful reading.

Just a part of his extensive classics collection at the library.

"Oh my God," I said. "Oscar Z. Diggs, the Wizard of Oz."

43

I Have a Feeling, Toto

And of course that led to everything else.

Or it led to most of what I thought was everything else.

"Dorothy Gale," I said, shaking my head and repeating myself. "Dorothy Gale."

"I know," Neil said, still amazed. "Why didn't we see it earlier?"

"Well, we did have a few distractions," I said, trying to make excuses for ourselves. "And I did think it was odd that she just dropped in on us so coincidentally."

"Coincidence my ass," Neil said solemnly.

"No kidding. I mean here's this mute cook coming in from the snow out of nowhere, wanting to work for us. Did it even once occur to us that we also had an ad in the Sioux Falls paper? The same paper where Del found her date, and where you"—I poked a finger into Neil's chest—"handsome, single, millionaire librarian were the lead local-boy-makes-good story last month. Did we wonder how the hell she got to Delphi? Did we call any of her references?" I asked. "Such as they were."

I stopped and then slapped myself on the head. "Jesus, her application even listed former places of employment in Nebraska. Look!"

I dragged Neil back to our original table, where I'd laid the folded piece of paper that I'd found in my coat pocket earlier.

The folded piece of paper that just happened to be Dorothy Gale's employment application.

The one with her references and former address listed on it.

I opened it and pointed to the entries.

"Did I even ask where she was going to stay before I gave her the keys to the cafe?" I asked myself. "So that she and her dapper English accomplice could rob us all blind?"

But I already knew the answer to that one.

We shook our heads in amazement at our own stupidity.

Presley wandered over to the table.

"What's up with you guys? You look like you found a ghost or something."

"We did," I said, laughing.

"Or we almost did," Neil said. "We still don't know where she is."

I thought about that for a minute.

But only a minute.

"Get your coat and follow me," I said to Neil.

44

....

...We're Not in Nebraska Anymore

Except for a brief interval in my own bed, which felt like a year or so ago, I hadn't been warm all day.

I was nearly frozen last night, and without heat anywhere in town, I had been deeply chilled ever since.

Because South Dakotan homes and businesses are well insulated against the deadly cold, most of the buildings in town were still above freezing indoors, even without heat for going on twelve hours.

The pipes may well have frozen underneath the trailer, but the water in the sink would still be liquid. The library would be a relatively toasty 60 or so degrees due to Neil's fireplace and the sparing use of his generator to run small electric space heaters.

The combined heat of moving, breathing, and occasionally fighting bodies and the flickering candle and lamplight kept the bar a good fifty degrees if you stayed away from the windows and the door.

Even so, we were all cold.

And we had been all damn day.

But we'd been mostly indoors and we'd forgotten just exactly how cold it was outside. And considering the clear skies and shining moon, it was apt to get even colder before daybreak.

Which meant that Dorothy Gale, a woman with likely no notion of how to survive in arctic conditions, could be in grave danger of freezing to death.

Especially since people here rarely bother to insulate their garages, much less heat them.

"You think she'll be okay after all this time?" Neil asked.

"As long as she stayed out of the wind," I said, remembering my long night in the cold, "she should at least be alive."

We'd already confiscated a couple of old wool blankets from Pat's storeroom (a handy place, that), and poured a thermos full of strong coffee that she'd had been keeping warm over a spirit lamp on the back bar.

Of course, our preparations did not go unnoticed.

"Where're you goin', Tory?" Pres asked. His left eye was already swelling and turning purple. He'd be very proud of his bruises come morning. "What's all the blankets and stuff for?"

"Never mind," I said, wrapping a scarf around my neck. I'd already put on my coat and mittens and earmuffs and a hat in preparation for another snowy jaunt. "Just stay here."

"No way," Pres said enthusiastically. "Whatever you're doing, I want to see. Hey John," he shouted back at the pool table, waving frantically. "Come on!"

I shot a pained look at Neil, who shrugged.

"You don't think she'll be dangerous, do you?" he asked.

"I suppose not," I said. "If she was intent on hurting anyone, she'd have done it by now. And if I am right about where she is, she'll be too cold for mayhem anyway."

"In that case, it won't hurt to have the boys along. They can run back here if she's in tough shape and we need help carrying her out."

"I'm coming too," Del said. She'd already zipped and wound and fastened her multiple layers of outerwear, a conglomeration that made her look a good thirty pounds heavier than normal, which would not have pleased her at all.

Her conversation with Gina had been short and to the point, and Gina had left the bar long before Neil and I had finished hashing out my latest crackpot theory, which I actually thought wasn't so crackpot after all.

Del had been pale and nearly silent. I was surprised that she wanted to come along.

"I'm a part of this too," she said quietly, reading my mind. "I want to see it through to the end."

She was pale but calm. And absolutely determined to come along.

I nodded at her, picked up my flashlight, gathered an armload of blankets, and headed for the door.

The frigid air cut like a knife. It was still well below zero outside. The cold was so sudden and sharp that it hurt just to open your eyes. The wind had gone down, so the probability of dying of exposure, as Ian likely had last night, was low. But it was still dangerously cold.

Too cold to dawdle.

Crinkling our noses against the sudden freeze, amazed at how good the air outside smelled, we started single file across the street, with Neil in the lead.

He stepped over the bladed snow along the sidewalk, and helped me to stomp my way across. Since the piles lining the street were not natural drifts, but lumps and globs of dirty, compacted snow rearranged by the plows, the going was uneven and difficult. Every third step or so, my foot broke through the crust and I sunk up to mid-calf. Or deeper.

Walking in snow is exhausting, like running in water, or wading through sand. It's amazing how quickly you can work up a sweat when the temps outside hover at the minus 20 level.

None of us talked on the way across the street. Not even Presley and John, who brought up the rear.

In fact no one said anything, until we worked our way around the back of the cafe and over to the unheated, unlocked garage where Oscar Z. Diggs, AKA Ian Douglas O'Hara, had been lying all day.

And even then no one said anything until after we opened the walk-in door (the overhead door having been blocked by a five-foot snowdrift), and our flashlight beams found, huddled under an old and smelly blanket, a shivering woman who sat, hunched and miserable, holding vigil beside the body.

We all stood for a moment, speechless.

As much as anything, I was surprised to have been right.

I tried to figure out what to say to her, remembering suddenly that I had not brought a pen and paper along for her to use. We had lots of questions for Dorothy Gale to answer.

But she broke the silence first, saying, in a perfect English accent, one exactly like Ian's, "I was rather hoping you wouldn't make the connection. But since you obviously have, do please, come in."

45

....

Gale Force

I should have known that no cook was going to suddenly appear in Delphi, ready made to solve our staffing woes at the cafe.

That's not how life works.

And to give her credit, Alanna had been against hiring Dorothy right from the beginning, based on some nebulous bad feeling about the whole enterprise.

I had been the one to insist that she be hired.

I had been the one to give her the cafe keys.

So it was my fault that she'd taken our two thousand dollars.

Well, technically (and legally) it was Dorothy's fault that she had taken the money, but I had made it absurdly easy for her to add to the booty that she and Ian had amassed in their few hours of professional life here in the snowy city.

So really, I was sort of mad at Dorothy.

She and Ian, who I assume was her husband (which

meant that she was really Emily Diggs and not Dorothy
Gale) had complicated my life no end.

And together they'd given Alanna a weapon to hold
over my head forever, or for as long as Alanna felt like
holding it.

Which would probably be forever.

Which might be as long as I was willing to hold a
grudge against Dorothy/Emily for lying to me.

I looked around for someplace to sit in the small, dark
and crowded garage. Our combined flashlight beams
kept it bright enough for us to see each other's faces,
but we cast long and weird shadows on the walls, and
looming, amorphous piles of stuff made the far reaches
seem even darker. It was a less than pleasant place to
have spent a whole day, with or without power.

Not to mention a dead body.

Which lay in Stu's truck box covered with a blue
vinyl tarp.

The cafe had used its portion of the shared garage
space to store old empty five-gallon pickle buckets and
big cardboard crates, as well as all the other junk that a
business can accumulate over the years that serves no
practical purpose but is too good to throw away.

My Uncle Albert, Junior's father, had used some of
his portion to store bales of straw.

I had no idea why, but at least they gave us something
to sit on. Dorothy had pulled a couple over near Ian.
Their insulating properties had probably helped to keep
her not only alive through the long cold day, but as far
as I could tell, relatively unharmed.

I sat down on another bale nearby.

"So, you can talk too?" I demanded, exasperated.

Damn, I hate being lied to.

"Yes indeed," she said, shivering. "Might I trouble
you for one of those blankets? And is that tea in your
canister?"

"Coffee, sorry," Neil said, being strangely apologetic
to the woman who'd burgled his library. He held a blanket and the thermos out to her.

"That will do nicely," Dorothy said, taking it from Neil. "I'd offer you all some, but I am in dire need of some warmth, and far too cold and tired to be properly hospitable."

We watched her pour and drink a cupful of coffee. She inhaled the warmth, and held the cup close to her cheek and then wrapped another blanket around her shoulders.

The boys were unusually still and silent, not speaking or shuffling. I think it might just have occurred to them that they currently shared quarters with a dead man.

Already, their fight was a part of the dim dark past. I'm sure they were storing up sights and sounds to repeat to all of their friends, who'd envy this grand adventure.

Of course, it had occurred to me on the way over from the bar that Dorothy/Emily might not only be a thief, but that she may have actually engineered her companion's death.

That silly notion was dispelled the moment I saw her face.

The English may be famous for the stiff upper lip stuff, but the grief etched in her eyes was absolutely real.

Dorothy had not killed Ian.

She finished drinking another cup of coffee and then turned to me. "I rather suspect you have some questions for me," she said, in that intoxicating accent.

If she weren't such an obvious bad guy, I would like to have sat and just listened to her talk.

Well, if we hadn't been in a cold garage with a dead man, that is.

"Uh, yeah, you might say that," I said awkwardly. "Or maybe you could confirm what we already know."

"Whatever pleases you," she said simply. "You do hold the upper hand at the moment."

Which was true enough.

"You saw the help wanted ad for the cafe in the Sioux Falls paper, right?" I asked.

"Yes, and a lovely little newspaper that is too. Such a font of information," Dorothy said, with a faint smile.

"No kidding. Like our needing a cook, and Neil here being almost uncomfortably rich, not to mention Delphine's spot in the personal ads."

Del looked straight at Dorothy, waiting for her reply.

Presley watched his mother closely, having been reminded, once again, that this wasn't just a game. He stepped toward her, and she gave him a small, tight smile.

"It did work out rather well," Dorothy said, slowly. "We decided that the fates were pulling us northward. From here, we were going to go to North Dakota and try our hand there. In fact, if not for this snowstorm, I would be on my way right now."

"You'd have left your husband, and not looked back?" Del asked sharply.

It was her day for confronting ugly truths about herself and those around her, I guess.

But instead of getting angry or defensive, Dorothy laughed.

"Husband?" she said, genuinely amused. "Oh my, no. Oscar wasn't my husband. We were business partners, yes indeed, and successful ones at that. And we were relatives too. But you needn't worry that I am an aggrieved wife, or that I am filled with smoldering resentment toward you, or any of the other lovely women with whom my nephew liked to spend his off hours. Combining business with pleasure."

I was a half a beat slow.

But I got it.

"Oh my God, you're his aunt aren't you?" I said. "Aunt Emily Featherstonehaugh Diggs."

The one who dispensed brandy on cold days to a young Oscar.

His Auntie Em.

Neil burst out laughing.

"I'm so glad to see that someone finally understands the joke," Dorothy said. "So few of you Americans even read your own literature."

Our burglarizing English visitor shook her head at the

sorry state of American education and taste.

"You know, we thought at first that our names would be a dead giveaway. We thought for sure that we'd have to adopt permanent aliases. But not a single person, until now, has even made the connection. We're very close to the same age. He is, or was, only ten years my junior. Oscar's father was my older half-brother, and we actually grew up together in the same house. It was easier to let people assume we were married. It generated less questioning about our relationship. However, I must say that I'm rather glad that the truth is finally out. I'm tired and I would like to retire. Especially now that I am alone."

She sat on the straw bale and folded her hands in her lap and waited, looking from Neil to me and back again. Del she ignored.

"So, you arrived in Delphi yesterday before the worst of the storm hit," I said. "Together I assume."

"Yes, we drove in and parked down the alley a bit, and then walked around the town awhile. Getting the lay of the land, so to speak. I thought that our cover had been spotted immediately. One old gentleman who had been gazing out the cafe window actually saw us talking together outside in the street, and I thought for sure that he was going to give us away. But then the wonderful woman with the baseball bat diverted his and everyone else's attention so very well that he seemed to forget all about me."

Actually, Eldon McKee had probably seen it all, and remembered it all, and had just not seen fit to pass any of it along to us.

I was going to wring Eldon's neck next time I saw him.

"So you came in and applied for the job. Why pretend to be mute?"

"Wouldn't you have noticed two strangers with English accents showing up in your small town on exactly the same day?"

She had a point.

Dorothy continued, "I never could master American diction. You all say you're A's so peculiarly. Oscar's speech seemed to enchant all who heard it, and the women told him the most amazing things."

I could feel Del blushing beside me in the darkness.

"It just seemed easier for me to pretend not to be able to speak at all. That way, no one questioned my accent. And given the American propensity to be awkward around the *differently abled*"—she said the term with a small laugh—"no one asked any uncomfortable questions at all."

I certainly had not. I had hired her on the spot.

Though to give myself credit, I would have hired cooks with no arms, as long as they were willing to flip burgers with their feet. And start that afternoon.

"So you lived and worked awhile in Sioux City," I said. "Doing little side jobs in the evenings in the small surrounding towns."

It was a guess, but a good one. Dorothy nodded, while pouring herself the last of the coffee.

"You pretended to be mute everywhere."

The landlord in Nebraska had mentioned that Emma, or whatever her name, was pretty quiet for a woman.

"You'd take jobs to get the feel for a place. Ian would meet women and charm information out of them for future robberies."

"He did so love his work, and very good at it he was too," Dorothy said. "But he also loved the bottle. I fear it was his undoing." She patted the tarp sadly.

"That and an incomplete understanding of how cold it really gets here," Neil added.

"Yes, we'd been working our way up from the South. We'd had no idea what real cold was until we got to the Dakotas. But we'd planned to leave here for North Dakota in the morning, and from there, to make our way west as the roads opened up."

"So you visited the library and then went back later to take such money and valuables as you could find.

Calling first to check and make sure that the place was really empty."

"We never expected a rich man to have so little cash on hand," Dorothy said, plainly disapproving. "We had a series of signals worked out with our mobile phones, ways to let each other know what was going on without having to talk . . ."

Rhonda had seen Dorothy using a cell phone in the bar. Presley and John had seen, or at least heard, Ian using one in the street. Both had called the library leaving hang-up, untraceable messages. Ian had even used the phone at the trailer to make one of the calls.

"You worked yesterday afternoon at the cafe," Neil said, taking over for me. "Then you robbed the library, then you came to the bar, and later back to the cafe, with the intention of taking that money too."

Dorothy smiled. "Yes, it was just our good fortune that you were staging a cash-heavy event the very night we were to visit. I spent all evening trying to devise a way to get back into the cafe later . . ."

"And then I handed you the keys to the till myself," I said, slapping myself on the forehead. "I practically invited you to take the money."

"Well I wouldn't have needed an invitation, actually. But thanks all the same."

We'd gotten answers to almost everything so far. But there was another mystery yet to solve.

"Where *did* you spend the night anyway?" Del demanded, thinking ahead of me for a change.

We knew for sure that she hadn't been with Ron Adler, at least.

Or Wayne DePaul.

Or Stu and me.

Everyone else was up for grabs.

"Right inside the cafe," Dorothy said, simply. "It was warm, and there was good food, and I had the keys. I planned to wait until Oscar's signal, and then grab the money bag and leave the keys on the countertop so you wouldn't have to look for them in the morning."

"How very kind of you," I said sarcastically.

Evidently they don't get American sarcasm in England because Dorothy welcomed me and continued.

"But the signal never came. I assumed that Oscar had found a warm bed in which to spend the night, so I curled up in a far corner in the back room. I was still there when your Alanna came in this morning. That's how I heard about . . ." She paused, her voice cracking. "That's how I knew what had happened to Oscar, and where he was to stay until the roads were opened."

"So you skulked around the cafe until after the body was brought in, right? And then spent the rest of the day here with him?" I asked, not ungently.

"More or less. No one paid any attention to another woman wrapped in many layers of outer clothing tramping through the snow. We all look alike in the winter. I entered the cafe several times today after the power went out and found myself some cold food. But mostly I've been here, staying with Oscar until such time as I could actually leave town. We had never planned to stay here anyway."

"So Delphi was just an overnighter. A little recon mission to tighten up your skills before you moved north, huh?" I asked.

I was offended.

"Well, we'd had high hopes for your handsome librarian"—she nodded at Neil—"but he was too crafty for us. So yes, we would have been many miles away before anyone knew that anything, goods or employees or transitory boyfriends, was missing. By the way," Dorothy said, putting the cup and thermos aside and standing up. She moved slowly, as though she was in great pain.

Or maybe like a late-middle-aged woman who was very cold and very tired and very, very sad about the unexpected death of a close relative.

She rummaged in a cloth bag and then handed Neil a small bundle of cash and an envelope filled with loose change. "Also," she said, reaching into her pants pocket.

She drew out a ring. "This is yours too, I believe."

Neil stared at the ring she placed into his outstretched hand. His fingers curled around it protectively.

"Did Ian . . ." I would never get used to calling, or thinking of him as, Oscar. ". . . have the garage money on him when they brought him in?"

"Pardon me?" Dorothy asked, confused.

"The money stolen from the garage. Do you have that on you now too?"

I figured that as long as she was handing loot back, we might as well all get in line.

John Adler stole a glance at me, eyes and mouth wide, and then he shuffled uncomfortably behind Presley.

"I wouldn't know about any money on Oscar's person at the moment. We didn't have time to compare notes last evening. He was, as you well know, *out of range* before I went off duty."

That was one way of putting it.

"I am understandably reluctant to search him now," Dorothy said calmly. "But you may if you like."

"That's okay," I said, uncomfortable with the very notion. "It can wait until the police get here tomorrow. But you must at least have my money on you," I said sharply. "I'd really like to have it back. We do need the working capital."

"Your money?" Dorothy asked, confused.

"Yes," I said impatiently. "The two thousand dollars that was in the blue bag on the counter by the till, that you schemed to steal all evening long."

"I certainly schemed to steal that money," Dorothy said, looking me straight in the eye. "And I most assuredly would have taken it without a backward glance, but I left it lay, waiting until Oscar's signal. I'd planned to leave the keys, take the money, and exit by the front door.

"But Oscar's signal never came. By the time I remembered the money bag, it was no longer there."

46

....

The Obligatory Exposition Chapter

It would be nice to be Nero Wolfe.

Then I could sit, secure in my brownstone empire, with orchids germinating overhead, and something wonderful being prepared for me in the kitchen, and a cold imported beer always at my side.

I could command the suspects to appear and sit in a ring around my desk while I toyed with them for the required seven pages or so, before revealing to everyone (except whodunit of course) the final secret, the key to the mystery.

But a certain physical resemblance to Mr. Stout's creation, notwithstanding, the mountain was simply not going to come to Mohammed.

And Mohammed was hopping mad to have to go out in the snow again for any reason other than to trek back to the warmth of the library.

Which was where everyone else was going.

Delphi had no jail, and besides which, we had no police available to make arrests.

We figured that Dorothy was too cold, and too cornered, to try to take anything else.

And she was stuck in town for the duration anyway.

We could not, in good conscience, leave her in an unheated garage with a dead body.

No matter what she'd stolen.

Or from whom.

"Call and tell them I'm coming over," I told Neil. "I don't want to get shot."

I also didn't want to stumble across any nude bodies in the lube pit, but I couldn't say that in front of the kids.

I had no desire to toy with Alanna Nero style, I just wanted some answers and I wanted them fast.

Neil knew better than to argue with me.

He gathered up his small troupe and headed back out to the street and down toward the library.

I veered off through the snow toward the garage side door.

It was dark inside, but that was to be expected.

It was dark inside everywhere.

But I knew they were there; Ron had answered Neil's call.

I marched right up to the door and raised my hand to bang on it, and then stopped for a second, wondering if I should duck anyway, and was run into from behind.

By Del.

Who was, in turn, run into by John Adler, who'd been looking at his feet and not at the person in front of him.

"What the hell are you two doing here?" I demanded.

"Till the end, I told you," Del said quietly. "I'm in this as far as it goes. Until it's over."

I shot an inquiring glance at the heavens, wondering why now, of all times, Del had discovered her secret desire to be a detective.

"And you?" I peeked around Del at John, who squirmed but said nothing. He did, however, blink just like his father.

I sighed.

"Get ready," I said. "He's hoping for more burglars. Neil called in advance, but that doesn't mean he won't fire off a load of buckshot anyway."

I pounded on the door and then jumped back.

Del and John hit the ground.

Nothing happened.

They stood up and brushed the snow off themselves.

I stepped up to the door and pounded again, and then ducked. Again.

Still nothing.

I opened the door a crack and hollered in, "It's me, Tory. And Del and John. We're coming in."

"Yeah," I heard a voice from inside. "Yeah, okay."

I looked at the others and shrugged.

They shrugged back, so we stepped inside and stomped the snow off our boots.

Old habits die hard. It was almost as cold inside the bay as it was outside, and yet we worried about tracking in and melting on the nice clean concrete floor.

"We're coming through," I said very loudly, just so there would be no mistaking exactly who was approaching, and no temptation to think we were burglars and fill us full of holes.

"We heard you the first time," Alanna said sharply, leaning out of the office door. She shined a flashlight directly in my eyes, thereby blinding me. "I declare, you make enough noise for six or eight people."

She peered around me. "You got six or eight people out there?"

"Nope, just Del and John," I said, rather enjoying her startled reaction to both.

I had a flashlight too.

Which I used.

Alanna was tired, of course. And she was disheveled. And she was cold. And she wore no makeup.

But she also looked worried.

That worried look pleased me enormously.

Ron sat in the chair behind his desk. I didn't see the shotgun, but I assumed it was within reach, though he wouldn't need it anymore after what I was going to tell him.

He eyed us warily, blinking every few seconds as usual.

He didn't say anything.

And we returned the compliment.

The office wasn't big, but the five of us fit in comfortably enough. I pulled up a chair and sat opposite the desk. Del leaned against the doorway with her arms crossed.

John came in and hovered by the far wall.

The silence dragged out for another moment or two.

"To what do we owe the pleasure—" Alanna began, as Southern as I've ever heard her.

I interrupted her. "Tell us again when you noticed that the money bag was missing," I said sweetly.

Alanna shot a glance sideways at Ron, looking for approval, support, confirmation . . . something.

He sat watching us, blinking impassively.

"I told you both, I came to work this morning and found the money gone," she said, working up some indignation. "And if you'd taken notes, you'd remember that stuff and not have to ask for repeats."

"Well, I'm sorry to burden you," I said, still sweetly. It was an effort. "But I just wanted to hear you say it again."

"Say what?" she asked, not looking at me.

"Say that someone else took the money when you know damn good and well that you did it yourself."

She actually gasped.

Just like in the books.

I had to admit that I enjoyed it.

Me and Nero, we got a good gig going.

"Now looky just a minute here," Ron said, standing up.

"Shut up," I said to him.

Amazingly enough, he did.

He also sat back down.

"So," I said to Alanna, "why?"

"I don't know what you're talking about," she sputtered. "That mute woman took the money, we both know that."

Dorothy had forgotten that Americans either tiptoe around *the others*, or they use them as convenient scapegoats.

I suppose it often worked, especially in insulated small towns.

But the plan backfired this time.

"Dorothy didn't take the money," I said calmly. "In fact she says that it was still there this morning. At least it was until you arrived."

Alanna swallowed, obviously considering her options.

"Well, you know, I did try to talk to you at the bar just a while ago," Alanna said, licking her lips. "I wanted to explain some things to you."

I spread my hands out. "Now's as good a time as any."

"Well, I wanted to talk to you in private about this," she said weakly.

"Del is in this," I said, shooting a small smile at her. "To the very end."

Del nodded.

Alanna sat down and actually wrung her hands.

"Well . . ." she said. "You're not going to believe me, but I wanted to make money for the cafe."

"You wanted to make money for the cafe by stealing money from it?" I asked.

Sort of a Vietnam era destroy-the-village-to-save-the-village philosophy, I guess.

She licked her lips again. "Well, Ron and me was talking about investments and the like. And he has this opportunity to get in on the ground floor of a new company, and alls they need is fifteen hundred dollars apiece from a few more investors and they can get the ball rolling. And I knew you'd never agree to do it. You never want to take chances. But we can quadruple our money in three months. You should take a look at the paperwork."

Oh Lord, Alanna was not only sleeping with Ron Adler, she was also taking investment advice from him.

"Alanna," I said softly, "look at Ron here."

She darted a puzzled glance at him and then back at me.

"Does he look like a Wall Street mogul to you?"

"Well, no, but everyone has to start somewhere," she said lamely.

Well, at least that explained the affair. Alanna smelled money.

Or she smelled the hope of money, which for some people is just as exciting.

I had wondered what the attraction was.

I knew it couldn't be his boyish good looks and his loyalty to his friends and family.

"So what were you going to do with the other five hundred?" I asked, mildly curious.

"Other five hundred?" she repeated.

"Yeah, there was close to two thousand in the bag, and you only needed fifteen hundred as your millionaire seed money. What were you going to do with the rest?"

I highly doubted she'd planned to return it to me.

"Well, for one, I was going to pay the boys to do some work. Those poor boys don't have nothing, you know. And I would be helping and . . ." Alanna risked a peek at Del.

It was a mistake.

Del actually showed her teeth.

"Anyway, I would have done something *good* with it, not spent it on myself."

"But you would have let an innocent woman go to jail, in order to help yourself get rich?"

"Oh she'da never gone to jail." Alanna stopped just short of pooh-poohing the idea. "They never put anyone in jail these days. Besides, who knew if they were ever going to find her? She could have been long gone by now."

And without the blizzard, Dorothy and Ian would have been gone.

With our two thousand dollars.

This way, at least I got a little back, and a major lever over Alanna in the bargain.

I turned to Ron.

"So you were going to help out by funneling money back to the boys too, huh?"

He looked at me and blinked.

He looked at John, who didn't blink.

"What do you mean? I make it a policy not to pay my own kid to help out around the business. You know that."

I looked over at John in the corner. He was pale, and unblinking.

And I thought about how long it had taken him to get back to the bar after seeing his father in the street.

And I thought about what he'd overheard.

And I remembered a couple of other little facts that should have fallen into place long ago.

And the lights went on.

Literally and figuratively.

47

....

Let There Be Light

I should have known.

I mean, I really should have known.

I shot a stricken look at Del in the doorway.

She nodded imperceptibly, which meant that she knew too.

She'd known for a while, which was why she was here.

I don't think I've ever felt this bad.

No, come to think of it, I have felt like this before. More than once. But it's a feeling that I hate.

One I'm tired of feeling.

One I am going to avoid feeling ever again.

If I have anything to say about it.

Which is not likely, considering where I live.

"John," I said wearily, shielding my eyes against the bright fluorescent light.

It had only been one day, and not a whole one at that, without electricity, for artificial light to seem unbearably bright again.

John winced, squinting his eyes, anticipating my next question, dreading the answers he would have to give, and his father's wrath.

I surprised him. "When did you give Ian's wallet to your father?"

Ron opened his mouth to say something, but I held out a hand.

"Let him talk," I commanded.

John blinked at me, clearly unsettled.

"Well," he said, thinking furiously. "Well . . . we were coming back into town. You know, late last night. In the snow. After we'd been stuck."

Alanna looked between Ron and John, and then to me, lost.

"And when did you mention the argument? The one between your mom and Ian."

"He never said nothing at all," Ron said slowly, telegraphing something to his son. "Nothing at all."

John looked at me, frightened.

"The argument, John?" I said, gently.

"Well, the same time, I guess."

Ron slumped in his chair.

Alanna started to say something herself, but one look from Del silenced her completely.

"On the way back into town last night?" I asked John again, just to confirm.

"I guess that was it. Then."

"Not when you saw him in the street earlier?"

"Oh," John said, relieved. "Yeah, I guess I did say something about it then too. But not a whole lot. Remember Dad?" He looked over at his father, who was looking down at his desk, rubbing his forehead.

"Go on," I said.

"We was out there just a minute, but I guess I told him about what Mom said."

I nodded.

That's what I had expected to hear.

Been afraid to hear.

"And then you went right to the bar and got Mardelle

and left town, right?" I said to him, staring at him mean-ingfully.

He hesitated for just a moment before he understood what I was doing.

I was giving him a reprieve for a day or so.

There were more important issues at the moment than the fact that John Adler had burgled his own father's petty cash box, out of revenge, or adolescent anger at erring parents. Or just because he wanted some cash to go to a New Year's Eve party.

I had no idea why John had really taken the money, but he had.

And he'd told Presley and Mardelle that his father had given it to them, and they'd had no reason to doubt his word.

So John had been harboring not only the twin horror/terror of seeing his parents' marriage disintegrate up close and personal, he had born the added burden of guilt for having stolen money from them.

No matter how justified he may have felt at the time, he knew it was wrong.

I assumed the money would reappear in its proper place shortly.

Or most of the money anyway.

"That's what I thought," I said to him. "Now get out of here. Pres is waiting back at the library for you. Go pop some corn and read a book or something."

No thirteen-year-old boy ever moved as fast.

Or with as light a heart.

I hoped he enjoyed his evening, because his heart was going to be wrenched out of place again. Sooner than he ever imagined.

A couple hundred in petty cash was a hill of beans.

At least compared to murder.

48

....

The Fellowship of the Ring

I'd known almost from the beginning that it all revolved around Gina Adler.

Her outburst set everything in motion.

It brought her to Ian's notice for the first time, and as Dorothy had said, he liked the pretty ladies. He'd made a point to come back to Gina the first chance he got.

Which was when Del stood onstage singing karaoke.

It had kept Eldon McKee so very entertained that he'd forgotten to mention that the cook who couldn't talk had actually been in the street talking to someone.

It had caught Joe Marlow's attention, and therefore he was more than willing to add to the budding Gina mythos by reporting what little he'd overheard in the street to anyone he could get to listen to him.

It had resulted in her son leaving town late at night and getting stranded in the country, which engineered the transferral of the wallet to his father. The same wallet that Ron had not even looked into, the wallet he had certainly meant to destroy, with none of us the wiser.

Of course it had resulted in my getting stranded in the country with Stu McKee, which had stalled, at least temporarily, the change in my relationship with Neil.

It had certainly ended with Gina entertaining the DJ during a whole night when we'd assumed he'd been burgling houses.

And in the end, it had caused Ian Douglas O'Hara/ Oscar Z. Diggs's death by exposure in the box of a burgundy pickup truck that just happened to have been parked in front of the bar on the fateful night.

"And it's all because of the ring," I said.

"My ring?" Gina Adler asked from the doorway.

She'd come up behind Del and they had been standing together for the last few seconds, though neither Ron nor Alanna had seen her yet.

Ron nearly fell out of his chair.

Being confronted in the same small room with one's wife, one's former lover and one's present lover (as well as one who would never be a lover, take my word for it) is the stuff of French Farce.

But there was no humor in this situation.

This was sad.

It was pathetic.

And it was slightly dangerous.

There was, after all, a loaded shotgun still under Ron's desk.

"Yeah," I said. "Your ring, though it might have happened anyway. But the ring was the catalyst."

"I was afraid of that," Gina said sadly. More than sadly.

She reached into her pocket and pulled her wedding ring, a smallish solitaire, the kind a young couple buys, expecting to be able to afford a larger stone later.

Gina had been waiting more than twenty-five years.

I think she was done waiting.

She tossed the ring onto Ron's desk.

Ron stared at it like it was radioactive.

"Is that what you were looking for this morning?" I

asked. "When you jumped up into the pickup and patted down Ian's body?"

He picked up the ring and looked at it numbly.

"Where was it?" he croaked.

"Pat Jackson had it. She found it in the storeroom this morning at the bar," I said. "It had been there since last night when Gina took it off, and it got lost because . . . well because she was startled and it fell to the floor."

That had been my contribution to the scenario. I had interrupted Gina and Ian, and Gina had accidentally knocked the ring to the floor and then later thought that Ian had stolen it.

I don't know why she jumped to that conclusion, maybe he'd been teasing her about taking it and buying her another. Or maybe she'd just picked up on his vibes.

But either way, she'd accused Ian of stealing her wedding ring, and her son had overheard.

And he'd told his father, who understood immediately the significance.

"She never took her ring off," Ron said, voice so low we could barely hear him. "It was a thing with us, a game. A vow. She always said that as long as she loved me, she'd never take her ring off."

"I took it off," Gina said simply, with the kind of finality that no husband wants to hear. "Not for the right guy, Lord knows. But I took it off."

"And you knew what that meant the minute John told you about the argument," I said to Ron.

"Well that don't mean anything," he said, shaking his head, blinking.

"Maybe it wouldn't have," I said, tilting my head and looking at him closely. "But not an hour later, you sat in the bar and listened to Rhonda and her friends rhapsodize about Ian and how he and Gina had been laughing together in the bar in front of everyone."

"So?" he asked, snottily. "You think I spend my time alone? You think I care?"

"Yeah, I think you care," I shot back. I also thought he'd be spending a lot of time alone from now on.

Del was through with him.

His wife had finally given up.

From the look on Alanna's face, I thought she was on the brink.

I had known Ron Adler all of my life, and I had liked him for most of it.

But way back last June, I had seriously thought he'd participated in a murder.

He hadn't, but the insight into his character had been correct.

Ron Adler hadn't killed in June.

But he had on New Year's Eve.

Of course, it wasn't the usual kind of killing. It was more of a Delphi style execution, brought about by leading a very drunk Ian O'Hara to the box of Stu McKee's pickup and leaving him there (or perhaps by discovering him in the box, still alive, and deliberately turning away). Ron had caused Ian's death the same as if he had whacked him alongside the head with a two-by-four.

"You don't know anything," he said.

It was a dare.

A bluff.

Which I called.

"I know that your son told you that his mother had accused another man of taking her wedding ring. I know that you knew exactly what that meant in terms of your marriage. I know that you had his wallet late last night, and that you frisked his dead body looking for your wife's wedding ring because you had no way of knowing that it had already been found. And I certainly know that you lied about all of it."

Finding the wallet had been the key for me, though of course, in true mystery fashion, I didn't know it at the time. I already had most of the pieces, and would have been able to put the rest together eventually.

After all, Del had.

I realized, somewhat late in the game, that Presley had already told her the same story about Gina and Ian and Ron and the wallet that he'd told to Neil and me. When she'd heard my version of the body search, and added that weird ten-minute delay from the time Ron had left the cafe to when Neil had said he'd shown up at the garage, arguing with Del and acting oddly, she'd realized what had happened.

She had known all day that her former lover and lifelong friend was a murderer. That's why she had not let me out of her sight tonight. She was protecting me.

I looked at her, pale and sad, and strangely beautiful in the harsh light. I thought Del had come through the fire and emerged on the other side. Singed but intact.

Gina had lied to me about arguing with Ian to protect her son, to keep him from knowing what Presley knew intimately.

She had a long way to go, but she was on a journey too.

Alanna—well, I didn't know what was going to happen with Alanna. I thought perhaps that the mystery calls to the library from the bar last night had been Alanna, looking for me while I'd been dozing in a booth at the cafe. Maybe she'd been going to tell me of her amazing investment opportunity before she stole the money from the business we owned together.

I hoped so.

As for Ron, he sat there, face hard and unblinking.

"I didn't do anything. You can't prove anything. Nobody can prove anything."

And he was probably right. In fact he'd probably already convinced himself that he had done nothing wrong.

But we knew. The three of us women knew.

And we weren't going to forget.

I looked at Del and motioned for her to leave with me.

I turned and walked out of the bright artificial light and stepped into the cold white of the snow.

I knew that Ron still had a loaded shotgun under the

desk, but I wasn't afraid he'd use it on me.

I was less certain that he would not use it on himself, given a private and cowardly moment.

But I wasn't sure that was such a bad thing either.

Epilogue

So, boys and girls, what have we learned?

We know that in South Dakota, winter is a bitch, that's for sure.

We know that life is complicated.

We also know that life goes on.

But we knew that already.

Ron Adler was either going to confess to causing Ian's death, or I was going to tell everyone what I knew, which was going to blow apart the social structure in Delphi. Though that little bombshell wasn't apt to wreak the kind of havoc that my mother was about to unleash, now that my grandmother was dead.

People were going to be surprised.

People were going to be shocked.

People were going to be hurt.

Even though I am the least athletic person in the world, I finally know exactly what they mean when they say "No pain, no gain."

It's a shit rule but we don't get to make the rules.

We just have to live by them, one day at a time.

There was a lot to process, there was a lot to learn, and there was a lot to accept.

But it was an amazing night.

The stars were out and the moon shone brightly, and the snow was as lovely as it was dangerous.

As Del and I walked back to the library to join the boys, I looked up at the light shining brightly from all of Neil's windows and thought I'd never seen anything so beautiful. I knew he'd turned them on just for me.

Inside was warmth.

Inside was light and laughter.

Inside, just maybe, was the rest of my life.